FROM UNSEEN FIRE

FROM UNSEEN FIRE

✦ BOOK ONE OF THE AVEN CYCLE ✦

CASS MORRIS

DAW BOOKS, INC.

DONALD A. WOLLHEIM, FOUNDER

375 Hudson Street, New York, NY 10014

ELIZABETH R. WOLLHEIM
SHEILA E. GILBERT
PUBLISHERS
www.dawbooks.com

First Printing, April 2018
1 2 3 4 5 6 7 8 9

DAW TRADEMARK REGISTERED
U.S. PAT. AND TM. OFF. AND FOREIGN COUNTRIES
—MARCA REGISTRADA
HECHO EN U.S.A.

PRINTED IN THE U.S.A.

To Bear O'Bryan

1947-2014

Who always knew I could and would do this

DRAMATIS PERSONAE

In Aven

The Vitelliae:
Aulus Vitellius, a Popularist Senator
Vipsania, his wife, a mage of Water, deceased
Aula Vitellia, their oldest daughter, a widow
Vitellia Secunda, called **Latona**, their second daughter, a mage of Spirit and Fire
Vitellia Tertia, called **Alhena**, their third daughter, a mage of Time
Helva, a freedwoman, mage of Time, and Aula's personal attendant
Merula, a Phrygian slave, Latona's personal attendant
Mus, a Cantabrian slave, Alhena's personal attendant

Vibius **Sempronius** Tarren, a Popularist Senator and a mage of Shadow and Water
Vibia Sempronia, his sister, a mage of Fracture
Taius Mella, her husband
Corvinus, a freedman, mage of Water, and Sempronius's steward
Djadi, an Abydosian slave, Sempronius's household clerk

Galerius Orator, a moderate Senator
Marcia Tullia, his wife, a mage of Air
Lucius Galerius, their son, a mage of Air

Marcus Autronius, a Senator and a mage of Earth
Autronius **Felix**, his younger brother
Gnaeus Autronius and Dula Spurinna, their parents
Vatinius **Obir**, client to Sempronius, head of the Esquiline Collegium
Vatinius **Nisso**, his brother
Numerius **Herennius**, Latona's husband
Aemilia Fullia, High Priestess of Juno

Ama **Rubellia**, High Priestess of Venus, friend to Latona
Quinta Terentia, a Vestal Virgin, a mage of Light
Terentilla, her sister, a mage of Earth
Maia Domitia, friend to Aula
Crispinia and Crispinilla, friends of the Vitelliae
Publius Rufilius and Proculus Crispinius, friends to Felix
Rufilius Albinicus and Aufidius Strato, famous generals

The Optimates:
Lucretius **Rabirus**, a Senator
Young Lucretius, his son
Arrius **Buteo**, a Senator
Licinius **Cornicen**, a Senator
Decius **Gratianus**, a Senator
Pinarius **Scaeva**, a Priest of Janus

In Iberia

Gaius **Vitellius**, a military tribune, son to Aulus Vitellius and brother to
Aula, Latona, and Alhena
Titus **Mennenius**, a military tribune
Calix, a centurion

Ekialde, chieftain of the Lusetani
Neitin, his wife
Bailar, a magic-man, Ekialde's uncle
Otiger, a magic-man, Neitin's uncle

Bartasco, chieftain of the Arevaci
Hanath, his wife, a Numidian warrior

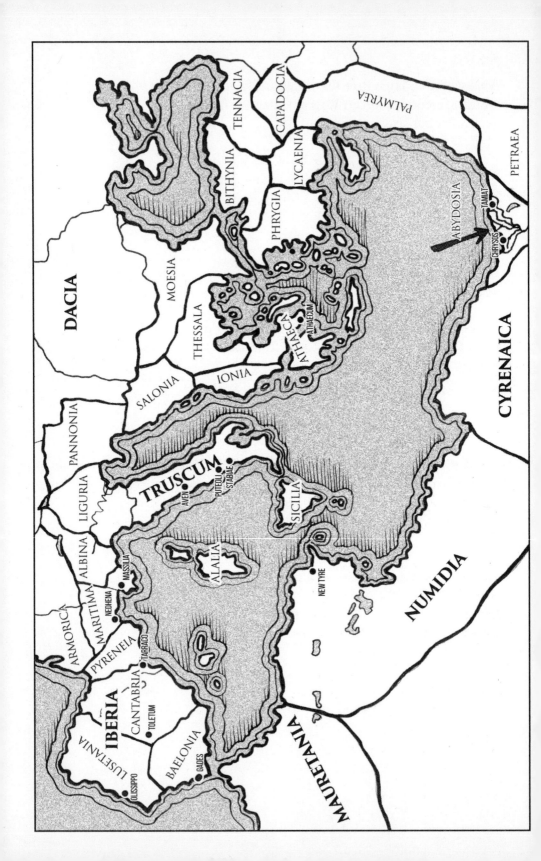

unde reconflari sensus per membra repente
possit, ut ex igni caeco consurgere flamma?

–T. Lucretius Carus, *De Rerum Natura, Liber Quarta*

How might sense be rekindled in the limbs,
As flame can rise anew from unseen fire?

–T. Lucretius Carus, *Of Natural Things, Book Four*

PROLOGUE

Lucius Quinctilius was not, by nature, a reflective man, so perhaps it was just as well that the Dictator's men gave him little time to contemplate his fate.

The morning of his execution dawned cool and fair, and no one in the household but Quinctilius himself had the slightest inclination that anything was amiss. Even Quinctilius suffered only a mild prick of unease, no more troubling than a splinter. His tongue had overrun him during his last public speech, but as a few days passed and retribution did not fall on his head, he convinced himself that the lapse had been overlooked. He had not meant anything by it, just a stray comment during legal proceedings, though it may have edged too near to criticism of Dictator Ocella. Lucius Quinctilius privately had many things to say that would have edged much closer, but he was of no mind to be a political hero for a lost cause. That had never been his intention. And surely no one was paying such close attention to the minor financial courts, not with the turmoil in the treason courts, not with riots threatening to erupt in the Subura. Surely, he was safe.

Still, suspicion twinged at the back of his mind. When he rose and dressed that morning, he considered confiding in Aula, his excellent wife. But she was so pleasant-spirited, so cheerful, even in this dark season of proscriptions and danger. He could not bear to disrupt the simple pleasure she managed to wring out of the tumultuous world.

It certainly did not occur to him to share his concerns with the other lady in his household, Aula's younger sister, Latona. For all Quinctilius knew, she was living with them only for companionship while her husband was touring his holdings in the provinces. It would have been a blow to his dignity, had he been aware of Latona's true motive: to watch after them, knowing that Quinctilius's foolish streak of nobility might get the better of him, all too aware that Aula was so dizzy with motherhood and marital bliss that it had turned her a bit feather-brained.

Latona had not kept her eyes and ears alert enough *outside* of the household, or she might have known in time about Lucius Quinctilius's final act of honorable idiocy. Had Latona heard of his lapse, she would not have hesitated, but packed the whole family off to her husband's country villa that very night. But though she had returned to watch over her sister and her niece in the city, Fate kept the tale of his indiscretion from her ears a few hours too long. When six pairs of hob-nailed boots thumped up the too-quiet street to the Quinctilius domus, when six pairs of burly arms forced open the front door, she was in the back garden, unaware.

Ocella had power enough to feel no need to carry out his assassinations under cover of darkness. The lictors set upon Quinctilius in his own study, early in the morning. Ocella's lictors were not the honorable attendants who usually accompanied politicians of consequence, but his own private killing force, a sacred and venerable office perverted to new and abhorrent purpose. They asked no questions of the man who gave their orders and issued their pay, and they made swift work.

Quinctilius hardly had time to rise from his chair. One short sword penetrated his gut; another slit his throat as he staggered to his knees; and then it was over. The expression of astonishment remained frozen on his face as his blood pooled on the geometric mosaic set in the floor, slipping like crimson mortar between the tiles.

"So much for him," one of the lictors said, nudging at Quinctilius's shoulder with his toe. "Where's the next one?"

"No." His colleague rubbed at the back of his neck. "Not yet. This one's got a wife and a tot."

The other lictor nodded. Proscription touched the family, as well. Quinctilius's brother and sister resided in a province, and so his wife, Aula Vitellia Prima, eldest of the Vitelliae daughters, would have to suffice for an example—an excellent one, really, from a noble and ancient family that had not yet presented Ocella with an opportunity for chastisement.

The noise attracted Aula's attention, drawing her across the atrium from her own rooms. A short scream escaped her before she choked it back. She scarcely had time to process her husband's death before she had to dive to stop Lucia from toddling in and seeing her father's corpse. The lictors had not even wiped the blood off of their blades, and in a wrenching moment, Aula realized they did not mean to do so. A shadow dimmed the pale sunlight streaking in through the open door: the Dictator himself, come to bear witness to the deed.

Ocella was a man of impressive presence, with the lean grace and threat of a panther. His hair was so fair it resembled the winter's dawn, icy and unforgiving, but his eyes were dark pits, a blue so deep as to be nearly black, and utterly unreadable. They rested on Aula for only a moment before he made a quick gesture to summon his lictors forward.

Aula collapsed, her knees unequal to the task of holding her upright in the face of such incisively cold malice. Lucia, too, started to cry, stared up at Ocella, mouth hanging agape. "Please, Dictator," Aula said. "P-Please. We are n-nothing. Not my baby. Sh-she's just a child, she couldn't—" But when Ocella held up a hand, Aula fell silent, though tears continued to stream from her eyes.

Latona flung herself through the doorway just as two of Ocella's lictors advanced on her prostrate older sister and the frightened child. Ocella flicked his wrist, and Lucia set up a tremendous wail. Aula grabbed the girl and clutched her close, holding a hand over her mouth to stifle her cries. "Pray, do not take this personally," Ocella said, even as Aula wept and Lucia struggled against her mother's grasp, her pale blue eyes wild with abject fear.

"No!"

Latona's cry cut through the air, and both Ocella and Aula's heads whipped about—Ocella indignant at the interruption, Aula horrified by Latona's nerve. Mastering her shaking limbs, Latona strode forward with mustered confidence. "No, great Dictator," she said, more softly, smiling at Ocella almost impishly, as though they were sharing a great joke. "Of course you don't mean harm to Aula or Lucia. I'm sure I've misunderstood."

"Have you?" Ocella said, his expression utterly unchanged. "Pray, tell me what has led you to that conclusion."

Though Aula, tears in her eyes, shook her head in a mute plea for Latona to leave herself out of it, Latona had a plan. Not, she admitted to herself, a wholly good one, but it was certainly better than watching her sister and her niece butchered in the atrium—and likely sharing their fate. What scrap of a chance they all had rested now on Latona's gifts.

Blessed by Juno and Venus, Latona had power over the elements of Spirit and Fire, and it was Spirit that would come to her aid now, if anything could. She could not consider the possibility of failure, and as she spoke, the words tasted of cinnamon on her tongue.

"There's no need, and it would look so ill. Everyone thinks well of Aula, and she thinks well of everyone. Especially you, Dictator. If her husband displeased you, I know she sorrows for the trouble it caused you. You can only have done right in disposing of him, we all know that. But Aula and Lucia? A cheerful woman and such a pretty child? Why, they should be allowed to speak your praises! Such magnanimousness would only make your star burn the brighter."

Latona's breath was shallow and hesitant, but she did not let the gracious smile fall from her lips, and she prayed that her eyes would not betray her. If Ocella suspected her of using magic against him, that would be the end of Aula, Lucia, Latona herself, and probably every other son and daughter of the Vitelliae that Ocella could get his hands on. His paranoia was even more acute concerning mages than his other foes. Never minding that ancient law prohibited mages from seeking higher political office, Ocella remained convinced that they would somehow surmount the prohibitions and use their powers to usurp his position. He had executed men and women on mere suspicion, and many more had fled the city rather than have the suggestion of treachery fall on them.

But she couldn't think about that; any flicker of uncertainty could give her away, and doubt could shatter the spell. She let the soothing magic roll off of her, a golden wave of positive emotions washing over Ocella, and she flung silent prayers at Juno that her efforts should move him.

"Aula never chose her husband, nor Lucia her father," she went on. "They renounce him if he caused you any misery. I pray you, mighty Dictator, do not punish them for the misfortune they've already suffered. Rather, show all Aven what a kindness you've done them, to free them from that pernicious man. They will tell all the city of their gratitude, I promise you."

Aula was ghastly pale, her hand still clamped firmly over the weeping Lucia's mouth. Latona had never seen her sister so frightened, a doe caught in the gaze of a ravening tiger. But after the long, horrible silence, Ocella nodded slowly. "Yes," he said. Latona fought to keep relief from coercing her into releasing the spell too soon. "Yes, I believe you are right, Vitellia Latona," he went on. "Your sister is such a charming woman, and this fair creature promises to be of her ilk. No need to harm them. In fact—" He twitched his finger at his bodyservant, a balding man who hovered several steps behind him and who moved immediately to scrawl Ocella's words on a wax tablet. "We shall invite them to holiday with us in Capraia this summer. You as well, Lady Latona." He stepped closer to her, too close. When his fingers touched her shoulder, toying idly with the brooch that fastened her gown, she held as still as death, refusing to let trembling flesh give away her terror. "We wish to see if rumor speaks true of your many talents."

Latona blinked. "I . . . am all astonishment, honored Dictator. I cannot think what anyone could say of a simple matron to be worth your notice."

"Come now, no false humility. Not from one blessed by Juno . . ." His thumb trailed along her collarbone, then pressed at the tender notch at the base of her throat. "And by Venus." His easy smile warred with the intensity swirling in his unfathomable eyes, but the threat in his voice matched that of his hand at her neck. "I have such a keen interest in the magical arts, you know, though the gods did not see fit to bless me with them. Would you come to Capraia and show me, Lady Latona?"

There was a bargain in the air, and the weight of it pitted in Latona's stomach. *'You have walked into the trap Father feared.'* Ocella collected women and he collected mages, and she was both—an irresistible prize. *'This is why Father wanted you married to a provincial, tucked safe away in the country.'* But neither husband nor father could stop Dictator Ocella pursuing what he wanted. Swallowing fear and revulsion, Latona nodded her assent. She would pay the price in flesh and soul, if it kept her family safe.

"Wonderful. So much better to be surrounded by charming women instead of bickering old men. And little Lucia Quinctilia might make a fine playmate for my boy. They're of an age." Then he laughed, that sudden burst that could come from nowhere, like the flash of lightning out of impenetrable clouds. "Perhaps we'll have to arrange a marriage."

And then he was gone, a storm swept out to sea, and as the footsteps of his lictors faded away down the stairs, Latona's knees buckled underneath her. Never before had she exerted so much energy in one go, and the sudden evacuation of her focal point, combined with the weight of the bargain she had taken upon her shoulders, robbed her of even the strength to stand. One of the slaves moved fast enough to keep her head from cracking against the floor, and the last thing she heard before fainting dead away was Aula dissolving into hysterical sobs of sorrow and relief.

◆ SEXTILIS ◆

I

Three Years Later

The hand was rigor-stiff when Lucretius Rabirus went to pull the signet ring off of it. Nearby, an Abydosian priest and an Aventan Earth mage prepared to set about preserving the body, so that it would not turn fetid and fester in the stifling late-summer heat before the time was right to bring it back to Aven for display and cremation. Neither showed any signs of minding Rabirus's interference. They had been well paid not only for their services but for their silence, and if either had privately held notions of carrying tales, the crucified forms of two slaves they had passed on their way into the villa would have dispelled such a temptation.

Rabirus had to tug hard. The golden band caught at the knuckle, long enough to let a tendril of doubt sprout up in his mind.

'The Dictator of Aven lies dead on this pallet. How long do you think you can keep this a secret?'

He stared down at Ocella's body, left pallid and waxy by the disease that had come so suddenly and ravaged through him so quickly. When he began to fall ill, Ocella had taken to the countryside—ostensibly for the restorative powers of fresh seaside air, but more to prevent the city from witnessing his all-too-human vulnerability. His eyes were open yet, but their glossy darkness had lost the power to intimidate. There was nothing behind them now: no otherworldly depths, no fathomless magnetism. Whatever shade had lurked in Ocella's soul, it lived with Pluto now, and what lay on the table was a bereft shell.

'The secret must stay with me as long as possible.'

That was why he had crucified the slaves, of course. They were two he had long suspected of passing information to the Dictator's exiled enemies. Rabirus had never told Ocella. The Dictator's paranoia had made him short-sighted, and he would have crucified the slaves on mere suspicion, but Rabirus had hoped to trace the spies back to their masters, the banished Senators still working against the Dictator abroad. Now, though, that potential usefulness had been rendered irrelevant, and Rabirus could not risk news of Ocella's death spreading any faster than could be helped.

He *would* have to send to Manius Maloricus, brother to Ocella's late wife and guardian of the Dictator's two young sons. Obedient, competent, and without ambition of his own, Maloricus had been the ideal man to hold the city in the Dictator's stead. *'But will he have the strength to hold it after his death?'*

Rabirus gave another tug, and the ring came off. He held it up, examining the sigil carved into the jasper: an eye with a thunderbolt for a pupil. With this, Rabirus could tie up loose ends, push through a last few decrees in the Dictator's name.

When Ocella had marched an army on the city and taken the Dictatorship by force, Rabirus had swiftly determined that while there might have been dangers in being Ocella's ally, they were at least known quantities. He weighed the benefits of making himself indispensable to the Dictator, and he judged them worth the risk. For years, he served Ocella not with fawning subservience but with entire and unquestioning obedience, a worthy lieutenant in whom Ocella could see much value and no threat. He learned to judge the Dictator's moods, knew when to conveniently absent himself from a room, and when to proffer advice in the form of flattery.

Yet as absolute as Ocella's power had been at his ascent, Rabirus's intuition told him that the flame would quickly burn itself out. *'No one lasts forever,'* he had often thought. And this summer his patience had been rewarded.

Rabirus briefly considered that he could do as Ocella had done: take command of a legion, seize the city before the exiles returned, turn Ocella's Dictatorship into his own—but however attractive that dream, his practical mind knew it would never do. The armies would not follow him as they had Ocella, famous victor of so many battles.

'Besides,' Rabirus reminded himself as he slipped the signet ring onto his own finger, *'Ocella's Dictatorship was an aberration—an offense, truly, to the mos maiorum.'* Rabirus was, at heart a member of Aven's traditionalist party, fervent in upholding ancient laws. Good governance by a select group of the best men, from old and well-established families—that was what the Optimate party stood for. *'I have survived a Dictator. Gods grant I need never survive another.'* While the Aventan constitution did allow for dictators in times of great crisis, Ocella had manufactured those

circumstances, and he had forced his rump senate to extend his term in the extraordinary office far beyond what the law allowed. *'It is right and just that the very office of the Dictator should die with him. Aven will correct itself now. Things will go back to the way they were. The way they should be.'*

He left Ocella's body in the care of the priest and the mage and returned to his own villa, high atop a hill surrounded by fields of browning barley. It was well past the middle of the night when he strode into his home and immediately began barking orders to have trunks packed, horses readied, and provisions set. His abrupt return woke his wife. Wide-eyed and wrapped in a thick robe, she padded barefoot into the atrium. "Husband? What's going on? Is there—? Is something wrong?"

"Ocella is dead. We're returning to the city."

"At this hour?" she said, holding her hand to her chest in what Rabirus considered an unnecessarily dramatic way.

"I am," Rabirus said. "And our son. You should go back to bed. Come along in a few days, once you've settled things here." But she trailed after him, a bewildered shadow, as Rabirus went to his son's sleeping cubicle and shook the young man awake. "Get up and put on traveling clothes. We're going back to the city."

Young Lucretius blinked several times, struggling to his feet. "Back to the city? Tonight?"

Rabirus suppressed a sigh. For years, he had been hoping that his only son would show some of the mental acuity which Rabirus prized in himself, but as the boy entered adulthood, it was becoming clear that he had inherited his mother's tendency towards vagueness. Rabirus did not deign to repeat himself, but opened the wardrobe standing in the corner, pulled out a tunic and cloak, and flung them at Young Lucretius. As he went back to his own chamber, he heard his wife attempting to explain.

Rabirus moved from room to room, snapping instructions at the slaves. Young Lucretius stumbled out of his chamber a moment later. "Dictator Ocella is dead?" he asked, shrugging the cloak on inelegantly.

"Yes. It will behoove us to be in residence before word gets out and someone thinks to recall the exiles. I have a few matters to see to." He grasped his son by the shoulder and spun him about, shoving him back towards his chamber. "Pack a bag. *A* bag. We'll be home in a few days, your mother will bring any forgotten necessaries with her when she joins us, so don't waste any weight on frivolities." With that final instruction to his son and no further word at all to his wife, Rabirus strode back out of the villa to await the horses. *'If we ride hard, change horses as frequently as we can, and the weather continues fair, we need spend no more than two nights on the road. Surely none of the exiles will make better speed. And we have much to set in order before they can start exerting influence again.'*

Rabirus had navigated Ocella's reign as deftly as he could manage, but it had been a stifling experience nonetheless. To exert power only on another's behalf, to work with no recognition, knowing that both failure and success could be punishable by death—it hamstrung his ambitions. *'But now . . .'* There was a chance, here, in Ocella's wake, to ride the rising current of power in a way that would re-establish the strength of the *mos maiorum,* the proper way of things, as set down by Aven's ancestors centuries before, eternal and inviolable.

Rabirus looked out into the night sky and nodded with grim satisfaction. *'It will be good to see the city again. To see it and to claim it, with the grace and sanction of the gods.'*

◇◇◇◇◇◇◇◇◇◇◇◇◇◇◇

TARENTUM, SOUTHERN COAST OF TRUSCUM

Sempronius Tarren read the words twice, carefully, to make sure he had not misunderstood the message. Then he rolled up the scroll and handed it to the freedman servant waiting at his elbow. "Burn it," he instructed. "Immediately." The man nodded his fair head, then melted back into the house. Tapping the knuckle of his thumb against his lips, Sempronius stared for a long moment at the sunlight bleeding into the broad, still blue of the bay. Then he stood, and with a cool breeze whipping at the frayed edges of his tunic, he stalked down towards the pavilion where his sister lay on a couch, enjoying the last fading rays of light.

As he came down the sandblown stairs, she looked up but did not stir. Even in repose, Vibia Sempronia Mellanis somehow never gave an impression of being at ease; she reclined too stiffly, as though the art of relaxation required great effort and concentration. Both siblings shared the same sable hair and plain brown eyes, and slender Vibia would have been a pretty woman if not for the perpetual scowl that seemed etched into her features. Her best feature was a keen and hungry mind, and for this, along with the many secrets they shared, Sempronius brought the news to her first.

"The dictator is dead," he said, simple and emotionless.

Vibia sat up, dark eyes narrowing. "Ocella?"

"Do we have another dictator?"

Her lips twitched in irritation. Sarcasm was something Vibia considered her personal weapon, and she never responded well to having it turned on her. "How did it happen?"

"According to Galerius Orator, a swift and sudden fever, at his villa in Puteoli."

"Ha." Vibia swung her legs around to one side of her couch. "I'm only surprised to learn it wasn't his spleen, finally bursting out of so many years of concentrated hate." Sempronius put out a hand to help her rise. "He heard from Marcia Tullia, I take it?" Galerius's wife, a mage of Air, had a particular talent when it came to gathering and disseminating information. "One of her little birds . . . You must go, as swiftly as you can," Vibia said, starting up the stairs. "You must be established in the city before the Senate reconvenes. Let me and Taius see to closing the house. Take only what you need and get as far up the road as you can."

"I will," Sempronius said. "But there's one thing I must do first."

Vibia caught the intent in her brother's eyes. "Make yourself ready, then. I'll send Corvinus to you with the mirror."

⬦⬦⬦⬦⬦⬦⬦⬦⬦⬦⬦⬦

As Vibia moved about the house, giving instructions for Sempronius's departure, Sempronius changed into a plain tunic, charcoal-gray and free of ornamentation. He washed his hands and face, sloughing off the grime of the day, and letting go some of his tensions with it. Corvinus, the fair-headed Albine freedman who was Sempronius's steward and chief attendant, waited outside Sempronius's sleeping cubicle. Balanced in his hands was Sempronius's most valuable possession: a dark mirror, procured at great cost from the East, not polished bronze or silver, but volcanic glass, black and glossy.

"Attend me," Sempronius said, taking the mirror from him. "Just in case." Corvinus nodded solemnly and followed.

The rented house had a small garden protected by high walls, blocked from the prying eyes of either neighbors or the household, ideal for Sempronius's purposes. Though he had never intended to stay in Tarentum long, he had taken care to set up an altar here. He would never want the gods to think him negligent.

As he sank to his knees, placing the dark mirror into its allocated place, he said, "I call upon Pluto, Lord of the Underworld; I call upon

Nox, Lady of the Night; I call upon Neptune, Master of the Seas; I call upon Lympha, Reader of Souls. Blessed lords and ladies, governors of Shadow and of Water, I, Vibius Sempronius Tarren, entreat you. Look here, gods; look here and hear me."

Corvinus had just enough Water magic in him to see the signs: a plum-purple haze, seeping up out of the terra cotta tiles; a silver rain, hailing down from the sky; indigo sparks setting on the shallow pool just beyond the altar. The physical manifestations provided both source and channel for magic to work, and the prayers were not those of a common citizen: Sempronius Tarren was blessed and, true to the Shadow of his nature, had hidden his blessings from the world.

By law, it was sacrilege to conceal his gifts, but Sempronius felt confident of the gods' tolerance. He believed he knew the thread the Fates were spinning for him, and that mandate took precedence over the customs forged by man. And so he defied the *lex cantatia Augiae*, the law laid down in the Republic's earliest days to prevent men of magical talent from assuming high political office. No one man should hold so much power, the Republic's founders had determined, after the first man to try to wield magic and government alike had nearly brought the fledgling nation to ruin with his hubris.

'My aims are different,' Sempronius avowed. *'Not for my own glory, but the good of the city. The gods know this.'* Behind that thought prickled another: that the law was, fundamentally, unjust—not merely a protection for the Republic, but a means of keeping magically-gifted plebeians from rising too high above their station. Bar them the rank, and bar them power. *'Talent,'* in Sempronius's opinion, *'ought to be encouraged to flourish, wherever it springs.'* And so he felt no moral quandary in working his will.

Shadow and Water both moved in him, a blend that lent itself to a strange intuition, an ability to hear words unsaid and see things not yet done. Drawing energy from the dark corners of the garden, from the dimming sky above, from the water that flowed into the peristyle, Sempronius concentrated on what it was he needed to know, willing the answers to come to him, etched on the surface of the obsidian mirror. His heartbeat slowed; his muscles relaxed as he eased into that place where body and mind flowed synchronously with his elements. Thus settled, Sempronius passed a hand over the dark glass and waited, all patience, for something to surface.

As was the nature of Shadow, the images did not come through clearly. Faces were obscured, shapes moving against the black of night. These were not the crystal-clear visions of Light, nor the coded symbols of Time; for Sempronius, they were far more valuable *because* they were less precise. They showed alternatives, possibilities, might-bes and not-yets. Sempronius cherished that lack of finality. The future was so marvelously open-ended—and that meant there was always room in it for a man to assert his influence. Too, the visions did not come unbidden, as they so often did for the prophets of Time; Sempronius had to dig for the answers he sought, like feeling his way through a maze of ever-shifting curtains. Only through great force of will could he direct the power to show him something useful.

"I have great opportunity before me," Sempronius said, his voice pitched low—not that he did not trust Corvinus, but some things were private, standing between him and the gods alone. "I seek guidance. What paths will be open to me, and which must I take?"

He worked hard to keep his mind clear while a smoky haze danced on the glass; the balance was a delicate thing to hold, and his suggestion could influence what he saw. An answer came in a swirling rush: a lush, rolling countryside, hills that teemed with trees and—ah! Mines. Iberia, then, where farmers and slaves picked up their hoes and forged them anew into swords. Leading them, a man crowned with the stars—young and fresh-faced, scarcely bearded, though his cheeks were painted with blood.

As quickly as they appeared, these images melted into something else: Shadows, tangling with each other by a river with water as black as the night, and a woman standing on the shore, holding a skull in her hand. She smiled, and the skull's empty eye sockets glowed with a strange blue light.

Finally, a third vision, briefest of all: the splash of blood across white marble, scintillating in the light of the sun.

Before Sempronius could grasp what that might mean, the image dancing on the glass swirled into something new, such that he seemed to see two things at once: the city of Aven, larger and more glorious than it was now, the teeming center of life for all the peoples of the Middle Sea, wealthy and prosperous and strong, so strong that no one could challenge its dominance; the city of Aven, diminished, failing, emptying, its temples stripped for their stones, the sacred fires gone cold. Intuition whispered to him that these were Aven's two futures. Swift and correct action would lead to the former, the Aven of his dreams, the nexus of a web of allied states greater than even Parthia could dream of—Aven, the beating heart of a strong body, where the brightest minds and most talented hands of a thousand peoples would join in federation. The image gave breath to the voice of his heart, a yearning that had churned in him since the first time he had looked out over Aven's ragged red rooftops . . .

But the alternate vision hit him like a lash: a city and a people blinking out of importance without making a mark on the world, subject to the mercies of more robust civilizations. The Curia would stand empty, no longer echoing with senators' arguments, and strange armies would march in Aven's streets. Even her magic would die out, weakened when its people scattered, lost faith in their gods, rejected their blessings in favor of those of their conquerors. This, the price of failing to meet the challenges the mirror had shown.

And then he saw himself: himself, wearing the distinctive scarlet cloak of the commander of legions; himself, with a chaplet of golden leaves bound about his head, cheered in the streets; himself, seated in the consul's chair, though with an empty seat beside him—first among men, first among the greatest that Aven had to offer. But there were others, too—a Sempronius Tarren dying, suffocated by dust on a foreign field; a Sempronius Tarren dying, choked with his own blood in a crowded street; a Sempronius Tarren dying, elderly and friendless and exiled in a cold and barren place.

That appeared to be all the gods were willing to impart, for the dark mirror took on a misty quality. With whispered thanks, Sempronius drew a hand down over the obsidian, wiping it clean. The swirling energy around him began to dissipate, receding to the adumbrate corners of the garden, sinking down into the water of the impluvium, evaporating back into the sky. Sempronius sat back on his heels, considering.

'I will need an army,' he thought. *'An army like this world has never seen, if I am to protect Aven from these ravages, to bind together what I mean to build . . . A legion, for a start . . . Then the allies, the auxiliaries, to marry their strengths to ours . . . Protection and support, for all the peoples of the Middle Sea . . .'*

Instinct told him the first conflict would be Iberia, and soon. *'And there's your chance to show Aven what you can do.'* At this moment, with the city still bleeding from the wounds Ocella had inflicted, power was there for the taking. *'Elections will have to be held before the end of the year. And I . . .'* Sempronius had already served as aedile, a city official responsible for festivals and public buildings—though his term had been rudely interrupted by his proscription and exile—and so the next step on the ladder was a praetorship. The office was venerable in its own right—praetors were judges, legal magistrates, military commanders, and regional governors, all wrapped up together—and only one step away from the consulship.

And a praetorship came with legions.

For this much the mirror had made plain: the key to Aven's survival lay with him. He would need the love of the people, the loyalty of the legions, and the wit to outmaneuver his opponents in the Senate. *'What a challenge,'* he thought, and smiled even as it chilled him.

Cradling the obsidian mirror protectively to his chest, he rose, feeling a stiffness in his legs. "I'll just take a small plate of bread and cheese in my room," Sempronius said to Corvinus, as he entrusted his attendant with the dark mirror. It would be wrapped in velvet, stored in its own box and then locked in an inconspicuous trunk among his luggage. "Let me rest an hour, no more, and then I will want to start north."

Corvinus moved swiftly to comply, and Sempronius walked, leaden-footed, to his room. Working that magic had taken much of his strength, and he would need time to submerge its signature, that no other mage might observe the mark of it on him. He had spent years building up fortifications in his mind, weaving the patterns of his magic into obscurity. From his earliest awareness of his gifts, he had nourished the secret close to his heart, hiding it even from his parents, young as he had been. Eventually he had chosen to trust Vibia and Corvinus, but none other. The instinct for self-protection went deep, and over time, Sempronius had crafted it to his best advantage. It would now take a dedicated mage indeed to discern his abilities, and they would have to know what to search for. Shadow was not just his gift, not just the name of the energy he could command and to which he was subject: it was the stuff that composed his very being, the natural fiber of his person.

◇◇◇◇◇◇◇◇◇◇◇◇

CITY OF AVEN, THE PALATINE HILL

"Dead!" The two older Vitelliae sisters, Aula and Latona, had been sitting in their father's garden, relaxing among the narcissi and hyacinths, when the youngest sister, little Alhena, burst in on them, shouting, "He's dead!"

Aula and Latona rose from their couches at once. "Who's dead?" asked Aula.

"The Dictator!" Alhena gasped, holding a hand to her chest; evidently she had run the entire way home.

"You're quite sure?" Latona, the middle sister, asked, reaching out to grasp Alhena's free hand. "How do you know?"

The question was not a flippant one, for Alhena had ways of getting information that went far beyond news-criers or slave gossip. "I'm absolutely sure," she said. "It . . . It *happened* again."

"You needn't sound so aggrieved," Aula reprimanded, settling her hands on her hips. "It's a magnificent gift. One of the most useful the gods can bestow." Like Latona, Alhena had a magical blessing, but for her, it was the touch of Proserpina, granting the prophetic gifts of time.

Less strident than Aula, Latona stroked her younger sister's cheek. "The more you embrace it, the less it will plague you," she said, brushing back a lock of fire-red hair. The Vitelliae were all flame-colored in one way or another, but where Latona's wealth of curls burned sun-gold and Aula's held the soft auburn promise of sunset, Alhena's head was a vibrant shock of fiercest red.

"I'm not plagued, I'm annoyed," Alhena huffed. "I was in the middle of shopping for new silks. I could've dropped right there in the macellum if Mus hadn't had the wit to drag me into a temple before I'd lost all faculty."

"Good girl, that," Aula said, toying idly with her fan, a spray of feathers dyed bright cerulean blue. "Good head on her shoulders, especially for a Cantabrian."

"They aren't *all* mindless barbarians, Aula," Alhena insisted.

"Did I say—?"

Latona interrupted, squeezing Alhena's shoulders. "Nevermind Cantabrian merits right now. Mus did well, yes, but what did you *see*?"

With a wearied sigh, Alhena wrenched away and flung herself onto a couch. "The sun set into an ocean of blood, and as soon as it was submerged, the waters ran clear and pure as a mountain spring. All the people of Aven rushed to the water's edge to drink and drink and had their fill."

Aula and Latona exchanged a significant look. "Auspicious, I think," Aula ventured.

"Yes, we must hope so," Latona said.

"It *is* so!" Alhena insisted. "You know it is. You remember what I dreamt when he came back to the city that last time? That was when the ocean ran bloody, and it's been like that in my dreams ever since. If it's clear now, he must be dead." She sat bolt upright on the couch, leaning forward avidly. "And you know what that means? Tarpeius will be coming home."

Tarpeius, a promising young man from a good family, had been betrothed to Alhena years earlier. As she had been only thirteen at the time, their fathers had decided to hold off on the actual ceremony until she reached full maturity. Unfortunately for both, Tarpeius had been assigned a post as military tribune to a general, who, upon making it onto the Dictator Ocella's proscription list, decided that fighting barbarians was quite preferable to being assassinated.

"I'm right, aren't I? With Ocella dead, there's no reason for General Aufidius Strato to remain in the field."

"Well, there is the small manner of all those Vendelicians yet to be subdued," Latona pointed out. When Alhena's face blanched, she hurried on. "I'm teasing, pet. Of course he'll come back. I wager Aufidius had quite enough of tramping around the swamps, and anyway, he'll want to stand for consul. A garrison will have to stay, but the tribunes will all come home."

Dozens of important men, patricians and plebeians, had packed up and left, either before or after finding themselves on the Dictator's proscription list, uprooting their families and households as well. Their father, Aulus Vitellius, had only escaped proscription by a hair; with his only son Gaius serving his own term as a military tribune in far-off Albina, Aulus devoted all attention to protecting his daughters. Alhena was then only ten, easily kept out of sight at home, and Aula had already married Quinctilius, but Latona he hastily matched to Numerius Herennius, a provincial aristocrat with considerable wealth, who was meant to keep her at his estates in the north, away from trouble. *'Men make plans, and the gods laugh at them . . .'* Quinctilius had not been so safe a choice as Aulus had hoped, and Latona had been unwilling to molder in a country villa—a choice that had saved Aula, true, but had also thrown Latona into Ocella's path. *'Neither marriage turned out as planned. Oh, please let Alhena have better luck.'*

"Before we start planning any weddings, we should see if we can reach anyone else to confirm the Dictator's death," Aula was saying. "Someone who might know more. No offense, my honey, but your visions aren't precisely abundant with tangible details."

Alhena sniffed. "You think Marcia would know—"

"I do," Latona said, "but I don't know how we could safely reach her."

"No, not without one of her birds coming to Father first."

Talent and ambition made Ocella see a conspirator and assassin where a senator stood. Such were the suspicions that had driven Galerius Orator from the city, along with his wife Marcia and their adolescent son. Galerius had used his wife's magical talents to keep up communication with some of his fellow senators in exile. With Galerius proscribed and Aulus trying to avoid the same fate, no letters could pass between their families without Marcia's help.

Aula's fingers drummed restlessly against her thigh. "I might be able to send word to the Domitiae. It would have to be carefully worded, just in case . . . And some of the Crispiniae are still in Truscum . . ." She sighed. "This scattering of our friends is really most inconvenient."

"I just hope enough of them are ready to return on short notice," Latona said, thinking of how long it might take just to get word to those farthest-flung.

"When word got out that Ocella had taken ill, I expect many would have started preparing themselves," Aula said. "They had to be hoping he wouldn't last forever."

The words prickled something in Latona's memory: Sempronius Tarren, a longtime friend of the Vitellian family, the night that he had not so much fled the city as sidled out of it. *"'This is Aven. No dictator lasts forever. Indeed, most of them do not even last very long. And I intend to be back as soon as this one trips.'"* Ocella had hounded him as far as Abydosia, though rumor in the Stabiae bathhouse was that he was one of those who had crept back into Truscum upon word of the Dictator's illness.

Latona found herself slowly pacing, her fingers trailing idly through the clusters of blushing oleander that grew beside the garden's shallow pool. A strange feeling was growing in her chest. It took her a few minutes to realize that it was relief, the easing of a tension that had been wrapped around her heart for years.

'It's over . . . If Ocella is really dead, then it's over.' She would never be summoned to his court again, never terrorized into submission. She would never again feel his eyes on her, assessing her physical and political worth. He could never again try to compel the use of the gifts of Juno against his enemies—nor command those of Venus for his own amusement.

The relief hit her with physical force: tears behind her eyes and a prickling warmth in her palms, a hot sunburn-like flush creeping over her skin. Magic, unbidden, rising to the surface. Accompanying it, there was a pressure behind her ribs, an impulse to act, like being pushed from the inside out. She didn't know if she wanted to sob or scream or set something ablaze.

She gripped her fists tight, hoping her sisters would not notice her discomfort. After a few deep breaths, the pressure eased and the tingle on her skin abated. *'Mind yourself.'* Since childhood, she had kept tight control over her emotions and her abilities, not wanting to draw a moment's more attention than could be helped. Ocella's death meant some reprieve, but she could not allow it to be like the breaking of a dam.

Slowly, she uncurled her fingers, smoothing her hands against her skirts. For her, there could be no loosing of discipline.

II

It had started out simply enough.

At first, Ekialde's feud was not with the Aventans. There *were* no Aventans, to speak of, where he lived, on the western side of the Iberian Mountains, which his people called the *mendi*, where the high steppes and rocky plateaus gave way at last to placidly rolling hills, flat river basins, and beyond, to the ocean without an end. But there were absentee Aventan landowners, and there were relocated peoples, moving westward from other parts of the empire, lured by tales of fantastical wealth and fertile land. And certainly there was gold in the region, so much that it was hardly a thing of value to the people who lived there. The women of Ekialde's tribe dangled it from their wrists and ankles, their ears and noses and, in the case of a few more intrepid ladies, their nipples; the men banded it about their arms and their throats. There was no peasant so wretched but owned at least one gold ring, a treasured heirloom protected from the ravages of time.

Word of the riches of the golden sands of the Tagus had spread, and the region was far more crowded now than it had been in Ekialde's father's childhood—at least by Lusetani standards. Though communities on the coast, influenced by the large cities of the mercantile Tyrians and Athaecans, were accustomed to such proximity, it was not so in the foothills and the mountains. The Aventans called it peace when the people they had beaten moved at their behest, adopted their gods and their language, wore their flowing, impractical clothes, and coveted the ever-elusive citizenship in their strange government. Aventans pushed in a way that the Tyrians and Athaecans never had.

The Lusetani had become anxious. They had not seen the legions yet, but they knew that the garrisons were not so very far away: over the mountains in Tarraco, in the southern plains at ancient Gades. Near, too near.

And so they began to push back against their arrogating neighbors. There was no official organization to it, at first. A forager who trespassed into Lusetani territory did not return home. A traveling party had their horses stolen and their purses filched. A village too near the nebulous border was put to the torch. Ekialde, son of a chieftain, was only one of a dozen or so men from various Lusetani villages who began leading raids.

Eventually, the tribal leaders held a council. Some of the older men favored peace, but there were too many fire-eyed youngsters in the group, too many hot tempers and vengeful heads who had never seen real war, whose only experience of battle and death was in raids like these. They were prime for it now, their bellies full of the sparking coals which make young men seek out bloodshed. Ekialde was only one of several who spoke at the council, but by the judgment of many in the mud-walled meeting hall, he had some of the finest words.

The young blood overpowered the old, and soon after that, the Lusetani began an offensive, striking not just at those who trespassed on what they considered their lands, but actively venturing into territory claimed by Aven or their traitorous allied tribes. Valley by valley, riverside by riverside, they moved over the conquered areas and reclaimed them. Through spring and summer, the groups splintered and vanquished and re-formed, and as they did, they drew in more followers, more men willing to fight, more women ready to pick up the spoils. And at twenty years old, Ekialde, with his wild black hair and yellow eyes, found that more and more men were looking to him for the answers, for guidance, for their next direction.

Eventually, pressing at the edges of more heavily settled areas, the Lusetani found themselves running out of tiny villages to overwhelm. The next circle out were fortified towns—not with immense walls, to be sure, but pikes and fences and ditches that many of them had begun to reinforce, as they heard of the western tribes rising up in revolt. So too, these fortified towns were more heavily armed. Some of the men there were veterans, at least of local skirmishes. They would not fall as easily as the smaller villages had.

And so Ekialde wondered: What to do now? Shy back from harder odds? Recede back into their wilderness, having made their point? It might work. Probably no one would pursue them, and it would be some time before the Aventans and their allies thought to reclaim the center of the peninsula.

Some time. But it would not last forever. The high plateaus were too rich in metallic ore, the river valleys too fertile, the woodlands too flush with game. The temptations of their high-peaked *mendi* were too great.

Rapacious Aven could not stand so near to it and not feel the desire to seize what it saw—and if not Aven, Ekialde allowed, then someone else. If they did not fight now, they would have to do so later. But now—now there might be opportunity. The scouts and merchants spoke of disarray among the Aventan people, their much-prized order thrown into confusion. Swift action now could take advantage of that weakness.

Ekialde had no magic himself, but as his victories began to pile up, he had found it beneficial to acquaint himself with those who did. It was to these men he went, one star-spattered night in the hottest part of the summer, when the air brushed arid against his bare shoulders. He had begun to realize how men, important men, were deferring to him, but he would not tempt fate by dressing the part. He was his father's second son, and no chieftain in his own right yet. He would wait to be proclaimed as such before donning a leopard-skin or binding a golden circle around his brow. Until that time, he walked bare-chested in the summer night, wearing only what armbands and greaves and belts he had earned the right to bear.

With the silvery sheen of the half-moon bleeding through the trees, casting a faint dappled light on the camp, Ekialde gathered the magic-men of the collected tribes. "I wish to know the will of the gods," he said, and explained what it was he desired. Other men might have sought more mundane counsel—if their plans were feasible, if they could join the tribes, what political alliances would need to be solidified, whose daughter would need to be traded to whose son. The magic-men did not discuss such things; that was not their province. Instead, they told Ekialde what he would have to do to get the answers he required, to submit himself to the will of the gods.

He let them bleed him, those magic-men with their bony headdresses and ancient pelts. He let them make little cuts in his hand and his upper arm, taking his vitality for their perusal. His wife, Neitin, sat by while they did so, rocking back and forth on the balls of her feet, murmuring little prayers. His wife did not trust the magic-men and perhaps for good reason; they were not universally recognized to be good men. Some could turn very bad indeed, if the lust for power overwhelmed them. But the men trusted to bear the knives were of his clan, and the blood they let was their own, for one of them was his mother's brother.

Three bowls they prepared, three bowls of polished bone filled with crimson drippings, and when they bandaged his hands and arms, Ekialde endeavored not to show the dizziness roiling in his head. One bowl they placed over a fire, to heat and bubble; another they poured at the base of a sapling; and the third, Ekialde's uncle swirled in the bowl, staring at the oscillating liquid for long, long moments. The other magic-men gathered around him, chanting and singing, drawing down the power of Endovelicos, the supreme god in his guise as an oracle, to know a man's fate and see the future. Then he dipped his fingers, raised them to his mouth, and tasted Ekialde's life-force.

Ekialde stood stoic as he watched all of this, ignoring the throbbing ache in his arms. The first magic-man rose from his place near the fire, taking the bowl in his hands with no sign that he felt a burn from the heat. "You have strong blood, Ekialde, and a man with strong blood may do many things."

Then it was his uncle's turn, who stood, still contemplating the taste of his blood. He rose, sinking two fingers in the bowl. With great solemnity, he passed his hand over Ekialde's head, then smeared his nephew's forehead with his own blood, drawing a faint reddish-brown streak across Ekialde's sun-darkened skin. "The gods have picked you out, Ekialde, my sister's son, to lead our people at this time," he declared. Ekialde felt his shoulder muscles tense up, heard his wife gasp, heard murmurs from his tribesmen, but he made no response as yet. His uncle continued. "Your strength will unite many tribes, as we were when we first crossed the mountains, so many hundred generations ago. You will call them. They will answer. So the gods speak: Endovelicos tells us this is so. Nabia implores you to protect her people. Bandue, lord of battles, claims you for his own. *Erregerra*, he calls you. It is written in your blood."

The word meant "war-king," a title only rarely bestowed on any man. Men of legend held it, men who had governed the Lusetani in the days when they first entered Iberia as one tribe, moving south like a massive flock of gulls. Ekialde could not have hoped for more. His closest men, his friends and younger brothers, erupted in whooping cheers; his wife mostly looked pale. But Ekialde, aware of the significance of this moment, maintained an expression of blank dignity. "Then it is well with the gods, that I seek to make war on Aven, to protect our people from their encroachments forever?"

"The gods have placed their faith in *you*, my sister's son. If it is your will, it is theirs."

He nodded, satisfied. "And the tree?" Ekialde asked curiously, jerking his head towards the sapling.

His uncle shrugged. "That has the longest story to tell. The tree's life or death is bound to yours, now. It may flourish as you do. It may serve as a warning if there is misfortune in your future further than I can see. Or if the gods' favor alters." Ekialde tried not to think that the warning would do him small good, if none of his people remained in this place to watch it, but it was part of the ritual, and perhaps they would pass this way frequently enough to check in on the tree's growth from time to time.

"Then there is much work to do."

III

CITY OF AVEN

Ocella's body made the journey from Puteoli shrouded in gray cloth, laid on a cart drawn by black horses. It meandered the long miles beneath the dappled shade of olive trees, then passed the mausoleums of centuries' worth of Aventans that lined the road into the city. Word of his demise had officially reached the city only shortly before, though Galerius Orator's arrival had set the rumors flying.

"I suppose we'll have to go, won't we?" Numerius Herennius asked his wife on the day before the funeral.

Latona only flicked her eyes up from her book briefly to look at her husband. He was not an ill-favored man, and he did have a thoroughly Truscan nose, but there was still little in him to inspire even casual interest in her. But then, theirs was a match made in haste and out of Aulus's desire to keep Latona out of the city and out of trouble. Neither romance nor ambition had played a part in her marriage, as had both in Aula's; Latona was bound to Herennius for security's sake.

"I had assumed," she said, endeavoring to keep impatience out of her voice, "that was why you came back from Liguria." Herennius had none of her love for the city, attending the Senate as infrequently as he could get away with, preferring to spend his days tending to his vast estates.

Herennius heaved a sigh, shuffling his feet against the blue-tiled floor as he paced around the atrium. "Yes, yes. It's only that . . . well, it's not likely to be a very pleasant affair, is it?"

"Funerals are rarely occasions for jollity," Latona said, adding silently, *'Though this one may be met with more good cheer than most.'* Around her husband, she had been careful not to demonstrate high emotion of any kind in regard to the Dictator's demise. What Herennius did not know for certain about the nature of Latona's bargain with Ocella, he certainly suspected, and Latona was loath to give him either confirmation or denial to hold over her head. "Our absence would be remarked on."

"Well. Yes, it would." Herennius furrowed his brow, and Latona could see various considerations knitting themselves together behind his eyes. A familiar expression, when he was arranging some money-making scheme or another. Herennius was not unintelligent, but in Latona's opinion, he had an unfortunately limited scope of the world, which he then proved by saying, "I wonder if I could pull Licinius Cornicen aside for a moment to speak about some of those tax revenues from Alalia . . ."

Latona let her scroll furl entirely and slapped it into her lap. "At a *funeral?*"

"Yes." Herennius shrugged. "I know he'll be there. And it isn't as though I can ever talk business properly in the Curia, and the Forum's always so loud and crowded . . ."

Latona thought about explaining just what a gross breach of propriety it would be to initiate such a conversation on a day of public mourning— even if it were state-mandated mourning for a man she was all too glad to see dead. But Herennius's face, broad and blank, indicated there would be no way of making him understand. Business took precedence over social niceties for him, and marriage to Latona had done nothing to change that. Besides, from what she knew of Licinius Cornicen, Latona thought he would be unlikely to take offense, since he was among the more mercantile-minded members of Senate. Ocella's funeral was unlikely to overwhelm him with sentiment.

So instead, she sighed, rising from her chair. "If you decide to hunt him down then, let me know and I'll arrange to go to my father's for dinner. In order to avoid being in your way, of course." Herennius nodded, fully in agreement that his wife had no place hovering around his business dealings, but as she left the room, Latona reflected with satisfaction that at least she would not have to bear witness to his self-engineered embarrassment.

Then again, as Ocella had taught a few score senators and mages, it was safer not to be *too* good at anything. Nor had Herennius himself felt such a burden at first. When their marriage began, he had been so thrilled at the advantageous alliance that he had been gentle and solicitous with his peerless patrician wife.

'Ocella changed that.'

Against Herennius's wishes, she had returned to the city to be with her sister, and when that put her in Ocella's path, he had no power to challenge the Dictator's summons. When Latona returned, she was brittle and fatigued from the strain of exerting so much control over her magic, her conversation, her smiles, nearly every aspect of her being, as was necessary in Ocella's court, and she found Herennius no longer so attentive. Their relationship had been cool and formal ever since. At first that had been preferable, a respite for her nerves.

'Now, though . . . ' The world was changing again, and there would be opportunity in it. Latona could not help wondering what Fortuna might have in store for her—and if she would have the temerity to reach for it.

⬦⬦⬦⬦⬦⬦⬦⬦⬦⬦⬦⬦⬦⬦

That afternoon, with the weather dryer and cooler than it had been in weeks, Aula and Latona went shopping, ostensibly for fabric for new gowns, but as much to discover what gossip about Ocella's funeral and the returning Senators could be heard in the marketplace. As was proper and fitting for patricians of such old blood as the Vitelliae, each of the daughters had her own personal attendant. The jewel of the household was Helva, the Athaecan freedwoman who had once belonged to their mother, Vipsania. She was invaluable, not only for her precision, her shrewd bargaining skills, and her ability to dress hair and style clothing, but because she had been blessed by Vesta and Saturn. She had a perfect memory. No need to pay a *nomenclator* to memorize vast lists of names; Helva could, at a second's notice, see a face and recall everything she had ever heard or read about that person and every member of his family or political circles. It was a talent Aula had made good use of over the years, employing Helva to keep track of myriad intrigues, shifting alliances, aristocratic family trees, and legal maneuvers.

In youth, Helva had been quite beautiful, with glossy black hair, creamy pale skin, and sky-grey eyes. Now her skin was no longer alabaster-smooth, and she tended to keep her hair wrapped firmly under a kerchief, but her eyes were still bright and keen. There was an oddity to her, not unlike that which sometimes surfaced in Proserpina-touched Alhena. It happened with those whose talents lay in Time; they saw the world on a different scale than those around them.

Latona's Merula was also an unusual attendant. With warm brown skin and a pointed ferocity in her dark eyes, she had a quick and keen look about her, for all that she was also boxy-faced, short, and prone to fidgeting. Among the other qualities which made her undesirable to most noble ladies was an abominable habit of speaking her mind. It had earned her plenty of beatings as a child, in her first household, and was the reason she had found herself on the market. But with that intuition born of Spirit, Latona had seen in Merula someone she knew she could trust implicitly.

Together, they kept a secret. Years earlier, Latona had made a proposition, and it was one that Merula, athletic and aggressive by nature, had leapt at the chance to fulfill. Latona wanted protection—protection that was inconspicuous and, more importantly, ever-present. Enormous, well-muscled bodyguards were all well and good, but they attracted such attention. Who could object, though, to a refined lady's handmaiden? Latona had, on the sly and with her allowance, hired a gladiatrix to teach Merula some tricks of her trade. Before her twentieth birthday, Merula was, by Latona's estimation, probably one of the finer combatants in the city.

Apart from Helva and Merula, Aula and Latona had a pair of male slaves clearing the way through the street for them. Alhena had declined the invitation to go out, as she often had lately. She gave many excuses, but her sisters knew she wanted to be home in case her betrothed—or, at least, word of him—arrived.

Perhaps, for the elder two, it was just as well; Alhena could be a little *too* much sometimes, and there were some things Aula and Latona could only discuss comfortably with*out* their baby sister present. "I think Father might start trying to find me a new husband once the Senate comes back to town," Aula commented, as they picked over a selection of linens, soft wools, and precious silks at the stall of their favorite vendor, a Palmyrean merchant and his wife.

"Would that be the worst thing?" Latona asked, rubbing a bit of cobalt fabric between her fingers.

Aula frowned, considering. "Not *the* worst," she admitted. "The city could catch fire. Plague could strike. Tennic tribes could invade."

"I'm glad you rate the welfare of the city above your widowhood," Latona laughed.

"At least a little." Aula lifted a swath of cherry-red fabric up to her face. "What do you think?"

"Too bright with your hair. Ask if she has anything darker." As Aula gestured to the woman who ran the stall, Latona continued. "Now, speak honestly, Aula. Aren't you tired of living at home?"

"Oh, it isn't so bad, most of the time, apart from Alhena's mooning. Father's hardly any restriction to my comings and goings." Aula lifted the fabric to show the stallkeeper. "Yes, do you have anything like this but a little darker?"

"I will check, Domina."

"Speak even more honestly, then," Latona pressed, smirking a bit. "Aren't you tired of an empty bed?"

Aula heaved a great sigh, casting her eyes heavenward. "Now there, my dear sister, you may have something. Three years alone is . . . well." Latona smiled, envying her sister's carnal appetite. Aula and Quinctilius had been extraordinarily well-matched. Passion had blossomed easily between them, and in the days before Latona's own wedding, Aula had delighted in regaling her sister with tales of rapturous pleasures. Latona had been thrilled, scandalized, and anticipatory, all at once; the reality had rather paled next to Aula's promises. She suspected she could go three years without Numerius Herennius's attentions quite easily. "But," Aula went on, twitching her hips and grinning wickedly, "who says I have to find a *husband* just to keep from having an empty bed?"

Prim and pious Alhena would have screeched in outrage, but Latona merely returned her sister's grin. "You'd hardly be the first widow in Aven to seek that solace."

"Perhaps this dinner will bring someone suitable to my attention," Aula said, as the stallkeeper brought forward a few lengths of cloth, ranging from vermilion to cinnamon to deepest crimson. "Oh, I know I could just go choose some sturdy buck from the markets, but I've always thought that a bit of a tawdry way to go about it."

"And I somehow suspect you'd have a hard time slipping a prize stud past Father's notice." Latona examined a bright fuchsia fabric, wondering if it was too garish or just daring enough to be interesting; she needed a new mantle for this year's Cantrinalia, and a shocking shade might be just the thing to spice up her typically demure religious garb.

"Well, if I'm going to go a-hunting, be it for a husband or a lover, I think it'll have to be the crimson," Aula said. "Could you be a dear and send the usual length over to Tura Petronia?"

"Of course, Domina."

"And some of that gold trim as well." She turned back to Latona. "I'll have to make an appointment with Petronia soon, then."

"Better hurry. I'm sure you won't be the only one sprucing up her wardrobe, and it'll cost a fortune if you have to ask her to rush anything through." Latona lifted the bright pink silk for her sister's inspection.

Aula's eyes widened. "Why my darling little sister, are you *finally* stepping out from those matronly disguises?"

"How dare you?" Latona said in mock indignation, though she knew the color was out of her normal mode. Since marrying Herennius, she had always dressed well, in fine fashion and quality garments, but without much real flash. Muted tones, modest cuts, splashes of brighter color in the trim and embroidery, perhaps, but nothing so unsubtle as this brilliant fuchsia. "I don't dress half so conservatively as Marcia Tullia."

"Mm, true, but modesty suits her so much better than it suits you. Here!" Aula snatched at another fabric, a lovely, shimmering pale gold, far less ostentatious, but exquisite in its own way. "Buy that pink for a gown, and promise you'll wear it, and I'll make a gift of this as a mantle to go with it."

Latona looked over at the stallkeeper, who waited patiently for instructions. "How can I refuse? Add the pink to my account and send it to Petronia as well, if you would."

"And add *two* lengths of the gold to mine," Aula chirped, her cheeks bright with merriment. "We'll dress to match," she added, giving Latona a friendly jostle.

They left the fabric vendors and meandered towards the Forum. They passed a gathering of children at one of the corners, where a magister had set up his school. A knot of boys, both patrician and plebeian, mixed with a few promising girls, sat on stools with wax tablets in their laps, listening with varying degrees of attentiveness to a togate man lecturing on grammar. "You know," Latona said as they rounded a corner onto the broad Via Sacra, "Ocella's death will leave quite a gap."

"Yes, I was thinking that as well," Aula said. "I wonder how it will fall out. So many are dead, and some who were stripped of their fortunes may choose to remain in exile."

"The Senate rolls will have to be reviewed," Latona said, "and I daresay a few new men admitted, to plump out the ranks."

Aula giggled. "Plebeians and provincials of all stripes. What a scandal!" It was the sort of adjustment the Popularists frequently agitated for, the better to represent Aven's growth, and as such, likely to meet steep opposition from the Optimates, who saw such measures as degradation. "Well, the elections should be lively and no mistake. A lot of men missed their first chances under Ocella." The Dictator had all but abolished elections, filling positions by appointment. "And when you consider that men like Lucretius Rabirus will be running—"

"Yes," Latona said. "He could be trouble. If too many Optimates like him get in, we can expect a year of public lectures on morality, tariffs on luxuries, exclusionary voting measures, and anti-Popularist legislation." Aula pulled a face, then began quizzing Helva's flawless memory for information on which men were eligible for which offices.

As they drew near the Forum proper, the preparations for Ocella's funeral became more apparent. A host of slaves were sweeping the steps of every long-columned temple and chunky administrative building that bordered the open plaza, and the statues lining the dusty pathways were getting a good scrubbing. Aula and Latona fell silent, staring up at the Rostra, the elevated platform in front of the majestic Temple of Saturn. Usually used for political speeches or grand announcements, the space had been cleared for display of Ocella's body. Latona shivered, pulling her mantle closer about her shoulders.

"Are you looking forward to it?" Aula asked. Her voice was low, subdued, far from its usual strident confidence.

Latona paused, regarding the barren stone before them. "Yes," she said, shuttering her mind against unwelcome memories. "Yes, I rather am."

"Good," Aula said. "Me too."

◇◇◇◇◇◇◇◇◇◇◇◇◇

The journey from Tarentum to Aven took eight days, even as swiftly as Sempronius could ride, and as such, he arrived in the city only the night before Ocella's funeral. Sending his trunk with his chief attendant Corvinus on to his domus on the Aventine Hill, he took himself directly to the Palatine Hill, where tapers burned bright in the windows of Lucius Galerius Orator.

"Sempronius, my friend!" Galerius wrapped Sempronius in a warm embrace, and Sempronius thumped his back lightly in return. Galerius was several years older and had been a model to Sempronius in his youth, first on the training grounds of the Campus Martius, then in the law courts of Aven and on the battlefields of Numidia. If Sempronius thought him sometimes too traditional and a touch hesitant in his scope, still he admired Galerius's valor and intellect. They had kept up their secret, magically assisted correspondence in exile, but scantly worded messages passed every few months did little to make up for three years' absence. "I am glad to see you well."

"As well as a man can be after eight days on horseback."

"Sit, sit," Galerius said, showing him to a couch. "Helion, fetch some bread and fruit up from the kitchens. And wine." He smiled, sitting across from Sempronius. "Your return to the city warrants a toast."

"And yours no less." Sempronius glanced around the domus. "Marcia and Young Lucius?"

"Well, but still in the country. I hadn't thought to find *you* as near as Tarentum," Galerius said. "Why did you leave Abydosia? And when?"

"Just before the Nones of Quintilis. I had heard—well, the same rumors that brought you back from Pannonia, I suppose, and I wanted to make sure I crossed before the seas turned too dangerous."

Galerius nodded. "Well, Fortune smiled on you. We'll need everyone we can back in the Curia as soon as may be. The Optimates are already trying to manipulate the change in circumstances to their favor."

"Rabirus?" Sempronius asked.

"And Buteo. Rumor has it he wants to block attempts to revoke Ocella's proscriptions."

Sempronius's mouth quirked up at the corner. "He'd like nothing better than to see us and our friends in permanent exile."

Sighing, Galerius gestured to Helion as he came back in, indicating that he should serve Sempronius first. "Our ranks are too thin as it is. So many didn't survive Ocella's reign."

Sempronius accepted a glass of wine, and they both drank to absent friends by the uncertain light of a single, low-burning lamp. Sempronius thought of men he had served with in Numidia, legates and quaestors and tribunes, cut down by Ocella for the promise they had shown; or the mages, patrician and plebeian, who took their own lives rather than submit their powers to a Dictator's use. Sempronius lifted his eyes to Galerius over the rim of his cup. "You realize you'll have to be consul next year. I don't mean you have to run. You have to *win*."

A wry smile touched Galerius's lips. "You show a lot of faith in me, friend. You know I don't share your enthusiasm for measures that are more . . ."

"Radical?" Sempronius supplied.

"I was going to say innovative."

"Be fair to yourself, Galerius. You're practical, not conservative, and your moderation is a boon," Sempronius said, leaning forward a bit. "It makes you an attractive alternative to the Optimates." Sempronius used their self-assumed title with a touch of bitterness on his tongue. The arch-traditionalists could be intractable and impossible to wrangle even in the best of times, so firm were they in their belief that ancient patrician blood made them the best equipped men to make decisions on behalf of all Aven. Sempronius shared that illustrious ancestry but considered their rigid adherence to custom both obtuse and impractical. Galerius Orator was a true moderate, respecting custom whenever possible, ceding to innovation where beneficial. "You will do what needs to be done," Sempronius began, "to get Aven's governing body back to full strength and operations. And if you oppose the stronger Popularist measures—"

"As I fear I may have to."

"—it only shows the strength of your character. And," Sempronius added, tearing a hunk of bread into small pieces, "I'd rather spend my energy tangling with you over things that *matter* than fighting with the Optimates on their general principle of stubbornness." Lack of worthy opposition could undo a man. Sempronius anticipated, even relished, the opportunity to showcase his plans in open debate, and he knew his own wits would only be sharpened against the bedrock stability of Galerius's pragmatism. Dealing with the conservative Optimate faction, on the other hand, was more like attempting to hone a blade by stabbing a sack of wet seaweed. "Aufidius Strato is likely to win one of the seats on sheer popularity, but his interests are military, not civil. He won't have enough of a care for setting things to rights. The city *needs* you, Galerius."

Galerius was quite still for a moment, then he sighed, running a hand through his sandy-colored hair. "Then I will serve." Some men would have said such words pompously, but Sempronius knew that Galerius's humility was genuine all the way down to marrow and bone. Such selfless lack of personal ambition was foreign to Sempronius, but he could appreciate its worth in others. "If, of course, we can get me elected."

"You'll do best to steer the middle course. I expect much of the electorate will be timid this year, fearful of leaning too far to either side. Fortunately, the opposing field is nearly as sparse as ours." The Optimates had fared little better than the Popularists under Ocella. Ambitious men with the strength of their faction behind them, and principled conservatives who opposed the very idea of a dictator as an affront to the Republic, had both fallen victim to Ocella's paranoia. Others simply had the wealth that Ocella needed for bribes or to appease his troops. Only those who had toed the line and toed it well had survived with position and power intact. "It's a mercy that Rabirus isn't eligible yet—"

"He'll be *your* problem."

"Too true." That Rabirus, the Dictator's former right hand, would likely never answer for his part in Ocella's crimes was bad enough. Having to compete with him electorally was a twist of the knife. "But I do think you'll have Buteo to worry about."

"You think he'll run again?" Galerius asked.

Privately, Sempronius thought that ancient, entrenched Arrius Buteo would be a thorn in his side until nothing more than a desiccated husk kept alive by pure spite, but, suspecting Galerius would little appreciate such a colorful assessment, he said simply, "No—he was last consul only eight years ago, so he's not eligible again yet. But his opinion will carry a lot of weight. We should try to figure out who he'll be supporting."

"Perhaps we can glean some idea of his intentions from how he behaves at the funeral." Galerius took a drink, then added, "I'm giving a laudatio."

Sempronius looked up sharply, but the surprise soon faded. Whatever else Ocella had been, he had been a Dictator of Aven, a consul and a senator before that. No doubt the coming weeks would be a flood of denunciations and repeals, but on the day he journeyed to the underworld, Ocella would be remembered with respect. It was not only piety, of course; it was political as well. Men like Galerius Orator had no desire to fan the flames of vengeance which might plunge the city into total chaos. Sempronius might have been willing to chance it, if he thought he could control the flow.

He stayed with Galerius until late in the night, and before he took himself home, the talk turned from political strategy to tales from exile. The next morning, Sempronius rose early, donning the toga pulla of mourning, little sorrow though he felt, and walked to the Forum with only Corvinus to accompany him.

∞∞∞∞∞∞∞∞∞∞

The curbs of the broad Via Sacra, the widest and straightest street in the city, were packed shoulder-to-shoulder with citizens watching the funeral procession. There were soldiers enough in attendance to keep anyone from attempting to dishonor the corpse, but the faces it passed were stony, marking but not mourning the dead man. The procession began at what had been Ocella's last home in the city, on the Esquiline Hill, when the sun was high on the last day of Sextilis. Before the body came floats bearing the spoils and honors of his career: the military honors, the gifts from foreign leaders, the captured works of art and statuary. Though the day was cloudy, threatening rain, a stiff wind took the odor from hundreds of pots of cinnamon and frankincense and wafted it through the streets.

Six trumpeters preceded the ivory litter bearing the corpse. The body, well-preserved by both Abydosian and Aventan magic, looked fresher than it had in his last moments, all marks of disease gone. He was dressed in a purple-trimmed toga, and a chaplet of oak leaves sat across his brow. The family walked behind the bier—what was left of it, anyway. Of his father's generation and his own, no blood relations remained. Both his wives had preceded him to the Underworld, but they had left sons. The elder was but four years old, more bewildered than solemn as he did his duty, walking first behind the corpse. His uncle Maloricus followed close at hand, carrying the younger child, not yet a year old.

Many attendant at the funeral had to do their best not to look too pleased, though the professional mourners, no doubt well-paid for their efforts, were certainly making a good show of it—dresses torn, red welts raised on their arms and breasts, ashes rubbed in their hair. The actors wearing the masks of Ocella's ancestors were doing a fine job of imitation. Ocella must have left considerable funds for his funeral. *'He certainly had enough to spare, after what he confiscated during his proscriptions,'* Latona thought. She stood between her sisters, all three draped in somber colors, with their father and Latona's husband, Herennius, behind them, both in dark mourning togas. As it was an official civic occasion, Latona and Alhena both wore tunics and mantles with the black mage's stripes on the borders.

Aulus Vitellius had insisted the family be prominent during the proceedings: Aula was far from the only patrician woman widowed by Ocella, but Aulus wanted onlookers to remember her sacrifice. *'And she does make a nice picture,'* Latona thought, watching as Aula bounced little Lucia in her arms. Lucia was growing too tall to be comfortably held for long, but today, Aula was willing to endure her wiggling in exchange for the comfort of having her close. Aula's coppery hair shone even beneath her charcoal-gray mantle. *'Young and beautiful and holding the proof of her fertility, no less. Perhaps Father's hoping to remind any eligible returning exiles of that, too.'*

Suddenly self-conscious, Latona pulled her mantle a bit farther around her face. *'If everyone's meant to be thinking of Aula's noble sacrifice and eminent eligibility, what in the name of Juno might they be thinking about me?'* Plenty of those in the crowd had been at Ocella's court at the same time she had, others might have heard rumors from slaves and servants, and not all would be generous with their assessment of her bargain, if they could ever confirm the gossip. In that regard, Herennius's presence was good for *some*thing. So long as he stood by her, it would be harder for anyone to believe the worst. *'But the thought that anyone might* *think me mourning in truth, the Dictator's woestruck mistress . . .'* Shuddering, Latona pushed her mantle back from her cheeks again. Let them look; let them see the truth of her hatred for Ocella written upon her face.

Lucretius Rabirus stepped up to the platform to give his laudatio, sparking a low murmur in the crowd. Not of surprise—everyone knew Rabirus had been as good as Ocella's right hand for the past year, so it was natural that he would give one of the sending-off speeches. Latona found it difficult to pay strict attention as she listened to what started out as a fairly uninspired recitation of Ocella's rise through the ranks of the *cursus honorum.* Her eyes were fixed, hardly blinking, not on Lucretius Rabirus, but on the purple-draped litter and the corpse atop it. Her rapt attention had nothing to do with piety or social concern. Like many in the city, Latona had come to the funeral just to assure herself that Ocella was really dead.

Latona knew her sister well enough to intuit that Aula's fidgety attentions to her daughter stemmed from the same sour memories as Latona's coldly transfixed stare. They never spoke of it, after all. Aula had treated Lucius Quinctilius's funeral as though he had died by accident, and when they had traveled to Capraia under Ocella's command, everyone had pretended it was their own idea, a simple holiday. After that, Aula had rushed to her father's house, hurriedly re-arranging her life. She responded to sorrow with forced merriment and a feigned sense of normalcy; Latona, by burying the shame as deeply as she could manage.

When Rabirus's words began to take on a more overtly political bent, it called Latona's attention away from the unpleasant past and back to the uncertain present. "Though we may disagree with his methods—even recognize them as brutal—he was a man seeking to save his city from the brink of collapse, the very edge of disaster. A man who did what was necessary." Murmurs rose up, far back in the crowd. Rabirus's words did not strike a favorable chord with all present. Too many had seen their families and friends fall, crushed lifeless beneath Ocella's idea of what was necessary. "Horatius Ocella picked up the rubble left by a generation's worth of feckless consuls, more devoted to their own feuding than to tending our noble city. If he was ruthless, perhaps the gods decreed that he be so, to stand up for our traditions in difficult times. The steps he took to bring Aven back to its days of moral integrity and pious devotion are incomplete."

Latona's blood felt near to boiling at the falsity of such platitudes. *'Morality and piety hardly figured in his plans for me.'*

No one applauded when Rabirus finished, for that was not the way of a laudatio, and then Lucius Galerius Orator ascended the platform with grace and somber regard. *'A rare man,'* Latona thought, *'who can find it in his heart to honor the tyrant who drove him from the city, threatened his wife and son, and murdered his friends and colleagues.'* Latona would not have been able to summon up the charity.

Galerius Orator was a good speaker, worthy of the cognomen inherited from his ancestors. Tonight, he spoke of the man, not the Dictator, telling stories that glorified Ocella as he had once been, and as he should have been, had he lived up to the promise of his youth. The city had loved Ocella in early days, and Galerius sought to remind them of why. He had been a hero of the Republic, saving his legion from ruin and disgrace in Phrygia. He had been kind to his wives and doted on his children. He had been charming. He had thrown excellent parties.

'And from that,' Latona thought, *'to such a demon as he became. Why would the gods create such a man and then let evil consume him?'* Blood splashing across mosaic tiles, the sharpness of cinnamon, Capraia's rocky outcroppings and the price of the gifts of Venus: thus, Ocella's legacy to Latona.

Dark clouds were gathering overhead, blocking the sun and bringing the cool, mineral scent of impending rain. Galerius finished his oration, and the priests stepped up to sacrifice the customary sow. It went down easily, a good omen. Latona could only assume the gods were as glad as the people of Aven that Ocella's rule had ended. The entire city seemed to breathe a sigh of relief as the attendants loaded the Dictator's body, sewn into its gray shroud, onto the pallet that would bear him outside the city limits for cremation. Latona felt a tingling in her hands, a hot prickle, as though her skin anticipated the flames that would consume Ocella's flesh. *'Would that I could cast the spark myself.'*

✦ SEPTEMBER ✦

IV

Life in Aven entered a strange stillness following the funeral. Not serenity—too much remained uncertain for that. It was more like doldrums settled over the city, an unnatural calm waiting to erupt into a storm. The Senate was waiting a market interval to reconvene, ostensibly out of respect for the Dictator's journey to the Underworld. The decision frustrated the Optimates, who had hoped to assert control before any more exiles could return from abroad; another eight days might bring in a larger quorum than would benefit the conservative party's intentions.

Each day, too, ships docking in Ostia or moving upriver to the Aventine ports bore more than wayward Senators as their cargo. Rumors had begun to bob their way across the Middle Sea, slow and uncertain but compelling nonetheless, of trouble in Iberia.

Helva always seemed to hear and know everything well ahead of anyone in either the Vitellian or the Herennian household, and so it was with rare pleasure that Merula was able to stride up to her one day in the bathhouse dressing room. All three Vitellian daughters were enjoying the steamy comfort of the baths, and it was the duty of the attendants to watch their clothes and other belongings until the ladies returned. While Helva glared at the bathhouse slaves, whom she considered unworthy to be trusted with her mistress's garments, Merula sidled up beside her. "I am hearing something this morning."

"You *heard* something this morning," Helva said, indulging in her perpetual quest to improve Merula's grammar, which still bore the marks of her Phrygian origins—not so much for the girl's own good as because Helva felt any slave or servant who spoke for the family ought to be able to do so with grace. And Merula *would* speak, invited or not.

Merula, who felt she made herself understood just fine, rolled her eyes. "I *heard* something, then. From the boy who brings the honey in from the country house. He is hearing—*heard*—it from a trader who landed in Ostia last week."

"And what did he hear?" Helva said.

"Rumors. From the west." Helva blinked, rather than verbally entertaining Merula's desire to bait her. "Some grand new warrior stirring up trouble in Iberia. His name . . ." Merula paused to wrap her tongue around the name, its syllables and cadence unfamiliar to her in either Truscan or her native Phrygian. "Ekialde."

Helva's nose wrinkled, for it sounded as exotic to her as it did to Merula. "What sort of a name is that?"

"Iberian, I suppose," Merula said, a touch tartly. "West, far west, the boy is saying. Almost to the Endless Ocean."

Helva frowned. Her grasp of geography was superior to Merula's—she remembered every map she had ever set eyes on—and so she wondered what news of interest could be coming from such a far-flung territory. "And did this boy's trader know anything about what sort of trouble he's causing?"

Merula laughed. "What other trouble on the borders? Rebellion, of course. Stirring up all the tribes, talking about throwing the Aventans out of Baelonia and Cantabria."

Nearby, little Mus stirred. Merula and Helva had, as usual, nearly forgotten her presence. She was so small and quiet, always happiest when standing in the shadows, and since she belonged to the youngest daughter, Alhena, she was of less consequence in the household hierarchy. Merula had caught her attention at the mention of Ekialde, though. Mus knew of no individual by that name, but it had the sound of her homeland, rocky and uneven like the mountains that jutted up above her village.

"Not just talk, either," Merula continued. "Already he is attacking some villages, taking some plunder. No Aventans killed, but Tyrians and friendly tribes. More than a few, the boy is saying."

"It isn't that unusual," Helva said. "The inland regions aren't nearly as well-settled as the coasts. Every few years, some young buck or another conducts a few raids, causes a panic, and then usually gets himself good and swiftly killed."

"Ah!" Merula said, her dark eyes shining. "But this one, he is making a pact with those blood-drinking priests they have. This one, they say, he is being something special. They are naming him leader of all Lusetani, not only his own people."

"*Erregerra*," Mus said, then, startled at herself, immediately bit her lower lip and cast her eyes down at the ground. Helva and Merula both turned, nearly as bewildered to hear her speak as she was to have done it.

Helva reached out, firmly lifting Mus's chin, forcing the young slave to look her in the eyes. "Say that again, and what it means."

Easily intimidated, Mus trembled. *"Erregerra,"* she said. "They name him . . . if he leads . . . then he . . . *erregerra."* She whimpered in frustration at her inability to find the right words, terrified of what Helva might do if she could not explain. Mus's Truscan was worse than Merula's, less frequently-practiced, and even more fractured when she was frightened. "He is . . . he is . . . Mars-king!" she gasped, finally seizing upon some construction of the correct concepts.

Merula scoffed. "Mars is not being king. Jupiter is being king of the gods, everyone is knowing this."

"Perhaps it's different for the Lusetanians," Helva said, still boring into Mus with her pale eyes. "I don't think they actually worship Mars, for one thing. But a king who is like Mars, perhaps?" Mus nodded frantically. "Blessed by a god like Mars, the way our mages are blessed by our gods?"

"Yes! Yes!" Mus nodded with frantic relief. "Mars-god is Bandue. Chosen of Bandue is *erregerra.* Blessed. Special."

Helva cut her eyes sideways at Merula, who shrugged, and then she released Mus with a sigh. She never had much patience with the girl, whom she considered an unfit attendant for a lady of an ancient house. She had been Domina Alhena's own choice, however, plucked from the market by some vision driven by Proserpina's blessing, and so Helva would tolerate her, though she felt the girl should have been relegated to kitchen drudgery or service in the fields of a country estate. "How did this trader come to know of it, then, Merula?" Though she turned her attention away from Mus, Mus continued to stare wide-eyed at them both, fascinated by Merula's story.

"Soldiers' gossip from Nedhena," Merula said. "Men who've been still and quiet too long, spoiling for a fight. All hoping for a transfer to Lusetanian border, to put down this Ekialde-king. Is causing discontent in the legions, they are saying along the roads. I ask the boy if he is knowing which legions. He does not, but might be the young master, I am thinking."

Helva nodded. "Very like," she said, closing her eyes to think for a moment. The benefit of her magical gift was obvious; the downside, less so. Her mind worked like one of the catalogs kept in the temples, rows upon rows of pegged holes in which to slot information. Finding one particular fact was always easy. Drawing connections between them took more skill. There were legions stationed on the Vendelician border in three Aventan provinces. Gaius Vitellius, the eldest child and only son of the Vitellian house, was with the Eighth Legion in Albina, where there had been no real action for quite some time. If they had heard of skirmishes going spare across the Pyreneian Mountains, they would be sure to want some part of it. "Have you told Domina Latona yet?"

"No chance yet," Merula said. "She is being mewed up with Dominus Herennius all morning, before Domina Aula come to fetch her. And then we come straight here. Did not want to holler about it in the streets."

"That shows some wisdom," Helva said. While Merula tried to decide if Helva's tone had implied an insult, Helva continued, "I expect if it's true, we'll hear from the young master soon enough."

And that, it seemed, was to be the end of it, for the ladies returned then, Aula half-dragging a sullen-looking Alhena. "At least you're *clean*, even if you will insist on moping through the whole thing," she was saying, fairly pushing her sister at Mus. "We'll have word from Tarpeius, I'm sure, but your mooning about won't make news come any faster. You'd do better to be helping me prepare this feast—" While Aula went on chiding her sister, Helva set to dressing Aula with brisk efficiency. Merula tsked over Latona's damp hair, and Mus gently wrapped her mistress up, all the while thinking of the *erregerra* Ekialde, and what might be going on so many hundreds of miles away.

◇◇◇◇◇◇◇◇◇◇◇◇◇

Latona parted ways with her sisters at the base of the Palatine Hill, continuing on with Merula to her husband's house. As she turned up towards the Caelian Hill, she saw a knot of girls giggling by a market stall, its shelves stacked high with amphorae of olive oil. Two looked to be sisters, with ebony curls and identical strong hooked noses; another was a dark Numidian with coltish long limbs; the last plump and fair with rosy cheeks. They were about Alhena's age: common girls and all Aventans now, no matter where their families had come from. *'The beauty of Aven, there.'*

They seemed happy. Had they been lucky enough that Ocella's reign had not touched them or their families? Latona hoped so, but she knew how few in Aven, patrician or plebeian, had truly escaped unscathed. Ocella may have focused his attention on bolstering his power against the wealthy and powerful, but plenty of his minions had taken advantage of his tenure in office to play tyrant in their own smaller circles: families evicted from their homes so a landlord could profit, girls and women snatched for a magistrate's personal pleasure. *'Just acting in the image of their great dictator,'* Latona thought, anger burning inside her chest. *'And who protects them, when another Ocella comes along?'* She, at least, had been able to make some sort of bargain out of it. Those who had nothing to trade fared less well.

As she and Merula continued towards the Caelian Hill, and her thoughts churned over the injustices she hoped would never visit Aven again, Latona began to feel slightly ill. At first she thought it might be a delayed effect of leaving the warmth of the baths for the rawness of the outdoors, but then she realized that the source of her discomfort was magical in nature. When she had first begun to stifle her talents as a child, then suppressed them further during Ocella's reign, she often came down with stomach cramps, as though her body revolted against the idea of holding so much inside of herself. The sensation had dulled, with time, but Latona was reminded of it now. *'But this is not the same.'* This was less a twisting pressure and more a rising, not of bile but of power, determined to retch out of her.

The pain grew stronger when they were still a few minutes' walk from the Herennian domus. Staggering slightly, Latona clutched Merula's shoulder. "Domina?"

"I need to get inside, Merula . . . fast."

Merula slipped an arm around Latona's back, draped Latona's arm over her own shoulders, and quickened their pace towards the Herennian domus. "Can you tell me what is wrong, Domina?"

"No . . . not really . . ."

"Am I needing to send for a physician? The Temple of Asclepius is—"

"No," Latona said. Her skin felt as though it was on fire, a sizzle that coursed from her fingers, up her arms, and all the way down her spine, burning inside her blood and setting a hot flush on her chest and cheeks. Despite the heat, she lifted her free arm and weakly dragged her mantle forward to obscure her face, so that no one they passed might recognize the Lady Vitellia Latona in such an undignified state.

As soon as they reached the house, Latona ran for the atrium, craving the coolness of water on her face. She fell to her knees by the impluvium pool in the center of the room, her stomach in a nauseated roil.

Then it happened in a rush. There were only a few small lamps lit in the atrium at that hour, standing at the shrine at the far end. But it was enough. Latona's fingertips burned, the prickling sensation crawled all the way up her arms, and then a blast of power erupted out from her, fanning the tiny glowing licks from the lamps into an enormous, gulfing flame. The spindly cypress next to the shrine caught fire immediately, as did the decorative fabric hangings draped above it. Latona was too startled to scream and too dizzied to try and use her magic to calm the flames.

Merula, however, suffered no such petrification. "Bring buckets!" she yelled, then snatched the mantle off Latona's shoulders and threw it into the impluvium pool. She jumped in, stomping on the fabric to submerge and saturate it more quickly, then dragged it out and flung it over the burning tree in the center of the conflagration. Sparks had already set on the vines beside the cypress, and the hangings were still blazing. One of Herennius's household slaves came in with a bucket, another with a large bowl, and they worked together, scooping water from the pool and flinging it at the fire.

Latona's skin was still overheated, but after a moment, she was able to control herself enough to try and exert some influence over the flames. Fire was ever more difficult to rein in than to ignite, but Latona forced herself to think extinguishing thoughts, turning the fire back in on itself. Then, once she felt sure that the slaves were beating out the last few smolders, she thrust her hands into the pool. It hurt, the sudden immersion in the inimical element, and she hissed through the pain, waiting for the sizzling energy coursing through her body to abate.

When Latona withdrew her hands from the water and stood up, her skin was raw and chapped. The backlash of dousing the magical energy seemed to have had a physical effect. Gingerly, she rubbed one hand against the other, and the redness faded. Her heartbeat slowed, and she felt entirely drained, as though she could fall asleep standing up.

"I think we are putting it all out, Domina," Merula said, coming over to her, the sodden remnants of scorched fabric still in her hands. "My apologies."

"Don't you dare," Latona said, as out of breath as though she had run a race in the Circus. The air, still smoky and acrid, didn't help. "If it hadn't been for your quick thinking, the whole house might have gone up. And it's not as though I can't buy a new mantle. You'll be getting one as well." She nodded at the other two slaves who had rushed in to control the damage. "As will you. Cloaks, tunics, shoes, whatever you would prefer, with my gratitude."

"Thank you, Domina," all three replied, and while the other two set to assessing the damage to the atrium, Merula considered her options. "Something new and warm for winter would be nice. In blue, maybe. I like blue."

"I'd give you Tyrian purple if you asked for it," Latona said, collapsing onto the nearest bench. She sighed heavily, as though she were breathing for the first time in minutes. "Oh, how am I going to explain this to Herennius?"

Merula snorted. "You are thinking he'll notice?" She dropped the ruined mantle and sat down beside Latona. "Domina, you should be going to a temple, if not to a physician. They have much knowledge. Perhaps it is . . . not unusual." Merula bit her lip, then pressed on. "For Venus's Fire, it is Ama Rubellia you would be wanting, yes? She is a kind lady, Domina."

The last thing Latona wanted to do, however, was to admit her deficiency to a priestess, not even one as effusively accepting as Ama Rubellia. She could picture how the High Priestess of Venus would react: her soft brown eyes would swim with empathetic concern, she would press Latona's hands in her soft fingers, and there would be naught but compassion writ on her lovely face.

To admit that she had lost control, though—a lapse she had been guarding against her entire life—struck her as intolerable. Rubellia might treat her kindly, but if anyone else in the temple carried tales of an undisciplined Fire mage whose emotions were getting the better of her . . . *'The repercussions to my reputation and my family's could be too much to bear. I can control this. If I must go to Rubellia, I will. But only if I must.'* She drew herself up, despite the lingering pain in her chest and tingle in her fingers. "I don't think that's necessary, Merula. I'm sure it's just . . . just that I'm overtired," she said.

Merula's lips twisted. For a moment, Latona thought she might hold her tongue, but Merula had always been given much liberty by her mistress, and she rarely missed opportunities to exercise it. "Let us hope, then, this passes before your sister's party," she said pointedly.

"Yes," Latona agreed. "I suspect we'll have quite enough to manage without unexpected conflagrations."

◇◇◇◇◇◇◇◇◇◇◇◇◇◇

One image had haunted Rabirus since the funeral. Not the grey-wrapped shroud. He knew too well what was beneath that. Not the well-rehearsed mourners or the flocks of citizens, few of whom had any real grief to spare. Aven loved a spectacle, whatever its cause. Not the rain clouds that had gathered as the cart rolled out of the Forum. All the better to wash away what was no longer useful.

No, what kept prodding at the edges of his awareness was the image of a stricken and confused child, trailing behind the cart—and the uncle standing behind him.

The Dictator had left children behind, too young to be important in and of themselves, but each a prime opportunity for political advantage. Rabirus had to consider the men now controlling them: how ambitious they were, to marry the women of their families to Ocella; how appropriately aligned were their sympathies; how well would they honor and defend the *mos maiorum*.

How much of a threat they might be to Rabirus's own ambitions, particularly with the possession and raising of a dictator's brats.

Rabirus did not come to a conclusion swiftly. He contemplated, observed, and analyzed the situation and the players. And then he gave his steward instructions.

V

The Vitelliae had lived in the same location on the Palatine Hill since the age of the kings, when the city had begun to expand from the increasingly crowded Aventine to the higher hills in the north. The domus itself had been torn down and rebuilt by the current Aulus Vitellius's father, and as a result, the interior was spacious and modern. Just beyond the entry hall, the atrium boasted a fantastically detailed mosaic floor and paintings by Athaecan masters all over the walls. The impluvium pool, a tribute to the late Vipsania Vitelliae's Water magic, was immaculately free of algae and grime, with small fish swimming above the tiled representation of the goddess Lympha bathing in a stream.

In the peristyle garden, a dozen couches had been set up for the evening—the usual triclinium dining room being, though spacious enough for family affairs, too small to accommodate all the guests expected for the evening's reception. Crimson-painted columns stretched up to a gilt ceiling, and Alhena kept songbirds in ornamented cages hanging from the row of fruit trees at the far side of the pool. Their cheerful melodies echoed throughout the space. Though the day had been warm and humid, the evening turned mild, and late-blooming flowers lent a sweet and inviting fragrance to the air. The sun had just gone down, and a heavy golden moon was curving into the sky, as though the Vitelliae had ordered it just for the occasion.

Sempronius, his sister Vibia, and his brother-in-law Taius Mella arrived just late enough that several other guests were already ahead of them in the receiving line, chatting with their hosts before proceeding into the garden. Vibia fidgeted impatiently, but Sempronius didn't mind; it afforded him the chance to observe the Vitellian family in action, playing host. Close friends that their families were, he was eager to discover whatever may have changed since his exile.

Aula, the widowed eldest daughter to whom welcoming responsibilities had fallen, was bright and cheerful, beaming smiles at each and every guest. Her copper curls were arranged in a new style, with tendrils dropping daintily in front of her ears. Sempronius guessed it would soon become the new rage; Aula had ever been a trend-setter. She held herself well, proud but not haughty, elegant yet approachable. Sempronius had always sensed there was more to her than fashionable vapidity. Her eyes were a little too keen, and her mouth sometimes twitched in a way that suggested it held back less-than-polite commentary. *'And no surprise,'* Sempronius thought. She had been serving as lady of one house or another since her mother's death, many years earlier.

At her side was Alhena, the youngest of the sisters, who had eyes like the sky before a storm, an intense swirl of blue and gray. In contrast to her sister's trend-setting appearance, Alhena wore her blazing-red hair plainly, pulled back from her face and pinned up to expose her neck. *'Too severe for a child her age . . .'* Not a child, though; she now wore a woman's garments and had put off the protective charm of the bulla necklace. Still, she looked quite small standing next to Aula, and her cheeks still bore traces of prepubescent roundness. Sempronius knew little of her except that she had been blessed by Proserpina—a rare and sometimes treacherous gift. Sempronius hoped, for the girl's sake, that her tutors had impressed on her the importance of grounding herself, and that whatever husband Aulus Vitellius found for her would prove to be a kind and patient man.

When Sempronius entered the atrium, the ladies were receiving Galerius Orator and his wife Marcia. Their son was present, too; the Vitelliae had deemed the evening a family affair and so, some guests had brought along even those sons who had not yet entered manhood.

Marcia Tullia, only a few years younger than Galerius, had a dignified beauty: dark hair with just a touch of silver, cool blue eyes, and an intelligent face. If she had been a common plebeian woman or one of a host of spare daughters, she might have stayed in the Temple of Mercury her whole life. Instead, she had wed Galerius Orator, and for all the trouble they had found themselves in under Ocella, the match was not only mutually advantageous, but tender, warmed by admiration and devotion. *'How might Galerius's life have been different had her path been different? Or my own, for that matter?'* Sempronius wondered, well aware of how much of his safety was owed to Marcia Tullia's warnings.

The son was obviously still growing into himself, gawky and awkward, at that age when the limbs fast outpaced the rest of the body. He took after his mother, dark and serious, with his father's hawk-like nose. He was already in training for the priesthood. If his father became consul, as he was likely to do, Young Lucius could not follow him there, under the restrictions of the *lex cantatia Augiae.* If he had a mind as good as his father's, Sempronius considered that another shameful waste of potential to add to the law's tally. Blessed with gifts of Air like his mother, the lad could at least look forward to a position as a pontifex someday, guarding the religious orders of the nation.

As the Galeriae moved away, middle daughter Latona appeared—and Sempronius realized, as an unexpected warmth filled his chest, that he had been hoping she would arrive in time to greet him. Of the three Vitelliae, Latona provoked the most intrigue. Since she had first entered adult patrician society, Sempronius had sensed in her some potential unfulfilled.

As a mage of Water as well as Shadow, Sempronius knew what dammed-up power felt like—and he could sense the pressure point where it threatened to burst. The intervening years had done nothing to dim his sense of trammeled potential in the Lady Latona; if anything, Sempronius perceived a widening breach in the dam.

Taller than either of her sisters and swathed tonight in a gown of shimmering bronze, to Sempronius's eyes, Latona shone like the sun. Her skin had a slightly honeyed hue, not ivory like Aula's and Alhena's, and her hair was pure gold. The similarities between the three Vitelliae daughters were evident at a glance. Aula and Latona had the same emerald eyes; Latona and Alhena both had tip-tilted noses; all had delicate, aristocratic bone structure and full rosebud lips.

Sempronius watched as the sisters greeted the cheerfully unsophisticated Autroniae. He thought well of the Vitelliae for inviting them, considering that they were an up-and-coming plebeian family unwelcome in many patrician homes. Marcus Autronius served with Sempronius in the Senate, but could never be consul, not as an Earth mage. His younger brother, called Felix, had recently returned from Numidia, lamenting the lack of suitable action there. He had a martial look about him, the sort who thrived on life in the legions, but with the ladies, his manner was easy and charming. Something he said made Aula titter, though it seemed to have startled Marcus. Their father had the contented roundness of a man of comfortable living, and his wife, though garishly dressed, was pink-cheeked and amiable.

When it came time for Sempronius, Vibia, and Taius Mella to greet their hostesses, Aula reached forward to grasp Vibia's hands, grinning broadly. "So glad to see you, my dear! We thought you might not make it."

Vibia's smile was not quite so freely emotive as Aula's, but she inclined her head graciously. "I should never have forgiven myself had I been unable to accept such a kind invitation." In truth, Sempronius suspected she would have been as happy to travel at a more leisurely pace, but he had sent a messenger to urge her haste.

Sempronius and Taius were not intimately enough acquainted with the ladies to offer greeting embraces of any kind, but when Latona lifted her eyes to him, Sempronius felt his heart seized by a tremendous impulse to touch her. His fingers burned for it, though he could not for the world have explained why. "I hope you've been well since we last met," Latona said. "Or, as well as can be expected, considering."

"Yes, thank you," Sempronius replied, then gained enough control of himself to bestow her with the grin that typically put women off their balance. "If one has to go into exile, there are certainly worse places for it than Tamiat."

Latona tilted her head to one side, the corners of her eyes crinkling. "No trouble with the locals, then?"

"Absolutely not," Sempronius replied. "They may worship crocodiles, dabble in curses and profane magic, and indulge in unspeakable depravities, the women may parade half-naked through the streets, and the royal family may be a nest of murdering vipers, but . . . I found them to be most charming, really."

Latona gave a little half-laugh, looking as though she were entertained but could not quite decide whether or not to believe him. "How pleasant your life must have been, then," she teased him.

"Entirely. I can thoroughly recommend it to any Aventan as an unexpectedly edifying vacation."

The smile curving her lips was more than polite, and she met his eyes boldly, though she dropped her voice below the usual tones of greetings and introductions. "I do so enjoy edification. You must promise to tell me all about it," she said, "especially the curses and depravities, half-naked or otherwise."

He couldn't help it; her frank statement coaxed a bark of laughter out of him, causing both his sister and Latona's to glance over at them questioningly. Sempronius found that he desired little else than to keep talking with this woman, to make her laugh in earnest. The feeling caught him quite by surprise. "I shall endeavor not to disappoint you, then, Lady," he said.

"And I shall hold you to that," she replied. There was something dancing merrily in her expression—a promise, or a challenge. Sempronius couldn't be sure. Nor could he stall in the entryway any longer, so he moved on to nod his greetings to Aula and Alhena, letting Mella file in behind him. His thoughts, though, lingered behind.

◇◇◇◇◇◇◇◇◇◇◇◇◇◇◇◇

Aulus Vitellius stood in the peristyle garden, welcoming guests as the slaves ushered them from the atrium and pointed them towards their seats. As the daughters of the house brought up the end of the line, Aula caught Latona by the elbow, hissing beneath her breath. "What on earth did you say to Sempronius Tarren?"

"Something that would shock the curl right out of Alhena's hair," Latona answered.

"Well, whatever it was, everyone who saw that's going to be talking about it." Mischief lit up Aula's eyes. "And I'll make sure anyone who didn't see it hears about it, for certain. Fancy my proper matron of a little sister causing the first stir of the evening."

Latona felt a blush come to her cheeks. Drawing that sort of notice had hardly been her intention. *'Careful, careful . . .'* she warned herself. *'You should know you can't play and tease like that. There are always repercussions.'*

A little rebellious spark, one that had ignited more frequently in these past few weeks, argued against that logic, begging her to do as she pleased. And it *had* pleased her to make Sempronius laugh. Aloud, she said only, "It's a sad state of affairs if making a man laugh is enough to provoke commotion. We truly *must* be starved for entertainment."

"Abydosia seems to have agreed with him," Aula commented, glancing down the line of guests towards the man in question's broad shoulders and dark head of hair. "Most of the men returning either lost forty pounds or gained them, but he looks positively improved by exile." Latona had no argument against that but shushed her sister as they entered the garden.

It had been decades since society had considered it promiscuous for women to dine while reclining, but since some ladies still preferred to sit rather than lounge, the tables arranged in the peristyle garden had both couches and chairs around them. The wife of Chief Augur, her wrinkled face split by a wide grin, eased herself down to a chair saying, "Ha! I remember when ladies who lay down to eat were considered *fast.*" And then, gimlet eyes sparkling, she leaned towards Latona, saying—in what was probably meant to be a conspiratorial whisper—"And I reclined on *plenty* of couches in my time! But these old bones, well, they just don't settle down the way they used to."

"I simply don't believe you can remember the time when this was scandalous," Latona insisted, with a dazzling smile. "You don't look a day over thirty, Crispinia."

"Good girl," she said, reaching over the table to pat Latona's hand. "Always liked you. Now, tell me what you thought of that play where I saw you last week. Damned frivolous piece of tripe, if you ask *me*—"

And so the banquet began. The slaves brought out table after table of delectables: hot sausages, fine white rolls with honey, olives, figs, a capon's liver steeped in milk, sturgeon, eel, prawns in a fine sauce; pheasant and thrush and fatted guinea hens. It had been easy to procure the very best. For so long, few patricians or plebeians of wealth had been in the city to throw such extravagant affairs. The merchants had practically slavered to provide the Vitelliae with luxury goods that had too long gone under-appreciated.

Around the couches, the buzz of conversation grew to a steady hum, broken with frequent laughter. The men returned from exile told tales from life abroad, and as was so often the case in times of trial, turned their misfortunes to humor. Not the false and brittle charm Latona had been forced to adopt in Ocella's court, nor the contrived merriment Aula had affected instead of mourning, but this, too, was a kind of coping. *'The past cannot be forgotten,'* Latona thought, *'but maybe—maybe—it can be set behind us.'*

By the time the desserts were served—nuts and fruits and almond cakes—the guests began to leave their appointed places to mingle freely between the couches, particularly those younger and less prestigious members of the company. Though the evening had begun with a certain degree of formality, with free-flowing wine, cheerful music being played by comely slaves and hired girls, and such a general feeling of good cheer and relaxation, it was not likely to continue in the same upright vein. The Vitelliae knew well how to ride the line that separated a loosening of stricture from a total lack of sophistication, and their guests were all too willing to set themselves at ease. The great men retained their seats while the young bucks moved about, jockeying for position near those who held influence—or near some of the lovely ladies.

Autronius Felix made his flirtatious rounds in the company of several friends, including Young Publius Rufilius, a good-looking young man who was son to the famous General Rufilius Albinicus. The two swains could not have appeared more different. Felix was broad and stocky, with solid shoulders and powerful thighs. His hair and eyes were dark, his skin ruddy, testament to his plebeian status and the freedmen somewhere in his ancestry, and he moved with a charmingly careless ease. Patrician Publius Rufilius, on the other hand, was tall and slim-waisted, with the smoothly powerful grace of a thoroughbred horse. He well deserved the nickname of Young Apollo, with his golden hair and blue eyes, bright with merriment and mockery. An unlikely pair in some respects, perhaps, but they shared a carefree irreverence that made them natural allies.

Sempronius gave up his seat beside Taius Mella to a young senator seeking financial advice—all the more readily when he noticed that a spot on Latona's couch had opened up. *'Where is her husband, I wonder?'*

∞∞∞∞∞∞∞∞∞∞∞∞

Latona's thoughts, as Sempronius watched her, were on her sisters. Alhena's natural reticence had been getting the better of her, and Latona had worried that her shyness might read as arrogance. Latona felt, beneath her sister's unease, not just discomfort, but insecurity.

'Of course,' she realized, with a pitch of her heart. Alhena had little experience in society and small idea how to behave. Latona had sent a charm Alhena's way—a boost of confidence to combat anxiety—and now Alhena was sitting across from old Crispinia and a priestess of Proserpina. Her expression was serious and her mannerisms still tight, but at least she was actively engaged in conversation.

Aula, meanwhile, seemed to have chatted with everyone in the room— and flirted with half of the eligible young men. Aula had a knack for putting guests at their ease. She lounged between the Autronian patriarch and a historian of considerable esteem. Latona would not have guessed the two men to have had much in common, but Aula had both chuckling with interest as she chattered animatedly.

"She *is* a marvel."

Latona startled. She had not even noticed that Sempronius had sat down next to her until he had spoken, and she remembered now his uncanny ability to pluck thoughts out of other people's brains.

He gestured towards Aula with the hand holding his cup of wine. "So long across the water, I had forgotten, but your sister is a remarkable woman."

"I'm sure she would thank you for the compliment, Senator," Latona replied, inclining her head slightly.

"Would she take it kindly if I tendered my long-overdue regrets regarding her husband's misfortune? Or would she not thank me for the reminder?"

His dark eyes were sincere; he meant no empty pleasantry, and so Latona gave him an honest reply. "I think she would rather not be reminded of it, sir," she said. "She does not speak of it often, even to me, and I believe the whole family would just as soon put those dark days behind us entirely. But I will thank you for the kindness of remembrance, on her behalf."

"Will she remarry now?" Sempronius inquired.

A playful smile toyed at the edge of Latona's mouth. "Are you asking, Senator?"

Sempronius laughed good-naturedly. "No, I fear not. As delightful as your sister is, we would be an ill match."

Latona laughed, too. "It will take a man of special temperament to make her happy, I think," she admitted. "She was quite fond of Quinctilius; I do not believe she would settle for a less amiable match."

"And *your* husband?" Sempronius asked, and for the blink of a moment, Latona thought he was asking if her husband made her happy. "He was in town for the funeral, wasn't he?"

"I— Yes," Latona replied. "Yes, he was, but he headed back to Liguria the next day. He has new slaves there, and he's worried this news of rebellion coming in from Iberia might have stirred them up."

"Isn't he eligible to stand for praetor soon?"

"Next year, but I don't expect that he shall," Latona confessed. "It's such an expensive venture, and I believe he'd rather keep reinvesting his funds in his business." She tilted her head to the side. "You'll be standing yourself this year, won't you?"

"I intend to, as soon as elections are set," Sempronius replied, though in almost too casual a manner. He masked it well, but Latona's magic gave her an insight. Spirit knew ambition, and she could feel the bite of it nested inside his words. "But," he went on, with a grin sliding onto his face that made her want to inch closer to him on the couch, "enough of politics. I don't think anyone here truly wants to talk of Curia matters tonight, and I promised to tell you about Abydosia."

She did move closer to him at that, though under the guise of repositioning herself more comfortably on the couch, leaning over to take a fruit tart from the table. "I'm gratified to find you a man of your word," she teased, voice merry. "Do begin with the grandest debauchery you can think of."

From across the room, their affinity caught Aula's attention as she glanced between her conversational partners. *'Well. Now isn't that something?'* Her mind rapidly set to turning over the possibilities presented by a strengthened alliance with the Semproniae. Sempronius Tarren was not so very great a man yet, but he had the aura of greatness about him. Aula didn't need any magic to tell her that.

Veteran of so many dinner parties and social functions, Aula had made something of a study of how men and women presented themselves, and she could see the sparks of interest between her sister and Sempronius. Their bodies were angled towards each other, just a fraction closer on the couch than was strictly proper. A flush danced on Latona's cheeks as she spoke to him, and Aula did not think it came solely from the wine.

Aula was not the only one who noticed the warm conversation going on between Latona and Sempronius. His sister Vibia caught sight of them when she turned in her chair to ask Marcia Tullia a question. Her brow creased; she misliked the too-warm, too-genuine smile lighting her brother's face. It bespoke an unguarded attitude that unsettled her.

For her part, Latona was enjoying herself too thoroughly to put much thought into how they must appear to any onlookers, but she was dimly aware of her own entrancement. It was rare for her to feel so captivated by someone, and yet it was a quality that Sempronius had always owned. His appearance was comely, but hardly extraordinary. Brown hair, brown eyes, a proper Aventan nose, a good strong jaw, but with no particularly notable features to set him apart. He was no paragon of masculine beauty, like golden-haired Publius Rufilius, nor sinfully dark, like Young Crispinius, nor even bearing the rugged attraction of the Autroniae brothers. But there was something magnetic about him all the same, a fathomless quality that made it difficult to take her eyes off him.

Eventually, with regard for the propriety requiring him not to monopolize the hostess, Sempronius yielded his seat to old Gnaeus Autronius, father to Marcus and Felix. But as he rose, his fingers brushed, ever-so-lightly, against her shoulder. It was almost imperceptible, nearly too feathery to notice, and yet Latona felt like she'd been scalded.

◇◇◇◇◇◇◇◇◇◇◇◇◇◇

Though now officially belonging to the Herennian household, not the Vitellian, Merula had nonetheless assumed a position of responsibility when it came to organizing the festivities. While Helva handled the niceties of decorations and menu-planning, as well as keeping the extensive guest list locked safely in her head, Merula applied motivation to the rest of the household, chivvying the cooks along, terrifying the servers into precision of movement, keeping the entire feast on schedule. Between her imposing presence and Helva's demanding standards, everything had gone quite smoothly. After the fruits had gone up to the tables, both women took a moment to step out onto the porch that ran behind the kitchen and breathe in the crisp night air. Soon, they would have to help with ushering the guests back out, making sure everyone's cloaks and mantles got back to them—but, in silent agreement, they had decided to reward themselves with a brief respite.

Almost immediately, however, a strange orange glow from beyond the wall caught their attention. "Fire?" Helva questioned. It was the fear of all Aven. Flames could leap so quickly between the houses in the city, butted up against each other as they were. Merula rushed to the gate and poked her head out.

"No," she called back. "Is something, though—not sure. Come look." Helva joined her at the gate. The side of the house faced down the Palatine Hill and out towards the Esquiline. Away from the noise of the kitchen and the music suffusing the party, the servants could now hear a dull roar coming from the streets below. A line of torchlights wound its way from the Subura and up the base of the Esquiline Hill.

Helva and Merula glanced at each other, then turned in unison and bolted back through the gate and straight through the kitchen door.

VI

Helva found Aulus and his eldest daughter sitting together with Galerius Orator, and after a quick calculation, Helva thought it appropriate that she share the news with all three. "Domina, Dominus," she said, her voice low and even. "Forgive my intrusion—"

"What is it, Helva?" Aula asked, sitting up straighter. Even Aulus did not object, knowing that Helva would hardly interrupt them for anything trivial.

"I thought you ought to know. There appears to be something going on over on the Esquiline Hill, near the Subura. Some unrest."

Aulus and Galerius both rose slowly, glancing at each other. "We should go see what we can learn," Galerius said.

"Yes," Aulus said, scanning the room. "Let's gather a few of the calmer heads. Not too many, though. We don't want to provoke anyone. Aula, my dear, keep everyone else here and entertained until we return."

Aula nodded, then looked at Helva. "Helva, find the usual boys to accompany Father. Haelix and Pacco, to be sure." She dropped her voice to give a distinctly unladylike order. "Tell them to take clubs. There might be a need to knock some heads."

Merula's explanation to Latona was more abrupt. With no apology, she simply dipped behind her mistress's ear and said, "Riot on the Esquiline. Looks big."

Latona's eyes shot wide. She murmured an apology to Gnaeus Autronius—"Just a small matter that needs my attention, do excuse me"—then rose from her couch and took Merula to the lee side of a column. "Explain."

"Don't know much more, Domina. Helva and I are standing on the porch, we see lights and fire, hear shouting. Her eyes are better in the dark, you know. She thinks there is some uprising in the Subura, moving up the hill." Merula jerked her head towards where Aulus and Galerius had their heads bent in urgent conference. "I am thinking, if it is so, the important men in this room will wish to see to it, yes?"

"Yes, yes, they will." Latona noticed who else was rising: General

Aufidius Strato and Sempronius Tarren, apparently summoned by Galerius, and young Felix, whose eager expression indicated he had sensed action and did not mean to be left out. "Merula, have someone fetch their cloaks. No togas, they won't want to be encumbered." Merula darted off, and when she returned a moment later, ahead of several other slaves attending to the departing men, she had her own cloak on and casually handed Latona's mantle to her. After only a slight hesitation, Latona took it, swung it over her shoulders, and pulled the edge up over her head. She could not put a name to the impulse that had seized her, but something was prickling at her, urging her out into the streets, despite the danger that surely roiled there. With Aula cheerily diverting the attention of the other guests onto a pair of dancers hired for the evening, Latona slipped out the door with a dagger-bearing Merula at her side.

∞∞∞∞∞∞∞∞∞∞

As Sempronius and the others descended the Palatine Hill, the dull roar from the Esquiline grew louder. Sempronius could see that the mass of bodies was moving with purpose, and from the tone of the clamor, he assessed that it was not a benevolent one. At night, the streets of Aven were usually clogged with delivery carts, not with human bodies, but this crowd seemed to have driven all other traffic away. If it was not quite a full riot yet, it was well on its way. "What set them off, do you think?" Felix asked, as the little group hurried across the Via Sacra.

"I think we'll know better when we can see where they're heading, precisely," Galerius said.

"We should have expected this," Sempronius said. "I'm only surprised it took this long to erupt." It had been on his mind for several days, that, with the funeral past, certain factions might finally feel brave enough to assert themselves. He knew of several potential targets for mob rage who lived on the Esquiline, not so much the arch-conservatives who had sided with Ocella out of genuine moral fervor, but the wealthy equestrians and lower-ranked senatorial families who had seen in the Dictator a path to greater glories. If the unrest had first stirred in the Subura—ever a cauldron likely to foment civil disturbances—then the Esquiline was the nearest location where anyone worth harassing would be. If not contained, however, the trouble could quickly spill into the rest of the city.

And then a sickening thought occurred to him. He stopped in his tracks, grabbing Galerius by the shoulder. "The Maloricae. Where do they live?"

Galerius blinked, then his jaw fell open as he understood. "Oh, sweet Juno's mercy," he said. "Ocella's children."

As the realization rippled through the rest of the group, they all quickened their pace. Every man of them had reason to hate Ocella, but the need to protect children—innocent boys, and patricians of ancient blood, besides—demanded immediate action.

The din grew louder as they ascended the Esquiline Hill, and the press of bodies became so dense that they struggled to stay together as they shoved their way through. Some had begun pitching stones at the shuttered windows of nearby houses. Some buildings had simply been closed up, but others now had men of their own standing outside, holding clubs or iron rods. "The Maloricae domus is on the other side of that tavern," Galerius said, or rather shouted in Sempronius's ear, so loud had the crowd grown.

Sempronius looked where Galerius indicated. "We'll never fight our way through that." They were already being roughly jostled by the bodies crushing in around them. "We have to bring this under control first."

A crash from a nearby building caught their attention: a door had given way, and the mob surged in, smashing pottery and glasswork, pitching furniture out into the street. Inside one of the nearby houses, a woman was screaming hysterically, and the men in the crowd were growing rougher. Their pitched stones hit backs and heads, not just shuttered windows. "The only thing that will control them," bellowed Aufidius Strato, "is a firm hand!"

A surge in the pack of malcontents pushed several of their party into a knot of men guarding the door to an impressive and clearly new-built house. Suddenly there were hands, hands everywhere, shoving at their backs, clawing at their garments, buffeting them between the seething mass of bodies. Sempronius was loath to answer with violence against Aventan citizens, but he also knew that the time for pacifist measures was after a riot, not during one. Someone's nails scratched at his forearm. Aufidius flattened a man who had the temerity to tear the shoulder seam of his tunic. Felix was brawling as enthusiastically as any of the rioters, though by both nature and training, he was far more fit to do damage. One of the Vitellian bodyguards who had accompanied them brought his club down too hard on someone's arm, and Sempronius heard the sickening crack of a bone splitting. As the man fell back, howling in agony, the mob answered his cry with their own, shouting in fury and indignation. Weaponless himself, Sempronius had to deliver a swift jab under one man's chin to keep him at bay, and then he saw a metallic flash in the crowd. Swords were forbidden within the city, but few men were so poor that they did not have at least a little eating dagger to their names.

'I could get out,' he thought. A little Shadow magic was all it would take, enough to make him not invisible but un-noticed, such that he could slip away. But that would be the action of a coward. He needed to control the situation, not escape it.

One older man, trying to escape the fray, got shoved down, his head dropping out of view as the mass of bodies pulsed in the street. Sempronius was not near enough to help. 'And if he's the only man trampled tonight, it will be a miracle.'

"Hey! Hey! You sons of bitches, listen!" One voice, pitched high and loud, carried over the crowd, and something in it made at least a few of the brawlers take notice. A dark-skinned man, near a head taller than his fellows, was pushing his way toward the senators. As he approached, he whacked one of the more enthusiastic rioters upside the head, then grabbed two more by the tunics, growled something at them, and shoved them backwards.

"Vatinius Obir!" Sempronius called in recognition. He was Mauretanian, an auxiliary soldier rewarded with citizenship for his exemplary service during the Numidian wars. When his years under the standard were done, he and his brother had settled on the Esquiline Hill to work for a crossroads college—one of the sanctioned civic clubs responsible for the upkeep of the shrines positioned at every major crossroads—and they had become clients to Sempronius Tarren. "Obir!"

"Sempronius Tarren?" Obir called back. "Stupid sons of— Stop fighting! Don't you know who that is? He's no enemy of yours!"

Enough of the combatants listened to Obir that it gave the bodyguards time to form a cordon around the embattled senators. "Obir, what's going on? How did this start?"

Obir's brief explanation confirmed that it was as Sempronius had guessed: discontents in the Subura, most of them men of the ever-bellicose neighborhood collegia, had taken it into their heads to exact belated revenge for the crimes of Ocella's reign. With the Dictator dead, cremated, and past retribution, their sights had fallen on his allies. "But not you, Sempronius Tarren, you have no need to worry," Obir said, with what he clearly thought was a reassuring smile—even as, somewhere behind him, Sempronius could hear the wet thud of a fist hitting flesh. "Everyone knows the bastard chased you out of town. You had no part in his wickedness."

The crowd surged again, and the bodyguards struggled to hold their footing. Jostled, Sempronius set a hand on Obir's shoulder to steady himself. "Obir, you have to help us quell this riot. We think some of these men mean to storm the domus of the Maloricae and kill Ocella's sons."

"The little babies?" Obir's eyes flashed, all the joviality leaving his face. "That would not be right with the gods." His attitude was not unusual in the city's collegia. A little fighting and thievery was one thing, but the murder of children was something only the lowest of the low would consider. "Say no more. We'll get you to the house."

"It's on the other side of the tavern," Galerius supplied. "I believe it's the house with the green door—"

Obir nodded. "This is my neighborhood, Senator. I know the place. Hey! Nisso!" Another tall, dark man pushed his way to Obir's side. He wiped at his bloodied nose as he approached, but he was grinning, apparently enjoying the brawl. "Brother, the noble Sempronius Tarren requires our assistance."

Obir swiftly explained what needed to be done, and why, and Nisso's expression turned serious. He put two fingers in his mouth and whistled loudly, a pattern of two short calls and a long. A number of heads turned towards him, and those men left off their shoving and punching in order to rally to the brothers. "Military discipline in the college, friend?" Sempronius asked Obir.

"Whenever possible, Senator."

Between the Vitellian bodyguards and the men of Obir's college forming a cordon around them, the strange group of senators and erstwhile rioters began making headway through the crowd. Obir and Nisso cursed and punched with liberty. "It's the Suburan scum, really," Obir called over his shoulder to Sempronius. "Our boys just like a good fight. Men from the slums—" His fist connected with the jaw of a short, screaming rioter. "No respect for how we do things here!"

Though they progressed faster with the Vatiniae's help, it seemed to take hours to wind their way around the tavern to the street on the opposite side, and Sempronius cursed every second of delay. Even as he worried over getting to the boys in time, he was forming plans for what they could do to bring the riot under control, lest it inflame the entire city.

◇◇◇◇◇◇◇◇◇◇◇◇◇◇◇◇

'What was I thinking?' Latona hugged the wall as they approached the top of the hill's western spur. She could not put a name to the impulse that had driven her out into such chaos, and with screams echoing in her ears, she was beginning to severely regret giving in to it.

Merula had snatched a small torch from somewhere and was brandishing it as though she were as likely to knock someone over the head with it as use it for illumination. Her other fist clutched her little curved dagger. Latona had her hands full of her skirts, and her feet were reminding her just how ill-suited fashionable sandals were for a trek down one hill and up another, particularly at a trotting speed.

Latona drew near to the shelter of a wall, finding a small nook between two houses. The sun had been down for hours, but the night had grown hotter, though Latona was unsure if that was due to the heavy humidity in the air or the close press of sweat-drenched bodies. Most of the fighting men were focused on battering down doors, but some nearby were starting to notice Latona's incongruous presence. Two suddenly advanced on her, and Latona had no intention of finding out if they had robbery or rape on their minds. Merula jabbed at one of them with the dagger, drawing a prick of blood from his arm, but the other got close enough to pull on Latona's mantle. "Lady. Hey—"

Merula made to slash at him as well, but Latona flung out a hand, palm out, and the flame from Merula's torch flared brightly, licking out towards the would-be assailant. It cast a red glow, heating his skin until it raised into blisters, pink and puffy. Eyes wide with fear, he backed away, clutching his wounded hand to his chest. "Well, Domina," Merula said, "that will be making them think twice, at least."

"Yes . . . but what are they doing to the women who can't set them on fire?" Latona muttered. Unfortunately, she knew too well. She had stood by in Ocella's court, terrified for her own life, for Aula's and Alhena's and Lucia's, as the Dictator and his cronies did what they pleased with whom they pleased. She, at least, had made a bargain, but others had not been given even that much choice. She had told herself she couldn't save everyone. *'But I could have done something . . . I chose not to . . .'* Ocella had watched her too closely; any sign of defiance would have put the knives back at her family's throats. Pain and terror had reached out to her from behind closed doors, and she had turned aside. *'It wasn't only your own body you purchased their safety with . . .'*

She could turn around, walk away. She could leave this part of the city, rush back to the Palatine, where she would not have to hear anyone's screams, nor put her own fears to the test. *'And what sort of woman would that make me? Ocella's not here now. I don't have to be afraid.'*

In defiance of the dead Dictator and every soul bruised on his account, Latona closed her eyes and reached out with Spirit magic, searching within the whorl of unpleasant emotions surrounding her for a familiar thread—someone who felt as Aula had felt, that night Ocella's men came to her door; or a ripple reminding her of what she had sensed too many times in the Dictator's court. Opening herself in such away invited so much else in, though: the hot burn of rage, the acid tang of bitterness, the cold tremor of fear. *'Concentrate, damn you.'* Filtering out unwanted emotions was something all Spirit mages had to learn to do early on, or risk madness. *'Just find what you need . . . There!'*

Like iron to a lodestone, she followed the sensation to a nearby building where the front door had been smashed in. As she stepped inside, picking her way over splintered wood, screaming echoed from somewhere upstairs. An insula, like thousands of others crowding the city: five stories tall, with apartments built around a central courtyard, the plaster on its walls cracked and flaking. "This way, Domina," Merula said. "The stairs will be over here."

The steps were wooden and uneven, and getting up them was made more difficult when a fresh wave of horror washed over Latona's primed empathic senses. Seeing her sway, Merula gave her a little push between the shoulder blades. Few slaves might have dared so much, but Latona had never minded her over-familiarity, least of all when it brought her back to her senses. Seizing her skirts in her hands, Latona climbed the last few steps to the second floor.

The apartments did not have their own doors, only curtains drawn over the openings. One of these had been torn halfway off its hanging. There were two men and two women inside—a girl of fifteen or so, and her mother. One man had the weeping girl pressed up against a wall. Her gown had been torn from her shoulders, and while one of the man's hands fumbled to bring up the edge of his tunic, the other was squeezing her breast. The other man held the screaming mother back while she scrabbled at him with her nails, trying to reach her daughter.

Rage ignited inside Latona. She yearned to set the man ablaze, and Merula's torch flared in response to that desire—but the close quarters made that action impractical, and Latona suppressed the compulsion.

Instead, with a sweep of her hand, she sent a blast of Spirit magic at him, gathering up the fear and revulsion and terror the young girl felt and dumping it back into her attacker. *'By Juno, I will see you suffer.'* Another nudge of her power magnified the emotions for him, overwhelming his mind's capacity to manage them. The man staggered, cursing and sputtering. Seeing an opportunity, Merula thrust the torch into Latona's hand, stepped forward, and gave him a solid shove out the window, sending him tumbling down into the insula's central courtyard. Latona found herself hoping the fall would break his back.

The other man released the mother, who ran to cradle her daughter. He took a step towards Latona, but she gave the torch a mental nudge, and its flames turned white-hot. "One more step and I roast you like the pig you are. I will not warn you twice."

She felt his emotions sputter, lust turning to anger, anger giving way to panic. "Y-You can't. The law. You can't—you can't use violent magic a-against—"

"Against a man I've caught in the commission of an abominable crime?" Latona snapped. Aventan law, under the *leges tabulae magicae*, did protect citizens against magical attack, but such did not apply to magic used in the defense of oneself or others, and this criminal knew it. Latona felt the strength his insolence had given him guttering out.

"Lady— Lady, please— Mercy—"

"Would you have shown them any?" she snapped. Now it was her fury against the crater of his cowardice, and she pressed the advantage until his knees wobbled.

Merula moved beside him, twirling her knife. "You want I should deprive this one of his manhood?" Merula said, her lip curling. "Probably little enough to start with. Doubt he will be missing it."

At Latona's nod, Merula moved so quickly that the mother shrieked again. Before the man could react, Merula was behind him, twisting one of his arms behind his back, holding her knife alongside his throat. "Walk, beast," she snarled. Latona watched them go, aware that her nostrils were flaring as she struggled to maintain a controlled demeanor. Under Aventan law, rapists had the choice to lose their genitals or their hands. Merula would simply speed the process along.

The mother regarded Latona with awe; Latona could feel her confusion taking over as the immediate threat passed. Grateful as she might be for a rescue, being saved by a mage, and one of an element so unpredictable as Fire, could cause mixed emotions. "Domina—" she began, but was cut off by the daughter, who burst forward, flinging herself at Latona's feet and sobbing.

Latona bent, lifting the girl's tangled hair and placing her hands on shivering shoulders. Skin to skin contact was best for this sort of magic. Closing her eyes, she tried to project calming, soothing sensations into the girl. *'I cannot undo what they did to you, child,'* she thought, *'but I hope you will find peace.'* Latona did not have to use her magic to know the revulsion, terror, and frantic shame that the girl was feeling—wounds which were scabbed over in her own heart, but still familiar enough to make bile rise in her throat. Latona, at least, had made something like a choice, and the hands invading her had been cold, but not violent. *'Blessed Juno, help her to heal . . .'*

Merula's footsteps stamped inelegantly back up the stairs. Moving slowly, Latona helped the girl to repin her torn tunic. Then she removed her own mantle and wrapped it around the girl, whose sobs were subsiding into quiet, ragged breaths. Latona looked up at the mother. "We'll see you out the back way, towards the macellum. You should be able to make it to the Temple of Venus. Their acolytes are gentle ladies. They'll take care of you both."

The woman nodded, still struck dumb by the ordeal. Latona herded them both down the stairs and around to the entrance on the other side of the insula. Merula stuck her head out first, then nodded back at them. "Much less trouble this way. Go quick."

Once they were out of sight, Latona turned, moving back towards the tumultuous side of the building, priming her Spirit magic to probe the crowd's roiling emotional landscape again. All too soon, another scream caught her attention, and another tendril of feminine fear and pain tugged at her: a cry for protection, for rescue. Latona caught the direction it came from, like a hound scenting the wind, and started off in that direction.

"Domina!" Merula said, moving to step in front of her mistress. Her duty was to protect Latona—a duty that the domina seemed hellbent on making as difficult as possible tonight. "Domina, it is a good thing you did. But there are many bad things going to be happening tonight. You cannot save all of them."

Merula's words were like a punch to the gut. How many times had Latona told herself the same thing? How many nights had she folded in on herself, closing her ears and her magic alike to those in need, convincing herself that any effort she made would be futile at best, a death sentence to her family at worst?

'He. Is. Dead. He cannot hurt you now.'

Latona's eyes had a brightness to them that hovered somewhere between fierce and mad. Her hands curled into white-knuckled fists as she said, with unreasoning vehemence, "I can damn well try!"

And then she was off again, and Merula had no choice but to follow, with torch and knife clutched in blood-spattered hands.

VII

As soon as he saw the green door, hanging ajar and splintered, Sempronius knew they had come too late. In the atrium, a trio of roughly-dressed men were taking turns beating and kicking a fourth man, whom Sempronius could only just recognize as Manius Maloricus, uncle to Dictator Ocella's two young children. General Aufidius, Vatinius Nisso, and the Vitellian bodyguards wasted no time in altering the odds. Aufidius laid out one of the attackers with a single blow to the head. Another, Felix grabbed and quickly subdued. Nisso was still wrestling the third when Sempronius, Galerius, and Aulus Vitellius rushed to Maloricus's side.

His mouth was a scarlet ruin, his throat purple and bruised, and one eye was swollen shut. Only then did Sempronius notice two other bodies strewn about the atrium: slaves to the Maloricae, he guessed, though whether they were dead or merely unconscious, he could not say. They lay amid shattered pottery, spilled lamp oil, and broken furniture, though it was impossible to tell if all the damage had been done by the few men still inside the house, or if others had contributed to the looting and already moved on.

"The children!" Galerius said, kneeling beside Maloricus. "What happened to—"

Maloricus could not speak, only made a wheezing noise as he pointed towards the sleeping cubicles across the atrium. Galerius started in that direction, then paused, as though his feet did not want to let his eyes make the confirmation. Laying a hand on Galerius's shoulder, Sempronius moved past him and into the little room.

For a moment Sempronius hoped that he was mistaken, that they had made it in time after all. The infant Horatius lay on the mattress, still half-covered by a blanket. But then Sempronius saw a few spots of blood on the pallet and noticed that the tiny chest was not rising and falling. He stepped closer to confirm. No one had wasted bladework on the boy, not when an infant's skull was so fragile.

Sempronius felt a flicker of Shadow magic seeping unbidden into his mind, an undercurrent bearing ideas of what this little Horatius might have grown into. *'He might have become a great leader,'* Sempronius thought. *'Or he might have been a pawn for men without scruples. He might have grown bitter and resentful at the fate Fortuna gave him. He might have burned himself out before his twentieth year. Or he might have imitated his father too nearly.'* Potential was not always a positive thing.

He pushed the nudging intuition of his gift aside. He did not want to think, with the boy's blood not yet cooled, that it might be better in the long run that Ocella leave no such legacy, that a child not grow to manhood under the shade of such a father's reputation. There would be a time for such considerations, but even Sempronius's pragmatism had its limits. He stalked back out into the atrium, where Nisso had pinned to a wall the only murderer left conscious. Obir and the Vitellian bodyguards stood ominously over the others, while Galerius was helping Maloricus to stand, blotting the blood from his face with a strip of cloth.

Sempronius moved beside Nisso. "Where's the other?" Sempronius demanded of Nisso's captive. When the man didn't answer, he gestured to Nisso, who shook him again, slamming his head against the wall. Groaning, the man gestured towards the back of the house. Sempronius ignored Galerius's stricken expression and Maloricus's agonized moan as he went to investigate.

Ocella's older son, it seemed, had tried to run—or someone had tried to run with him. *'And they nearly made it.'* Sempronius found the boy crumpled on the kitchen floor, just inside the door leading to the alley behind the house. The slashing wounds on his nursemaid's hands and arms showed that he had been defended, however briefly. The murderers' knives had found both their hearts all the same.

Sempronius returned to the atrium and shook his head in answer to an unasked question. Maloricus slumped to the floor again, keening. Galerius was trembling with rage as he approached the man Nisso held against the wall. "The punishments of Tartarus," Galerius said, fiercer than Sempronius had ever seen him, "will be a mercy compared to what I intend for you. I will see you chained and bound in some dank Pannonian mine and left there to rot, until one day you choke on your own— Do you realize, do you even comprehend what a disgrace this is? Not only to yourself, but to the *city*? We do not— We *do not murder children!*" Galerius's horror, Sempronius knew, was not for Ocella's children themselves so much as for the sacred protection that gods and men alike were meant to extend to all innocents. It was not naivete, but faith, and the pain of its wreckage was writ clear on Galerius's face.

"Whelps," the murderer spat, finding courage in the surety of his doom, as men sometimes did. "Their father butchered his share of children. It's no more sin to rid the world of his brats than it is to drown a cat."

Nisso growled, wrapping a hand around the man's throat. "I can deprive this accursed beast of his tongue, if it pleases the Senators."

"Not quite yet," Sempronius said, holding up two fingers. "We'll make an example of him." He swiftly analyzed the assets available to him with the men in the room. Aufidius and Felix were spoiling for a fight, and Galerius looked angry enough to join them in it. The noise from outside suggested the riot had in no way abated. "Aufidius, this may get worse before it gets better. Go, fetch some of your men from the Campus Martius. No blades!" he hastened to add. "You're bringing them within the bounds of the city, so they may bear clubs only, and should not use them unless at dire need. Felix, go with him."

It was a bit of a legal dodge, to allow soldiers within the city at all, but with no elected officials serving at the moment, there were no lictors and no urban praetor to dispatch any kind of pacifying force.

Sempronius looked down at Maloricus, still half-swooning. "Aulus, he needs a healer, and fast. If you take him out the back, you should be able to skirt down the far side of the hill towards the Temple of Asclepius. Obir, can you spare a man or two to accompany them?"

"Yes, Senator."

"And you and I, Sempronius?" Galerius asked.

By way of answer, Sempronius gestured out at the portico. "Time to live up to your cognomen, friend."

∞∞∞∞∞∞∞∞∞∞∞

In two more houses, Latona had interrupted crimes in progress, though fortunately neither had gone so far as the girl in the first house. Merula's face was set in strict lines, and Latona guessed she was torn between worrying over her mistress and enjoying the acts of retribution. Latona had never shared the excitement that Merula found in a fight, but now, she began to understand. There was a thrill in vengeance. Years' worth of stifling herself, of squelching her power so it would not draw unwanted notice, of closing her eyes to injustices beyond her capacity to correct, all now poured forth, setting a rush of fury in her blood and fingertips.

She paused, drawing strength for another empathic search, when Merula jostled her, crying, "Look!" Latona followed her pointed finger and saw Sempronius Tarren and Galerius Orator climbing the outdoor stairs which led to the second level of the tavern at the corner. There was a little platform at the top, barely large enough to hold them both. They had taken the traditional oratory pose with one hand held aloft, despite their lack of togas, and both were shouting to be heard. Two dark-skinned men stood at the bottom of the stairs. One had a whistle in his mouth, which seemed to summon some of the brawlers to order. The other bellowed instructions, pointing emphatically. Both Sempronius and Galerius were known to the mob, by name if not by face, and as word spread that there were senators present, famous exiles from Ocella's reign, curiosity began to turn some heads. They could not win full silence, but it did quell the shoving matches and fistfights in the immediate area, and several of the stone-throwers paused mid-hurl.

Latona stared, wondering what they were doing, where her father had gone, how they had enlisted the aid of the men of the college. Then something lurched in her chest, as though a fist had clenched around her heart and given a little tug. *'Oh, what now?'*

Sempronius Tarren began to speak, and she realized how she could help.

"Citizens!" Sempronius began, and his voice cut as well over the din from the surrounding streets as it would over a battlefield. "Citizens, hear me! I *implore* you, cease this brawling! Three men here are already guilty of heinous sacrilege! Do not join their number!" The word "sacrilege" pricked a few more ears. Latona noticed then that there were a few bloodied men at the bottom of the stairs, their hands roughly bound. Two barely seemed conscious. "These men," Sempronius went on, gesturing to them, "have used your discontent, your righteous anger, as a cover for their own misdeeds. They are *infanticides*. Lucius Galerius Orator and I have seen, with our own eyes, the broken bodies of the *children* these men murdered, children who were under the divine protection of Juno and Diana. They have defiled themselves, and they have risked bringing the wrath of the gods down on us all!"

As Sempronius went on, Latona focused on the platform, trying to block out all other noise. *'I can do this. I can help. Please,'* she silently implored. *'Juno, great lady who protects this city, please, let this work.'*

It would have taken an extraordinary mage to influence the crowd itself, to siphon off the harmful emotions and douse the rising heat of the situation. Trying to move multitudes in their full vigor was a power beyond what any Spirit mage in generations had evinced—not to mention that it occupied shady legal ground. She might not be able to control the crowd itself, but she could help the two senators to achieve a similar effect through their words. She concentrated now on pouring that edge of influence into Sempronius and Galerius, particularly as Galerius took over. *'Let his words be golden, let his charisma shine through him, let him find the right way to reach their hearts . . .'* she thought, feeling her skin grow warmer with the force of the magic pouring through her.

<hr />

"Gentlemen!" Galerius Orator said. "I know you have suffered! I know you feel yourselves wronged! But this is not how we settle such disputes! We are not barbarians, to solve our problems by slinging rocks and mud! We are not animals, to befoul our own home out of spite or ignorance! And we *do not* punish children for the sins of their fathers! We are Aventan. We are better than that." He took a deep breath. "Any grievance you have will be settled in the law courts once there is a new urban praetor—elected by *your* votes. But we cannot hold those elections if the city is in chaos!"

As Galerius went on, speaking of ancient laws, legendary heroes, the will of the gods, and anything else that he thought might strike an empathic chord with his audience, Sempronius surveyed the crowd, watching for any shifts in their temperament, or for Aufidius, Aulus, or Felix's returning. What caught his eye first, though, was a shock of golden hair showing above a shimmering bronze gown: Vitellia Latona, staring right up at the tavern stairs, mouthing words to herself.

He looked away quickly, suspecting she would not like to find herself caught out by him, but he couldn't help quirking a small smile. He knew an invocation when he saw one. *'Well done, my lady. Well done.'*

Her incongruous presence reminded Sempronius of another night, years earlier, when they had encountered each other in similar circumstances. Ocella had sent his lictors out to execute more proscribed unfortunates, but several neighborhoods had erupted into rebellion. Ocella had been forced to dispatch his troops to quell the unrest, but the sight of them in the streets had only fueled the panic. Sempronius, aware that his name had landed on a proscription list, took advantage of the chaos to slip out of the city and into exile—but before leaving, he made one last sacrifice at the Hut of the Twins, swearing to the Founders of Aven and all his gods that he would return. Amid the turmoil, he had encountered the Lady Latona and her handmaiden, alone in the streets, tearful and harried.

Sempronius had never found out what had brought her into the streets that night; she had not volunteered an explanation, and he did not ask. He had simply been grateful to encounter a friend—one of the last he would encounter for many months.

Now, seeing her in such incongruous circumstances, his curiosity pricked up. *'Not only wandering the streets during a riot, but using her talents to help calm it . . . What other woman would dare such a thing?'* Most Aventan patricians would have been scandalized by such boldness, but while Sempronius did feel some concern for her safety, he was far more impressed by her bravery. He could no more have abandoned the Esquiline to the present danger than have severed his own arm. *'Perhaps she feels the same.'*

Between Galerius's skill and whatever edge Latona's magic gave him, the mood of the mob was changing, swiftly and significantly—at least on this street. The brawls had ceased, the roar had dulled to murmurs, and some few that Sempronius could see even had tears in their eyes. He guessed them to be of terror and shame more than of genuine sorrow, but he was willing to accept whatever advantage he could get.

"May I count on you?" Galerius asked. "May I count on you to help us see to it that we can hold proper elections—a right that you have been denied for so long?" A few men hollered back in the affirmative. "May I count on you to restore the order for which Aven is famed? The order which has made us respected throughout the world?" There were more supportive cheers this time, when Galerius paused for a reply. "And may I count on you, good men that you are, to guide your fellow citizens?" Yet more cheers, allowing Galerius to smile. "I thank you, friends. And to show my gratitude, I volunteer my service. I see some leaders of the crossroads collegia here tonight. You come from the Subura, from the Esquiline, from the Quirinal and the Viminal. If the rest of you agree to go peaceably back to your homes, and to tell your friends and neighbors to return in peace as well, I will stay, and speak with these men, that I may know your troubles and bring them to the Senate at the earliest opportunity." That won him genuine applause—and likely, Sempronius thought, more than a few votes, when the time would come for elections.

∞∞∞∞∞∞∞∞∞∞

As the crowd began to break up, the leaders of the Suburan crossroads colleges who had started the unrest moved towards the tavern. Galerius and Sempronius came down the stairs to speak with them—though Latona noticed they were careful to keep their particular friends from the collegium close at hand. Some men they dispatched to neighboring streets, to call off their fellows from inciting any further violence. Others gathered near the senators, eager to have their concerns heard by those who promised to see action taken. As the tension bled out of the atmosphere, Latona swayed into Merula, who moved quickly to shore her up. "Domina?"

"I'm fine, Merula, I am. I just . . . I may have over-exerted myself." The defensive outbursts had taken reserves enough; channeling so much power into Galerius had drained her entirely. "Let's just . . . get me home before Father realizes I'm here."

VIII

Merula spirited Latona in through the back entrance of the domus, and they found Helva waiting there. "They are still inside, most of them," she explained. "Most seemed to have deemed it prudent to remain here and safe rather than risk traveling across an uneasy city." Her eyes flickered critically over Latona, smoke-smudged, disheveled, and fatigued. "Come into the kitchen. We need to wash your face and repair your hair before you can go back in. Merula, *what* did you let happen to her?"

Exhausted though she was, Latona had to return to the dinner party. It seemed incredible, after what she had just gone through, that their guests could still be eating and chatting away unconcernedly. After a few cosmetic repairs, Latona could resume her seat without provoking comment. As Helva had reported, some few guests had drifted away, but many remained until Aulus himself returned, reporting that the "slight disturbance" had been dispelled. If anyone else noticed that Sempronius and Galerius had not returned, no one commented on it, and not even Aula seemed to have realized that Latona had slipped out during the uproar too. It was well past the middle of the night when the last of the guests departed, and Latona elected to stay in her old cubicle in her father's house rather than make the trip back to Herennius's domus.

Sleep proved elusive, however. Latona lay flat on her back, staring up at the window-slit as the black of night gave way to the faintly luminous deep blue of pre-dawn. *'What did I do? What did I think I was doing? If anyone found out . . .'* They would think she had gone mad, at best. A priestess *might* do as she had done, but only under direction of the Senate or the Pontifical College, and only with substantial protection. That a well-born Aventan woman would take it into her head to place herself in such danger was unheard of.

For years, she had clamped down so hard on any impulse that she had almost forgotten what magic she could do. As a child, she had feared the danger inherent in her powers; as an adult, she had been terrified that Dictator Ocella might force her to put them to nefarious use. But now, it was as if Ocella's death had taken away a suffocating pressure, and the air that rushed in was so sweet . . .

'Ridiculous,' she chided herself. 'Just because he's gone doesn't mean you're safe.' As the intoxication of vengeance faded, Latona realized just what danger she had placed herself in. 'This is why Father thought you need looking after . . . why you're supposed to stay in the province . . .' She pounded a hand into her pillow, frustrated at her own foolishness. 'You could have been killed. You see? This is what happens, just as everyone always said. Too much led by your emotions, too easily moved . . . You leap at an impulse and get yourself into trouble. Haven't you learned your lesson by now?'

Still, beneath how shocked she was at herself, pride blossomed. She had helped people—citizens of Aven, her beloved home. Women who had no one to stand between themselves and danger, as she had stood before Aula and Lucia. 'And surely that's what Juno would want.'

When she managed to clear those thoughts from her head, their replacements were nearly as unsettling. She thought, then, of the man who had stepped forward to talk with the discontented plebs and of the happy minutes she had spent in conversation with him earlier that evening. Sempronius Tarren, who had radiated righteous fury yet kept a cool head in the midst of chaos. Sempronius Tarren, nobility etched in every line of his face, so earnest, so intent. Sempronius Tarren, who had been a friend, in those days before Ocella's clouds blotted out the sun.

She chided herself for the absurdity of her fixation. She was hardly the only woman at the party who had shared a couch with Sempronius Tarren for a few minutes. So why on earth were thoughts of him keeping her from her rest?

A faint scratching noise sounded at her door, and Latona grinned in the darkness; it was the old signal that she and Aula used ever since they first had separate bedrooms. She reached over and rapped twice on the wall. Her door slid open, and her sister's slender form padded in, bare feet slapping against the bricked floor. "Scoot," Aula said in a whisper, and Latona slid over on the bed to make room. The pallet did not hold two bodies as comfortably as it had when they were younger, but Latona didn't mind. Her head flooded with memories of so many hushed conversations and muffled giggles. They had clasped hands and sworn vows to each other. They had gossiped about their friends and complained about their tutors. They had huddled together like this the night before Aula's wedding, gushing over her bridegroom's merits and how lucky she was to wed such a promising man. They had held each other in silence, the day after Ocella had him murdered, unwilling or simply unable to dare any words.

"I've had an idea!" Aula whispered, pushing an arm up under a pillow to better cradle her head.

"You always have an idea, Aula."

"Thank you," Aula laughed. "This is a good one, though." Latona waited, patiently, knowing Aula wanted her to ask, but knowing just as well that her sister wouldn't be able to resist spilling for long. Sure enough, after another beat, "I think you should become better acquainted with Sempronius Tarren."

Latona was absurdly grateful for the cover of darkness, feeling a hot blush crawl onto her cheeks that Aula would never have let pass without comment. "What in Juno's name do you mean by that?"

Aula's voice was too-innocent in its reply. "Only that . . . well, he seems to be very well placed, making nice with Galerius Orator and all, and with Gaius still coming up through the ranks . . . he could use a mentor. Someone other than Father, I mean. It does look best if you can get someone outside of the family to take an interest." Aula was talking a little too fast and at a little too high a pitch, always a hallmark of ulterior motives. "And since you seemed to have had a very profitable conversation with him tonight, I thought perhaps you might be the right one of us to cultivate him."

"Cultivate?" Latona asked, thinking that that was a new word for it.

"Yes, precisely."

"You know," Latona said, poking Aula in the ribs, "he mentioned to me how highly he thinks of you."

"What?" Aula squeaked, clearly alarmed at having her scheme redirected.

"Mm-hmm. He did. He thinks you're the epitome of charm and grace."

"Well, that can't be right."

"That's what I told him."

Aula smacked her lightly. "That isn't what I meant. I just . . . I was certain . . ."

"Relax," Latona said, "he didn't mean anything by it, for all that you're an eligible and temptingly available widow."

"Well, that's a relief," Aula said. Her voice had lost all of its coaxing suggestion. "I mean— Not that I wouldn't appreciate it. He is a very fine specimen. But . . . well, I just don't think we would suit."

"Strange. That's precisely what he said."

"See? And he has good instincts as well."

"So pray tell, dear sister," Latona went on, "why are you pushing *me* at him?"

Aula fidgeted, wriggling a bit under the covers. "I think you . . . would suit," she offered, after a moment's hesitation.

"And has it escaped your memory that I do still have a husband?"

Aula snorted. "I'm not pushing you into bed with him—not that I would judge you if you should take that particular path. Numerius Herennius is not nearly as attentive to you as he ought to be. All those long journeys to the hinterlands . . ."

"I don't *mind*, Aula," Latona said, but even as the words were leaving her mouth, she realized that she was speaking in the wrong tense. She'd never minded before; suddenly, though, it occurred to her to be bothered, as much by her own indifference as by his absences.

"Yes, well, you're very good and all of that. But that isn't what I meant, in any case. Not necessarily, at least, though what you do for recreation is really your own business and no one else's, and you'd hardly be the first woman in Aven to avail herself of opportunity. But what I *meant*," she rushed, before Latona could interrupt her, "was just that there might be tremendous potential for an advantageous friendship. He has such experience, and his brother-in-law let slip that he intends to stand for the praetorship. And you certainly seemed to be getting on quite well. I don't see there's anything wrong in pursuing that association. All for dear Gaius's career, of course!"

"Aula, you have the cunning of a weasel and the subtlety of a falling boulder."

Giggling, Aula gave her sister a playful shove. "It's a shame his sister isn't as amiable, or I'd suggest we work harder to befriend her as well. And it's not as though her husband makes much of an impression."

"Not everyone can strike a tremendous figure." Latona stared up at the ceiling. Her eyes had adjusted enough that she could pick out the painted geometric pattern, so familiar from her childhood. "He's a superlative attorney and was quite a good quaestor, as I recall. They don't have any children, do they?"

Aula shook her head, knowing Latona would feel the motion on the pillow beside her. "I asked Helva earlier. Twelve years of marriage, a few miscarriages, no living children."

"Poor thing," Latona murmured, feeling a sudden pang of pity for the woman. She found Vibia Sempronia too aloof and prickly to encourage overtures of friendship, but she could sympathize with that particular woe.

"Rumor has it," Aula went on, "that they're considering adopting out of the Ulpian clan."

"That makes sense. Ulpius Turro is a good friend of Taius Mella, I believe."

"What I wonder is why they waited so long to start looking. I mean, *twelve* years?"

"Sometimes," Latona said softly, "you don't want to give up hope."

Aula fidgeted, embarrassed. "Sorry." Latona murmured dismissively. "Well," Aula said, voice brightening, "that rosy gown she had on might not have done much with her coloring, but I *did* like the embroidery on the sleeves. And did you see what Crispinilla had in her hair? Is she really trying to bring Bithynian styles into fashion?"

Latona smiled, grateful for Aula's change of topic. The sisters chattered on sartorial matters until dawn was streaking the sky, and they fell asleep clasping hands.

◇◇◇◇◇◇◇◇◇◇◇◇◇◇◇◇

Galerius Orator and his wife were both early risers by habit. Galerius liked to spend the dawn hours readying himself for his clients, Marcia Tullia preparing the household for the day. Their son was yet abed—an indulgence they allowed him, for he was at the age where his body was growing so fast that it exhausted him.

"Well, Lucius," Marcia said. "You had rather a more exciting evening than you counted upon, I take it."

"Yes," he agreed, smiling as Marcia fussed with the arrangement of dishes on the table between them. Breakfast was a casual meal and on the small side, but still, Marcia liked for things to be just so, and it quite put her out of sorts if the array of bread and fruit was not attractive. "I suppose we ought to have expected it," he went on. "In some ways, I'm surprised it didn't happen sooner."

"Do you think there will be more incidents?"

"Undoubtedly." Galerius was too grounded to believe otherwise.

"When I think about those poor boys—" Marcia shook her head sadly.

"I know, my dove." Galerius reached across to squeeze his wife's hand, as much to quiet his own anger as to soothe her. Then he sighed. "Apart from them, the damage was minimal. The local healers will have their hands full today, but it could have been worse. Much worse."

"Thanks to your way with words," Marcia said, with pride, but Galerius was shaking his head.

"Thanks to Sempronius Tarren's quick thinking, my dear. If it hadn't been for his assessment of the situation last night—to say nothing of his friendship with the collegia men—the Esquiline might be in riot still."

"You sell yourself short."

"Perhaps. But he was the one who realized the danger to the Maloricae. And he was the one who got the crowd's attention. His mind works fast, so fast, and he has a way about him . . ."

"You don't think it smacks a bit of demagoguery?" Marcia had always had her reservations about Sempronius Tarren, even as she had facilitated his exiled conversations with her husband. It was odd, a patrician with such familiar ties to Aven's tangled network of enforcers—potentially a dangerous eccentricity.

Galerius shook his head. "No. I've known him long enough not to fear that. But he plays the game well, Marcia, and he is not unwise. He doesn't mean to stir the people to revolt. He knows their uses—and their limits, as I believe he ably demonstrated last night."

"If you say so, I'm sure it must be so." There was no agitation in Marcia's voice; she accepted her husband's word as truthful and accurate. After all, she had not heard Sempronius speak in the Senate, or even in the Forum. Some of the more daring ladies might crowd about the rostrum, but Marcia Tullia did not consider so public a sphere appropriate for women. And in any case, she could never abide the jostling. Marcia picked idly at the rind of a citron; she liked it to be well-clear of excess before she ate it. "Do you expect many clients today?"

"Oh, I should think so, especially after last night. Many of them will want reassuring that the city isn't going to come down around their ears anytime soon." Galerius liked some of his clients very well, and many of them were men who genuinely needed his aid and guidance. He could not shirk his duties, as too many patrician patrons did. For Galerius, the patron-client relationship was inviolable. A patron was benefactor and protector to his client, sponsoring his business endeavors or political career and lending his superior clout to legal proceedings. In return, the client would support his patron's political maneuvers, campaign on his behalf, and stand as part of his public entourage. The system of mutual obligation was one of the fundamental bricks on which the city had been built and grown to prominence. Neglected, it could jeopardize the foundations of their social order.

And, in any case, Galerius Orator needed his clients as happy as may be, with the elections forthcoming. Many were wealthy or powerful men in their own right, and had clients of their own; the Galeriae stood at the apex of Aventan society, but many strata of interweaving obligations permeated throughout the ranks. In this way, Galerius's reach extended far past the men who would be in his tablinum today. Those men would return to their clients or to their underlings in a crossroads college or to their guilds, and they would spread whatever message it was Galerius set them to. It was their end of the bargain. In exchange for Galerius's assistance, advice, and protection, they would faithfully support his endeavors.

"You'd best make ready, then; I'd imagine there are several at the gate already," Marcia said, also rising. "I will speak with you this evening."

Whatever Galerius had been prepared for that morning, however, the sight at his front door baffled his expectations. In addition to his own clients, dozens of men from the Esquiline had come, each bearing some small gift of thanks for his intervention. Galerius was touched by their gratitude—and astute enough to realize that he had, perhaps by accident, won himself a great many future votes.

One plebeian cobbler, however, after tendering his thanks, had a question that left Galerius curious and confused. "Dominus, who was the lady who was helping you?"

Galerius's eyebrows arched upwards. "The lady? There were no ladies with us."

The man looked nonplussed. "I'm sorry, Dominus, I thought . . . My wife said there was a woman, clearly a patrician lady, one of great magic, who . . ." His eyes found his feet, shuffling from side to side. "I had gone out to try and secure our shop. I should not have. It left my wife and daughter unguarded. They were set upon, in our own apartment."

Feeling pity for the man's perceptible shame, Galerius reached out to clasp him on the shoulder. "I'm sure you did what you thought best. You are not responsible for another man's villainies."

The plebeian looked grateful, though disbelieving. "Well, sir . . . My wife said there was a lady who found them, who saved them. I thought, perhaps, your noble wife—"

Galerius laughed softly, though at least partly to cover his confusion. "I assure you, I would never have led my wife into such chaos."

The man nodded. "Of course. I apologize for the misunderstanding."

"There is no need."

"If you do hear, though— Should you find out who it was, I should be grateful to know. We owe her a great deal."

IX

CAMP OF LEGIO VIII GEMINA, ALBINE-VENDELICIAN BORDER

Gaius Vitellius was beginning to have very strong feelings about Vendelicia. Namely, he was beginning to have strong feelings about the weather, the food, the mud, the boredom, and the weather again, which was considerable enough to merit a second mention. None were feelings that Gaius Vitellius would qualify as positive.

There had been a time, he allowed, when it was necessary for Aven to station a full legion between their provinces and the wilderness. More than once, Tennic tribes had tried to flow through the mountain passes towards the peninsula of Truscum; more than once, they had gotten a little too close for comfort. It had been over three hundred years since they had reached the city of Aven itself—but the city had a long memory, and no desire to repeat that humiliation. Just forty years ago, invaders had managed to press into upper Truscum, raiding villages, sacking towns, and generally making a nuisance of themselves. So there were times, of course, when Aven needed the strongest military presence possible on the northern border.

That time did not appear to be now.

By fate or chance, the Vendelicians had quieted in the last year. No one had trusted it at first, because everyone knew you couldn't trust Vendelicians. They would swear pacts, vow to behave themselves, and then the second the legions turned their backs, there they were again, raiding and pillaging and pushing at the borders, just like before. They always claimed to have a good reason for it—the vows had not been bound in the right way, with the right words or the right spells; or the revived rebellion was the result of internecine strife amongst the Vendelicians themselves; or one chieftain had died and another, less friendly to Aven, had taken his place. And so, although a few months passed quietly, no one allowed themselves to relax too much, assuming that the relative peace would be unlikely to last.

But then more months had passed, and more, and then the whole summer went by and drifted into autumn with not so much as the theft of a sheep to break up the monotony.

It boded ill for the troops. A small garrison could get along quite well on its own, but a full legion, cooped up for months, meant trouble. There had been fighting, of course. Gaius Vitellius and the other tribunes had had their hands full keeping it at a minimum. The official legion punishment for brawling was a rather severe flogging, but too many of those could incite mutiny rather than serving as a deterrent, and none of the tribunes currently stationed with the Eighth Legion were the sort to enjoy doling out punishments. There had been complaints from some of the locals, particularly regarding the officers' failure to preserve the unmeddled-with state of their daughters. A crop of bastards was coming in along with the autumn harvest. As though all of that weren't bad enough, it had been raining for nearly three weeks solid. The men who could be fit into the fortress were doing well enough, but the cohorts still in tents were experiencing no end of trouble. The tent stakes slid in the mud and the weight of the rain made the canvas sag and sorely tested its oil-slick proofing. And the constant damp bred disease and fungus.

It was all a headache that Gaius Vitellius would far rather do without. He had entered the army at twenty-one and had been in Vendelicia for most of the five years since. He had attained the highest rank among the tribunes and was approaching the age when he would be eligible to join the Senate. *'The military is certainly one way to attain honor,'* his father had written, *'but with the Dictator gone and the city again safe for a son of the Vitelliae, you must consider establishing yourself for your quaestorship. I have some good friends who would assist you in the law courts.'* A necessary tedium, putting in his time as an advocate, and life in the city would certainly have more social advantages, but part of him would be loath to leave the legion.

And so it was with these thoughts on his mind, idly planning out the next few years of his life, that his governing legate, Sallust, found him.

"Tribune!" Sallust barked. Vitellius snapped to attention but was not alarmed by his superior's tone. He had learnt, in his years at this post, that Sallust only had one volume, and it was strident. "At ease, tribune!" Sallust said, though sounding no more at ease himself. "I have a task for you."

"Eager to serve, as always, Legate," Vitellius said, trying to sound as stoically dutiful as he could manage, though internally hoping for something active and exciting that did not involve, for example, overseeing the relocation of the camp latrines. They had flooded three times in the past two weeks; no ground seemed safe.

Fortunately for Vitellius, his superior officer had something other than inundated waste facilities on his mind. "We've heard some strange rumors from Iberia." Vitellius nodded. The men had spoken of little else since the traders from Nedhena had brought up the autumn supplies. "I'm sure it's nothing, lads, just a few tribesmen irritating the smaller villages when they think no one's looking, but it's worrying the traders. They're starting to squawk about what good is Aven's protection if it can't keep trouble like that down. Can't have that, can we, lad?"

"No, sir."

Shaking his head, Sallust drew a parchment out from his belt. "I've had a letter from Governor Fimbrianus, in Gades. Fine politician he is. Damn lot of dithering to get to the point, which seems to be that the Fourth Legion is already tucked into its winter quarters, and he doesn't want to send them out."

Vitellius tried not to let his face betray his confusion. Digging in for the winter was hardly necessary so early in the year in seaside Gades. *'So why wouldn't Fimbrianus want to send out his men to deal with the problem?'* Vitellius could think of no reason—except that the threat was more serious than anyone had let on, too serious for the undermanned, undertrained, and unblooded Fourth to handle.

Sallust seemed to catch the thought on Vitellius's face. "I hope all it means is that his men are too soft for tromping about in the wilderness. It *could* mean that they're aware of conditions we're not. Well. Whatever his reason, Fimbrianus asked me to send someone down towards Toletum to sort things out. Fancy stretching your legs?"

"A vexillation, sir?" Vitellius asked, not wanting to mistake Sallust's meaning. A vexillation meant a small command of his own—a chance for a young tribune to make a name for himself—and putting down rebellious tribesmen in Iberia was far preferable to watching the mud rise in Albina.

"Of course, Tribune!" Sallust bellowed. "I thought one cohort, but the arms-master talked me up to two after what he heard from those southern devils he trades with. If you need cavalry, you should be able to pull it from the local allies in Iberia. I'll give you some names to inquire from. Let me know if there are any centurions you're friendly with that you'd like to take along."

"Yes, sir," Vitellius said, a few names jumping to mind. Then, another thought sparked. "Sir, might Titus Mennenius accompany me?" Vitellius's closest friend in the legion, Titus Mennenius, was younger than Vitellius and most junior of the legion's six tribunes.

Sallust frowned. "Two tribunes with a single vexillation? Seems a bit excessive."

"Yes, sir. But he might benefit from the exercise, sir. Young as he is, there hasn't been much chance for action here."

Sallust's florid face was still furrowed, but Vitellius knew the expression for one of consideration, not necessarily disapproval. "Very well. Take him as far as Nedhena and see what you can learn there, then decide if he needs to go along further or not. I'll expect regular reports, Tribune."

"Of course, sir."

◇◇◇◇◇◇◇◇◇◇◇◇◇◇◇

CITY OF AVEN

A few days after the riot, the Senate was finally able to convene, though it was with the barest of quorums. The Curia felt hollow, too few voices ringing against its white brick walls. Galerius Orator sat in the front row of wooden benches with the other ex-praetors, watching as the rows of men filed in, most wearing only the senatorial red stripe on their togas, not the purple stripe that indicated the man had held the rank of aedile, praetor, or consul. Ocella had been most afraid of men of proven worth.

The hastily appointed interim censor took his place of honor in a low chair. The office was an august one, responsible for the electoral rolls, administration of state finances, and matters of public morality, and in the absence of consuls, the most powerful of elected offices, presiding over Senate business. Usually there were two, but in such circumstances, scraping up one man with the necessary qualities had been challenge enough.

Behind him stood six men in black-bordered togas: the Augian Commission, all devoted to the arts of Water, Light, Air, or Spirit, those elements which could most easily see the magic of others at work. They were a cohort sworn to administer matters of magical justice and order, including the prevention of thaumaturgical craft within the Senate's bounds.

Galerius heard Arrius Buteo before he saw him; true to his cognomen, which meant "buzzard," Buteo squawked and hollered and generally raised a fuss wherever he went. *'Now what could have set him off so stridently in the short time he's been back in the city?'* Not, he recalled, that it took much to set Buteo off. Ever-conniving Lucretius Rabirus was at his elbow today, nodding along at Buteo's stream of opinions even as he scanned the Curia with an acquisitive eye.

The entrance of General Aufidius Strato diverted all attention. He was an imposing figure: tall and broad-shouldered, with deeply bronzed skin and fathomless dark eyes. The chaplet of oak leaves wound in his glossy black curls, a marker of great honor, only emphasized his likeness to Mars. The more enthusiastic Senators rose to their feet, applauding him with considerable vigor. Not everyone, Galerius noticed, was so encouraging; the General had won great victories, to be sure, but many Optimates disagreed with his methods, believing that he provoked conflicts rather than settling them. As one of the few ex-praetors present, Strato joined Galerius and Aulus Vitellius on the front bench.

The last of the stragglers settled in, yet the senators' rows were not half-filled, and the consuls' chairs remained conspicuous in their vacancy. The interim censor, chosen by virtue of seniority, rose shakily to his feet. "August fathers," he said, "it is good to see you returned." He paused, worrying his lower lip. "Even if there are too few of you. Far too few. There is much that must be remedied. Our priority must be to hold general elections for all offices. Venerable fathers, does this seem right and just to you?"

With general agreement voiced, there was no need to show a division with a formal vote, and the Senate moved to the question of how elections would proceed: an issue on which everyone had an opinion, and few in accord. Arrius Buteo rose, proving that the Optimates had not wasted their time. "Before we speak of holding elections and setting dates and opening ourselves to the flood of inadequate campaigners," he said, his harsh voice bouncing off the walls, "we ought to examine the circumstances that brought our hallowed congregation to such a dismal state. The past few years were not a misfortune, august fathers, no—they were a *punishment*." Galerius resisted the urge to rub his temples; Buteo's implacable moralizing could give a man a headache faster than anyone he'd ever known. "The gods saw how we have degraded ourselves. We have allowed foreign influences to pollute our noble Aventan purity. Even our oldest families—whose sons and daughters occupy some of our most sacred offices—have allowed eastern harlots and northern barbarians into their bloodlines." His eyes flickered towards the cluster of Terentiae, a noble family known for their famously eclectic taste in marriage matches—and who had a daughter who was a Vestal Virgin. "We have allowed degenerates and savages within our walls, even within this very Senate! We scarce deserve to call ourselves Aventan, muddled as we have become. We deserved no better than we got. But now—*now* we have an opportunity! We can regain our noble origins, rededicate ourselves to the founding principles of the Republic, and conciliate the gods, that they never visit another horror like Ocella on us." Buteo cast a supercilious gaze around the Senate, clearly imagining that the assembly hung on his every word. "I propose that, as we re-fill our ranks, we hold the number of men in the Senate to one hundred, as suited our Founders." He gave a sharp, self-satisfied nod.

Galerius sighed. Absurd, of course. Aven had grown too large and too complex for a mere hundred men to manage. Adjudication of the law courts alone would consume the time of any Senator left in the city under such a proposal. *'Fools,'* Galerius thought, pursing his lips at the few of Buteo's loyal cronies nodding along with him. *'Damn fools.'* This sort of thing had always kept Galerius from throwing in his lot with their faction, even when it might have benefited him to have friends with their sort of clout. He sympathized with the affection for days past, but they were precisely that—*past.*

"Furthermore," Buteo continued, "we should roll back all those laws which have allowed the dilution of the Senate's purity. No descendants of freedmen or immigrants can be allowed within these hallowed halls. No provincials, and no plebs but those whose family names appear in the initial rolls. And—" Here his eyes found the few black-bordered tunics in the room. "No mages. This is my call—my *challenge* to you, august fathers. Do we have the fortitude to be the good men, the *great* men that our gods demand that we be?"

Buteo ceded to Rabirus, speaking in support, then a chain of other men rose in succession. For all his morally superior bluster, Buteo was not popular, nor was his proposal. There were too many men in the Senate who might lose their standing if Buteo could convince a majority to agree to the rescinding of rights.

Rufilius Albinicus eloquently voiced opposition and managed to turn attention towards setting dates for an election, but that set off a squabble about the eligibility of men who had been forced to abandon previous offices mid-term by Ocella's proscriptions. His attention wandering, Galerius's eyes fell on Sempronius Tarren, who had a keen expression on his face. *'What might that be about?'* When the current speaker finished, before the interim censor could appoint anyone else, Galerius said, "August fathers, I move that Vibius Sempronius Tarren offer his opinion."

A slight murmur went up at the idea of a man of only thirty-four years, comparatively low in rank, being asked to speak, but Sempronius rose with dignity, holding up one hand in the traditional oratory pose. "I thank you, Galerius Orator, for the honor. Venerable fathers, I propose that *all* offices and commands be elected anew. Including—" He paused, glancing around the room. "—the governance of our provinces and legions afield." A murmur went up; generally those positions went to men who had recently vacated the office of praetor or consul. Ocella's mandates had stymied matters, however, and many of the current governors had been settled into their regions for years. "Furthermore, I think it imperative that we assign all praetorships and their attendant legions before the end of the year. The news coming out of Iberia concerns me, venerable fathers, concerns me greatly. I anticipate that we will see a need, before the year is out, to prepare for war. Indeed, we ought to begin preparing now, that the commands be settled in ample time to muster the extant legions and to make travel provisions."

'Well, that's put the cat among the pigeons,' Galerius thought, as Rabirus shot to his feet to argue.

"Iberia? We hardly have matters here in hand, and you would have us launch a foreign campaign?"

"You would certainly be in an excellent position to know the city's troubles," Sempronius said, "having been at the right hand of the man who authored them." That set Buteo and several others to sputtering in indignation, but Sempronius pitched his voice over theirs and continued. "Certainly there are enough men of worth left in this city—particularly if we're willing to expand our narrow confines to see them—to handle matters at home and abroad. If we cannot defend our provinces when they cry for aid, we lose all respectability." His eyes flicked, quickly but significantly, towards the famous generals present, Aufidius Strato and Publius Rufilius Albinicus. Strato, man of little political acumen though he was, knew an invitation when one was extended to him.

"The lad's right," Strato said, getting to his feet. His voice boomed sufficiently to quiet all the others, though Buteo and Rabirus still had their heads bent together, furiously whispering. "If we let these Lusetani bastards nibble at one province, we'll have trouble on all fronts before long. We've just gotten the Vendelicians quiet, but they'd start up again if they thought we lacked strength to resist. And then what? We become easy prey for all the old enemies still holding a grudge—Numidians and Pannonians and Armoricans. Who knows what fool ideas the Menaphon might get into his head down there in Abydosia? Even the Athaecans might find a backbone, and then where would we be?"

"Back where we were four hundred years ago," Buteo said, though he spoke it with pride, not as a detriment. "Honest and pure, undistracted by these—these frivolities!"

"I am surprised at you, friend Buteo," Sempronius said, though his tone was neither surprised nor friendly. "You, who have such reverence for our noble forefathers, would see us lose all that they have gained?"

Buteo spluttered some sort of response, but it was lost in a buzz of accusations and reproofs from one side to the other. Galerius raised his hand for attention, then stood when the interim censor nodded to him. "Sempronius Tarren has the right of it when it comes to electing new positions. We ought to start fresh, rather than rewarding Ocella's promotions. However," he added, "I cannot share his certainty on the matter of Iberia. We simply do not know enough yet. I propose this: that we set our elections for December, if our worthy interim censor believes he can continue to govern the Senate until then. This will give us time enough to sort out matters both domestic and foreign. The people can then make the best possible decisions, and we can decide the Iberian matter with a full Senate, not the scraps of one."

"We cannot wait that long." Sempronius's feet were firmly planted, as though a strong enough stance would ward off opposition. "Each boat arriving in Ostia carries new tales of woe. What further proof do we need that the gods require our action?"

"Be reasonable," Galerius said. "We can hardly focus on a war effort while the Senate is still at such depleted numbers. We must see things done in the appropriate order."

Strato's mouth was set in a thin line, and his chin had a stubborn angle to it, but after a moment, he nodded. "It may be for the best—*if* we may be assured that the matter will remain up for exploration and debate in the meantime." He cast a dark look at Rabirus and Buteo. "Silence will serve no one, and the people of Aven have a right to all intelligence pertaining to the security of our provinces."

Buteo purpled, ready to start up again, but Rabirus laid a hand upon his shoulder, silencing him. They were both watching Sempronius, who clenched and unclenched his right hand, but eventually nodded, too. "December, then."

◇◇◇◇◇◇◇◇◇◇◇◇◇◇

Sempronius was careful to keep his expression stormy until he was well out of the Curia. He exchanged few words with anyone as he passed, only a brief promise to call upon Aufidius Strato and Rufilius Albinicus soon. They were neither of them staunch Popularists, but they were men of war, and Sempronius intended to secure their support as firmly and rapidly as he could. Only when he had passed the Circus Maximus, on his way towards his home on the Aventine, did Sempronius allow himself to relax.

"Sempronius! Hoy, Sempronius!" He paused at the call and turned. Autronius Felix was bounding across the street, his brother Marcus trailing behind him with an apologetic grimace. "Marcus just told me—you're for war in Iberia?" Felix, on the other hand, looked like Saturnalia had come early. "What can I do? I can't believe the bastards—"

"Felix!" Marcus smacked him in the back of the head.

"Well? They are! I can't believe they're making you wait till after the December elections to start planning."

But Sempronius was laughing, shaking his head. "That went better than I could have expected. I assumed Lucretius and Buteo would want to delay me—but to have it come from Galerius? My known friend? Fortuna smiles on me."

Marcus and Felix exchanged confused looks. "Er, Sempronius?" Marcus asked. "I'm afraid I don't take your meaning."

Sempronius clapped Marcus on the shoulder. "Marcus, there's no point in rushing towards war. We need to prepare for it, most certainly, but no legions could move now, with autumn setting in. We can't risk the storms at sea in the autumn, and we'd never get provisions enough to make it over the Albine Mountains, not with snow slowing us down as soon as we reached the heights."

"Then why raise the matter to begin with?"

"It gets the idea in everyone's heads." The answer came not from Sempronius but from Felix. "And with Aufidius insisting it remains in discussion, by the time the official vote in December rolls around—" He spread his arms wide. "Everyone will think of it as a done matter! And it'll better your chances in the praetorial elections, if the people are excited for a war they see as your project."

"You think you'll convince them later?" Marcus asked.

"I won't need to," Sempronius said, starting to walk again. The Autroniae fell in step beside him. "The Lusetani will do that for me long before it comes time to vote."

"If you get the common folk talking of it, they'll demand action," Felix said. "Half raging to defend the honor of Aven, the other half hungry for spoil and new trade ventures. Rabirus and Buteo won't be able to stand in your way if all the city cries for war."

"But you've handed them a win," Marcus said. "You allowed them to score a point off of you—"

"But gave nothing away!" Felix said. "What a hollow victory for Lucretius Rabirus."

"I don't doubt he'll realize it soon enough," Sempronius said, "though Buteo may not have the wit to. And in the meantime . . ." He cast a grin over his shoulder at Marcus. "You notice how easily my suggestion about sloughing off Ocella's appointments went over?"

Marcus blinked. "Well, yes . . . Rabirus and Buteo sort of . . . forgot to argue with you about it."

"Because you dangled such juicier bait in front of them with the Iberian business," Felix said. "Oh, you clever devil."

"But Sempronius," Marcus said, "with Buteo agitating for a reduction of the Senate—"

"I'm not worried about him. Rabirus is the real threat. Didn't you notice? Every one of the men who spoke looked to him. That's a dangerous proposition; to stamp it out, we'll need men like Aulus and Galerius to stand on our side. Men who are known to sympathize with that affection for days past, but who recognize that they are just that—past." He grinned. "How fortunate, then, that Galerius's credit in the Senate remains unimpeachable, since he's willing to stand up and oppose his known friend."

Marcus was agape. "Do you mean to say that you *intended* that he oppose you on Iberia?"

"I had hoped someone honorable would," Sempronius said. "To have it be Galerius? Perfect. He proves to the Optimates that he's not gone over to the Popularists, but he still keeps them in check as a moderate voice."

"But *Iberia*, Sempronius!" Felix cut in.

"Yes, Felix, I have plans for that as well. I'll have to come in first in the lists." Once, the twelve men elected to praetorships had been assigned their duties by lots following the election, with random chance determining which magistrate would govern which province—and who would remain in the city, seeing to urban matters. Since reforms a century earlier, whomever the electors returned first, with the most votes across all the Centuries, had his pick of any open magisterial positions or provinces. It was one of the modern degradations of the *mos maiorum* that Arrius Buteo was fond of decrying, but a practicality as Aven's territories expanded.

"But what are you *after*?" Marcus said.

"Cantabria, I'd bet," Felix replied. Sempronius gave him a sideways smile. "Of course. You don't just want us to go to war—you want to lead it!"

Sempronius stopped suddenly, clasping Felix by the shoulder and looking him straight in the eye. "May I count on you?"

Felix answered with a grin. "Take me to Iberia with you, and you can count on me till you run out of numbers."

"Good. If—*When* I am elected praetor, I'll want you for my laticlavus." Felix beamed as Sempronius glanced to Marcus. "We'll need you for tribune of plebs, if you're willing."

Marcus was staring, slightly agape. "I'm sorry, Sempronius, I still haven't gotten past the part where you engineered your own upstaging in the Curia."

"It's engineering my election I'm more concerned with now. I need you—both of you—to help me make contacts throughout the city. Friends of your father's, merchants, farmers, men of the Subura—" Another enigmatic smile flashed on his face. "Ocella interrupted my term as aedile. The way I see it, that means I owe our fair city a great deal."

"What do you mean?"

Sempronius opened his mouth to speak, then shook his head and started again. "Come to supper tomorrow, and I'll explain more fully. Bring your father."

"Certainly!" Felix said.

Marcus shifted his weight from one foot to the other. "I just hope you know what it is you're putting into motion, Sempronius," he said. "Come on, Felix."

The Autroniae split off north towards the Quirinal, leaving Sempronius to walk the rest of the way back to the Aventine Hill alone, taking the long way around, through the side-streets and crowded alleys that most men of his class barely knew existed. The Aventine and the neighborhoods that sprawled at its base were an odd mix: half illustrious, half impecunious, where the enclosed homes of wealthy nobles butted up against multi-tiered insulae, homes to dozens of families and freedmen, shopkeepers and clerks.

Sempronius Tarren lived in his family's ancient domus on the north side of the hill, near the Temple of Juventas. *'The Palatine may have the flash and the cash—and, perhaps, the beauty,'* he thought, considering the Vitellian domus. *'But the Aventine is where our nation began and where it truly lives.'* The city had expanded past its bounds centuries earlier, when the kings of Aven had built themselves new homes on the less-crowded Palatine and Caelian Hills. Certain neighborhoods, particularly those around the Hut of the Twins, retained their historical dignity, but much of the hill had changed as Aven had. A shame, said some of those same men who now inhabited the more fashionable neighborhoods, that the founding hill had fallen so far to now play home to so many immigrants and working plebs. Sempronius saw, instead, great wonder in the mosaic of demography.

Living on the Aventine made for a hike to and from the Forum, but Sempronius had never minded. He liked strolling, liked *feeling* the city bustle around him. Today, his senatorial toga made him a touch conspicuous, but many days, if he had no official business, he would forgo the cumbersome garment and pass by unnoticed. He enjoyed the polyglot clamor of the common people of Aven going about their daily lives. Fullers beat cloth, mothers wrangled their children, masters yelled instructions to slaves, butchers hewed meat, vendors hawked wares, all as they had for generations and would do as long as the world lasted.

Walks like this reminded him of what he meant to achieve—the reason he baited dogs like Rabirus and Buteo with his own flesh. The city had a great and glorious future, and it did not belong only to the citizens of the Palatine. All of Aven's citizens had a share in the city's great and glorious future—and Aven's citizens ought to encompass the best the world could offer, from one end of the Middle Sea to the other.

The visions that both drove and haunted him seemed to pass before his eyes like ghosts: he could see the streets bedecked with flowers, teeming with new citizens, a flourishing mass of color and sound. Too easily, as well, he could see the buildings crumbling, a dark and oppressive silence falling over empty streets. *'These risks, this boldness . . . I do what I must to secure one future and avoid the other.'*

Corvinus met his master at the door, ready to unfold him from the toga and pass the cloth to the house slaves for cleaning. "We'll be entertaining the Autroniae for supper tomorrow. Let the kitchen folk know so they can go to the markets early."

"Of course, Dominus."

Knowing he could leave preparations well in Corvinus's hands, Sempronius went to his study, then pulled out parchment and ink. *'December. Three months. Time enough to get quite a lot done, I think.'*

X

A few days before the Kalends of October, Aula and Alhena sat together at their looms, though the elder sister was not attending to duties nearly as diligently as the younger. Weaving had never been among Aula's favorite activities—in her opinion, performing menial tasks you'd rather avoid was what slaves were *for,* and she employed several far more talented in textile matters than she would ever be.

Alhena, however, attacked the loom with manic energy, her focus absolute. She wasn't really supposed to weave or spin; there was a chance such repetitive activity could bring on one of her Time-related episodes. And while, of course, it was a blessing and a gift from the gods, Aula rarely felt up to dealing with it. But Alhena had insisted, claiming the work would help her take her mind off things.

It did not, to Aula's observation, appear to be working. While Aula pushed her shuttles lazily, chatting with Helva about the news from the Curia, Alhena's fingers flew. Her jaw was clenched tight, and her teeth worried her lower lip raw. Faster and faster, her shuttle rocked back and forth, until suddenly it slipped from her fingers and clattered to the floor.

Aula looked sideways to see Alhena white as a sheet, hands shaking, tears brimming in her eyes. "My honey!" Aula exclaimed, setting her own shuttle aside. "What's the matter?"

"Tarpeius," Alhena breathed. "He should . . . He should have come by now."

Aufidius Strato had brought home with him only a cohort of retiring soldiers; most of the legion remained in Albina, and those military tribunes whose terms were up were straggling behind as ships became available to make the transit from Massilia to Aven.

"Oh, sweetheart, you know they never release the tribunes from duty immediately," Aula said, patting Alhena's hair.

But Alhena shook her head, then jammed the heels of her hands into her eyes. "Ohh, I don't know. I just have this feeling . . ."

"A feeling?" Aula echoed, brow creasing in worry. "Or a . . . well, you know."

"No. Maybe. I don't think so. Ahh!" Alhena stamped her foot and straightened, flinging back her hair. "It hasn't been anything like that. It's all cloudy. I just . . . I just see clouds, that's all."

"Well, that might not be so bad," ventured Aula. "Clouds might mean, oh, anything! The fortune of Jupiter, riding in on a lightning bolt. Nourishing rain for the next growing season."

Alhena bestowed her elder sister with a withering look. "*Clouds*, Aula. If it were Jupiter astride a lightning bolt or nourishing rains, I'd have seen those. Not *clouds*." She started to rub at her eyes again, but Aula caught her hands.

"That won't make it stop, you know, and you might blind yourself if you keep it up," she chided. Alhena crumpled slightly, letting her head fall against her sister's shoulder, and for a moment, she was a little girl again. Eight years separated the eldest and youngest daughters of the house; they had never been as close as Aula and Latona, but they had a different bond. Vipsania Vitelliae had died at such an inconvenient time, and though she had loved her children desperately, the bulk of her attention while she was alive had gone to Gaius, her only son. Aula had been the one to take care of Alhena, to kiss away the early tears of childhood, bind up scrapes, teach her the ways of womanhood. It didn't mean she always had patience for Alhena, but it meant she always tried. Aula stroked her sister's fire-red hair, murmuring soothingly, too much the optimist herself to allow the possibility that Alhena's fears might have foundation.

∞∞∞∞∞∞∞∞∞∞∞∞

The man who eventually *did* arrive at the threshold of the Vitellian domus, on the day before the Kalends, was not Tarpeius, but rather one of the legion's senior legates. "Aulus Vitellius Caranus, I salute you," he said, snapping to attention.

"Please, be at your ease," Aulus said, gesturing for them to sit. "What brings you here, legate?"

"Ill news, I regret to say." He had the deep neutral tone so crucial to military command. "It is my sad duty to inform you that military tribune Tarpeius died three days ago, while we were at sea."

For a moment, Aulus could only stare in shock. "He— But how?"

"There was a storm," the legate said, pursing his lips slightly. "Part of the rigging tore loose and struck him."

Aulus clutched at his breast, filled with sorrow—for the young man, for the young man's family, but most of all, for his daughter. "And that killed him?"

"Not immediately."

Aulus winced; he would have liked to have been able to tell his daughter that it had at least been quick and painless.

"It crushed his chest, you see. Our surgeon did what he could, but there was, apparently, a lot of internal damage, and being at sea . . . there was little he could repair. He died the next night. A hemorrhage, I believe."

With a heavy sigh, Aulus got to his feet. The legate stood also, recognizing the signs of his imminent dismissal. "I cannot thank you for bringing this news to my house, legate," Aulus said, "but I can commend you for doing a difficult duty. You have, I assume, already seen to his family?"

"Yes, sir. His father."

Aulus shook his head sadly. At least the elder Tarpeius had another son—but he was only eight, no replacement for a young man in his prime, with such a bright future ahead of him. "I will have to visit him as well. Forgive me. Will you take bread and water?"

"I thank you, sir, but no." His was brusque but polite. "I must be on my way."

"Other duties to fulfill, I suppose, of a similar nature." There was no rancor or malice in Aulus's tone, though some pity. The legate gave another salute and departed. "Sabino." Aulus gestured for one of the house slaves. "Please go find Alhena. Tell her I need to speak with her. And— And make sure Mus is with her."

While waiting for his daughter to arrive, Aulus paced the peristyle garden. Alhena's birds chirped merrily all around him, oblivious to the ill wind that had just gusseted through the house. He wasn't wondering how to break the news to her; nothing would do but the truth, as plainly as he could manage. Sugarcoating the matter would not make Tarpeius any less dead.

No, Aulus's primary concern was for what happened *next*. Alhena was, he knew full well, not like his other daughters. Aula had borne Quinctilius's death with proper Aventan endurance. She mourned, in private, for as long as was appropriate, and had then moved on to the rest of her life, assuming normalcy as well as she could during the Dictatorship. As for Latona—well, Aulus's worry was more that Latona might display a rather unseemly lack of regret if anything tragic befell Numerius Herennius. But for Alhena, Aulus had significant concerns over how she might handle the shock.

Alhena was his baby, the last of his brood. Vipsania had lost two children following Alhena's birth, and the last of those had taken Vipsania away as well. Aulus had arranged her marriage to Tarpeius not with more care than Aula's or Latona's—he had, of course, tailored the decision to what he thought best for each in her turn. But for Alhena, he had made the decision with rather more tenderness. Alhena could not be given to a political husband. She needed someone solid and dependable, someone who would cherish her—someone who would never think to make ill use of her Proserpina-given gifts.

Tarpeius had been ideal: from a good family of backbenchers, high status enough to be important, but lacking the ambition that would put too much pressure on Alhena. Even better, they had been childhood friends, and mutual liking had grown over the years into genuine affection, even in Tarpeius's absence. Alhena treasured the letters she had received too infrequently from Albina.

Aulus was still pacing when his daughter came to him. She wore a dove gray stola over a crimson tunic, which Aulus thought had once belonged to Latona. It clashed, he thought, with her too-bright hair, but that sort of consideration never occurred to Alhena. She looked pale and a touch brittle, as she had ever since word had come that General Aufidius was back in the city. Alhena's Cantabrian shadow trailed in behind her.

"You sent for me, father?"

"I wish I had had no need." Aulus swallowed. "I have had word from General Aufidius."

Alhena's azure eyes lit up with interest, but it was a brief flash of lightning that quickly clouded over. Alhena was clever enough to know that her father's tone did not presage good news, or perhaps her gifts spoke to her in that instant. "And . . . what word would that be, father?"

"I am sorry, daughter." The blood started to drain from her face even before he continued. "There was an accident crossing from Nedhena. Tarpeius died at sea."

Alhena blinked several times, as though uncomprehending. "He . . ." She swayed slightly, and Mus moved to catch her, but she held up a hand to ward her off, determined to remain upright on her own. "How?"

"Some rigging tore loose during a storm. He was struck and died from his injuries." Alhena nodded almost unconsciously, as though his words had confirmed a suspicion—or a premonition. She kept so much close, held so many things private. In times like this, it left Aulus feeling at a loss, unequal to the task of guiding the daughter who so rarely expressed her feelings, much less her needs.

"I . . . am sorry to hear of it," Alhena said at length, her voice sounding as though it came from very far away. "I will need to tender my regards to his family."

"I will be pleased to do so on your behalf, daughter," Aulus said. "You need not visit yourself, if it is too—too troubling."

She nodded again, a blank, emotionless bob. Then she turned, neatly, and walked away. Aulus did not stop her, but trailed behind. With even footsteps, hands folded neatly in front of her, Alhena walked calmly to her sleeping chamber. Mus followed her in and shut the door behind her.

A long moment of silence passed, and then a wail that would have harrowed the Furies went up from inside Alhena's room. Aulus nearly sighed with relief. With a crook of his finger, he summoned his steward. "Where is my eldest daughter?"

"With Lady Latona," answered the Athaecan freedman, who was well-bred and well-trained enough not to glance at the doorway from behind which such a woeful keen resounded. "I believe they meant to visit the baths."

"Send to the house of Numerius Herennius," Aulus instructed. "Tell them both to return here, as soon as may be. Say that Tarpeius is dead, and that Alhena has need of them." The steward nodded, bowed, and departed. Aulus rubbed at his temples. All he had ever wanted was a placid, well-organized life—and for a brief time, he thought he would get it. Ocella's reign had upturned so much, brought his eldest daughter back under his roof, along with his only grandchild, and now, if indirectly, it had robbed his youngest of her husband before they had even managed to exchange vows. As for Latona, lately he could not escape the feeling that he had erred, failed her in some critical way. She never reproached him, not with words, at least, but sometimes he caught sight of a deadened gloss in her eyes.

At least there was Gaius, properly on track. Ocella's reign had not kept him from his duties, and Aulus had heard nothing but positive reports of his action on the Vendelician border. It was a comfort, for a man to have such confidence in his son's career. There would be more to worry on later—Aulus was already tucking money away to assist Gaius up the *cursus honorum*, as every responsible father did—but for the time being, all was well.

He knew what to do with his son. That was easy. *'One daughter widowed . . . now a second, before she could even be a bride . . . and Latona . . .'* Aulus sighed. Not for the first time in the past few years, Aulus regretted not remarrying after Vipsania's death. Girls, it seemed, didn't stop needing a mother just because they themselves were grown.

XI

Twenty feet of white wool. Beaten, fulled, bleached, and finally chalked until it shone startling white. Twice as tall as a man, fully stretched out. Formal and precise, its every fold and tuck carefully prescribed. Most importantly, a signal. A challenge, to some. A rallying cry, to others. An Aventan man donned the *toga candida* when standing for political office, that all and sundry knew to watch his public words and actions and judge him accordingly.

Sempronius rotated his shoulders in anticipation of bearing its weight. Tradition could be hell on a man's musculature. "Very well, Corvinus. Let's begin."

As Corvinus wound him into the garment, Sempronius thought out his day. First, a formal greeting of his clients, some of whom he had not seen since his exile. Then a procession to the Forum. An analysis of who else was there. Conversations with important allies, at least one of which ought to yield an invitation to dinner. In the afternoon, when the crowds were thick, a speech. Back home to change into more comfortable attire, then, with luck, a long and profitable meal with a friend. It would be a long day, out early and back late.

He smiled at the thought. Life in Abydosia had been idyllic—far too much so. Life in Aven, Sempronius found far more stimulating.

As early as Sempronius had risen, his clients were already waiting in his atrium or outside his house when he emerged from his chamber: a collection of distant but well-born relations, a selection of equestrians and plebs of the First and Second Classes with whom he had served in Phrygia and Numidia, and a sizable herd of lesser plebs whose loyalty he had earned through various favors, big and small. Rarely did he call them all in to attend him in public, but today the show would matter. He needed to arrive at the Forum with as massive a horde as he could manage to assemble. *'Maybe,'* he thought with a wry smile, *'I can convince the former centurions among them to get everyone to march in formation.'*

Vatinius Obir and Nisso were there, admiring the stylishly-painted interior of the domus with gregarious smiles. Sempronius could not neglect his higher-ranked clients today, of all days, but the brothers' frank lack of ceremonial pomposity did tempt him. They were certainly better company than some of his cousins. And so, holding in a sigh, he nodded his greeting to all, then took a seat behind the lacquered desk in his study, arranged his toga at the proper angle over his shoulder, and said, "Send them in according to rank, Corvinus."

∞∞∞∞∞∞∞∞∞∞∞∞

Late in the morning, Sempronius Tarren left his house on the Aventine and proceeded downhill, trailing a few dozen togate men of varying station in his wake. He was far from the only man taking the opportunity of the first clear day since the Senate's reconvention to publicly announce his candidacy, and as such, the Forum was even more of a crush than usual. The noise of so many men shouting at or over each other rose to a thunder before Sempronius was even off the Aventine, a dull roar of ego rising over terracotta rooftops.

Sempronius stood at the edge of the Forum for a moment, taking in the scene before him. The valley between Aven's hills teemed with life: white-togaed politicians, like himself, and scores upon scores of businessmen and traders, sealing their contracts in this sacred space, surrounded by the watchful eyes of so many gods.

For a man who could see the blurring haze of deceit and obfuscation, the day seemed cloudy, not fair. He closed his eyes for a moment, deliberately dampening Shadow's awareness, since he knew from past experience that remaining alert to every shady misdirection, disingenuous promise, and dubious quibble flung about the Forum would result in a particularly nasty headache. Then he opened his eyes and began scanning for friends and enemies alike.

Galerius and General Strato were at the Rostra, both announcing their candidacies for consul. Sempronius watched them strike up a conversation and thought that they made unlikely, though not necessarily incompatible, allies. One of the few ex-consuls present, Aulus Vitellius, declaring that he would stand for the office of censor, completed the triad of venerable dignitaries.

Buteo, who had also decided to run for censor, was nearby, chewing his tongue. For consul, he seemed to be throwing his support behind Gratianus, a portly man who had hidden out Ocella's dictatorship in the comfort of an eastern court, but Sempronius could not imagine that such an uncharismatic lump of conservatism would stand much of a chance against Strato's military popularity or the appealingly moderate Galerius.

The field of praetors was more concerning. The Optimates were out in force and standing together, vowing to restore the honor and dignity of the Republic after Ocella's transgressions. Sempronius overheard one echoing the benefits of Buteo's plans for a hundred-man Senate. "These new men, these merchants and immigrants, they are motivated by short term gain, not civic duty! They care for their own coffers, not those of Saturn!" Whatever sins they cloaked in such words, Sempronius had to admit it was compelling rhetoric—and they had chosen a powerful place to declaim it, clustered at the base of the Temple of Saturn, home to Aven's treasury.

Despite his former status as Dictator Ocella's right hand man, Rabirus still had political traction. In his speeches, he re-framed himself as a defender of the Republic. *'A neat trick,'* Sempronius thought, *'to tell the populace you were holding Ocella back from his worst atrocities, rather than co-authoring them.'* Rabirus stood with several other prominent Optimates around him, including Licinius Cornicen. A man of uncertain allegiance, Cornicen concerned and frustrated Sempronius. He generally stood with the Optimates, but Sempronius had always harbored hopes that his pragmatic streak might move him toward the center.

Making matters worse, the Popularists standing for praetor were not all that Sempronius might have hoped for. He would need strong allies beside him, particularly in the provinces that would field legions for an Iberian campaign or field the money to fund those legions. One prospect was an affable round-cheeked gentleman of low birth, whose wealth could easily buy him an office; another came from one of Aven's Founding Families, but hardly had a sestertius to his name these days, clinging to the bottom rung of the senatorial rank; a third was so timid that he could barely string two sentences together in public.

'What a challenge.' There was something simultaneously depressing and invigorating about it. Sempronius had much to do and much to prove. He glanced over his shoulder at his herd of clients. They had all been briefed back at his domus on what he expected of them. A showy entrance, as tradition dictated, but then they would divide and, with luck, conquer. To sentimental audiences, they would play up Sempronius's status as a banished hero returned to the city, driven out by Ocella's jealousy for his brilliant mind and popular ideas, who had nonetheless continued to work for the Republic in exile. To the mercantile, they would trumpet

Sempronius's dedication to improving trade routes and the emporiums. To the military-minded, they would drum up support for the Lusetanian campaign and his vision for expanding Aven's influence around the Middle Sea. "Well, gentlemen," he said, gesturing towards the Forum. "Into the fray."

◇◇◇◇◇◇◇◇◇◇◇◇◇

"You're worried."

Corvinus stood in the quiet of the recently vacated Sempronian atrium, staring at the front door. He glanced over his shoulder at Djadi, the dominus's Abydosian household scribe. "What makes you say that?"

"Because you haven't called half the household in to put the chairs back at right angles, refill the water jugs, and sweep up the dust."

Corvinus turned, taking in the disarray that several dozen clients had left in their wake: dusty footprints all over the floor, potted plants askew, chairs and cushions out of place. "Ah."

Djadi strolled forward, smoothing a lock of Corvinus's pale hair back from his face and tucking it behind his ear. "What's troubling you, *resh-weti*? Think the dominus can't manage himself for a few hours without you at his elbow?"

Corvinus moved Djadi's hand away from his face, but gave it a brief squeeze before going to examine the atrium. "The biggest concern there, is what he might say to one of those cousins of his if they try his patience."

"That wouldn't leave you staring at the door so long."

Corvinus nodded absently, bending to return a footstool to its proper place.

"You can tell me, you know," Djadi urged.

"I know," Corvinus said, only regretting the lie a little.

They had picked Djadi up in Tamiat—a necessity, to establish a new household in exile, since they had been able to bring so few slaves with them on their flight from Truscum. Standing in the market with kohl-rimmed eyes and oil in his raven hair, Djadi was hardly what Corvinus had expected from an educated colleague. The placard around Djadi's neck, however, had proclaimed him fluent in four languages and able to write with a neat hand. As soon as he proved those skills, Sempronius had taken him on as a scribe and an assistant to Corvinus.

They had never spoken of it, but Corvinus felt sure that his dominus had kept Djadi on when they moved back to Truscum not out of appreciation for the young man's neat handwriting and obsessive attention to detail, but because of Corvinus's affection for him.

Sempronius Tarren had never given Corvinus reason to regret his loyalty.

And so, even to Djadi, he would not voice his deepest fears. That Sempronius's ambitions were blasphemous was of little concern, directly; Corvinus assumed that the dominus could manage his own *pietas*, his spiritual well-being, without anyone's assistance. What troubled him was the perception of transgression should anyone else learn of Sempronius's long-hidden magical gifts, to say nothing of the legal consequences. No one had been executed for violation of the *lex cantatia Augiae* in nearly a century. But then, no one else was known to have violated it in that long.

Corvinus knew the stories; Sempronius had explained them all when Corvinus's own weak magic had bought him his freedom. When Dolosus brought the city to ruin, it had been over a century before the populace would even allow a mage to be a senator. To dare more than that remained a capital offense.

Stepping out of doors in his bright *toga candida* was a clear sign that Sempronius Tarren was reviving his secret violation of the *lex cantatia*, pursuing high office despite his magical gifts. The Dictator had unwittingly interrupted his earlier attempt, during what should have been a glorious term as aedile, but Sempronius had neither taken that for a discouragement, nor an indication of the gods' disfavor. What this second attempt might wreak, Corvinus had no idea—but the stress of speculating on it might have been turning his hair white, if it weren't already so pale.

So instead, as he directed the cleaning of the atrium, he told Djadi of purely mundane concerns: the vitriol of the Optimates, the weakness of certain of Sempronius's clients, the rough nature of associates like the Vatiniae. All valid concerns in their own right, but none of those had left Corvinus staring at a closed door, vaguely wishing his master had not stepped through it.

◇◇◇◇◇◇◇◇◇◇◇◇◇◇◇

Lucretius Rabirus had a narrow line to walk.

The people needed a show of strength, a reminder of his capability and administrative acumen—but he had to somehow convey that without also reminding them how near he had stood to the Dictator. His best tactic, then, was an appeal to self-interest.

"The office of praetor should be magisterial, not bellicose. Measured and cautious, focused on the good of the state, not war-mongering, not caring more for foreign provinces than for Aven's own citizens!" Rabirus gestured openly at the crowd that had gathered around him. "Good men, hard-working men, like yourselves. You deserve the attention and support of dedicated praetors."

"What about praetors who will bring money into Aven?" someone shouted from a few rows back. "Don't we need them, too?"

"Sempronius Tarren would send your wealth overseas!" Rabirus bellowed, stretching a hand out over the crowd towards his opponent. "He would fund foreign wars to benefit Iberian tribesmen in their animal skins, not the toga-wearing men of Aven! The money he would generate— if he generated any at all, instead of just spending it on his own glory in a foreign war—would go to Tyrian traders, not into your purses!"

Some men were murmuring in agreement, but others—too many others, to Rabirus's eyes—seemed skeptical. "We do business with the Tyrians, though, don't we? And the Athaecans?"

"We *need* Iberian metals," someone else hollered. "Why shouldn't we support the man who would bring more trade our way?"

"Such men are misleading you," Rabirus called back. "They see your noble intents and turn them to ill use! Mark me, gentlemen, an Iberian war would not improve *your* lives."

"And what do you mean to do, Rabirus?" Sempronius said, pitching his voice to carry above the crowd. "If you care so much for the citizens of Aven—" He spread his hands wide. "Tell us your platform. What improvements will you make?"

"I will defend their rights against encroachment by foreign influences."

"How?" Sempronius said. "Those are fine words, and no mistake, but I hear no plan behind them, no *action* you will take."

Rabirus's face was paling slightly, but he went on. "I will support their businesses, that Aventan acumen and ambition may thrive in the world."

"How?" Sempronius asked again. "What initiatives do you propose?"

"I will support the *good* men of Aven, the *righteous* and the *pious* men on whose backs this city is built—"

"*How?*" A third time. "Good friends, Lucretius Rabirus wants you to believe that his focus is on the people of this city, but he offers only empty words."

Furious to have been thrown off his mark, Rabirus glowered across the Forum at his opponent. "And you, Sempronius Tarren? What will *you* offer them?"

Sempronius smiled. "I am not so foolish as to think I have all the answers right now, Rabirus. As you have so rightly pointed out, I have been kept from the city for some time. So I am asking questions—asking what the people *need*." He gestured across to a plebeian who had made himself extraordinarily wealthy off the dye trade. "Papirius Dolus tells me we need improvements to the dockside emporiums, so that goods are protected from both weather and theft." Then, he moved his hands towards a man in a blue tunic. "This man's wife is a priestess of Lucina, and she says the temple is in disrepair and understaffed. It needs money from the city's coffers, or it cannot tend to the women who need its services." He pointed next to Obir and Nisso, who straightened, grinning broadly at the recognition. "My friends in the crossroads collegia inform me that daytime traffic remains a problem. We have roads that need widening, perhaps, or better system for bringing carts in and out of the city." Sempronius dropped his hand to his side. "And traders up and down the Forum tell me they hear ill news out of Iberia, and that they fear for the security of their goods if we do not heed the call from the local tribes to intervene. I do not offer empty words, Rabirus. I offer a willing ear, a capable mind, and the desire to make the city truly better, in deed as well as in thought."

And with that, he turned and moved away, plunging back into a crowd where many men now plucked at his toga to gain his ear. Obir was already at his side, muttering invectives against Rabirus in his native Mauretanian. Then, "I wish I could say otherwise, dominus, but his deceitful message . . . it will play well with many Aventans."

But Sempronius quirked a smile. "But not with others. Not with such fine men as yourselves, and if you can sway the other collegia—"

"Some, yes," Obir said. "The Subura, the Esquiline, the Aventine where they love you . . . but the Palatine collegia? The Caelian? The men who live a stone's throw from the Forum?" He shook his head. "They're as staunch as Rabirus, in their own ways. Proud to have been plebs for five hundred years, because they've been *Aventan* plebs. They fear we foreign citizen-mongrels as much as any invading barbarian."

Sempronius shook his head. "Short-sighted." The narrowness of such men's views dismayed more than angered him. "They are so desperate to cling to what is and what has been that they have no eyes for what *could be*."

Obir raised a hand to clap Sempronius on the shoulder, but thought better of it at the last second. The gesture was too familiar for the Forum, for one thing, and his *toga candida* would have raised quite a cloud of chalk dust, for another. "They fear, Senator. Perhaps not wrongly." He grinned. "What chance do fools have when clever men like me move into the city to take all their jobs?"

Sempronius snorted, but he knew there was some truth to what Obir said. An influx of immigrants and slaves alike could affect employment levels in the city. But, foreign expeditions that required the mustering of more legions would also employ many men who might otherwise be in need of work. Signing on with the legions meant sixteen years of financial security and a decent pension—so long as you survived it. Plenty of men had proved themselves willing to take that risk ever since the Senate had opened up military registration to the lowest rank of Aventan citizens, the landless Head Count. There was, too, the chance that veterans of Ocella's wars would re-enlist. Men who became used to the battlefield often found themselves at loose ends in peacetime, and the citizenry might well prefer that they be off in the Iberian wilderness than causing tavern brawls and engaging in petty thievery in the city.

"I must frame the entire expedition as something that will expand economic opportunity across *all* classes." He glanced up at the sky. "I must find the right words . . ."

∞∞∞∞∞∞∞∞∞∞∞∞

Sempronius received several invitations to dinner, but decided to forgo pleasure in favor of politics, accepting Crispinius's invitation over those from the Autroniae and Rufilius Albinicus. He returned to his domus to divest himself of both his clients and his *toga candida*. As he scraped away the chalky residue the garment had left on him, he dictated to Corvinus and Djadi a list of promises made during the course of the day. Bribery was a time-honored illegal tradition in Aven, but Sempronius preferred to do favors—expensive favors, often, but the tangibility had considerable benefits. ". . . a brace of trained pigeons for the Temple of Mercury. And finally, Papirius Dolus has a daughter I should send a wedding gift to and a son serving in Numidia who, perhaps, could use some new boots, blessed by an Earth mage."

"These are in addition to your public plans, Dominus?" Corvinus asked, as Djadi etched the final benefice onto his wax tablet. "The feasts and improvements to public buildings?"

"Yes, Corvinus. These are personal gifts, not public endowments."

Corvinus nodded, still scribbling. "And how are we paying for all of this, Dominus?"

Sempronius shot his servant a significant look. "Ocella didn't manage to seize *all* of my assets, you know. I do still have resources. And my sister and her husband have pledged their support as well, since Taius Mella's political career is never likely to cost them much."

"Even so, Dominus . . ." Corvinus regarded his tablet, adding up figures in his head. "I think these initiatives will well exceed those funds."

"Then I will borrow," Sempronius said. "The Athaecan oligarchs are always happy to have an Aventan senator indebted to them. And I have friends abroad I can sound out for the rest."

"Ah." Corvinus's eyes remained carefully on the tablet, though his eyebrows had drifted towards his hairline.

"You disapprove?"

"It's not my place to approve or—"

"Corvinus," Sempronius said. "When I ask you a question—"

"Yes, Dominus. It seems an . . . unsustainable plan."

"I wager against my future, it's true," Sempronius said, setting his strigil down onto a towel. "The men I'll borrow from won't just be making a loan, they'll be investing in my career. I have every confidence of repaying them within five years."

Another eloquent twitch of Corvinus's brow. "You will need to return from Iberia a very rich man."

"I have to get there first." He tapped the edge of Corvinus's tablet. "This will ensure that."

◆ OCTOBER ◆

XII

CENTRAL IBERIA

"I wish you wouldn't drink that."

Ekialde stopped with the cup halfway to his lips, looking over its brim at his wife. She had followed him on campaign, as was right and proper for the wife of an *erregerra*. Even better, she had become pregnant over the summer, and now her rounding belly was testament both to his manhood and to the favor of the gods. It compensated for the anger burning in her eyes as she glared at the clay cup in his hand. The magic-men had been giving him tinctures sauced with the blood of fallen enemies. They said it would give him strength to continue his conquest, and thus far, Ekialde had experienced nothing to cause skepticism. "It is our way, wife," Ekialde said.

Neitin sniffed. "The war-god's way, maybe."

At that, Ekialde had to grin. "I am *erregerra*, my sweet rabbit," he said. "Whose way should I better follow?"

Neitin grabbed his hand and held it to her swollen stomach. "It is not only Bandue who makes a man," she said, fierce determination burning behind her eyes, the same warm brown as the stones of the mountain he so loved. She had courage, to be sure, courage befitting the wife of an *erregerra*, and Ekialde was proud of her even when she spoke thusly. "You owe much to blessed Nabia and Trebarunu as well. Will you risk cursing your son with your uncle's magic?"

Ekialde sighed. "It is no curse, wife. It is what the gods intend for me." His gaze turned faraway, and Neitin could see the shadow of Bandue clouding his eyes. "They have given me a grand purpose—a sublime one. A new Lusetania—a *free* Lusetania!"

Neitin was unimpressed by his rhetoric. "Lusetania is free," she said with a snort. "It has been for centuries."

"The Tyrians—"

"The Tyrians in Olissippo give us no trouble! They sail their ships and they buy our cloth and our olives, and we buy their tin and their fish. What is so wrong with that?"

"It encourages others to think they can likewise encroach," Ekialde said. "And the others are less benign. The coastal peoples are already nearly lost to the proper Iberian ways."

"Because they trim their beards and some of them speak a little Athaecan?"

"Because they turn away from their gods and the ways of their ancestors," Ekialde said. "You remember that messenger that came from the Edetani in the spring, who wanted our tribes to establish trade with Gades? Did you see the son he brought with him? He wore one of those charms the Aventans put on their whelps for protection, because the Aventan gods are so cruel, they will not look after the innocent without some bribe."

Neitin's hand rubbed her stomach. "Nabia will know her own, no matter what they wear."

"But *is* he her own? If he worships her in a clay-brick temple, shut away from her world? If he calls her by the name of Juno?" Ekialde fairly spat the unfamiliar name, its low, mournful vowels so foreign to his tongue.

Neitin stared a long moment, then nodded. "Yes. I think she will. The gods are less petty than we."

"And you, wife, may be too trusting. If we abandon our culture in favor of these eastern peoples'—if we sell our traditions to have access to their trinkets—then how will our gods even know to find us?"

"Even if you are right, you think baiting the Aventans will keep them away?" Neitin shook her head. "You think it won't just bring their iron-armored legions down on our heads?"

"We must fight them to show we can defeat them. Then we will have not just a free Lusetania, but a free *Iberia*."

Scowling, Neitin folded her arms beneath her breasts. "And how free do the Bastetani feel right now, with your swords at their throats? The Arevaci?"

"The Bastetani and the Arevaci are traitors to our people," Ekialde said, struggling to stay patient. It did not help Ekialde's temper to know that his wife was not alone in her thoughts. Some of his own people had questioned the decision to make war on other Iberian tribes, not only on the Tyrians and Aventans. "They were given a choice—"

"Your blade or the Aventans'?" Neitin snorted. "Some freedom you've offered them. Or does Bandue feel that the dead are freest of all souls? If so, then to be sure, you've done a great many men a good service." Her swift tongue usually impressed Ekialde, and allowances did have to be made for her condition. Perhaps it was that, the tug of the child inside her, which brought her anger shifting without warning to tears. "This will only come to sorrow, Ekialde," she said. "I feel it in the depths of my heart. You have turned away from your family and the way of . . . of rightness and health. And for what? To drink the blood of men you need never have killed?"

He took her face between his hands and kissed her brow. "There is nothing in this world dearer to me than you. What sorrow do you find in being the wife of an *erregerra*?"

"I am the daughter of a chieftain," she countered, "and so I know full well there are other ways to rule than by the sword." She waved a hand vaguely in the direction of the east. "Take your people home! We have enough spoil to satisfy your son's son yet unborn. If you must heed this blood magic, return to the tree that drank of your life and nurture it, so that it cannot betray you. Live there in prosperity, guard your people, tend the pastures." She nodded emphatically. "*That* is the action of a true man, a good leader."

"And what happens when the Aventans come there, hm?" Ekialde said, his cheeks growing hot, though it was not in anger towards his wife, but rather the heat that he knew was the righteous furor of Bandue filling him. "What will our son's son do then? Do not think that because the Tyrians have let us live as we please that the Aventans will do the same. They are not merely traders, as the Tyrians are. They seek to control, to dominate. And if you do not believe me, you can ask the Edetani about that."

"I could ask the Bastetani," Neitin retorted, "if I could find any left."

Whatever answer Ekialde might have made to that was forestalled. The flap of their tent swung open, and in came Bailar, Ekialde's magically inclined uncle. Bailar and Neitin stared at each other for a moment, mutual disdain barely concealed, until, with a derisive sniff, Neitin turned and stalked to the other end of the tent. She lay down on her cot and pointedly snuffed the nearest lamp. "Perhaps it would be best if we spoke outside, uncle," Ekialde said, in deference to her. *Erregerra* though he was, he was yet young enough to feel awkward when it came to family quarrels.

"No matter," Bailar said. "I was going to bring you out anyway." There was a cold gleam in his eyes. "Your scouts have returned. There's a party of merchants picking their way through the forest to the south."

Ekialde wasted no time reaching for his greaves and sword belt. "Let us welcome them, then."

◇◇◇◇◇◇◇◇◇◇◇◇◇◇

It never took long for the ravens to find them.

After each skirmish or raid, they descended, a black flock tracking their movements along the Tagus River and throughout the high plateaus. They were clever birds, and they had learned how to assure themselves of good meals on a regular basis.

Soon, they would feast on Tyrian traders and the Iberian mercenaries hired to guide and protect them. Ekialde's men had made swift work of the little band, and the birds descended while the Lusetani were still looting the bodies. One of the mercenaries was burbling feebly through the blood half-choking him; Ekialde put a swift end to his suffering.

However, the people of the mountain towns were becoming cleverer. For weeks now, Ekialde and his men had reached villages only to find them already deserted, their people and goods packed up and fled. Where to, he was not certain. Perhaps they were simply gathering for numbers, but it was possible they had raced south and west, pleading to the walled towns of the Tyrians and Aventans for shelter. Ekialde did not know his foes well enough yet to guess whether they would receive refugees or turn them away at the gates, but either way, he did not like it. It meant that his net was not tight enough, that his disparate forces were not strongly enough yoked together to pin their opponents down.

It prickled at the same issue his wife had raised. *'If I am to make the stand the gods intend for me,'* he thought, *'I must have all the peoples of Iberia with me. And if they are not with me . . .'* He had been pressing hard at the Oretani, offering them freedom and riches if they joined him, but dealing swift vengeance upon those who would not. They had not yet broken faith with Aven, but Ekialde heard that their chieftains were coming together for meetings. In that, he saw the start of their capitulation.

The skirmishes with traders were growing harder; anyone who wandered in the Iberian forests these days was careful to go armed. Merchants had begun hiring mercenaries for protection; this train had only brought a quartet of swordsmen along with them, but it had been enough to give Ekialde's band a solid fight.

They relished it. Some had grown restless with the easy pickings, finding little sport in running down sapling boys and well-fatted merchants. Angeru had taken a wound to the arm, his blood splashing out hot and fast onto the soil, but he would live, and he had well-paid the man who gave it to him. Another warrior had caught a shield under his chin, rattling his brains and breaking several of his teeth, but he had laughed it off and kept on fighting.

They were men to be proud of, and Ekialde was grateful and humbled to lead them.

As his men set up camp for the night, Ekialde wandered a little ways away, down the path the merchants had been traversing. Axe holstered at his shoulder, two knives sheathed at his belt, he hoisted himself into a tree, climbing nearer to the stars. He liked to be near them, breathing in sweet air, when it came time to think things over. An *erregerra* could not only maim and slaughter, after all. He had to have a plan.

He wanted to move eastward, toward Toletum and Corduba, and had given thought to taking both cities. *'What a victory that would be.'* But Toletum and Corduba had proper walls, not mere earthworks like the villages Ekialde had overrun, and he had a realistic expectation of his warriors' inabilities to besiege a defended city. Sooner or later, the Aventans would emerge from Gades in force. He had not yet encountered a legion, but the thought beat eagerly in his blood. *'My heart yearns to engage with these Aventans,'* he thought, *'but my mind tells me the time is not yet ripe. So what to do?'*

The hills spread out before him, and Ekialde considered the directions in which the world rolled. His strength was to the east. The Lusetani proclaimed him their leader with one voice, and the *mendi* were entirely his. *'If they believe I can really threaten Gades . . . they will come.'* And then Ekialde, *erregerra* of Lusetania, would prove his worth.

Mulling it over, Ekialde waited patiently in the tree. Hours he waited, watching the path, watching the ravens, until at long last came the patter of footsteps, slapping against the packed earth.

A lone figure emerged from the gap in the trees, breathing hard: a figure in an Aventan-style tunic, Tyrian patterns woven into its border. He had run into the woods and hidden at the beginning of the fight, had lain in a ravine for hours, waiting until he felt sure the Lusetanians had made camp and would not notice his flight. He glanced around as he ran, counting the bodies, but he did not look up into the branches waving softly above his head. He did not look to the veiling clouds in the sunset-streaked sky, and so he did not see Ekialde, caressing the smooth wooden handle of his axe, cocking the blade back over his shoulder, muscles tensed and ready to spring.

Ekialde had fresh blood to mix in his wine that night, a drop from each enemy felled by his own hand, and though he could not taste the iron tang of it, he felt their strength swelling in him, made his own. Each drop brought him closer to conquest.

◇◇◇◇◇◇◇◇◇◇◇◇◇◇◇

NEDHENA, PROVINCE OF MARITIMA

The slog southward had taken weeks, moving through marshy ground and dismal, sleeting rains. Gaius Vitellius was grateful for the vexillation's small size, for it meant fewer pack animals and carts to get stuck in the mud. Rather than risk crossing the Pyreneian Mountains when the weather might turn even worse, Vitellius had elected for a water crossing—but that provided its own challenges. Lining up enough large boats to transport two cohorts was difficult enough, even without the rumors coming out of Iberia and the autumn winds whipping up off the coast.

Initially, Vitellius had thought it would be no hardship. A treat, really, to spend time in Nedhena, a town famous for how it welcomed soldiers. A frequent stopping point for the Aventan legions, it was now a sizable village belonging to Vulcan and Venus. On the one hand, it boasted a coterie of Fire-forgers, armorers, and other metalworkers; on the other, it also housed more prostitutes, in Vitellius's estimation, than any city west of Truscum.

The girls in Nedhena were prettier and cleaner by far than those on the Vendelician border, and a far sight more willing to entertain soldiers with coinage to spare. But too many of Vitellius's men were spending too much of their wages on sport, and he intended to have a word with the centurions about holding back some pay and sending it directly back to Aven. At least most of the men seemed to have the sense to douse themselves with vinegar after a visit to the *lupanar,* or else to procure fish bladders to block against infection, but Vitellius worried that, if their stay in Nedhena was of long duration, he might, nonetheless, be facing decimation by disease.

Then there was the brawling. Not amongst themselves, for the most part—except for one quarrel over a particularly pretty girl, which left two men with broken noses. But these men were fighters who had already gone too long without an outlet for aggression, and in Nedhena, the opportunities for trouble abounded. Adding drink and gambling into the equation, Vitellius's centurions experienced difficulties maintaining order. Vitellius, to his dismay, had been forced to dole out punishments. So far, he had been making do with garnishing wages and assigning extra shifts of unpleasant duties, but he was worried that if matters got much worse, he would have to have some offender or other physically castigated. Instilling discipline was of utmost importance in the Aventan legions, and Vitellius loathed the thought of being known as a commander who had lost control.

Even the weather wouldn't cooperate. Vitellius had always heard that Nedhena enjoyed a fair climate year-round, but every night had been surprisingly cold, and every day miserably damp. One early October night found Vitellius and Titus Mennenius taking refuge in a local tavern, sitting close to a fire and sharing a jug of hot spiced wine. They were discussing whether triremes or quinqueremes would be better for their eventual trip to Tarraco when the door to the tavern swung open to admit a half-soaked band of men. As they stripped off sodden cloaks, Vitellius could see that half of them were in Tyrian-style wrapped robes and fully bearded, while the others boasted tunics, trousers, and shorter-clipped beards of Iberian style. It was enough to pique Vitellius's interest, and he held up a hand to pause Mennenius mid-sentence. "We'll continue east in the morning, if the rain lets up." Vitellius overheard. They were speaking Athaecan, still a dominant language on the western shores of the Middle Sea. "Damned weather, feels like we can't get more than a few miles in a day. I think we've hit every town with so much as a pier to dock for three hundred leagues."

Vitellius raised a hand to hail the group. "There's room by the fire," he called in Athaecan. "Come, gentlemen, warm yourselves."

The newcomers looked at each other questioningly, then their leader nodded, striding over to them. One of the centurions gave up his bench to squeeze in beside the other; the Tyrians took it over, and the Iberians sat on the floor. "I thank you, soldier," the leader said, nodding at Vitellius's identifying cloak. "I am called Marthanes. This is Soterich and Gregoras." He introduced his fellow Tyrians, but not the Iberians. "And you?"

"I am Tribune Vitellius, and this is Tribune Mennenius. Do you speak Truscan, friends?" Vitellius asked.

"We do," Marthanes said, switching to that language. "At least, we do and that one." He nodded at the youngest of the Iberians. "What is your business in these parts? I had not thought there were any legions stationed in Nedhena at present."

"No legion," Titus said, "only a few cohorts, headed south soon."

Marthanes exchanged significant looks with his comrades. The young Iberian was talking quietly, apparently translating for his friends. "I can't blame you for waiting for clear weather," he said, "not with how long it's taken us to come this far. All the same . . . the sooner you do get there, the better."

"Marthanes," Vitellius said, "we've been stationed far away, in Albina, and we've heard only rumors about what's happening in Iberia."

"All of that third-hand," Mennenius added, "and much the worse for wear for traveling those miles."

"Would you be willing to tell us the truth of the situation there?" Vitellius asked.

"Nothing good," Marthanes said. "We trade with the tribesmen in the central plains and plateaus, that whole region. We trade on the coast, but many of our goods come from further inland. Oil and marble. Lately, though . . ." He flicked a wrist, his nostrils flaring. "Shipments are unreliable. Many have been stolen."

"The rebels have spread so far east?" Titus asked, alarmed.

Marthanes flapped a hand. "No, no, not in the least. But they've disrupted all the routes through the mountains. No goods are making their way out. So, I'm returning to my father in Massilia, to tell him what's going on. Better we refocus our efforts elsewhere, until things quiet down."

There was a minor commotion from the Iberians sitting on the floor, all three of them talking at once in their native tongue, then one stood up swiftly and spoke in Athaecan. "Meaning no offense to the honored Marthanes—" and he nodded, with no trace of irony in his voice, "—but we can speak more directly to what is happening inland."

"It's true," Marthanes said with a shrug. "We only know how it has affected our end of matters."

"We have traded with the Tyrians for very long. We are a good people," he said, "a noble people, old in our territory. We have held it for many centuries. We do not fight the Tyrians when they come, and we do not wish to fight the Aventans. But this Ekialde, this so-called war-king, he stirs up trouble. He says, fight with him or die in front of him." Behind him, one of the other Iberians spat, and the speaker's expression indicated his agreement with that sentiment. "Some of our people can run and hide, but we? We are too tied to our land. We cannot pick up our olive trees and move them from one village to another. My honesty, sir? We are frightened. A year or two of bad trade, we could endure. But we hear that this Ekialde is setting fire to fields and orchards further west. If he should do so to us . . . we would be ruined. Forever."

Vitellius could see the passion for his land in the young man's eyes, and he felt his chest tighten, feeling, for the first time, the vital importance of Aven's keeping faith with its allied tribes. He was about to ask for more information, specifics on where his people lived and where they thought this Ekialde was moving, but one of his junior centurions came rushing into the tavern then, breathless and red-cheeked. He saluted Vitellius, then stammered, "A-Another fight, sir. With respect, sir, I think you're needed."

Vitellius stood and extended a hand to Marthanes. "I thank you for your wisdom, trader." Then he bent to shake hands with the Iberians. "And yours, friends. Would you be willing to tell more of your stories to Tribune Mennenius?" They nodded their assent, allowing Vitellius to dash out and deal with his newest headache.

XIII

The morning of the Cantrinalia, held on the day before the Nones of October, dawned fair, bright, and cool. All freeborn citizens divinely gifted with the talents of magic were required to show their duties at this time, or risk losing the gods' favor; and so Merula woke Latona at dawn to prepare her. There was a ritual to dressing on the morning of a religious ceremony. Latona had to bathe in a specific way, with water drawn from a fresh spring, not piped in through an aqueduct.

Merula dressed Latona in the colors attributed to her primary Element. For Latona, in whom Spirit reigned stronger than Fire, this meant Juno's pink. Latona rather wished she had another option. Soft pinks flattered her sisters, who were rosier-hued than she. Latona's skin was a touch darker, with golden undertones, and they failed to make her look as fresh and blooming as Aula and Alhena. *'Someday,'* she vowed, while Merula fussed over the folds of her dusky rose palla, *'I'm going to wear Jupiter's purple to this thing, custom be damned.'* She wished she could wear the shocking fuschia she and Aula had bought in Sextilis, but it was ornamented with golden beads and, for the ritual, she could have no metal at all about her. Her pins, brooches, and hair ornaments had to be bone or wood. Fortunately for Latona's vanity, nothing prevented the wearing of pearls, and so she had several strands draped about her neck and another wound through her curls. Her hairpins and the brooches at her shoulders were finest ivory from Numidia, and she was to forego the cosmetics she usually applied to her lips and eyes. The voluminous robes were belted with a special cord, knotted nine times around her waist, an unmistakable mark of religious purpose to any who saw her, to go along with the mage's stripes on her tunic.

Herennius did not trouble to see her off. While Latona was at the ceremony, Herennius would receive his clients; by the time she returned, he would likely be down in the Forum, conducting business. So much the better. She had quite enough on her mind this morning without adding her husband to the equation.

On her way to the ritual, Latona stopped by her father's household to retrieve Alhena. A yawning Aula greeted her in the atrium, bundled up in a cozy crimson robe, her hair loose about her shoulders. "She'll be out in a minute. I gather," Aula said, a mirthless smile on her lips, "it took Mus rather a while to get her going this morning."

"At least she's coming out," Latona said, folding her arms beneath the wrapping warmth of her palla. "I was worried—"

"As was I. But it seems her piety won out over her gloom."

"I suppose that's something." Latona hoped that this ceremony would prove a comfort to her—all women, all mages, all joining together in a display of devotion.

When Mus finally managed to produce her reluctant mistress, whispering encouragement in Alhena's ear, it did little to alleviate Latona's concerns. For Alhena, the day's color was a silvery gray. No actual cloth-of-silver or silver thread could be used, of course, but the fabric itself was a wool so soft and finely woven that it seemed to shine. Her bright hair was covered by a thin, moon-gray palla. Her eyes, though, were red-rimmed, and her skin was pasty. Nonetheless, Latona embraced her, adjusted one of her curls, and told her she looked beautiful. Alhena mustered the ghost of a smile before trundling herself into the litter. In deference both to Alhena's sensibilities and to the chill in the air, Latona kept the curtains drawn, protecting them from gawking eyes and crisp winds alike. She did not venture much conversation on the journey, beyond idle comments on the weather and the length of the ride. It was too early to be witty, in any case.

The rites were always held at the home of a prominent mage of the city. The pontifical association determined who would have the honor, and this year, the women's lot had fallen to Marcia Tullia. Despite their ancient blood and wealth, the Galeriae lived modestly on the eastern slope of the Palatine, an eminently respectable address, though not so fashionable as the Vitellian neighborhood, higher up on the south-western side. They had been known as staunch moderates for generations, voices of reason since the time of the kings, never a family given to producing wastrels or spendthrifts. If they did not seem to own the inimitable talent for attracting wealth that some families did, nor did they have the propensity for losing it.

For all its modesty, however, the house was large and quite well-kept. The outer walls were freshly painted with a broad red stripe to disguise the mud from the street, and a coterie of neatly-dressed slaves waited to assist the arriving guests. Latona and Alhena had to wait a few moments before their own attendants could settle the litter and help them out, as several well-to-do ladies had arrived ahead of them. Merula and Mus were dismissed at the door. Religious rites of this kind were one of the few instances in their lives when patrician women went unattended. It was a shame, Latona thought, that someone as talented as Helva was barred from the ceremonies. Freedwomen could not attend, though their free-born children could—just one way the conservatives had found to mediate the threat they perceived in talented newcomers to the city.

'*Stifle, not mediate,*' Latona thought, swallowing annoyance. Still, it was useful too, offering the same kind of protective obscurity that Helva had in working for the Vitelliae. '*But if she were respected as she should be, she would not need to hide her talent.*' How many others were there like her, Latona wondered, freedwomen and immigrants whose brilliance went unobserved, unappreciated?

The Cantrinalia was, however, a religious rite that welcomed free-born plebeians alongside patricians. Mixing with the Vitelliae daughters, Marcia, Vibia Sempronia, the Terentiae sisters, and all the rest of the noble ladies were a host of plebs from the Subura, the less prestigious hills, and the dockside districts; some of them priestesses, like Ama Rubellia, others working women like Davina of the bath-houses.

Marcia looked perfectly correct, adhering to the letter of every prohibition. Her slaves milled about, offering all the women sips of water out of wooden bowls—no metal, and no drink but pure spring water. Her peristyle garden had been cleared of furniture for the occasion, to make room for the scores of women who would crowd in this morning. The altar stood beneath the portico at the far end, empty but for a plain white runner cloth.

The autumn air was thickened by the ambrosial incense smoking in a half dozen alcoves. "You'll be all right?" Latona asked, pressing Alhena's hand. Alhena's answering nod was tight, but Latona had to leave her sister's side and join the eight other officiants, each with a subservient acolyte, at the right side of the altar. They were women that Marcia had deemed best to represent their elements—usually those with the most raw power, though sometimes those with a unique talent or who had demonstrated notable piety might serve. Latona had been relieved when Marcia chose her. By affirming Latona as worthy to represent Juno, Marcia made a public statement—and a political one—of her faith that Latona had not been tainted by Ocella's touch.

The rest of the women gathered in the garden, shoulder to shoulder, to bear witness. Their presence was no less crucial than that of the officiants. The gods had to know that the devotions were communal, the work of the whole city, supported by all the blessed mages in Aven.

As hostess, Marcia Tullia began the ritual with an invocation. "Blessed Fortuna, Supreme Jupiter Cantatius and Juno Cantatia and all the gods of Aven, watch over us this day and stand by our sides as we enact this sacred ritual. Look here, you gods; look here, you who have blessed us with these abilities; look here, you who have entrusted us with these responsibilities. We stand in the sight of all gods to offer renewals of our ancient compact with you. Please accept our offerings and our vows, truly and freely given, and witness our devotions in your names."

The procession of the elements began with Light. The *de facto* officiant for this element was the Vestal Virgin Quinta Terentia. Terentia had some six or seven years left in her term before retirement, though she had been serving the goddess of the hearth longer than Latona had been alive. Power and temperament alike made her a natural fit for the service of Vesta—patient, honest to a fault, and as thoroughly dependable as the rising sun.

She approached the altar, bearing a polished piece of rock crystal—the physical representation of her element. Terentia's acolyte placed a clay lamp, painted yellow, on the altar, and Terentia set her precious burden down in front of it, to catch the light and beam it out in a dazzling array.

Hands outstretched, palms up, Terentia focused her eyes on the crystal and intoned, "I charge you, Apollo, God of Light and the Sun, truth-bearer, music-maker, to witness our devotions; I charge you, Vesta, Lady of Light and the Hearth, truth-revealer, hearth-guard, to witness our devotions. I dedicate myself to you, on behalf of myself and as representative for all those bearing your gifts. Look with favor upon us; protect us from harm; allow us to continue in your glory."

Next was Marcia herself, representing Air. With tremendous dignity, she approached the altar bearing the symbol of her element: a glistening white feather. Marcia's acolyte bore a lamp painted a pale blue. Both symbols joined the yellow lamp and the crystal on the altar, and Marcia said, "I charge you, Mercury, Lord of Messages and Travel, quick-witted, most clever, to witness our devotions; I charge you, Minerva, Lady of Wisdom and Strategy, aegis-bearer, inspiration-giver, to witness our devotions . . ."

Following was Rubellia, High Priestess of Venus, calling on her patroness deity and on the goddess's husband, Vulcan, as she lay a small staff of polished wood onto the altar. Rubellia was in her mid-thirties and a vision of loveliness, a true avatar of Venus: small of height, round-breasted and full-hipped, with dusky skin and a tumble of rich, dark curls. Her smiles were full of promise, and her every gesture spoke of sensual delight. Latona couldn't help but give a rather irreverent grin as she watched Rubellia sashay her way to the altar. "I charge you, Vulcan, Lord of Smiths and Flames, mountain-burner, metal-shaper, to witness our devotions; I charge you, Venus, Lady of Love and Beauty, heart-warmer, passion-provoker, to witness . . ."

Rubellia stepped away from the altar a moment later, cheeks aglow, even more beautiful for her joy in the ritual, and then it was Latona's turn. She had served her role in this ritual before, and knew that whatever her private fears, she had to approach the gods without trepidation. She took a deep breath before moving forward, feeling only the softly building energy of the ritual, which created a frisson all its own.

Her acolyte was a pink-cheeked girl of ten or eleven, a plebeian child far from mastering the element. Though some others in the gathering had Spirit as a secondary element, no one else had strong enough dominion in it to serve. Latona tried not to frown as she struggled to recall the child's name. *'Fausta.'* That was it. A noble name on a quite common child, suggesting slave stock somewhere in her background, an ancestor freed and bestowed with his former master's name. *'I should offer to tutor her,'* Latona thought. Outside of the temples, it was rare, though not unheard of, for a patrician mage to take a plebeian child under her wing. *'My own training may not have been all I would have wished, but . . . Well, no other woman in the city has had better.'* Spirit, like Shadow and Fracture, was a gift more rarely bestowed than the other elements; there were but half a dozen women in the city so blessed. None had Latona's raw power, and if she had only benefited from six years of instruction with Gaia Claudia, the most gifted High Priestess of Juno in three generations, that was still six years more than anyone else. *'I should offer. To try, at least, little though Aemilia Fullia will like that.'* The High Priestess of Juno, who had no magical gifts herself, had a long history of contention with Latona and would no doubt take a dim view of Latona's taking on an apprentice.

Fausta bore a lamp painted the same rosy pink as her gown, and Latona held the symbol of Spirit: a fine-wrought golden crown. The irony had never escaped Latona—Aventan society abhorred kings, disdained the eastern potentates who wore the diadem, yet revered the King and Queen of the gods and were more than happy to wield magical power with so strong a correlation to monarchical authority. Perhaps in deference to Aventan republican sensibilities, the crown was wrought more in image of a military *corona* than an imperial diadem. That, at least, was fitting. How many victors of war, whether from legends and stories or from Aven's history, had been said to be blessed by Spirit? Even if they could not work magic on the field of battle, their very personalities translated well to command.

Latona spoke in a strong, clear voice, holding the crown up towards the opening in the roof. "I charge you, Jupiter, King of Heaven and Lord of the Sky, lightning-bearer, nation-builder, to witness our devotions; I charge you, Juno, Queen of Heaven and Protectress of Women, grace-bestower, womb-blesser, to witness our devotions. I dedicate myself to you, on behalf of myself and as representative for all those bearing your gifts. Look with favor upon us; protect us from harm; allow us to continue in your glory."

As she lay the crown upon the altar, she felt as though her heart were swelling within her chest, top-full of magic and heightened emotions. The crown seemed to glow all the brighter, set in line with its fellows of other elements, paired with the rosy lamp, and invested with the full strength of her prayers.

◇◇◇◇◇◇◇◇◇◇◇◇◇

From across the room, Vibia Sempronia watched as Latona moved to the side and Davina the bathhouse-mistress, representative of Water, took her place. Vibia knew she ought to have been paying more devoted attention to the ritual itself, but she always had trouble at the Cantrinalia. It was, in essence, a coming-together and, as such, went against the grain of Fracture magic. She strove to remind herself of what she had been taught: that Fracture was not the domain of fickle Fortuna alone, but of Janus as well, he who looked forward and back, that it was not only the rend a knife could make, but the edge of the blade itself—the hazard of chance, the point on which the world could tip.

It was difficult to master, though, when the strain of magic that came most easily to her was the ability to see the places where others crackled and split. She struggled to focus, as in a brisk, clear voice, Davina said her words to Neptune and Lympha, and then a graying priestess croaked her invocation to Ceres and Diana on behalf of Earth. The stronger the force of magic within the room grew, the more that Vibia had to fight the urge to let loose her instinctive inclinations. One woman's insecurities, another's envy, another's distraction—all of them called to her, little bells softly ringing in the back of her heart. Ignoring them in the spirit of the ceremony took a great deal of concentration, and she knew that she would suffer for it with a headache later in the day. *'Small wonder,'* she thought with wry detachment, *'that Fracture mages are known for coming unhinged.'*

Every element had its dangerous aspects. Even Light could blind, after all. Time mages were at risk of madness, Shadow mages could fall into darkness—a risk Vibia watched for in her brother—*'And Fracture mages tend to crack.'*

A young woman from an up-and-coming family gave devotions for Time's mages, then came a patrician acolyte of Nox, representing Shadow. The progression ended with Fracture. As Sexta Rufilia approached the altar, Vibia's limbs tensed, but not now with the effort to keep herself under control. This was jealousy, pure and simple, and if Vibia was not proud of it, she could at least admit it to herself. It rankled that she, a daughter of one of Aven's oldest houses, had to stand by and watch another perform these sacred rites.

Adding to the unintentional insult was that Sexta Rufilia, despite her aristocratic name, was no patrician of pure Aventan descent. Her full name was Sexta Rufilia Mulugonis, and she was the free-born daughter of a former Numidian slave. Like Davina, Sexta's power was too great to be overlooked on account of her low birth. Sexta had never performed her duties with anything less than total devotion and capability, but perversely, her competence irritated Vibia all the more. *'The gods bestow their gifts where they will, and there's no gainsaying it . . . I just wish they had seen fit to provide me with strength befitting my rank.'*

Vibia considered the altar, at the sequence of symbols: the crystal and feather, rod and crown, the cup bearing Water, the dirt-sprinkled dish for Earth, Proserpina's pomegranate seeds to represent the passage of Time, a black veil to stand for Shadow, and finally, a bronze razor for Fracture. For a moment, her heart beat faster. The power in the room was strong enough now that even she could sense it, the compulsion forged when the elements stood together, united in their appeal to the gods.

At the altar, Marcia Tullia was presiding again, beginning a rhythmic chant, an incantation which the others took up until the garden resonated with humming vibrations. At a signal from Marcia, all the women there assembled held out their hands, waist-high, palms up, and joined in the final stage of the supplication. The energy hummed like music from a cithara, the rise and fall of the vibrations drawing nearer together, nearly frenetic in its tension, drawn out until it seemed, surely, the threads must snap.

Vibia felt a sharp shock in the midst of this joining, and her eyes flew wide, searching for the source. Sexta had noticed it, too, from the way she was glancing around, but no one else seemed disrupted in the slightest. *'Except . . . Rubellia?'* But Vibia could feel no indication that the disturbance had come from her. *'How would she—?'* Vibia noticed Rubellia looking sideways at Vitellia Latona, and when she followed the gaze, she saw why: Latona's face had gone scarlet and her eyes were unfocused.

'Fracture mages may crack,' Vibia thought, frowning, *'but Spirit and Fire can be an unpredictable mix.'* And that which was unpredictable, Vibia would always consider dangerous. *'What has her so riled?'*

XIV

Latona gritted her teeth, focusing all her energy on maintaining her part in the ritual. This was usually her favorite portion of the ceremony, but she found herself unable to moderate the influx into her own mind and heart. Her tongue felt the sharpness of cinnamon, and a faint golden sheen dropped over her vision. It was not Fire, but Spirit betraying her this time. It twisted in her gut and throbbed in her head, and each heartbeat seemed to spiral her deeper into the emotional vibrations of everyone around her—dozens of mages, all projecting currents of their own, all with their own hopes and intentions and concerns. Latona felt it all.

And then—a blasting release, a wave of enchanting energy, surging outwards from the altar, rushing over the ritual participants like a flood. Some of the women sighed with relief, others swayed slightly. Latona staggered, then felt a hand at her elbow: Rubellia, keeping her upright. "Breathe."

"My sister—" Latona said, casting across the room for Alhena.

"She's fine. She's with Tilla." Around them, the other mages were starting to mill about and chatter. Some would depart immediately, others would join Marcia Tullia for a meal, others would walk to the Temple of Juno Cantatia for private rituals on this sacred day. Latona felt Rubellia steering her aside and heard Rubellia say to her acolyte, "Berenike, would you go ask Terentilla if she would see Vitellia Alhena home? Tell her I need a word with the Lady Latona. Thank you, dear."

'Good,' Latona thought, 'there's someone who can look after her.' Quintilla Terentilla, most often just called Tilla, was an Earth mage cast in a different mold from her Vestal older sister. Her clothes never seemed to hang on her correctly, always slipping off a shoulder or twisting asymmetrical, and her family indulged her in many eccentricities. But she had a good heart and was not much older than Alhena. Perhaps her presence would be not just a momentary comfort, but the start of a friendship that could draw Alhena out of her shell.

Rubellia pulled Latona behind one of the portico columns, away from prying eyes. The flux of emotions did not ebb. Latona could find no outlet to push them from her own heart and back into their owners'. They pulsed overtop of each other, one invasive influence rising to the forefront only to fall back in favor of another. Latona was worried for a sick mother, dizzy with the flush of new love, fretting over her children, anxious over the autumn rains, excited to purchase a new farm, frightened for a brother trading in Gades, each thing in rapid succession, flooding her with sudden intensity and then receding in a painful gasp.

"Count your heartbeats." Rubellia seized her hands, her fingers rubbing slow circles on Latona's palms. "You know what to do. This is in you. Listen to the air passing through your nose and mouth, feel it fill your lungs." Latona tried to follow her instructions, though it was difficult even to hear her over the torrent of magical energy inundating her. Tears swam to her eyes as the press of sensations threatened to overwhelm her.

But then there was Rubellia, determinedly calm. Latona desperately tried to narrow her focus on Rubellia's composure, Rubellia's tranquility. Slowly, she was able to push out the other influences, drawing in the soothing energy from her friend. Latona did not know how long she stood there, siphoning Rubellia's serenity into herself until it quieted the rest of the emotional cacophony. Eventually, she could breathe easily again.

"There," Rubellia said, "that's better, isn't it?"

Latona nodded. "Thank you, Rubellia. And my apologies. I— I seem to have opened myself a bit too wide."

Rubellia tilted her head. "A surge of uncontrolled empathy, I think?"

Latona dropped her eyes to her hands, still clutched in Rubellia's, and gave as small a nod as she could manage. The shame she felt now was all her own, but no less painful for that, and mixed with fear. "Has it happened before?"

Her thumbs moved gently over Latona's knuckles, and that gesture, so small and familiar, gave Latona the courage to explain. "Not the empathy. Fires, though . . . It's been happening since . . . well, since the Dictator's death, I suppose." And perhaps that was the answer: Without the need to suppress her magic, it now flowed too freely. *'Control, control . . . You see what happens when you lose control?'* She glanced up again, into Rubellia's warm brown eyes. "Please don't tell anyone."

"Of course not, my dear."

Rubellia looked about to ask another question, but Latona could not bear any more well-meant examination. She pulled back from Rubellia.

"Excuse me. I'm so grateful for your assistance, but I really must . . . I should get home, to check on my sister."

Rubellia did not release her hand immediately but gave it a press. "Very well, Latona. Just know . . . I am here if you need me."

Latona nodded tightly, then bundled her mantle about herself and hurried away.

∞∞∞∞∞∞∞∞∞∞∞∞

Merula frowned as her mistress exited the Galerian domus. Without a farewell, she left the girls she had been chatting with. "Domina?" Latona's face was streaked with a red flush, and she moved without her usual open grace, but instead closed-off, holding her arms close to her body as though afraid she might break. "Domina, are you unwell?"

"I— No, Merula, I'm afraid I'm not. It happened again."

"Not . . . not the flames, Domina?" Merula cast her eyes back at the Galerian house, reassuringly intact.

"No, it was . . . different." Latona rubbed irritably at her forehead. *'Claudia taught you better than this . . .'* she chastised herself. But then, Claudia had been teaching a child, and one who had never known want or fear or violation. *'And she didn't know what tribulations the grown woman would have to face.'*

Merula fussed at Latona's mantle, re-draping its folds. "What are we needing to do?" She saw little point in offering condolences or getting flustered. If Domina Latona had a problem, they would simply have to find a solution.

"I ought to go to my father's house to check on Alhena, but, I think I should like to go to the Temple of Juno Cantatia first. Perhaps there will be . . . some sort of an answer there."

Merula nodded in agreement. Going to the temple would do her mistress more good than seeing to the wayward Vitellian sister. "Domina Alhena is seeming fine when she left. The Terentiae had her well in hand." Merula snorted softly as they started down the street. "Indeed, she is almost seeming to enjoy conversation with the Vestal. No smiles there, still, but perhaps she is looking slightly less like drowned nymph."

"Good. That's good . . ."

Unsettled by her mistress's faraway tone and brittle manner, Merula kept up a steady, distracting chatter as their walk took them through the shallow valley angling towards the Esquiline Hill.

◇◇◇◇◇◇◇◇◇◇◇◇◇◇◇

The Temple of Juno Cantatia, devoted to the goddess in her aspect as governess of mages, was far smaller than the Temple to Juno Maxima on top of the Capitoline Hill, but was Latona's choice for her devotions. *This* temple, with its small, cerulean-painted portico and its bright mosaic floors, had never been home, and so was unhaunted by Latona's past.

Latona knelt before the terracotta statue of the goddess and put forward a honey-soaked cake as an offering. Juno was beloved by the women of Aven, because she understood them. She was there at the marriage altar and the childbed; she knew the pangs of birth and the sweetness of giving milk. She ached with wives and mothers when their men and boys went to war; she wept with wistful pride when their daughters became women in their turn. She was everywhere in a woman's life, sharing all sorrows and all joys, and Latona thought it a great comfort to know that someone in the heavens paid attention to even the smallest and most usual concerns of mortal life.

'But she is, also, the Queen of Heaven,' Latona thought, remembering the words she invoked during the ritual. *'She is a ruler, in her own right. She pursues her interests and defends herself aggressively. And—'* Latona's lips quirked up at one corner. *'I wonder who it is that sees to the running of things on Olympus when Jove neglects his duties to dally with shepherdesses.'*

The goddess's carven face was kinder than many people would assume—beautiful, too, sweet and round and wide-eyed, but not without majesty for all of its feminine loveliness. *'What do you want, Lady? I would do your will, if I knew what it was. Help me to understand, help me to stop this . . . this unbridling of the gifts you've granted me. Or at least show me how to make use of it . . .'*

After leaving Juno Cantatia, she only had to turn a corner, and the grand Juno Maxima was visible, looming over the Forum and Subura next to the Capitoline temples of Jupiter and Minerva. Nearly twelve years on, Latona could still hardly look at it without flinching internally. It had taken her a long while to learn to keep that flinch off of her face.

Today she stared it down, willing herself to peel back the years and remember standing before Aemilia Fullia, the weight of a child's protective *bulla* charm still heavy around her neck, and trying to negotiate with a woman two decades her senior. Aemilia was a good priestess, always precise and thorough in ritual, but her eyes had been cold and pitiless as she had spoken with Latona after the death of Gaia Claudia, from whom Aemilia had inherited her position. " *'Claudia was indulgent, but regrettably, there is no-one here who can now handle you. You've learned enough to keep from hurting yourself or anyone else.'* " Latona knew it was as much as most female mages got, unless they made vocational use of their gifts. Claudia had intended more for her, but Claudia had died. " *'I think it best we restore you to your family now. Without another mage in residence, there's little reason for you to stay here. You'll learn to apply your gifts appropriately in the domestic sphere.'* "

Latona had been grief-stricken and young, but she had still been able to read more into Aemilia's meaning: No one at the temple would have any time for her. Where she had once been a cosseted favorite, she would be forgotten at best, a nuisance at worst. Rather than face that misery, she had agreed to Aemilia's suggestion that she return home.

Now though, she wondered if there weren't something more to it, if Aemilia's insistence on her explusion was really such a matter of practicality. Or was it professional jealousy, fear that a gifted child might outstrip her authority in a decade's time?

The thought filled Latona with indignant resentment. *'Aemilia, afraid I would outshine her. My mother, afraid a temper fit might get the better of me. My father, afraid I was weak enough to be manipulated by another's ambition. I let those fears—other people's fears—make me afraid of myself!'*

Latona realized her fists were clenched, crushing the rosy fabric of her skirts between her fingers—fingers that were swift growing hot with her rising fury. *'Easy . . .'* she told herself, taking a deep breath. Control was still, and ever would be, essential where her gifts were concerned. *'But that doesn't mean I should live in terror of them.'* She glanced over her shoulder, where the goddess's statue was visible beyond the columns of the portico. *'I hid for too long, and maybe it was necessary while Ocella lived, but now . . .'* Now she could not escape the feeling that Juno demanded better of her, for the protection of her family and her city. *'And if I'm going to serve you, Lady, I need to know more . . .'*

XV

The morning chill had burned off under the bright autumn sun, and so Latona and Merula took their time walking back towards the Palatine. The Esquiline was a strange mix of high and low society, where fashionable homes shared streets with rickety insulae and bustling shops. As she worked on reconciling the day's tangle of thoughts, Latona walked with her head up, taking in the city in all its unrefined splendor. Next to a thermopolium selling quick, hot meals to passers-by, a group of eastern clerics huddled near a cubbyhole which must have passed for a temple to them, their threadbare robes dragging dust as they paced back and forth. A knot of Cantabrians brawled in front of a tavern, whilst a pair of whores yelled encouragement from an upper window. Latona nodded amiably at men who tugged their forelocks in recognition of her religious garb, ignored the few disrespectful comments thrown her way by those who didn't know better, and was amused when one man smacked his comrade upside the head for whistling at her. The black borders on her tunic meant something to Aventans, and they were quick to educate newcomers to the city. Even plebeian women wearing the *tunica magica* got a little extra elbow room.

Rounding a corner near the base of the hill, she was surprised to find, standing across the way, Sempronius Tarren. He wore no toga, only a wheat-colored tunic and a light cloak, and there was a sheen of sweat on his brow as he called up to a man who was coming down a ladder. The building, Latona realized, was the same crossroads tavern he had spoken from on the night of the riot.

Latona came to a halt at the side of the road, pulling herself out of the main rush of traffic so she could watch. "Merula, let's wait a moment, until Sempronius Tarren appears finished. I should like to speak with him." Latona chose to ignore the little smile curving her servant's lips. It was a bit unusual, and they both knew it, waiting in the street to speak to an unrelated man. But Latona couldn't help it. There was something fascinatingly bizarre about seeing him outside a crossroads college, chatting easily with a common workman. Genuine curiosity as much as anything else prompted her to want to ask him what was going on. She tugged Merula a little closer, so they could hear a bit of the conversation.

◇◇◇◇◇◇◇◇◇◇◇◇◇◇◇◇

"You're absolutely right, of course," Sempronius was saying. "The wood's warped. That patching ought to help keep the chill out, but one strong storm through here, and the whole thing will come crashing down." He sighed, shaking his head. "I'm afraid it's far from my purview, Nisso, and with no urban praetor until the elections, it may be hard to get anything done. I'll speak to Galerius about it, though."

"Thank you, Dominus," the man replied. "I know what people say about the collegia, but—"

"Only half of it is true?" Sempronius challenged. "You might remember that, Nisso—and tell your fellows as well. You are privileged with a certain amount of leeway because of your sacred duties. A little less petty crime and a little more piety might serve your purposes as well as applying to me."

The man did not look terribly chagrined by the chastisement. "We do what we must do, Dominus. It's no different from what all the other collegia do—"

"And a great deal less harmful than some. Yes, I know." Sempronius's brow had a hard line down the center; he was gazing thoughtfully at the streetside altar which gave the college its reason for existence, the shrine to the spirits of the crossroads. Every major intersection in the city had one of these, and they were the responsibility of the collegia to maintain. The balance of the city would be upset if they were ever to fail in their duties—and, indeed, no few accidents had been blamed on the neglect of one college or another. Despite this sacred charge, in many areas, the collegia had grown into little more than armed gangs. The crossroads taverns became havens for criminal exploits, and the men they employed noted for thuggery. It was a common complaint in the city, but no one had yet sorted out how to settle it. "I have some thoughts on that score as well," Sempronius said, then shook his head again, as if clearing away plans already forming in his mind. "I'll see what I can do about your roof. I may be able to call in a favor with the carpenters' guild. A collapse here would be dangerous."

Nisso nodded in agreement, then made a little jerking motion with his head, lowering his voice. "Eh, Dominus, you have some company, I think?" Turning, Sempronius strove not to appear surprised at the incongruous presence of Vitellia Latona and her spitfire of a slave-girl standing a short distance away, curious spectators to their conversation. "She's a fine little piece, if you don't mind me saying so, Dominus."

"She is a great and noble lady, besides being one of the most powerful mages in the city," Sempronius said. Nisso's eyes opened in surprise, and he glanced at Latona with a touch of bewilderment. "Her husband," and he stressed the word ever so slightly, so that Nisso would not get any mistaken ideas about the nature of his friendship with the lady, "has many mercantile interests, and her blood is of the very best in Aven. If you and yours ever see her in these parts again—well, keep any mischief from happening to her, and you'll have my gratitude."

"A lady like her is not often in this neighborhood," Nisso said. "And I think she might not be all too glad for our protection, rough characters that we are."

"Oh," Sempronius said, "she might surprise you."

"Well, Dominus, I think you'd rather be talking to her than to an ugly brute like me," Nisso said, good-naturedly. As they shook hands and said their farewells, Sempronius reflected on the oddity, that a man from a crossroads college, whom many would consider a common criminal without being too far off the mark, should feel familiar enough to tease him in such a fashion. It did not offend or discomfit Sempronius, but it was, he knew, strange. Many men would criticize him for allowing the breach of respect. Sempronius rather intended to use it to his advantage.

But for the moment, Nisso was right. Sempronius was far more interested in finding out what had the Lady Latona wandering the streets of the Esquiline.

◇◇◇◇◇◇◇◇◇◇◇◇◇

Latona knew it was no good pretending she had been doing anything other than watching Sempronius, so she hailed him in friendly terms as he approached. Sempronius strolled towards her, not looking the least bit embarrassed to have been caught out in so unusual a setting or such informal clothing. "Good afternoon to you, Lady Latona. On your way home from Juno Cantatia this morning, I take it? Are the fortunes of Aven's mages well-tended for another year?"

"As well as they ever are, I expect," Latona replied. She nodded her head back at the building Sempronius had been inspecting. "What has you doing business in this part of town?"

"The crossroads collegium has a faulty roof. If it collapses, it could bring down half the block—which would be far more expensive than merely fixing the problem. With no urban praetor and no aediles, things have fallen into disrepair."

"That still doesn't explain how you came to be responsible for the problem," Latona pressed.

"No," Sempronius agreed, "it doesn't. The head of the college and a few of his boys are clients of mine. They were auxiliaries in Numidia while I was a tribune there," he added by way of explanation, at Latona's questioningly raised eyebrow. "I've done them a good turn before, and they thought I might be able to do so again."

"And I expect they'll remember the good turn in the December elections," she teased.

"If they do, I shall certainly be grateful," he said, grinning. "I missed most of my year as aedile thanks to Ocella's proscription. Now, I must earn their regard. Besides—" His voice took on a more earnest tone. "These are the people—for better or for worse—on whom the success of the entire city depends. If they suffer, Aven suffers."

"A noble outlook."

"Practical," Sempronius corrected. "If you must put a word to it, always err on the side of calling it practicality. If word got out to my political opponents that I'm going around being charitable, I'd never hear the end of it." There was a mocking spark in his eyes, though whether it was directed at himself or at those opponents, Latona didn't know. "Forgive me," he said, switching focus, "I'm a brute to keep you standing out in the street. Are you headed home? And would you allow me to escort you?"

He offered her his arm, and Latona slipped her left hand out from under her mantle to take it. Since he was not togate, she should, for propriety's sake, have let the fabric remain wrapped around her, a barrier between them, but it had been a challenging day, and she would not deny herself the pleasure of feeling his skin against hers. "I shall be grateful for the company, at least as far as the Palatine. I'm heading to my father's so I can check on—" But she broke off, no more eager to reveal Alhena's troubles than her own.

Sempronius looked sideways at her for a moment, and though Latona had no notion of it, he tapped into some of his Shadow reserves, sensing a secret, compelled to know what it was. With most people, he would not have cared. In fact, he spent a great deal of time trying *not* to notice what others were keeping to themselves. So many banalities, so much *smallness* that they all considered to be of such great importance. Shadow mages, Sempronius knew, often fell prey to the temptation to concern themselves with minor scandals, white lies, tiny omissions. Sempronius tried to keep his concerns loftier, aimed only to invoke his power when it mattered, to the state or to his career. The golden-haired woman at his side intrigued him far too much to ignore the urge, though, and so he peeked, just a touch, just enough to let him know that she had family matters on her mind. His own knowledge could fill in the rest. "How did your younger sister weather the ceremonies today?"

Latona flicked her eyes up at him, a little startled. "It's kind of you to ask," she said. "I didn't get to speak with her afterwards. I was . . ." She searched for an adequate excuse. "The priestess at Juno Cantatia wanted a word. So I'm headed to the Palatine to check on Alhena before I go home."

"She was engaged to be married, wasn't she? Someone from the . . . Tervian clan?"

"Tarpeian," Latona corrected. "Yes. She ought to have been. But he . . . he died, on his way back from the Vendelician border. We just had word a few weeks ago."

"My condolences," Sempronius offered, with genuine if detached sentiment.

"I barely knew the lad, but I'm terribly sorry for my sister. She took it hard."

"Is there anything you could do for her?" he asked. "With your gifts, I mean."

There was a keenness in the question, but Latona missed the significance of it. "I tried a bit, at first. Mostly I just seem to be able to lull her to sleep, when she'll let me try. It's always difficult to exert influence on someone who knows what you're trying to do, and harder still when she's determined not to be cheered up."

"I can see how that would be challenging. Has it affected her gifts at all?"

Thinking back on the conversation later, Latona wasn't quite sure how he had managed to draw quite so much information out of her. She hadn't intended to divulge so much, especially not so many details of her sister's condition, and to a man who was not an intimate of the family. Yet somehow, with careful questions and a gentle voice, he coaxed much of the story out of her. She could not fathom the reason for his solicitous interest. What concern could a heartbroken sixteen-year-old girl provoke in a man with so much on his mind? Yet it seemed to go far beyond the bounds of strict politeness. And it had, at least, deflected from her own concerns about her magic.

They were only halfway to the Palatine Hill when they had exhausted the subject, however, and instead she got him talking about some of his other political plans. "Do you intend to visit every collegium in the city? Or simply the ones where the brutes-in-residence are so amiable?"

Sempronius laughed. "No, though I do have some other plans for improvement. Dictator Ocella was careful of his own power, neglectful of the city at large. There are roads that need repairing, docks in want of attention, grain doles that need re-apportioning . . ." He gestured at the shops and stalls they were passing. "Not to mention market disputes and judicial matters. Fortunately, Ocella was also a miser, so the city's coffers aren't as poorly off as they might be. I intend to help where I can. The city can't wait until after the elections to start putting itself back together."

"Will they let you?" Latona asked, surprised. "The Optimates, I mean. Strictly speaking, un*til* the elections, such measures aren't within anyone's purview."

"I don't intend to leave it to men like Rabirus or Buteo to decide what I am allowed." Sempronius held his chin a little higher, as though in defiance of his absent foes. In such a dignified man, Latona found it an almost charmingly petulant gesture. "This is . . . private charity. There really isn't anything they could do to stop it, even if they had the nerve to try."

"No one would be so foolish, not with half the city still a breath away from riot." Latona shook her head, unsure if his keenly incisive ploy impressed or frightened her.

Their walk had brought them to the eastern edge of the macellum cuppedenis, the spice and flower market, where the wafting aromas from the spicers' stalls reminded Latona that she had not eaten all day. Here, it was too loud to converse, unless they felt like shouting. Many merchants called to them, hawking their wares. Above the general din came the noise of a flute; a nearby flower-seller was using a musician and a juggler to attract passers-by to her stall. The crowd around them grew denser, and Latona's religious garb no longer won her a respectful radius. She knew Merula's fingers would be itching for her dagger; she was ever uneasy in such a press. Latona should have felt claustrophobic, with so many emotions pressing in around her, but her revelation at the temple appeared to have done some good; she was able to breathe freely, letting the sensations roll around her like water at a boat's prow, a part of her world, but not something that would sink her. *'This . . . this is what you need to master, to be of use . . .'*

Sempronius showed a deft ability to navigate the ocean of people, waving off the vendors who approached, each insisting his goods were superior to his neighbor's. When a beggar with crooked legs stretched out a hand, however, Sempronius withdrew two bronze coins from the pouch at his waist and pressed them into the man's palm.

He drew Latona back by the elbow, just in time to pull her out of the way of a cavorting pair of street urchins, barreling through the streets with no mind for their surroundings, then guided her around a pile of refuse. A heavily-loaded mule approached, prodded along by a bearded driver cursing in an eastern tongue. When they paused to let it pass, Latona noticed Sempronius appraising their surroundings with a strange, satisfied smile on his face. It was a scene of chaos: the ordinary, everyday chaos that dictated Aventan life, but Sempronius regarded it with evident joy—and he allowed himself to indulge in it, in a way that Latona envied. *'I never let myself give in to that . . . I was always too afraid . . .'*

Latona felt like she could hear music—and of course it was all around them, from flautists and a dozen other players hired to draw the attention of passers-by to certain shops. But that was a pleasant cacophony. What Latona sensed ran deeper than that, the melody of the city itself, composed daily by thousands and thousands of souls. Here in the market, the city danced as nimbly as any girl hired out for a banquet, and it made Latona want to dance, too. *'What people this city breeds,'* she thought, laughing as a shopkeeper's monkey juggled apples while balancing on the edge of his stall. *'And what people it attracts.'*

"Where will you start, then?" Latona asked, once they had pushed their way out to the relatively open air of the Via Sacra. "With so much to do, that is."

"Oh, something to do with a temple, I suppose."

Latona wondered if she would ever feel as casual as Sempronius sounded in that moment—but she also suspected that nothing with him was as offhand as it seemed.

"Not as crucial as the grain dole," he continued, "but far more impressive for an opening volley."

"And good for fostering a reputation of piety," Latona said. "A few priestly endorsements will help balance out the Optimates' accusations that you're set on the destruction of the *mos maiorum* and the Aventan way of life."

"An astute observation, Lady Latona." Sempronius regarded her with a sideways glance. "Wherever I decide to build, I'll show you in person, if you like. And if your husband will allow me to pay you the call, that is."

He seemed to have added the last as an afterthought. Latona held in a sigh. "Ah," she said, squeezing his arm lightly. "Well, there, Senator, you find me in similar spirits to yourself."

"How do you mean?"

"I find I am increasingly disinterested in what other people will allow me."

◇◇◇◇◇◇◇◇◇◇◇◇◇◇

By the time they reached the top of the hill, the sun was already beginning to ease itself down towards the horizon. The autumn days grew ever shorter, and Latona had spent longer in the temple than she had thought. They paused outside Aulus Vitellius's red-painted door to take in the southern cityscape before them. The sky was a languid, lazy yellow, shading to purple only at the eastern edge, and the pale gold of the sun cast a queer yet captivating glow on the brick walls and vermilion rooftops of the sprawling city beyond. From this vantage, none of the buildings seemed to stand at proper angles to each other, but jutted and collided every which way, as though elbowing each other for space just as their inhabitants did in the streets.

"She is magnificent," Sempronius commented.

Latona snorted softly. "She is an upstart. A sprawling mess, ill-planned and impudent, overflowing her proper boundaries, with no respect for her elders."

"You find fault with her, for that?" Sempronius asked, looking sideways at her.

Latona answered him with a grin. "I never said that." She gazed over the uneven skyline: the long stretch of the Circus Maximus, crowded all around with workshops and emporia; the thin ribbon of the Tiber River, curving its way through the urban knot; the triangular pediments of the Aventine temples, their bronze ornaments reaching up towards heaven. "I rather admire her for it. She doesn't give a fig what anyone thinks."

"If we had wine in our hands, I should like to drink to that," Sempronius said.

Latona glanced southward towards the Aventine. "It's quite a thing to think of, really," she said. "From a strand of huts on the river bank, built by fishers, hunters, and thieves, to all this. I've always wondered if Remus chose the land, or if the land chose Remus."

A grin from Sempronius. "A worthy question, my lady. Would Aven be Aven in any other place?"

"Would our people be who *we* are, had we grown up on Crater Bay or in the Ligurian foothills?" A smile twitched her lips. "I think . . . not. Just as these hills career into each other and jostle for space, we're a city of those who cannot be content with what we are handed." The thought prickled. "The eastern nations, they all sneer at our pretensions, think us nearly as barbaric as the Tennic tribes. Even Chrysos, with fewer than three centuries to her name, puts up her nose at unruly Aven."

"They won't always," Sempronius said, and it sounded more like a vow than like speculation. He turned to meet her eyes, and she saw a steadiness in them as sure as Mount Atlas, as enduring as the seas. Something in Latona thrilled to it, resonating with his certainty. "This city has a destiny, one I intend to see it reach. The Tyrians scoffed at us once, too. No civilization, no matter how great, will have the chance to do so again. Not the fallen Athaecans, clinging to their shattered pride, not ancient Abydos, not the so-called King of Kings sitting on his gilded throne over there in Parthia. No one will mock what I intend to build."

A warm breeze sought to wrap Latona in its pleasant comfort, and yet despite golden light all around and the impressive vista of their tumultuous city spread out before her, Latona found it impossible to perceive anything but Sempronius's eyes, dark and absolute. She felt a nesting ache nudged by his frank admittance of his ambitions. It ought to have terrified her, or else it should have made her laugh, or question his sanity. No man—no *normal* Aventan man—would make such a claim, and Latona did have to wonder why he was making it to *her*. There was no boasting in his voice. This was not the over-puffed rhetoric of a delusional politician. He stated his goals as fact, as if affirming that the ocean was blue or that grapes grew on vines. Something about that plainness not only made the assertion seem impossible to deny, but also reached inside Latona and plucked something out that she had scarcely known was there. "I do believe you mean that," she breathed, when she found the air for it.

The shadow of a smile, partly of satisfaction but also of self-mockery, crossed his face. "I do know how it sounds," he said, answering her unspoken thoughts. "It certainly isn't something I go around saying to everyone. But you, Lady Latona . . . I suspect you understand. I think you know, if you would be honest with yourself, what it is to feel that you are someone who is capable of glory."

He had managed to hit upon precisely what had dogged her thoughts all day. Dark remembrances: a blazing tree, pressure in her chest, the cracking of control, and eyes watching her, waiting to take advantage of her successes or exploit her failures—but, too, the exhilarating satisfaction of using her powers in benevolence to save Aula and Lucia, to help those girls on the Esquiline, to lend a hand to Sempronius's and Galerius's speeches. Beneath it all, a growing sense of burning defiance.

"You'll admit it someday," Sempronius said. "It must pull at you. How could it not?"

Latona's arms prickled, though not with any chill in the air. Her emotions were too close to the surface today, and his words bewitched. His rich, smooth voice drew her in; he spoke with such knowing, such insight into her, as though they were alike. She wanted to let these feelings consume her, and everything in his voice and eyes seemed to be inviting her to do so . . .

"Vitellia Latona," he said, hardly louder than the soft breeze buffeting around them, "who is, I think, destined for more."

His words cut through to a part of her that had gone unacknowledged for too long. *'But am I prepared to face the repercussions?'* More, she had come to realize, did not necessarily mean *better*. Yet there was sureness in his eyes. This man, this incredible, ambitious man, evinced such faith in her. *'What does he see when he looks at me?'* Latona felt a tingle rolling through her, part anticipation and part fear. Sempronius was dangling a golden dream in front of her, a dream of herself and what she might become if she dared to reach for it. A temptation—but a danger, too. Strengthening her power would also strengthen the damage she could do. *'Do I have what it takes to grow with discipline, to reach for the sun without losing control?'* Latona wasn't sure, but Sempronius stated her destiny as certainly as he did his own, almost impossibly formidable though each seemed. And he seemed to perceive their destinies as yoked together.

The enticement of it all had Latona's heart thumping. Or was that the result of Sempronius's close warmth and the intensity of his gaze, of how her heart leapt to stand so near and share their dreams? She ached to reach out for him—no, she wanted to *fling* herself at him, to step into his embrace and be damned with the havoc it would cause. She wanted to find out if this fire continually igniting inside her could find liberation in his arms. *'Losing control,'* she chided herself. *'Your blood is too hot, you have to have better control . . .'*

Sempronius blinked and turned away, releasing her from the captivation. "We appear to have arrived. Do give my regards to your father and your sisters." Latona simply nodded, letting him walk her up the stairs as Merula opened the door for her. He did not come in, but bade her a quick farewell from the doorstep. "I will remember my promise, to show you my plans for the temples," Sempronius said, before Merula, scowling at him with her typical insolence, shut the door quite decisively behind her mistress.

Aula emerged from around the corner only seconds later, mouth already open to start asking questions, but Latona started first. "Where's Alhena? She didn't look well when the ceremony was over, but I was called to the Temple. Is she well?"

"Quinta Terentia brought her home all puffed up with piety, so at least she's left off moping for the afternoon," Aula replied. "What *I* want to know is, why did Sempronius Tarren walk you home?"

"I ran into him while we were passing over the Esquiline," Latona said, letting Merula unwind her mantle, "and he offered to accompany me."

"Mm-hmm. And what were you two conversing about for so long out there?"

Latona narrowed her eyes. "Were you *spying?*"

"I was just *looking*. Helva said she'd seen you were coming up the hill. I didn't know I shouldn't *look* for you." Aula pinched her arm and dragged her to a sitting-room, then practically shoved her onto a couch. "Come on. Spill. A man like that doesn't just take a fancy to walking young matrons home from their religious obligations."

"I don't know what to tell you, Aula," Latona said with an attempt at a casual shrug—an attempt severely hindered by the heat still pounding in her blood. "We crossed paths. It's nothing to be in a tizzy over. Our families are on friendly terms, particularly with the elections coming up. There's nothing unusual about his offering to escort me home when we met by chance."

Aula was quiet for a moment, scrutinizing her sister's face: a carefully innocent expression spoiled by rubescence. "I just thought you might've been taking my advice," she said, "about cultivating him."

Latona rolled her eyes. "Not all of us set out each morning with those machinations in mind."

"You should," Aula said, admonishing. "Everyone else in this city does." Then she settled back, beaming contentedly. "That's why it's such a good thing you have me for a sister, to think of these things for you." The smugness of her poise lasted only a moment, until the pillow Latona threw hit her in the face.

◇◇◇◇◇◇◇◇◇◇◇◇◇◇

Sempronius was not so maudlin as to stare at the door after Latona disappeared behind it, but she remained on his mind as he descended the Palatine Hill and continued towards the Aventine. *'An extraordinary woman.'* His Water magic sensed the power in her, banked embers just waiting for a spark to set them off—and the same, he thought, was true of her essence. *'A keen mind, an active imagination, and, I think, ambition she has never been allowed to acknowledge. But all wrapped up so tightly, so under-utilized.'*

Sadly, the tale was all too common among female patrician mages. Earning money from their talent, as Davina and Tura Petronia did, was admired as resourceful in the lower classes but considered vulgar among the upper. Unless they dedicated themselves as priestesses, patrician women with magical blessings had few meaningful outlets. And with no purpose to put their blessings to, their families often scanted their education, giving them enough to make sure they were not a danger to themselves or others—but nothing deeper in either theory or practice. *'For someone like Latona, with both the power and the intellect to train and focus it . . . Oh, what a waste.'*

The laws that prohibited magically talented men from the upper echelons of politics, and barred freedmen and freedwomen from religious rights and certain occupations, were a different matter. But to Sempronius's mind, they all stemmed from the same flaw: an adherence to tradition so steadfast that it overshadowed possibilities for growth. Such a thought was abhorrent to Sempronius Tarren. Offensive, even anathema to the mandate of his soul. He hated waste, and that loathing drove many of his political goals. Making Aven the city of his dreams would require making the most of *all* of its citizens.

It was a frustration to him, to want to see Latona spread her wings and not know how to prompt her. That desire thrummed in her; he was sure of it. He had *felt* it, towards the end of their conversation. *'Did she even realize she was casting her emotions so strongly?'* Most Spirit mages, like some Fire and Water, had a degree of empathic talent, but very few had power enough to set that empathy in reverse and cast emotions out to influence others. He knew Latona had the ability, though, had watched her use it the night of the Esquiline riots. Then, it had been a controlled release; today, a wild tumult, the rage of yearnings kept close for too long. For a moment, the force of her emotions had been so strong that he had been able to think of little besides how intensely he wanted to draw her into her arms and kiss her until that passion broke free.

'But perhaps there is a more appropriate way to reach and inspire her . . .'

◇◇◇◇◇◇◇◇◇◇◇◇◇◇

Two days later, a slave arrived at the doorstep of the Vitellian domus bearing a tightly-wrapped scroll and a message to deliver it to the Lady Alhena. "With regards from Sempronius Tarren," the slave said, handing it over to Mus, since Alhena did not see fit to stir herself to the door for a messenger's presence. "With his hopes for her edification and improvement."

Mus delivered both the package and the message, Aula had hovered over Alhena's shoulder as she unwrapped the unlooked-for gift. It was cased in a sturdy leather cylinder, copied in a fair hand onto high-quality vellum. Alhena unrolled it far enough to reveal the heading, which proclaimed "A Commentary on the Truscan Auguries," a text examining the divinatory practices of the pre-Aventan peoples of Truscum and their eventual integration into the current magical and religious systems. Aula wrinkled her nose, thinking that it was the sort of thing she could not be persuaded to read under either the most lucrative of bribes nor the most refined of tortures. But Alhena's reaction was different, grateful, and almost misty-eyed. She did not quite smile, but there was a lightness in her expression that Aula had not seen in quite some time, a lessening of the woe-graven misery that had dominated her countenance since Tarpeius's death. "How thoughtful of him," she murmured, holding the tome to her chest. She blinked over at her sister. "What do you suppose compelled him to extend such a kindness to me?"

Aula, owning a greater awareness than the absorption of Alhena's mourning had afforded her for months, twisted her lips in a wry smile. "I'm sure I've no idea," she said, "but perhaps we ought to ask Latona."

XVI

'If only there were a damn road between here and Tarraco,' Gaius Vitellius thought, not for the first time, as he tramped through muddy streets to Nedhena's temple to Neptune, dragging a pig behind him. The unfortunate porcine had no notion that his destiny was to serve as a placeholder in Vitellius's plea to the god of the sea to grant him favorable conditions for travel. *'Who knew white bulls were so difficult to come by in Maritima?'*

They had finally found enough vessels to carry the cohorts to Tarraco, quinqueremes hired out from Tyrian merchants, but no sooner had Vitellius settled on payment with the captains than the heavens had opened. After three days of solid downpour and high winds, Vitellius was desperate.

The priests held the pig while Vitellius sliced its throat open with a sickle-shaped blade. Reeking of blood, he raised his slickened hands towards the statue of the god standing across the atrium, and tried not to think of how its rough-hewn wooden features hardly compared to the impressive representation back in Aven. *'Lord Neptune, please accept this creature as a symbol of my dedication, and if you can clear the seas and see me and my men safely to Tarraco, I will find a fine white bull to sacrifice to you there.'* Surely, he reasoned, there were bulls going spare in Iberia.

That done, Vitellius slogged his way back across the city. Nedhena had no walls, but he had still ordered the men encamped further upriver from the established neighborhoods in the hopes that it would mitigate conflict with the locals. On his way back, he encountered Titus Mennenius, herding half a cohort back into the rows of tents. Seeking to keep the men in fighting form and out of trouble, Mennenius had been drilling them relentlessly on the empty fields, even in foul weather. If nothing else, it was an outlet for their energy, though it hardly improved morale. "They're grumbling," Titus confided as the tribunes watched the men file back into camp. "Calling this a fool's errand, wanting to go back to Vendelicia, of all things."

"They think they'd be less bored there?" Vitellius scowled up at the sky. "Or less wet?"

"Perhaps it's just the matter of a boredom they know." Mennenius rubbed at his forehead, leaving a muddy streak on his skin. "You don't think they'd desert us, do you?"

Vitellius wasn't sure. Abandoning a tribune would technically be mutiny, but if they could make a case that the tribunes in question were negligent in their own responsibilities, there might not be much of a penalty to pay. Vitellius knew there was nothing else he could have done, but he could not count on everyone else seeing it that way.

With that threat brewing behind the cohorts' discontent, when the sun finally broke through the clouds two days later, Vitellius wasted no time in driving them onboard. The journey to Tarraco should have taken no more than three days, but as the sun began to set on the second, the wind turned bitter cold. The sun, rather than fading into yellows and oranges, fell into a pewter-colored sky. "Bad sign," the ship's captain said. "I'm thinking of turning back to Nedhena."

"I'm paying you well not to," Vitellius said, out of patience for delays of any kind. "You said you could get us to Tarraco."

"If we turned in towards Emporion, even—"

"We go on. We'll hug the coast as much as necessary, but we must move quickly." The ship rolled lightly, forcing Vitellius to grab onto the mast to stay upright. The captain shook his head, sucking air in through his teeth. "Look," Vitellius said. "Aven is generous to its friends. See us safely ashore—in *Tarraco*—and your bravery will not go unrewarded." Bravery might not have been the prime motivator, but avarice served its turn. The captain nodded his agreement.

A few hours later, Vitellius was regretting the decision. Clouds had utterly blotted out moon and stars, and the wind had grown so strong that it was fraying the edges of his tunic. His men, thinking, perhaps, that if they rowed hard enough, they would steer themselves out of trouble, did not seem to flag in their efforts. Even those who ought to have been off-shift, sleeping for a few hours, had put themselves back on duty. With the wind growing stronger and the sea pushing harder at the boats, Vitellius gave the order for his men to lash themselves to their seats, lest they be thrown overboard.

By the middle of the night, the three quinqueremes had been spun and tossed about so much that Vitellius no longer knew which direction shore might be. The ships became separated, not that he could see far off his own prow anyway. For his own comfort, he regretted having put Titus on a different boat, though he knew it was the safe and sensible choice. It bettered the odds that, if any of the boats made it ashore, they would still have a commander.

An enormous wave picked Vitellius's boat up high, then slammed it back down with a gargantuan crashing noise. He had no idea that ships could make such a sound, much less do so and remain intact. The quinquereme rocked terribly, water sloshing over the sides. The Tyrian captain shouted to his gods, but also to the Aventan men, swearing that his boats were sound and would not capsize. Vitellius hoped his assessment was correct but was not encouraged when one of the smaller sails tore loose of its rigging under the force of a howling gale, flying off into the sea, where it quickly became invisible, lost to the torrential downpour and turbulent waves. The quinquereme swirled as though kicked by a great wave, and Vitellius found himself hugging the mast for support.

'Neptune,' Vitellius thought, 'great and blessed Neptune, forgive my arrogance, to trespass on your roads when I should have turned back. If you let me and my men see the dawn, I will make a great sacrifice in your name. The finest white bull in Cantabria, or as many rams as I can find.' Another roll of the waves nearly up-ended the boat, sending the men tumbling, oars ripped from their hands. Vitellius could no longer tell if the water on his face was ocean spray, rain, or tears. 'Please. Just let me see the sun.'

◇◇◇◇◇◇◇◇◇◇◇◇

TAGUS RIVER, IBERIA

Blood drained into bowls from the bodies hanging suspended from a rail. Then, the magic-men mixed that blood with soot from the campfire. The smell of it had infected the whole camp, and while the warriors breathed it in and bellowed about inhaling the work of the gods, Neitin burned sage in her tent and tried to forget what she had seen.

It was Bailar's fault, Bailar leading him down this path. "He hears no other opinions," she muttered to herself, pacing around the tent with one hand cradling her swollen belly. "He listens to the magic-men, and they tell him nothing but certainty of his glory. His war-band is no different. And Bailar guides them all."

So when Ekialde had announced that they were setting up a new camp, farther up the Tagus River, Neitin had taken drastic action. She had sent her sister Ditalce home on a mission, to retrieve someone that Neitin hoped would be an ally to her.

When he arrived that afternoon, striding through the smoke of the pyre, Ditalce was scowling and sullen, annoyed at having been away from the excitement of the camp for days. But Otiger smiled when he saw his favorite niece standing in the doorway of her tent. "Neitin," he said, a broad smile breaking out in the middle of his braided red beard, "how good it is to see you." His embrace was as rib-squeezing as she remembered. "Your mother sends her love, and I've a few treats here in the pack for you and your sisters."

"That's very kind," Neitin said. "Please, come in."

Once Otiger was settled in a comfortable chair, Neitin offered him a cup of Ekialde's best wine—without the blood additives he had taken to drinking. "You look unsettled, dear one," Otiger said, for Neitin continued to pace about. "Sit down, child. Ditalce did not have much to say about why you wanted me to join you on this campaign."

Neitin smiled self-consciously, easing onto the edge of her bed. "No. I did not give her much information."

"What is it, then, that troubles you?"

She jerked her head towards the opening of the tent. "What is going on out there. Ekialde has brought us so very far from home. What have we to do with the upper plateaus? What is Gades or Toletum to us? We drove the encroachers back from our borders. We should go home and tend our lands." Neitin missed the olive groves of Ekialde's village, and lately, she found herself missing even more the blue river waters of her childhood home, down the mountain from her husband's territory. The rivers here were thin, the rocks harsh and grainy. Good enough for Arevaci and Vettoni, but it was not the proper place for the Lusetani.

Sighing, Otiger sat back, cradling the cup of wine in his lap. "Dear one," he said, "you must know what a hero your husband is to our people. It is for you to be proud—"

"I am," Neitin interjected. "Or, I was. But it goes too far."

"Conquest is the right of the strong," Otiger said, "and Ekialde is helping we Lusetani to prove ourselves strong."

"We are not only a people of blood! Are we not also of the river waters and the olive trees?" Neitin got to her feet, gesturing sharply out towards the still-smoking fire. "And it is not even the blood of foreigners he is taking! Those are Vettoni, cousins to our people!"

Rubbing his chin thoughtfully, Otiger gave a little grunt. "They *are* our old enemies."

"And our old allies," Neitin pointed out. "This is not only about taking their strength for himself. It is meant to show the penalty for not falling in line against the foreigners."

"I expect it's quite effective."

"With some. The rest of the Vettoni have pledged themselves to spilling my husband's blood in turn! He welcomes new men to his cause with open arms, and too rarely does he question what hand might hold a knife to his own throat. His war-band cares for nothing but the exhilaration of the fight, and Bailar makes sure that none of the magic-men let him hear anything that might make him question his course."

"Your husband is not a stupid man," Otiger said, cutting into her fury with his calm reason. "He must have a reason for pursuing this course so vehemently."

Neitin rubbed at her forehead. "He thinks . . . he thinks he is doing right. That our people are in danger of abandoning our ways, losing sight of our gods . . . And Bailar's stargazers have told him there is a great force coming. Ekialde thinks he must be ready for it." Neitin's hands were balling into fists, and she felt the frustration of knowing how impotent was her rage. "But what if they are coming *because* of his actions! We might live in peace, if he were content to have it so. He thinks so much of glory and conquest that he has forgotten to think of good sense. And now, do you know what he is doing? Bailar has convinced him to tattoo himself with blood."

"This is not an unknown—"

"*Human* blood, uncle! The blood of fallen enemies, to take their strength into him. As though drinking it wasn't enough!"

"These are deep magics, indeed," Otiger said, "but not necessarily a concern. He is listening to the advice of magic-men, like me."

"*Not* like you," Neitin said. "This Bailar, he is *trouble*. He's whipped all of this up, I don't know to what purpose, but—"

Otiger's lower lip folded over the upper: a pensive look, one he shared with Neitin's mother. She held her tongue, giving his thought time to process. "You may," he said, "have a point. Even an *erregerra* must make informed opinions. How else can he know that he chooses the path of the gods?"

Neitin released a long breath. "Just go *listen* to him. Join the war council. He'll have to let you, since you are kin to me. Listen." There was fire in her dark eyes as she added, "And be brave enough to speak if you feel my concerns have validity."

Otiger's hands fell onto her shoulders and he pressed a kiss to her forehead. "*Erregerra* or not, little one, Ekialde chose well in making you his wife. You have a fine and noble spirit."

Despite the praise, Neitin pursed her lips. Again, the cold burn of futility. "And I am a woman grown, uncle," she said. "I do not need patronizing. I need your support to stop this madness."

"And if madness it is," Otiger said, "then you shall have it."

XVII

'Vitellia Latona,' Sempronius Tarren had said, *'who is, I think, destined for more.'*

The words had haunted Latona for days, as had Sempronius's expression. His eyes, half-admiring, half-pitying, with the blended eagerness and frustration of a hunting dog being held in check when it had spotted a quarry. With that curious insight of his, he had hit upon the very point that had been working its way into her like a burr.

'But what next?'

She could go to Ama Rubellia at the Temple of Venus and receive both comfort and guidance. She could, and she would, she vowed, in order to make sure her incendiary tendencies stayed under control. *'But that will not be enough.'* She had to be better than that, braver than that. Juno had given her blessings, too, blessings that she had ignored for too long.

And, at the Temple of Juno, she had something to prove.

So, wrapped in a currant-colored mantle with prominent black borders, Latona made the long hike up the Capitoline Hill's steep slope, Merula at her elbow, seeking a meeting with High Priestess Aemilia Fullia.

The massive triadic temple complex atop the Capitoline was the seat of the gods on earth, filled with their divine spirits. Jupiter Maximus's temple was centermost, sitting with his wife Juno on one hand and his daughter Minerva on the other. Legend said that in Aven's earliest days, the enormous terracotta statues within the temples would come to life from time to time, inhabited by the spirits of the gods, who wished to better observe the growing city as it spread over the seven hills and overtook the neighboring towns. As she ascended towards them, Latona remembered, when she was about seven or eight years old, asking Claudia why the gods had stopped visiting in such a fashion. Were they simply contented with the city's progress, or had they lost interest? Claudia had only grinned, asking Latona what *she* thought, encouraging her to speculate.

The memory brought a small smile to Latona's face. Claudia had been more than a mentor. While Latona's own mother had been wary of the power brimming in her child, Claudia had loved Latona like a daughter, encouraging every question, indulging every curiosity, shaping Latona's interests with a careful bent, so that she would keep her duty to her family, her gods, and Aven always in mind. However badly Latona's time at the temple had ended, she had been cherished there for many years. She let those recollections, not the sadder ones, carry her up the dusty path, emboldening her for what she would have to face at the top.

Latona asked Merula to wait outside; Merula nodded, going to sit with a few other attendants on a bench near a small fountain. Within the temple, the first attendant Latona encountered was one who recognized her. Enough older than Latona that they had known each other but not well, the woman's face gave away her shock. "Vitellia!"

"Good afternoon. I hope you're well. I was hoping to see the High Priestess, if it is convenient."

"It . . . it may be. Do take a seat. I'll . . . see if she's available."

As Latona expected, she had quite some time to sit alone and let long-cold memories creep in around her before the High Priestess finally appeared. Some memories were warming—running barefoot across the mosaic floors, delighting in the temple's library, sharing a happy glow as Claudia taught her how to cast benevolent emotions outwards. For seven years, the temple had been far more a home to her than her father's *domus* on the Palatine. But the remembrance of her departure cast a pallor over that time; even the joy, she could not now remember without pain. Claudia's death had changed everything. Now, Latona had the opportunity to learn if Aemilia Fullia was really the figure of intimidation that lived in her memory.

Aemilia was small-boned, her eyes and hair both near-black. She wore a plain tunic with a robe of pale dyed wool, and her hair was plaited up in a conical fashion and bound with a purple band that covered most of the crown of her head. She moved with practiced grace, her hands clasped neatly in front of her.

Latona could have managed quite well never seeing the woman again in her life.

"Vitellia Herenniae," Aemilia said. Latona did not miss the pointed use of the marital form of her name. "What a surprise."

"Indeed, honored lady," Latona said, inclining her head as she rose in greeting. As bitter as the words tasted, she was determined to show respect. *'For the goddess you serve, if not you, Aemilia.'* Thanks to Aemilia, she had learned the graces of a socialite rather than a priestess, and she had Aula's example for how to wield them.

Aemilia's smile did not meet her eyes. "It must be quite some matter to send you, of all people, seeking my aide."

Latona took a steadying breath. "It is Juno's business I'm about," she said. "Or, more accurately, Juno's business that I *wish* to be about."

Aemilia's fixed smile did not waver, but her voice was sharper when she said, "When you left the temple, we all understood it was permanent, and for your own good. What could you possibly be seeking here?"

Latona lifted her chin, endeavoring to remember that she was no longer a scared and vulnerable ten-year-old, staring up into cold dark eyes as she was told that no one had time for her anymore, here in the only home she had ever known. *'I will not cower,'* she thought. *'I let her scare me away as a child. Let her look me in the eye now that I'm grown.'* Seeing Aemilia in the regalia of her office, it rankled even more to think that she had been coward enough to send a child away for fear the child would outshine her. It bolstered Latona's determination to assert herself.

"I've come seeking Juno's *knowledge*. As you are aware, my magical education was . . . foreshortened." A tightening around her eyes was all the recognition that Aemilia offered, so Latona went on. "Juno still has plans for me, however, and those plans cannot be fulfilled without further guidance—magical, ethical, and practical." Feigning a casual tone, she made a small dismissive gesture with her hand. "You need not concern yourself with it, nor with me, at all. I ask only access to the library."

One of Aemelia's hands lifted in a halting gesture. "Before I could make such an allowance, Vitellia Herenniae, I would need to know more about your intentions. What, precisely, do you believe Juno is calling on you to do?"

"Help the women of this city." Latona's eyes flicked towards the front of the temple and the sprawling streets beyond it. "As my father and other men have discovered upon returning to Aven, there is much to be done in Ocella's wake."

Aemilia tilted her head to one side. Latona remembered Aemilia affected that gesture when she was searching for something to object to, whether an offense existed or not. "Do you think the Senators cannot handle matters themselves?"

Rather than give her honest assessment of the Senate's efficacy, Latona answered, "I believe it is the duty of Aventan women to do what they can to support the city's health and growth, as our mothers have done since the days of the kings."

Aemilia frowned. "And how do you imagine your magical gifts could aid you in this?"

Latona refrained from pointing out that since Aemelia had none of the blessing herself, she had no idea what it might or might not help with. "The empathy to know where suffering is, certainly. The compassion that points towards healing. Whether they need further counsel or a place to go, or another kind of help, I can let the Spirit of instinct help me to better serve them." She spread her hands in an open gesture. "The truth is that I do not *know* the full extent of how my blessing might help me or the women of Aven. That is why I want to research and further develop my skills, as Gaia Claudia intended I do. I need to know what may be possible from the examples set by my forebears."

"Charitable donations," Aemilia said pointedly, "have been a fine enough show of philanthropy for many of your forebears."

Latona could feel the muscles in her neck and jaw tightening. "I believe I can do more. The magic will be my—" She almost said servant, but no, that was not the right sense of it. "—my partner in this."

Aemilia shook her head. "This is an irrational and unnecessary proposal. If the women of this city have troubles, they can—and do—come to the temples for aid."

"With all respect, honored lady," Latona said, "if the temples could do enough to fix all Aven's troubles, we would not still have so many hungry children, desperate widows, and beaten wives." She ought to have left it at that, but Aemilia's petty obstruction was wearing at her nerves. "You deal with the problems that are brought to you, here, and I have no doubt you do so commendably." Whatever else she thought of Aemelia Fullia, the woman was precise and thorough. "But not everyone brings their troubles here. Not everyone has that temerity. Pluto's hellfire, Aemelia, not every woman in the city is healthy enough to drag herself up those steps!"

All that earned her was a scowl. "You will watch your language in Juno's house."

Latona ignored her; Aemilia's stubborn and short-sighted self-preservation had ignited her temper. "You fix what is in front of you, but when was the last time you went walking through the city, Aemilia? I don't mean being carted to a dinner or a ritual in a curtained litter. When did you last *see* what Aven's people endure?"

"Enough!" Aemelia said, her raised voice echoing off the painted temple walls. "I have heard quite enough. I cannot in good conscience offer you assistance, Vitellia Herenniae, nor anyone else who would seek to usurp this temple's rightful role in serving the women of Aven."

A thousand words were in Latona's mind, trying to break onto her tongue: that she had no wish to usurp, only to supplement; that charity need not belong to the religious orders alone; that it was a civic duty, and that mages, with their blessings, had more responsibility to the public than most; that anyone who *could* do good, *ought* to. But with an ache in her chest, she realized none of it would matter to Aemilia. Not coming from her, not when she was proving the very fear of usurpation that had prompted Aemilia to bully her from the temple in the first place.

"You chose your path long ago," Aemilia went on. "You determined, as was entirely proper, to return to the domestic sphere and serve Juno within the bonds of matrimony."

Latona wanted to scream: *'I was a child! I was lonely and unwanted! Of course I decided to leave this place where I was no longer loved!'* She bit the inside of her cheek; Aemilia did not deserve to see that vulnerability.

"It is a noble thing, to do Juno's work as a wife *and* mother. A *holy* thing. If you feel unsatisfied . . ." Aemilia nodded towards Juno's statue. "Reflect on that. Perhaps your unwomanly ambitions have affected the balance of your womb. Attend to your domestic concerns and put these inappropriate political urges aside. Then, I am sure, your humours will balance and Juno will see fit to allow you to give your husband his heirs."

Aemilia turned neatly and started to stalk away from Latona, clearly considering the conversation over.

Latona's jaw was clenched so hard her head ached as she searched for words that would not cause her to blaspheme herself in Juno's house. "Forgive me, honored lady," she ground out at Aemilia's back. "I should have realized you would not be *capable* of helping me."

◇◇◇◇◇◇◇◇◇◇◇◇

As Latona stormed down the Capitoline Hill, Merula trotted in her wake. "Domina— Domina— I am wishing you would— Domina, if you are not slowing down, you may trip—Domina, *please*."

But for once, Latona had little attention to spare for Merula's concerns. The fury born from Aemilia's words still stung, and each time her foot stamped down, another castigation echoed in her mind. *'Usurp the temple's role . . . affected the balance . . . unwomanly . . . The nerve of that woman, blocking my path to preserve her own self-important sense of stature!'* Latona felt a heat growing in her fingers, and she shook her hands irritably, as though it might dispel the compulsion. *'Oh, sweet Juno, I'm going to set a tree on fire again . . .'*

The warning built as she stalked home, her footsteps treading ever quicker. *'All my life,'* she thought, *'someone has been telling me what I must not do. Mother, father, husband, priestesses . . . How did it take me till now to realize how heartily sick of it I am?'*

Her father's home was closer than her husband's, and so it was to the Palatine Hill that Latona stormed after leaving the Temple of Juno Maxima, hoping a sympathetic ear and a glass of wine with Aula might quell any incendiary impulses. When she arrived, however, she learned that Aula had accompanied their father on a visit to the College of the Augurs. "Damn." She tugged the mantle from her hair in frustration. "Do you know how long they'll be, Paenas?"

The steward shook his head. "Regrettably, no, Domina. Would you care to wait? I'll send a boy with water and anything else you might—"

"Wine," Latona said, raising a finger. "Half-watered, please, Paenas, and whatever fruit looks best. I'll sit in the peristyle."

As soon as she settled herself, Merula started fussing at her hair and clothes, muttering in Phrygian. Latona had not said anything to her yet about the confrontation with Aemilia. She would get the story eventually; she always did, but she lacked the patience to wait for it, and polylinguistic grumbling was her way of encouraging Latona to speed the process along.

While Merula played at detangling Latona's wind-tangled curls, Latona reached for the bolster pillow on the bench beside her. At first she was only squeezing it, feeling the stuffing squash under her fingers, but soon she was smacking her palm hard against it, then punching it outright. "Domina!" Latona felt Merula's hands on her shoulders, but she kept pummeling the pillow, with both hands now. "Domina, you are growing warm—"

Merula was right. Latona felt again the sizzle on her skin and in her veins, warning of Fire magic, heating fit to burst. *'Damn, damn, damn.'*

She gave her head a little shake, trying to bring herself to rights. She pointed at a decorative dish resting on a plinth in the corner. "Water, please." Merula was moving before she had even finished asking, filling the dish with water from the garden pool and bringing it back to Latona.

Latona tossed the pillow aside and shook her hands a few times, trying to clear the hot tingling. Then she plunged both hands wrist-deep into the water.

The pain was sharper than it had been after the fire in Herennius's atrium, when causing a conflagration had at least bled off some of the energy first. The shock of the slippery water helped Latona to refocus her thoughts. Merula held the dish, still as a leopard in the stalk. Latona took several long, deep breaths, letting the cool air fill her up from nose to gut.

'*Tamp it down, tamp it down . . .*' But rather than crashing the gate of her power shut, as was her usual recourse, Latona tried, instead, to adjust the flow more smoothly. '*Relax . . . Relax and release it . . .*' After a few moments, as her white-hot fury towards Aemilia cooled, so did her skin. The impulse to act, the sparking inclination of her Fire magic, tempered itself down until Latona felt it safe to pull her hands out of the water.

As Merula scurried to dump the water back in the pool, a head of curly red hair appeared around a column. "Latona?" Alhena said. "You sounded— Uhm . . ."

"Alhena, darling!" Wiping her hands dry on her mantle, Latona blushed to realize she had not thought to ask for her other sister. It had been Aula she wanted to rant to and commiserate with, and her rage at Aemilia had overshadowed any other concerns. She smiled nervously. "I'm sorry. I didn't mean to disturb you."

Alhena padded forward. Her feet were bare, and Latona thought she saw ink smudges on her arms. Alhena curled up on the bench beside Latona, tucking her feet up under her. "What happened?" Latona hesitated, not wanting to burden her younger sister with her problems. But Alhena's azure eyes were earnestly wide, and Latona reminded herself that the baby of the family was swift becoming an adult. '*She deserves my trust as much as Aula.*'

She sighed, pushing her hair back with both hands. "I seem to have had a . . . sharp disagreement with the High Priestess of Juno."

"With Aemilia Fullia?" Alhena said. "I thought you two weren't on, uhm . . . the best of terms to begin with."

"Mm. And I suspect we're unlikely to become so anytime soon."

"So why did you . . ."

"I wanted access to the temple's library." Latona flexed her fingers, which were cold and stiff from the water. "I'm trying to . . . that, is, I want to . . ." Alhena took her hand, and somehow Latona found herself spilling the entire story to her baby sister—her loss of control, the desire she'd been feeling to use her magic, the urge to claim what had been denied her. Alhena knew some of her history with Aemilia, but she had only been four when Latona's service at the Temple ended, and so was hearing many of the details for the first time.

Brow furrowed, she said, "I don't understand why she's so afraid of you." Latona started to shrug it off, but Alhena squeezed her hand. "I know that look. You're going to pretend it doesn't matter." Latona blinked at her a few times, wondering when little Alhena had become so observant. "It does, though. Tell me."

Their entwined fingers reminded Latona that just a few minutes earlier, hers had been burning with unspent energy, primed for destruction. "*I* scare me sometimes. Why shouldn't others be afraid?"

Alhena snorted in a way that reminded Latona of Aula. "You've been listening to the wrong people."

"You may have a valid point."

"Not everyone's as fearful as Aemilia, is what I mean," Alhena went on. "Claudia wasn't. And in Stabiae . . ." Her lips twisted in consideration. "This city. It does something to people. Everyone's tense and scared and fighting for position." Latona stroked the back of her sister's hand with her thumb. She could feel the confusion of Alhena's emotions: sensations of feeling out of place, fear of failure, discombobulation, but beneath them all, something Latona recognized viscerally—the desire to *do* something, to be useful, helpful. But Alhena shook her head, as though dismissing that line of thought, and said, "So. You were looking for more information about Spirit magic?"

"I *know* there are texts there that would be useful. Claudia had started me on some of them before she died. But Aemilia refused me, and then—" She pulled her hands from Alhena's to gesture at the dented bolster pillow. "I lost my temper, a bit. But I didn't set anything on fire this time, and I don't want to worry you, little bird," she said, teasing out one of Alhena's curls. "I'll figure something out."

Frowning, Alhena leaned closer to Latona, searching her face as though she could read auguries in it. '*Maybe she can . . .*' Before she could share any insights, however, the door creaked open and slammed shut— Aula and Aulus returning.

Alhena stood up. "She'll want to talk politics with you," she said, "and I'm just not sure I have the energy."

"You're always welcome, you know."

Alhena smiled. "I know. Thank you." She started off toward her room, but paused, turning back over her shoulder. "It wasn't wrong, you know, leaving the temple," Alhena said. "You, I mean. That's not . . .

that's not where your path goes. I don't think it ever was." Her eyes, Latona noticed, were slightly unfocused—and when Latona reached out with a tendril of Spirit magic, she felt the cool, slippery sensation of Time magic at work. It faded quickly, however. Alhena gave her head a little shake, then rushed back to Latona and bestowed a swift kiss on the cheek. "Don't worry, sister," Alhena said. "We'll figure something out."

XVIII

"Damn the man! Damn him!"

Buteo had stormed his way from the newsreader's rostrum to the other end of the Forum, where Cornicen and Rabirus stood beneath the shade of the Temple of Castor, listening to the gossip from the lawyers and bankers as they conducted their business.

"I take it you've heard about Sempronius Tarren's latest plot, then?" Rabirus said, his expression calmer but no more pleased than Buteo's.

"Damn him!" Buteo rubbed at his thinning hair. "He's a menace. A damned menace. We've barely started campaigning, and he charges in with these, these grain doles and building projects!" He waved a hand back at the newsreader. "And now he's announced a feast!"

"Yes, it is damned menacing of him, to take the initiative on actually *governing* this city we're all squabbling over," Cornicen said, without any of Rabirus's evident concern. Cornicen seemed more interested in digging through his pouch of almonds. "The nerve of the man. Oh, don't make that face at me, Buteo. He's not doing anything the rest of us couldn't, if we chose—and if we had the wit to think of it."

Buteo's face grew ever more florid in his rage. "It's beyond highly irregular. He is—" Buteo waggled a fist mid-air, searching for the appropriate invectives. "He is usurping duties that do not belong to him—the duties of an aedile or urban praetor. It's a gross violation of precedent, an offense against the *mos maiorum!*"

"I don't see what the fuss is, really," Cornicen said. "It's not as though he's undermining any elected official's authority, since we *have* none at the moment. He's simply filling a necessary gap."

"It is highly irregular!" Buteo repeated.

"And the man has a point," Cornicen went on, unperturbed. "He was exiled in the middle of his term as aedile. This is really just paying the city what he owes."

"But no one sees it that way, Cornicen." Rabirus shook his head, disappointed by his friend's lack of vitriol. "The people will see this attention as a gesture of great generosity."

"Magnanimous." Buteo's face was creased with sour mockery. "The good Sempronius, the *noble* Sempronius, unjustly exiled and returned now to bestow his largesse upon the people of— of the Subura and the Esquiline!"

"Where'd he get the money for it, is what I want to know," Cornicen said, leaning back against a column and popping another almond in his mouth. "Building projects are expensive."

"He did well in Abydosia," Rabirus said. "Cozied up to the Menaphon's cousins and all manner of eastern merchants."

"Foreign interests," Buteo said. He jabbed a finger towards the Basilica that loomed above the north-eastern side of the Forum; people of all sorts poured through the yellow-veined marble archways of its long arcade, seeking or offering legal and financial services. Once, none but freeborn Aventan citizens would have been allowed to set foot there. "Corruptive influences."

"And I believe he's taking some loans from Galerius Orator."

"In return for using his influence with the mob to get Galerius elected consul, no doubt," Buteo sniffed. "Popularists everywhere. And he'll want the office for himself in time, don't mistake that."

"Of course he does," Cornicen said with a dismissive laugh. "That can't surprise you, surely. He's a man of good family, adequate income, and some intellect."

"What will surprise me," Buteo said, "is if he's satisfied with that. I wouldn't put it past him to do as Ocella did, make a Dictator out of himself, with all of that pandering he does— Would you *desist*?" Buteo said, glaring as Cornicen cracked down on another almond. Cornicen grinned irreverently.

Rabirus paced a few steps, envisioning the damage a man like Sempronius Tarren could do with the power that Ocella had wielded. Aven had seen demagogues before. They usually came to swift and bloody ends, and more often than not, through their own missteps and poorly calculated maneuvers.

Rabirus did not think Sempronius would be quick to stumble in that way. *'With the backing of the populace, the lower Classes, and the Head Count . . .'* They were easy to lead by the nose, loving a good show and empty charisma, and Sempronius had already shown himself willing to pander to them. *'If he has Ocella's instincts . . .'* Ocella's true genius, the quality which had brought him to power and kept him in it, was an instinct for knowing when the people were about to turn against him and then forestalling it. Ocella would push them to the brink of outrage, but whenever he went beyond the brink, he would distract the masses with a feast or games or races. Even on the occasions when riot erupted, he would find a way to turn the people's fury on someone else—a scheming senator, a corrupt adviser, an ambitious legate. Anyone but the Dictator, who acted, he assured them, for their own good. He would remind them why they had once loved him and handed him the power he wielded so viciously, and the trinkets he threw would quell their tumult, bringing their discontent back to manageable levels.

Ocella might not have been able to stay on top of the current forever—sooner or later, there would have been, if not a murderous mob, then a hidden dagger or a poisoned dish—but he might have stayed afloat for years longer had illness not felled him. *'Everyone falters eventually, no matter how secure they think themselves,'* Rabirus thought. *'But could this city survive the damage Sempronius could do in the meantime?'* It was not a risk he wanted Aven to take. And living under such a man was not a condition he would endure.

"So what do we *do*?" Buteo said, breaking into Rabirus's consideration. "How do we stop him?"

"We delay him, as best we can, in whatever he means to do." Rabirus's lips twitched. "And then excoriate him for every flaw, every fault we can find."

"Easy to say, harder to do," Cornicen said. "He's made some powerful strategic alliances. Aulus Vitellius and the Terentiae are hardly a surprise, liberally inclined as they are. And the Autroniae—"

Buteo made a choked noise. "Surely you don't mean to consider *them* consequential? Peasant stock. *Slave* stock!"

"But they have many friends," Rabirus said.

"And perhaps more importantly, a lot of money," Cornicen added. "And then there are the Galeriae."

"That's the real trouble there," Rabirus said, "that he should net such a powerful moderate, a man who *ought* to be standing with us, by all rights."

Cornicen nodded, tossing an almond in the air and catching it. Buteo glared at the offending drupe. "It's an interesting mix of allies. The power's not all political, I mean. Four families with seven mages between them, in addition to his own sister."

Buteo sniffed. "*Female* mages, for the most part, plus a child and a peasant."

Rabirus shook his head. "Don't be so short-sighted, Buteo. Just the fact that they're god-touched at all will impress many." Liberal or conservative, many Aventan plebs considered magically gifted families to be favored by the gods and therefore particularly fit to guide the nation. The aura of piety and authority extended from the mages to their kin.

"All he needs is for Quinta Terentia to smile at him in public," Cornicen said, nodding towards the round roof of the Temple of Vesta, halfway down the Forum from where they stood, "and he'll win over every pious-hearted equestrian in the city. They'll think Vesta herself wants Sempronius Tarren to lead."

Ocella had kept the temples in line with threats and bribes plus help from his own pet mages, but Rabirus knew that tension was unlikely to hold with the Dictator gone. They could not afford to overlook the symbolic power of Popularist mages. "As for the others, Marcia is perhaps the foremost Air mage in the city, Marcus Autronius is a well-respected Earth mage, and Vitellia Herenniae—"

He paused mid-thought, remembering the golden-haired Spirit mage as he had seen her on Capraia. The Dictator had never considered her a threat, as he had Marcia, but he *had* thought her worth further investigation. Rabirus had never been sure if that was strictly related to her talent or if it were a side effect of Ocella's interest in her more tangible charms. *'And which is it that Sempronius is interested in?'*

Using Spirit magic to tamper with electors was illegal, of course, but that did not mean it had never been done, especially if the influence was spread well before the election. *'Would he dare?'* But he hardly needed ask himself the question; Sempronius Tarren, he was convinced, would dare anything. Could *she* be convinced, then?

"What we need," Rabirus said, "is a pet mage of our own."

All three were quiet for a long moment, Rabirus in consideration, Buteo scuffing his sandals on the dusty ground. Then Cornicen, finally closing his pouch and tucking it back into his belt, said, "I may know someone. Walk with me."

Buteo and Rabirus exchanged a curious glance, then followed Cornicen as he trotted off the steps of the Temple of Castor and started across the forum. They passed the three sacred plants, grape, fig, and olive, each bedecked with ribbons and offerings, and pushed through several knots of conversing men. The Forum was neither solely political grounds, nor just a collection of temples. Business of all kinds went on here, and every contract in the city had to be sealed in the Forum, or it was not valid.

Rabirus's lip curled at a group of bald-pated Abydosians negotiating with two togate men. '*Shameful. They ought at least to have an Aventan factor to conduct business on their behalf. That foreigners can behave thusly, here, in the heart of Aven . . .*'

Cornicen drew to a halt in front of the Temple of Janus. Its massive bronze gates were closed—for now. The Gates of War opened when Aven had active engagements. They had last been open when the Vendelicians stirred up trouble in Albina, but with the northern tribes quiet, they had closed. If Sempronius Tarren had his way, they would be flung wide in Iberia's name by the end of the year.

"I want to be clear," Cornicen said, rubbing his sandy hair with an expression of mild chagrin. "I may not favor his politics, but I wish Sempronius no ill will. What you do with the information I give you is your own business, but I want no part of it."

"Very well, Cornicen, I understand," Rabirus said, though in his heart he castigated the man for a lack of commitment. Protecting the *mos maiorum* was not work for the weak-willed.

Cornicen sighed, nodding his head towards the temple. "There's a man in there, a priest by the name of Pinarius Scaeva." Buteo jerked slightly; the name was inauspicious, unlucky. Cornicen shrugged. "You want dark deeds done? Ask a man with a dark nature." Cornicen folded his arms, hugging his chest. "He's a Fracture mage with . . . well, I suppose you'd have to call it skill, though what you make of a talent for destruction . . ." He shook his head. "I saw him at the rites of the *Mundus* last year. Apparently he insists on being the one to open the portal to the netherworld. No one else has done it as long as he's held his position."

That told Rabirus quite a bit about the man's character. The *Mundus* was a subterranean gate located beneath the Temple of Janus, opened only three days a year—cursed days, *nefasti*, when unsettled spirits roamed the land of the living. The man who opened the gate risked his own soul. Just the thought made Rabirus shiver, despite the sun bearing down on them from the broad, empty sky.

"If anyone can disrupt Sempronius's plans," Cornicen said, "he'll be able to. But it'll cost you. From what I understand, Pinarius doesn't come cheap."

"It would be worth it," Rabirus said. "Whatever it costs . . . it *will* be worth it."

XIX

For the politically-minded in Aven, October was a whirlwind of negotiations, speech-making, and alliance-coagulating. As the month wore on, the women of the Vitellian household found themselves in the thick of it all. Aulus's clients had proved ever more attentive since he had announced his candidacy for censor, turning up before dawn to await their chance to speak with him. Aulus had a reputation for beneficence towards those the Optimates deemed "the rabble." Half of his clients were of families only in the first or second generation of holding Aventan citizenship—and many of those had relations still bearing only the lesser Truscan rights. Buteo's proposals had them all anxious. Aulus's election could secure a great many futures, and his clients were eager to make sure he was aware of their devotion.

Aula believed it was her filial duty to further the family's ambitions, and she received visitors with Aulus or in his absence—not only clients, but allies as well. Though Alhena could scarce be coaxed from her room to assist, Latona spent many afternoons at Aula's side, finding the entertainment better than what could be had at the Herennian domus.

Galerius came often, sometimes with his son in tow, discussing strategies for the election. General Strato blustered in on occasion, roaring amiably, as did Rufilius Albinicus, offering advice on Gaius's military career and seeking news from Iberia. With him came his son, Young Rufilius, giving Aula someone to flutter her eyelashes at. The Autroniae were frequent guests, and Felix gave Aula merry flirtations as well. If Latona happened to visit on the afternoons when both Felix and Rufilius were present, she could sometimes hardly breathe for laughing at their antics.

And Sempronius Tarren would stop by, to discuss matters military and political. Aula would laugh and tease and beg for Forum gossip, which Sempronius happily provided. Sempronius was even gracious enough to tolerate Lucia's presence. He brought the little girl a toy model of a lion with moving arms and legs, which she now prized alongside her favorite doll. But sometimes, if Aula was napping or had wandered out on some errand or other, Latona would have a few precious moments alone with Sempronius.

Something had happened in the weeks since their strange conversation following the Cantrinalia. Their growing friendship spurred something warm inside her, an unexpected tenderness—but too, she felt freer in his presence. There was less need to draw down the persona of polished grace and cool regard that she found useful in other social situations. It was not merely a matter of relaxation: It was a liberty, to needle him and allow him to push back, a mutual challenge that sparked something in her mind and heated her blood.

She had a suspicion it was going too far.

With so many comings and goings, it was little surprise when the steward let Sempronius into their atrium shortly after the Ides of October. "I came to invite Aulus Vitellius and his daughters out for a walk," he explained. "I have a new project in the works and would be grateful for your master's opinion."

"Dominus Vitellius is out for the afternoon, Senator," the steward, Paenas, answered. "As for the ladies—"

"Alhena is indisposed!" Aula chirped, coming around the corner with Latona in tow. "But perhaps Latona and I could still join you, if you don't mind strictly feminine companionship."

Paenas fluttered a mild objection, though Latona wasn't sure if it was more at their sudden appearance or at the suggestion that they join Sempronius without their father present. Sempronius, however, inclined his head politely. "I would be honored to escort you, ladies."

Aula's eyes flicked to Latona, then back to Sempronius, then a broad grin broke over her face. "Oh, *no*," she said, in a tone that utterly failed to convey any sorrow, "I'm afraid I've just remembered. I'm due over at Maia Domitia's this afternoon. Lucia's such friends with her girls, you know, and she's just got her heart set on seeing them. But we couldn't possibly leave you bereft of company when you've come all this way, Senator. Latona, you should *certainly* go with him."

Latona stared at her sister, shocked more at her utter lack of subtlety than at the suggestion that she alone should accompany Sempronius. For his part, Sempronius's chest was shaking with suppressed laughter. "Well, Lady Aula, I shall mourn the loss of your excellent company."

"And where will we be going?" Latona asked.

"I think I'll keep it a secret," Sempronius said, his eyes crinkling up at the corners. "You'll be perfectly safe, on my life . . . though I will caution that you may be dressed a touch too finely for the occasion."

"She can borrow something plainer from me," Aula offered, before Latona could get out so much as a word. "Come on, my dove, let's alter your plumage."

Once secluded in her own chamber, Aula wasted no time unpinning Latona's stola and shucking it off her. "What in Juno's name are you playing at?" Latona asked as Aula tossed the azure gown to Helva and went to a trunk to pull out a plainer garment. "That was somewhat lacking in your usual social grace."

"Well," Aula said, shrugging, "I had to think quickly—"

"You might've had longer if you hadn't dragged me out of the library as soon as you heard him cross the threshold."

"—And I *told* you we ought to cultivate Sempronius Tarren."

"No, you told me *I* ought to cultivate him."

"So?" Aula grinned brightly as she draped an unembellished stola of burgundy wool around her sister's shoulders, fastening it with bronze pins. "I thought, after the Cantrinalia, that you'd taken my advice, and now here he's given you a fine opportunity to gauge his mettle outside of the *triclinium*. And I can't think you truly object to spending the afternoon with such an intriguing gentleman."

Latona could feel her cheeks turning scarlet. Her heart had no objection at all, but good sense was willing to provide what instinct lacked. She had to hope the delight she took in Sempronius's company wouldn't be as obvious to anyone they encountered as it was to her sister. She settled her hands on her hips, though it was difficult to affect a stern demeanor when faced with Aula's relentless cheerfulness. "Meeting him by chance on the way home was one thing, Aula, but this is quite another. It's going to look like he's—"

"Come courting?"

"No. I mean, yes! I mean—" She huffed. It was hard to think with Aula fluttering around her. "I *am* married, you recall?"

"Yes, you are married, to a man who's chosen to forsake the city weeks before the first proper elections we've had in years. Who thinks it more important to look after his olive trees than his political future." Aula snorted, snatching up a tawny mantle and pinning it into Latona's hair. "As such, I think he could hardly fault you for doing what you can to further strategic alliances for the *rest* of the family. You do have Father and Gaius to think about."

"You might be surprised to learn that Herennius's ideas of what he can fnd fault with differ somewhat from yours."

Aula spun Latona around, fussed with her curls, and smoothed out her mantle. "In that case, I see no reason why your husband ever need *know* about the friendships you choose to nurture on your family's behalf."

"And what do I do when gossips' tongues start wagging?"

"It isn't as though you won't have Merula with you. Feisty little thing makes a perfect chaperone." She pinched color into Latona's cheeks, making her yelp. "Go on now. I expect to hear *everything* when you return."

∞∞∞∞∞∞∞∞∞∞∞∞

Latona and Sempronius, with Merula trailing behind them, stepped out under a sky heavy-hung with gray clouds. As October dwindled away, autumn's fingers had finally reached down into Aven. The pines that dominated much of Truscum stayed evergreen, but other trees burst into flagrant color, then shrunk to brittle spindles. Even in downpours, the Forum had been crowded with candidates hawking their platforms, surrounded by clients and detractors alike. Latona expected that Sempronius would lead her in that direction, but instead, they turned south and west, towards the Aventine Hill and the Tiber River. "Don't worry, Lady Latona," he said, as they passed the Circus Maximus, "I'm not leading you down towards the docks—though I do have some projects ongoing there as well."

"You've been a busy man, Senator."

"What was it the old Athaecan fabulist said, of the noble virtues of the bees? Ever busy is ever happy?"

"Then you must be the happiest man in Aven," she teased.

"Not yet, Lady Latona," he answered, inclining his head towards her with a playfully conspiratorial smile. "Not quite yet." He helped her down from the uneven bit of sidewalk where a tangle of sidestreets collided, then tucked her hand into the crook of his elbow as they went on—an intimate gesture that Latona was only too happy to indulge. Merula coughed meaningfully behind them, but Latona ignored her. She was too delighted with him and with this adventure.

They skirted the Circus Maximus. Outside the Temple of Hercules, a plebeian Light mage was performing some basic illusions to the delight of a knot of squealing children, while their nursemaid, a flaxen-haired girl with a northern look to her, tried unsuccessfully to herd them away. Latona was glad when Sempronius took the path closer to the wharves rather than the temple-lined street closer to the Circus: the neighborhood was less savory and potentially more dangerous, but so alive! Sempronius pointed out the sails of a few boats that were known to him, those which brought Abydosian goods up from Aven's main port of Ostia, at the mouth of the Tiber. Here was the lifeblood of the Aventan Republic, its vigor flowing in from a hundred sources. However unorthodox the outing, Latona beamed with pleasure, enjoying the simple, everyday chaos of the streets.

The Aventine Hill was, like the city at large, a strange mix of grandiose and grubby. Even the patrician domuses here were smaller, older, crowded closer together than those on the northern hills. Nothing on the lower end, here by the river, had been allowed to become decrepit; the area near the Hut of the Twins was still revered, and the neighborhood collegia kept things in line. It was a different story on the southern side of the hill.

Before dog-legging up the hill, the lane opened up into a small forum in front of the temple complex dedicated to Ceres, Liber, and Libera, the plebeian counterparts to the supreme triad of Jupiter, Juno, and Minerva who sat atop the Capitoline. The three temples stood at right angles to one another, with a great open area and a decorative fountain in the middle. On this afternoon, however, the space was filled with a hundred tables, around which a crowd thronged. Slaves carried trays and platters back and forth, so that the assembly could eat their fill. "A public feast?" Latona asked. "It's not a holiday. Is this your doing?"

"A small portion of what I owe to them. Ocella robbed me of the chance to throw games and feasts during my aedileship. I am trying, in some minute way, to make it up to them now." Sempronius had a brightness in his cheeks as he regarded the crowd. "These people are the backbone of Aven, little credit though they get for it. They deserve recognition."

"And hoping that they'll remember your beneficence in two months' time?" Sempronius inclined his head in recognition. "It's a magnificent sort of bribery." Not only bread, nuts, cheeses, and vegetables, but roast fowl and boar, fresh fruit, goose eggs, fish, mushrooms, and delicate honeyed pastries loaded the tables. Latona even saw a dish of snails go by—an extravagance most citizens of the Aventine could only dream of tasting.

"Only the unscrupulous bribe outright," Sempronius said. "I prefer the indirect method." He gestured out at the scene. "Shall we?"

"Indeed."

Latona was surprised at how many people Sempronius already knew, not only the wealthier merchants, but also the lower orders of shopkeepers and artisans. *'He seems so at ease here, with them all.'* It ought to have been incongruous, for a man of such prestige and such ancient family to seem more comfortable moving among the people of the Aventine than he did in the finest patrician dining rooms, and yet, for Sempronius, it felt entirely right. Latona took pleasure in watching him in his element—and more, each time he put her on his arm or placed a hand at her waist to gently steer her around the crowd. He was treating her, she realized, the way Lucius Quinctilius had always treated Aula: keeping her close at hand, introducing her to his friends, sharing jokes and private observations with her. And, so casually that it had almost not occurred to her to notice, he was treating her not as a guest but as a partner.

'What would it be like,' she wondered, her heart giving a pang at the thought, *'if this were my everyday?'*

When they drew near the platform at the top of the courtyard, Sempronius paused, adjusting his toga slightly. "I did the formal dedication of the feast this morning, of course, but not *all* of them have camped out here all day. So, if you will permit me, I shall leave you in Merula's excellent care, just for a moment."

As Sempronius ascended the platform, a nearby attendant blew on a horn for attention. The plebeian crowd fell, if not silent, at least quieter, considering that a few minutes of listening to a speech was a small price to pay for a free meal. "Good people of the Aventine!" His voice carried as easily as it had the night of the riots—a commander's voice. Latona flushed with admiration. "I am Vibius Sempronius Tarren, and I bid you enjoy this feast, given in the names of Ceres, Liber, and Libera, protectors of you all!" This met with a good-natured cheer, which Sempronius allowed to subside before repeating the general dedication of a feast to the gods.

Latona kept her eyes resolutely forward, looking at the assembled plebs rather than Sempronius. She sent out little tendrils of Spirit magic, reading the mood of the crowd. She found it contented and appreciative, if not overwhelmingly enthused. The people of the Aventine were a notoriously tough crowd, proud of the lives they built for themselves and disdainful of attempts to influence them. They were not so easily bought as the Optimates claimed.

Latona again felt that desire to help where she could. As at the Esquiline riot, she knew herself unable to influence an entire crowd at once. *'And that might, technically, be perceived as illegally tampering with an election, in these circumstances.'* But she could, perhaps, give Sempronius a little nudge.

And so, even as she began to turn the golden tendrils of her Spirit magic towards boosting him, Sempronius finished his invocations and glanced around at the temples. "And yet, citizens, friends, I think we owe the gods more." A bit of a curious murmur arose. "For look—" With his right hand, he gestured at the three surrounding porticos. "Their houses fade and crack! Is this right and proper for the goddess whose bounty has allowed our city to grow? Whose beneficence nourishes you even today? Is this right and proper," Sempronius asked, curling his free hand into a fist, "for the god and goddess who guarantee you your rights? Your votes? Your freedom?"

The cries of "No!" were loud and forceful. Latona could feel a swell in the assembly; pride and indignation mixed together.

"No, it is not!" Sempronius echoed. "And I mean to remedy it. I vow to you, I will see these temples restored to glory!" That elicited some cheers. Latona spun the positive energy back around, funneling it towards Sempronius. "My men have already begun work restoring the friezes depicting Ceres's search for her daughter. They should, fittingly, be completed by spring."

There was applause, and pounding of tables, and a few cries of his name, a few of "Liber!" and "Aventine!" Sempronius let it go on a moment, echoing out into the street beyond, then raised his hand to call again for quiet. Latona gave him another encouraging push of energy. He seemed to stand taller, his eyes shone with bold intent, and even his toga seemed brighter, gleaming as though the sun shone on marble, not on chalked wool.

"But this is not all I mean to do!" he announced. "I shall not only restore these fine and ancient temples to the dignity they ought to own, but I intend to construct a new temple as well—a temple to Victoria!"

'Oh dear,' Latona thought, mildly concerned that she may have overdone it on the magical encouragement. *'I hope he had already intended to do that .'*

He went on: "A temple to honor the spirit that has carried our people forward through the centuries. A temple to honor the legions, the men who defend our borders and expand our realm. A temple to honor the greatness of the city—this city, this grand nation, born *here* on the Aventine!"

'Neatly done,' Latona thought. He could certainly not manage to build a whole new temple before the elections, but the promise was a brilliant one, and all the more because he had so deftly linked the city's welfare and the Aventine's pride to the idea of conquest by the legions.

"I thank you all for your time," Sempronius said, "and most humbly implore you to continue to live good lives, do your duty to the state, and show all devotion and piety to the gods." With a final wave, Sempronius stepped down from the platform, returning to Latona's side.

It took them some time to make their way out of the Aventine Triad complex, with even more men and women coming forward to speak to Sempronius or press his hand. When they finally did emerge, Sempronius took a moment to divest himself of the cumbersome *toga candida,* handing it over to his attendant.

"My apologies," he said, taking her arm again, "but they expect such things, from the host of the feast."

"Of course," Latona said, smiling. "You're quite entertaining to watch."

"I'm pleased you think so!" he laughed. "I confess it can be wearying, day in and out in the Forum. I think I prefer speaking to the people more informally."

Remembering his casual familiarity with the men of the Esquiline college, Latona nodded. "Aula used to drag me along to the Forum to watch Quinctilius speak, but he never had the gift for oratory."

"My father thought it the most important component of my education," Sempronius said. "'Words move the people,' he said. He hired so many rhetoricians that there were hardly enough hours in the day for all my lessons."

Latona tilted her head; Sempronius had never spoken to her of his father, not that she could remember, nor of his childhood. She knew little of Old Vibius, who had been a venerated elder before her own father had ever entered the Senate. "He must have been quite devoted to your education."

"He was devoted to making sure neither Vibia nor I embarrassed our ancient name," Sempronius said. "Well. Three wives pre-deceased him, and he only had the two of us to show for it. By the time I came along, I think he knew there weren't going to be any other opportunities for legacy, so he invested quite a lot in making sure I came up to scratch. Nothing less than perfection for the scion of one of Aven's founding families."

Latona sensed an unusual emotion in that moment, far more tender and quiet than she was used to from him. Sempronius typically exuded an aura of unshakable solidity, so confident and forthright. Even when relaxed and among friends, he never seemed less than entirely self-possessed and sure of his place in the universe. Not many, she guessed, had the opportunity to glimpse what lay beneath that conviction. *'What a privilege.'*

They turned uphill, towards the Aqua Appia. "I can't imagine he could have found fault with you," Latona said. "I'm sure he was very proud."

"He died before I had made anything of myself," Sempronius said, a touch of wistfulness in his voice. "I hadn't even been selected as a military tribune yet. He knew the path he had set me on, though, and I believe he died with confidence I would achieve what was necessary." His faraway gaze dissolved into a smile. "Though I confess, I hope to outstrip even his expectations. And this will be a start." He guided Latona off the road and onto a broad, rocky outcrop of undeveloped land. "Here. Future site of the Temple to Victoria Gloriana."

She turned in a slow circle, taking in the location. "It has a good view of the river."

"Not that the docks are always much to look at, as I'm well aware." He nodded in the direction of his own home, not much farther up the hill. "But see if you can picture this. The entrance there, then long porticos with columns of Abydosian granite, and along the sides, murals detailing Aven's greatest military victories. Veii, Vocontia, Callipolis, the Padus River." Sempronius spoke the names like they were his intimate friends. "And the more recent as well—the Tyrian Wars, the conquests of Athaeca and Albina, and, gods willing, the restoration of order to Iberia." He put a hand at the small of her back and guided her in a half circle. His head dipped next to hers, close enough to set her heart into a rapid patter, as he pointed across the outcrop at a space between two spindly trees. "The *cella* with her statue there, so that the rising sun will fall on Victoria's face—but anyone paying homage to her will have to face west."

"Towards *your* victories," Latona commented, smiling over her shoulder at him.

"Naturally," Sempronius replied. His hand, Latona realized, was still around her, and she had no desire to move away. Quite the opposite: she found herself fighting the maddening instinct to curl into him and rest her head on his shoulder. "It's hard to envision now, I know. I'll have to show you some of the sketches my architects have done."

Just as Latona was wondering if she were far more affected by their cozy proximity than he was, Sempronius turned to face her. When their eyes met, Latona felt a swell of emotion from him, so passionate it near staggered her. *'Oh . . .'*

His fingers came up to her face, as though to brush a hair back behind her ear, but hovered there, untouching. For a moment, Latona wondered if he were going to kiss her. For a moment, she desperately wanted him to—but then a crashing noise from somewhere downhill made them both look away, shattering the illusory privacy of the moment.

At the stark reminder that they were in public view, Latona drew back from him in an attempt to reassert some form of propriety. "Well, I eagerly anticipate the project's completion." She swiveled to take his arm, and they started towards the southern slope, back towards the Palatine Hill. "You're doing incredible work."

"You could, too, you know."

"I'm hardly likely to contribute to the city's architectural glory."

"I don't mean in that way."

"I know you don't." Latona pressed her lips thin. "Perhaps I shall." She caught his grin out of the corner of her eye. He had been expecting another demurral; the idea that she had surprised him was strangely satisfying.

By the time they reached the south end of the Circus Maximus, not far from her father's house, darker clouds were gathering overhead, suggesting another rain storm would not be long off. Sempronius pulled her aside, out of the street, to stand beneath a juniper tree whose branches swayed with the strengthening breeze. "Lady Latona. I hope you believe you can trust me."

A heat rose in her blood that had nothing to do with unruly magic. *'Yes, Sempronius Tarren, I would trust you if I had the liberty to do so . . . but what trouble that might cause, I don't know if I am prepared to find out . . .'*

Before she could make any answer, Merula rushed forward, taking Latona's arm from Sempronius's and pulling her aside. "My apologies, Senator," she muttered, "but you should see—" As Latona turned to see what had put her companion into a panic, a sudden darkness clouded Sempronius's face.

"Sempronius Tarren." Rabirus, accompanied by several tough-looking clients, had joined them on the knoll at the crossroads, and between their own absorption in conversation and the bustle of Aventan life around them, they had not noticed his approach until he was nearly upon them.

Unable to keep her expression from displaying her disdain, Latona felt her lip curl as Rabirus drew nearer. For her, Rabirus was a reminder of Ocella's court and things best left in the past, and she could not swallow her discomfiture at his unexpected presence. Sempronius, however, greeted him with all outward semblances of civility. "Lucretius Rabirus. Hail and well met."

"And Lady . . . Vitellia Herenniae, I believe?" Hearing the marital form of her name, which she never used, either formally or informally, irked her, almost as much as that he should pretend not to know her, but she nodded. "What brings you to such an unconventional promenade?"

"I might ask you the same," Sempronius said. He moved forward, placing himself between her and Rabirus. "I would ask if you were merely strolling this area for pleasure, but considering your dress and your entourage, I must assume you're about on business." For Rabirus was togate, fully swathed in the red-bordered senatorial garb.

"I heard there was quite a to-do on the Aventine," Rabirus said. "I thought it would behoove me to check in. The last thing any of us want is more unpleasantness such as followed Dictator Ocella's funeral."

"Then I am happy to put your mind at ease. It is no riot, but a feast thrown in honor of the Aventine Triad," Sempronius lifted his chin in anticipatory defiance. "At my expense."

Rabirus gave little outward sign of consternation, but a few of the men behind him shifted subtly into a fighting posture. Close beside Latona, Merula tensed. "Be ready, Domina," she whispered. "If trouble starts, you run."

"You have been such a busy man," Rabirus said. An echo of Latona's earlier words, but from Rabirus, they oozed with vitriol. "It's difficult to keep up with all of your good works."

"And yet you have spared them such attention," Sempronius said. "With such administrative dedication. Why, I think I should put out that I'm supporting you for *urban* praetor." A twitch in Rabirus's cheek indicated that he had caught the implication. The position, though critical to the city, was known to be exhausting, expensive, and largely thankless. "I would be happy to share my thoughts on what else needs improvement.

So much got neglected these past few years, as you no doubt know. The road to Ostia, perhaps? Improving the drainage of the Cloaca Maxima? Or perhaps you're more interested in pure construction. I've spoken to architects from Abydosia about tenement conditions in the Subura—"

"That won't be necessary." Rabirus's gaze went beyond Sempronius, lingering on Latona in a way that that she found too bold. She resisted the urge to pull her mantle closer about her shoulders, instead clenching her hands into fists as she tried to avert her Fire magic causing another accidental conflagration. "Lady Vitellia, I wonder that it did not occur to you that your presence at such an event might be inappropriate."

Latona lifted her eyebrows. "I had no idea the Aventine had been declared off-limits to women. What a disappointment for the thousands of them who reside there." Rabirus's silence managed to convey how little her quip impressed him. Though Latona knew she ought to feign meekness, as she had so often done to escape notice in Ocella's court, she could not seem to govern her tongue sufficiently. "If the Senator has been good enough to indulge my interest in his charitable works, I hardly think that a matter for intervention."

"Cavorting about the lesser neighborhoods of the city is most unusual for a *patrician* woman."

Latona felt her temper rising. "Unusual is not unfit." She knew how to quiet the heated emotions, knew how to bite her tongue and endure humiliations, had done so over and over again for years. *'But why should I answer insult with civility? Not now, not any longer. Not for such a vile creature as Rabirus.'*

As much curiosity as contempt lived in Rabirus's eyes as they roved over her. "And just because a thing is not forbidden does not mean that it is proper. The place for a patrician woman is in her home, seeing to domestic felicity." Rabirus's eyes flicked meaningfully towards Sempronius. "I wonder what your husband thinks of your dabbling in such curious matters, and with such company."

"I'm sure you are the very *last* person whose opinion I would—"

Sempronius touched Latona's shoulder. "Lady Latona," he said in a low voice, "you should go."

"I can hold my own, if that's what—"

"I have no doubt." The shadow of a smile touched the corner of Sempronius's mouth; Latona dared to hope it might be born of pride. "But he's here for me, and he's not likely to let us alone until he gets whatever it is he came for."

"I would stand with you," she replied in a fierce whisper, "and I have things of my own to say to that man."

"Latona." Her empathic magic felt a sudden flare from Sempronius: fear, little though she would have expected it. Fear for her and for what he might do if Rabirus menaced her further. "He's baiting you to get a rise out of me, and if he keeps it up, I am likely to satisfy him in that respect."

She pressed her lips in a tight line. However great the temptation to give Rabirus a piece of her mind, she would not want Sempronius to bear the indignity of losing his composure on her behalf. "Then I shall choose a more advantageous field of battle for that conversation."

The sharpness of his fear, prickling at her senses, gave way to relief. "Thank you." Despite Rabirus's presence, he risked taking her hand and pressing it briefly. "I regret that our afternoon must end so abruptly. I shall endeavor to make it up to you."

Latona gestured to Merula, stepped around Sempronius, and addressed Rabirus again, in a voice of perfect honey. "Senator, I thank you. Your consideration for the welfare of Aven extends to the moral virtue of every citizen, it appears. I shall take myself home to contemplate what damage my uncommon proclivities might do to the threads which bind our nation together." Head bowed, hands folded together in front of her, Latona floated on down the street, Merula, still tense, at her side.

◇◇◇◇◇◇◇◇◇◇◇◇◇◇◇

A less perceptive man might have taken her for sincere. Sempronius did not think Rabirus missed the sarcasm. *'What a lioness.'* Latona would have stood by him and given Rabirus the tongue-lashing he desperately deserved—a boldness he had long sensed in her but knew she had suppressed for most of her life. *'How glad I am to know Ocella was not able to douse that fire, even when it was kept to embers.'* As she disappeared up the street, Sempronius forced himself not to watch her, instead letting his gaze drift appraisingly over Rabirus.

The two men stood in simmering silence for a moment before Rabirus said, "So. Feasting the plebs. At considerable expense, I would guess. Your ambition is considerable."

"I seek to do well by my city and my gods," Sempronius said. "The citizens of the Aventine deserve as much recognition and honor as those who live on the Palatine or the Caelian."

Rabirus's nostrils flared. "You flatter these menials to buy yourself an election."

"Their votes are their own," Sempronius returned, "but it is the business of a politician to demonstrate that he will best represent their interests."

"Pandering." Rabirus's lip curled into its familiar sneer. "You cannot convince them to support you on your merits, so you toss them trinkets and promise them the moon. You are the weaker for it—and they are the worse off for allowing themselves so cravenly to be bought."

"If you think that," Sempronius said, "you have even less understanding of this city than I credited." It was not only the insult to so much of the city that infuriated Sempronius, but the stubborn blindness to intrinsic worth; the utter inability to value what other people could do. Men like Rabirus, with their insular arrogance, jeopardized the city's future.

"This is the same belief, I take it, that drives you to such demagoguery in the Forum."

"You may call it what you like. But I have at all times acted in accordance with the laws of our ancestors and the will of the gods."

"Not just ambitious," Rabirus said, stepping swiftly forward, "but arrogant. I've warned you before, Sempronius Tarren, what the gods think of men who overreach."

Sempronius did not flinch. "And the very moment *they* reveal their displeasure to me, I assure you, I shall alter my course."

Rabirus opened his mouth to speak, then closed it again, with an odd satisfaction in his eye that Sempronius found concerning. When he spoke again, his tone was too placid, too falsely harmonious. "Well. I'm sure we're all eager to find out what else you have in store." He turned to leave, then said over his shoulder, as his clients hastily rearranged themselves around him, "And I will be keeping a close eye on your projects, I assure you."

XX

As Latona stalked home, she felt the tingling in her fingers that she had come to recognize as a warning. Rabirus's words had ignited the fire in her blood, and her indignation gave the violent magic space to rise, hot and insistent. *'Domestic felicity, indeed.'* It was too like Aemilia Fullia's chastisement and too presumptuous by half, even if he weren't a vile specimen to begin with. *'And bringing Herennius into it, as though—'* She could feel her nostrils flare in irritation, not least because, as righteously indignant as she wanted to be, she knew her emotions regarding Sempronius fell short of the chastity expected of Aventan matrons.

Desperate for an outlet other than arson, she went to her own home rather than her father's and sat down at the loom, hoping busy hands might forestall another flagrant catastrophe.

The shuttle flew beneath her fingertips. Through weaving, Latona could refocus her energy, bleeding off the heat of her anger and entwining it instead into constructive magic. *'And anyway, Gaius must be needing new tunics and socks.'* Women often provided the men of their family with clothing when they went on campaign, and in the Vitelliae household, that duty often fell to Latona because of her gifts. She was not particularly clever with needle and thread, nor even a very swift weaver, but her talents gave something more to the garments than style or form: she could give them protection.

No one quite knew the reason, but magic and the battlefield never went well together, at least not directly. Mars was jealous of his domain, and since he blessed no mages, he would not allow them to tip the scales of war. The annals of history were full of tales of men being sucked dry by the effort. Summon a fire, and it would flare back in your face. Summon a gale, and find yourself blown away by it. Summon the rocks to hurl against your enemy, and find the ground opening into an endless maw beneath your own feet. Disaster befell every man who made the attempt.

Mages might duel in private—indeed, such spectacles were often staged as part of public games and festivals—but never on the battlefield.

According to the priests, magic in warcraft was a right the gods reserved for themselves, and they did not take it kindly when mortals usurped that power.

Fire, though, retained a connection to the battlefield, albeit in an oblique way. Fire was the dominion not only of Venus but of her husband Vulcan, forger of the weapons of the gods. Used defensively, Fire magic could make a tremendous difference on the battlefield, so long as its power was placed in protection, not in weaponry. As such, one of the chief functions of the Temple of Vulcan was to oversee the blessings of military gear. Generals made sacrifices there before setting out on campaign, to ask that their legions' weapons be sharp, their armor sound, their endurance unflinching.

Every legionary tried to have at least one item of his kit blessed, though it was, of course, best to have it *created* by someone with magical talent. Many legionaries, even those who came from humble backgrounds, considered it well worth the investment to visit a Fire-forger as soon as they had the sesterii to spare. These men would put their gifts into every scale of a legionary's segmented armor. For the right price. Others, whose craftsmanship ran in a different direction, sold amulets and charms; these were far less expensive than armor, and even the most impecunious soldier generally managed to hang at least one about his neck. It wasn't always enough; men still died, even in enchanted gear, but it did help to turn blades, to resist blows, to reduce the damage done by wounds.

According to Gaius Vitellius, the choice could be an important illumination of a man's character. It said a lot about a man if, for instance, he chose to have his sword blessed instead of his shield. But the very canniest legionaries, in Gaius's opinion, hied themselves not to a Fire-forger, but rather to an Earth mage, and got their *caligae*, their hobnailed leather sandals, blessed. "Nothing," Gaius had written to his sisters after his hike from Legio VIII's camp to Nedhena, "is more important than taking care of your feet." Latona easily understood how that could be so. The legions marched everywhere they went. Only the senior legates and the generals rode horses. Everyone else walked. A Fire-forger's protection charms could guard against injury to the feet, but for the promise of comfort, to escape blisters and bunions and aches of all kinds, smart soldiers went to the Priestesses of Ceres and asked that their shoes, which would have so much connection with the mother earth in the months and years ahead, not fail them.

Latona's gifts fell more naturally under Venus's domain than Vulcan's, but she could still work protective Fire magic when she wove. It was not quite as vital as armor or a shield, but, all the same, a man could go nowhere without a tunic, and so it might as well be a magically enhanced one. Latona's tunic would keep Gaius warm and dry in damp weather; with Fire's power for purification, it would resist the grime and filth that could lead to infection if he got wounded. It would give him a boost of courage and faith, a sense that victory was possible, when most he needed the bolster. With such methods, the Aventan armies conquered, even without using magic in battle itself. It had worked for centuries, it would work now.

And so, as Latona's fingers flew, she let herself fall into a deep concentration. The work put her in a sort of meditative haze, bearing the sense of peace and contentment she felt when the magic found its natural channels. Latona let the shuttle rock back and forth through her hands, pulling the crimson threads tightly together. She whispered prayers as she wove, and her fingers tingled with a slight reddish glow—the proof of Fire magic at work and under her control.

Hours passed, and it was well into the evening before footsteps brought her out of her work—fast, light steps, padding rapidly from the atrium, with a more even set behind them. Then a cheerful voice calling, "Aunt Lala, Aunt Lala!"

Latona froze, set oddly off-kilter by the imposition into her pleasantly thoughtless cocoon. Slightly dizzied as she surfaced from the magically induced haze, Latona became aware of the weariness in her hands, the prickling pain in her fingers, the ache in her shoulders and neck. Then she let the shuttle rest, turning just as her niece hurtled into the room, with Aula's voice echoing from the atrium. "Lucia, do not run—"

Latona was blinking rapidly, trying to re-accustom her vision to something other than the back-and-forth motion of the thread. Oblivious, Lucia crawled right up into her lap. "Aunt Lala, Gera helped me learn a poem. Do you want to hear?"

"Aunt Lala" was a nickname generated before Lucia could pronounce Latona's full name, but it had stuck, and Latona now suspected she would bear it until Lucia's maturity. Trying to ground herself back in the moment, she stroked Lucia's hair. "I would indeed, darling. What did Gera teach you?"

"She said it's called the 'Poem of the Nine.'" Latona nodded. Lucia's foreign-born nursemaid might not know the significance, but the Poem of the Nine was a typical component of every Aventan's early religious education.

"Go on then, little love."

Lucia interlaced her fingers, worrying her lower lip, then took a deep, searching breath and started. "Earth supports, Air directs; Water nourishes, Fire protects; Spirit inspires, Light reveals; Time measures, Shadow conceals; Fracture marks the lines between; Thus do all the Nine convene." Then she blinked large blue eyes up at Latona. "Was that right?"

"Exactly so."

As Latona was pressing a kiss to her niece's forehead, Aula strode into the room, looking harried. "I'm sorry, Latona, she got ahead of me, and then Merula didn't want to let me in, but when I heard how long you'd been at it, I decided that was—Oh, Bona Dea," Aula lamented, crinkling her nose at the loom. "I've a message from Father, but I didn't imagine I'd find you quite so . . . domestic. Please tell me that's not for Herennius. I don't know if I could bear being in the presence of such a display of marital devotion."

"It's for Gaius," Latona chided. "To send to him in Iberia." It felt so strange to focus on something other than the back-and-forth motion of the thread, it almost hurt to look at anything else, and Latona rubbed at her eyes with the heels of both hands.

Aula's tone changed. "Oh. I'm sorry, you *were* in the middle of something, weren't you?"

"No, no, it's best you interrupted me," Latona said, still rubbing. "It wouldn't do for me to lose myself like this for much longer. I'd sleep for a week after."

Aula came to sit next to Latona. "Well, it's good of you to be doing it," Aula said. Lucia peered with interest at the loom. Latona gathered she didn't often see one in use in her mother's home. Aula had such distaste for it, and for Alhena, the repetitive motion might trigger a prophetic trance—not an endeavor undertaken lightly—so most of the weaving for the Vitellian household took place in the slave quarters.

'I should teach the girl, though,' Latona thought, as Lucia reached a tentative hand up to stroke the crimson wool. 'She might end up hating it as much as her mother, but she at least ought to have the skill to her name. She'll be five soon. That's not too young to start.' Latona handed her niece a ball of wool to pluck at and stretch out, then asked Aula, "You came for a reason, I take it?"

"Yes, I'm afraid I did," Aula said. "Father wants us. Both of us. He sent Haelix to fetch me from Maia Domitia's, with instructions to collect you on the way."

Latona stood up quickly. Their father was not given to summoning them from work or leisure. "What's wrong?"

"He didn't say. He came home with a letter of some sort. Apparently it warrants discussion."

∞∞∞∞∞∞∞∞∞∞∞

When Latona and Aula entered their father's house, he was in the garden with Alhena. Lines of worry creased his face. "Girls. Sit down, please." All three daughters dropped themselves onto couches, and then Aulus turned to Helva, Merula, and Mus. "You may go." Aula and Latona exchanged nervous looks. Aulus rarely bothered to dismiss attendants, ever-ubiquitous in a wealthy Aventan household. Whatever he needed to talk to them about was either deeply personal or of great import. "I've had a letter about your brother."

"About?" Latona echoed. "Not from?"

Aulus shook his head. "A magistrate in Tarraco sent it. I didn't want to worry you three, but I last heard from Gaius a few weeks ago, when he was about to set out from Nedhena. And now it seems . . . there was a storm." Alhena made a strangled little noise, prompting both Aula and Latona to swiftly relocate to either side of her. With a stricken expression, Aulus rushed on. "He's fine! At least, he made it safely to shore. Lost a few men on the way, but not so many as he might've. And Gaius is fine." Whether from release or sheer emotional stress, Alhena slumped, not quite fainting, but simply as though all strength had flooded out of her at once. Aula put an arm around her to keep her upright, and Aulus looked chagrined. "I'm sorry, my dears, I'm a bit flustered, and it's making me tell the story out of the proper order. The storms forced them to put in farther north."

Fanning Alhena's face, Latona said, "There, dear, you hear? Gaius is fine. Nothing happened." She looked back at her father, hoping that the rest of the story would help calm Alhena. "Why didn't he write himself?"

"Apparently there was some rush," Aulus said, his eyes on his youngest daughter. "Should I call for—"

"She's fine," Aula said, jostling Alhena a bit. For her part, Alhena wiped her eyes and made an attempt to sit up under her own strength.

Aulus hemmed for a moment, then went on. "Well. When Gaius landed, he learned there was no time to spare. Word had already spread that far of tribesmen ravaging the local populations around Toletum."

"Toletum?" Latona asked. Though her gasp of Iberian geography was far from perfect, she did know that Toletum was near the center of the peninsula. "I thought it was the Lusetani giving them trouble," Latona said. "Aren't they further west?"

"Clear on the other side of the mountains," Aulus said. "But it seems this Ekialde character has inspired others. The Vettoni in the central mountains are in revolt and warring against our allies the Arevaci." He sighed, and took a letter out of the folds of his toga. "The magistrate says Gaius hardly had time to pause in Tarraco on his way down the coast, but Gaius asked him to pass the message along. He doesn't want to take two spare cohorts to face a full-scale revolt—if it is that—so he's trying to rustle up the allied tribes. He will write himself as soon as he can."

"But the magistrate would have written . . ." Aula did the calculation in her head. "Nine days ago? Ten?"

"Closer to fifteen," Aulus said. "The seas have stayed so rough, the ships have been crossing slowly."

"He could be halfway to Toletum by now, then," Aula said.

"He could be dead by now," Alhena whispered.

All four Vitelliae remained quiet for a moment, neither willing to confirm that possibility, nor to risk the gods' ill favor by denying it. "Well," Aulus said after a moment, "if he did manage to write before heading inland, we should know in another two weeks. If he didn't . . . we shall just have to wait." He cleared his throat, and stood up a little straighter. "In the meantime, I'll be reading this to the Senate," he said, voice suddenly fierce. "I fear we have been grievously underestimating the situation in Iberia. If this many tribes are involved, if the fire from these Lusetani is spreading within the borders of our provinces . . ." He shook his head. "It must be seen to. I can hardly blame Governor Sallust for not wanting to abandon his post in Albina, but that no one else is willing to stir more than a few cohorts is flatly absurd. And with Vendelicia so quiet—"

Aula's mind was working fast, figuring out which of her acquaintances she could press, whether the wives and sisters of important men, or the senators themselves. A personal appeal always helped, and with her brother now in harm's way, she felt certain she could conjure up just the sort of emotional overtures which would tug at a few well-placed heartstrings. Alhena was still shaking with terror, too stricken by the idea of her brother Gaius dying at sea to follow the thoughts through to what might happen to him in battle. It was Latona who spoke. "They won't want war now," she said. "Not with the city still struggling to get back on its feet. They'll say our resources must stay here."

"I'm afraid you're right, my dear," Aulus said, sighing. "We shall just have to find the right method of persuasion."

"May I?" Aula asked. Aulus nodded, and as she read, with Latona peering over her shoulder, Aulus paced about the garden, wondering how he could best serve his country and protect his only son at the same time.

Though Helva, when dismissed, had taken herself off to speak with Lucia's nursemaid, both Merula and Mus had hovered near the entrance of the garden. Merula's eavesdropping was shameless; Mus would not have plucked up the courage to listen had she not been able to huddle in the other woman's shadow. When the talk turned to the Lusetanian rebellion, however, Merula fixed Mus with a hard stare. "Which were your people?" Merula asked.

"Lacetani," Mus said, then rushed to add, "North. Much north. Good friends to Aven now."

"Well," Merula said, giving Mus a light pinch, which might have been either playful or threatening. "Don't go getting any ideas."

◇◇◇◇◇◇◇◇◇◇◇◇◇◇◇

CENTRAL IBERIA

Vitellius and Mennenius had hardly taken the time to wring themselves out from their sea voyage before setting off again. For Mennenius and one cohort, a mad dash down the coast; for Vitellius and the second cohort, a trek into the high plateaus. Between their efforts, they had managed to rally allied tribes from the area around Tarraco, in the foothills of the mountains and on the coast. Vitellius had also sent envoys further south, to try and rouse some support out of the garrison at Gades and to sound out the Tartessi tribesmen in the surrounding hills.

Vitellius expected less success further inland. Aventan authority was mostly concentrated close to Gades, jewel of the peninsula, the oldest and largest city in Iberia. The population further north was smaller and more dispersed, with the result that Aven had little influence beyond the coast. The cohort had already encountered several blockades on the road and fought their way through. No trouble as yet for a trained Aventan legion, but these were scouts and opportunistic bandits, not the true Lusetani-led fighting force.

He worried about the weather as well. So far, the days were much the same as in Truscum, but the nights were growing chill. *'At least it's been* dry.' After years in Albina, weeks in Nedhena, and nearly drowning in the Middle Sea, Vitellius had almost forgotten the feeling.

As he rode along the river valley, he eyed the surrounding peaks anxiously. His men were used to the wet chill of the Tennic lands, but they only traveled through the Albine Mountains in spring or summer. Vitellius had no idea how the Iberian chain compared for wind or snowfall, but he was not overeager to find out.

Vitellius had learnt a town some hundred and forty miles north of Toletum, the largest inland city, was the home of the current chieftain of the Arevaci, a man called Bartasco. The people there were long the fastest friends that Aven had in the central part of Iberia.

As he had learned was respectful to the Iberian tribesmen, Vitellius dismounted his horse outside the hewn-timber fence that served for the town's only approximation of a wall. He gestured to his highest ranking centurion. "You and your two best rankers will come with me; everyone else stays outside the walls for now. Best to make the initial approach with a small group, I think."

Though larger than the other villages he had passed through, Bartasco's town appeared in other ways the same. The buildings were mostly circular, brick or thatch built upon low stone foundations, and Vitellius could see signs of wealth similar to those in small Truscan towns or along the roads through Maritima: colorful woven curtains, painted pottery set outside the doors or resting in windows, gold bangles on the arms and ankles of the people he passed by. The citizens eyed him and his companions with interest, but only one made bold enough to speak to them, in halting Truscan: "Aventan, yes? Chief you are wanting, yes?" The bearded fellow gestured down a haphazard path. "Is there."

"I thank you," Vitellius said with a nod. He followed the path past several market stalls to an open square, smaller than most Aventan forums, but which seemed to serve a similar purpose.

In the middle of the square, a man and a woman were arguing. The man was typical Iberian stock: short and lean, with ashen brown hair and a close-cropped beard. The woman, however, was clearly not a local. She had the dark skin and slim, straight profile of a Numidian, and she wore her black hair shaved close to her scalp. She dressed in Iberian fashion, though more like a man than a woman. Her forest green tunic pulled up short, exposing slender calves and ankles ringed with gold. One hand gripped a rolled-up scroll, and she looked near to beating the man about the head with it.

They were shouting in Iberian, and none of the words seemed to be the few that Vitellius had so far picked up. The man seemed to be getting the worst of it, and when he noticed them approaching, he broke off the conversation with almost desperate relief. "Hail—" He said in Truscan, then squinted at Vitellius's uniform for a moment before adding, "Tribune?"

"You have the right of it."

The man squinted at him. "Aventan? Not some auxiliary?"

Gaius resisted the urge to rub at his gingery hair. Its paleness, along with his height and musculature, did give him somewhat Tennic coloring, at least to men more used to dealing with the northern tribes than with those born to Truscum. It had been no end of amusement to the Vendelicians. But he nodded, affirming, "Aventan. Gaius Vitellius, of the Eighth Legion."

"Eighth?" The man's brow furrowed in surprise. "Not the Fourth out of Gades?"

Vitellius shook his head. "Governor Fimbrianus has not sent men this far north."

The woman snorted derisively and spat something in Iberian. The man waved his palms at her in a gentle hushing gesture.

Vitellius continued. "Governor Sallust sent our vexillation from Albina. I have a single cohort with me. Another tribune went south with a second cohort."

"You've come all the way from Albina, yet they won't move the legion out of Gades." It was not a question, and the man made a sucking noise through his teeth. Then he looked Vitellius in the eye and tapped himself in the center of his chest. "Bartasco. Leader of the Arevaci—"

"For now, anyway," the woman behind him muttered.

To Vitellius's surprise, Bartasco showed no ire at her interruption. Instead, he gestured to her. "My wife, Hanath, leader of our women."

"Which is why I am so concerned," Hanath said, pushing forward. She shook the fist holding the scroll. Despite the total lack of physical similarities, Gaius was nonetheless put in mind of his eldest sister Aula. "We hear from upriver and down how much trouble these wild Lusetani are causing. They have even set the damn Vettoni on us!" Her Truscan was even finer and less accented than her husband's, though her Numidian origins danced in the sharpness of her consonants. "The Arevaci are no barbarians, Tribune Vitellius. We farm, we mine, we trade. And we have no desire to lose our livelihood to these marauding thugs."

"Our concern," Bartasco broke in, laying a hand lightly on his wife's arm, "is whether continued alliance to Aven will help or hurt us. If Aven cannot protect us . . ."

"I am here to assure you that we can, and we will," Vitellius broke in. "That is not only my pledge, but my purpose."

Bartasco glanced behind Vitellius at his small escort, as though hoping to see more legionaries suddenly manifest. "And how many men in a cohort? A few hundred, I think?"

"More will come," Vitellius said, with more conviction than he felt. "I've sent messages to Aven at every opportunity. I'm sure even now they are readying more legions to ferry across the sea or march across the mountains." He shifted uneasily, not wishing to raise hope higher than he could deliver on. "But, with the seasons changing, it may be spring before they arrive."

Bartasco nodded in understanding. "Winter will slow the bastard Lusetani and Vettoni down, too, thanks be for that. But you need to establish quarters, not go running around the peninsula chasing them. The higher mountains become icy very early, and even here, it can grow quite cold. And I must warn you, Tribune, I do not know if this area can support so many extra men in the lean seasons."

"We hope to make it to Toletum," Vitellius said. "I understand it has some fortifications."

Hanath snorted. "I doubt they will impress an Aventan soldier," she said. "I saw the fortresses you built in Numidia. Toletum's are more than our little fence, but nothing to hold out an invading army for very long."

Vitellius met her gaze evenly. "Then we shall spend the winter improving them." Hanath arched a thin eyebrow in a gesture that Vitellius could not interpret as either impressed or skeptical. "If we can winter there safely, we should still be able to send out patrols. The more we can study our enemy in the meantime, the better off we shall be when the full legions arrive." He looked back into Bartasco's placid hazel eyes. "Of course, the more aid I have from tribes like the noble Arevaci, the easier that will go as well. And so I come to ask: Can you spare men, good fighters and riders, to guide me to Toletum and winter there?"

Bartasco rubbed at his bristly jaw with the back of one hand, cautiously avoiding his wife's burning gaze. Hanath was staring at him so intensely that she nearly vibrated with the force of it, fists clenched at her side. But whatever certainty she had, she could not pass it through the air to her husband. "Tribune . . ." he began, in a wavering voice that Vitellius usually associated with haggling merchants. "It is much that you ask. To send men with you, I must leave this town, my people, ill-defended. We already have refugees, women and children, the ill and injured, from the villages to the west. I must think of them, Tribune. If you could winter here . . ."

Vitellius swallowed, trying to ignore the growing pit in his stomach. Without the support of the Arevaci, it would be nigh-impossible to secure the plateaus. "Your devotion to your people is commendable," he said. "Truly, all I have heard of the honor and strength of the Arevaci has not been overstated. I fear this town could not support our vexillation in addition to your people and the refugees. Toletum can—and Toletum has walls. I ask you to consider that you may best serve your people by assisting us to put down the threat to them."

"It is not that I do not see the sense of what you say," Bartasco countered. "But it is such a risk . . . venturing much for hope, rather than fortifying our security—"

"Enough!" Hanath cried, throwing her hands up in the air. As Vitellius gawped, she stalked into a nearby house and returned a moment later with a spear that was as tall as she was. Bartasco did not seem to share the Aventans' astonishment; he was rubbing his temples with the thumb and middle finger of his left hand, for all the world as though this were an accustomed domestic dispute. Hanath pounded the butt of the spear into the dirt in front of Vitellius. "I will accompany you, Tribune." Her eyes were on Bartasco as she said it. "I was born Numidian, but I am Arevaci now. And my husband tells me that the Arevaci are friends to your people. At least *one* of us should be with you in this fight."

Bartasco muttered something in the Iberian tongue beneath his breath. Vitellius caught only a few words: invocations to their gods, though whether in thanks or as a request for patience, he dared not guess. Bartasco's hands flopped helplessly to his sides, and he began a tentative sentence directed at his wife in Iberian. Almost before he gave the words breath, she fired back at him with another vehement stream. Through his tightly pinned hope that this woman would be able to influence her husband to their cause, Vitellius still felt wry amusement. This was no mere henpecking; more like a lioness cuffing courage into her mate.

"*Bene!*" Bartasco hollered at last. He turned back to Vitellius, straightening his shoulders and jutting out his chin. "I, Bartasco, decide this thing." The knot in Vitellius's stomach tightened in anticipation, then melted into relief when Bartasco said, with a decisive nod, "We will take you to Toletum."

XXI

As October waned, Latona considered her circumstances. True to her word, Aemilia had ensured that Latona could not acquire the texts she needed to study: the priests at the Temple of Saturn and the Basilica Tullia alike refused her entry. The evening after the last rejection, she had been so furious that she had accidentally caused an oil lamp to overheat and explode before she got her temper under control.

It had, however, redirected her focus. Clearly, rediscovering the strength of her emotions and allowing them space to breathe was detrimentally affecting the discipline she had held close for so many years. *'Escalation in one requires escalation in the other.'* Fortunately, Latona knew who could help her with that, and so the day before the Kalends of November found Latona sitting by a small fire in the garden of the Temple of Venus with the goddess's High Priestess, Ama Rubellia, sharing fruit and gossip over a bowl of mulled wine.

Latona was about to turn the conversation to her request for aid when a group of young acolytes came into the garden, all in matching wheat-colored tunics and red belts. They were shepherded by a priestess, who glanced over at Rubellia as they came in; Rubellia waved her permission for them to be about their business. One of the girls looked familiar, it took Latona a frowning moment to figure out why. There, arms linked with one of her companions, was the first girl that Latona had rescued on the night of the Esquiline riot.

Rubellia followed her gaze. "Pontia said she had been sent here by a golden-haired paragon," she said. "I *had* wondered . . ."

"How is she?"

"Healing. Slowly, but healing." Rubellia reached over and gave Latona's hand a comforting squeeze. "You did the right thing, sending her here."

"I only thought it might bring comfort," Latona said. "I didn't think she would decide to stay."

Rubellia nodded. "She and her mother talked it over. Her mother was concerned . . . Well. There might have been rumors, and a nasty stigma attached to her name. But there's no virtue lost if she's dedicated to Lady Venus. If she wants to marry someday, well, her people are of the Fourth Class, and she should have no trouble finding a good man to match her. And if she never wants to, there will never be a need. She will always be cared for here."

"You took her on charity?" Most families sent "donations" to pay their children's way into the temples, but a family of the Fourth Class was unlikely to have so much to spare without advance planning.

"We did."

"I'd like to make a donation," Latona said, her eyes still lingering on the girl, "towards her boarding."

Rubellia was quiet a moment, then: "You don't feel you've done enough." As was her way, it was not quite a question; she spoke through intuition.

Working in pairs, the acolytes were cleaning out the dovecotes at the far end of the garden. One of the other girls flung a fistful of feathers at Pontia's head, and she laughed, shaking them from her hair.

Latona felt a tug in her chest. "What could possibly be enough?"

They sat quietly, watching the girls at work. *'They look happy.'* Latona was glad for Pontia—glad for *all* of them, to have a place where they were useful, productive, but could still feel relaxed and at home, surrounded by friends. Rubellia's steady presence was a blessing. She had spent most of Ocella's reign protecting her acolytes and priestesses from the dictator and his court, and now the Temple of Venus had a warmth that few others in the cities could claim.

Latona's skin prickled: Spirit magic, aware that someone else was using magic on *her*. With a rueful smile, she turned back to face Rubellia. "You're reading me."

"Guilty," Rubellia said. "You Spirit mages hardly ever let me get away with it." Like Spirit, Fire could give mages an enhanced sense of empathy. As a result, Latona had manifested a double-dose of the gift.

Latona's lips quirked. "Rubellia, you're Venus's High Priestess. If you didn't *want* me to know you were reading me, I wouldn't. Probably not even if I were expecting it."

"I think you underestimate yourself," Rubellia said, lifting her wine. "But you do have a point." A grin. "I am *very* good." Despite herself, Latona laughed. "It doesn't take the High Priestess to see that there's something troubling you, dear. What happened at the Cantrinalia—that wasn't the first time, was it?" Latona's eyes fell to the wine, swirling slowly in the cup between her hands. She shook her head. "Nor the last?" Another shake. For a moment, only a breeze stirred the silence. Then Rubellia sighed. "Damn your Vitellian pride, Latona." Latona looked up, expecting the pity she had feared, but instead, Rubellia wore only a gentle smile, with infinite kindness in her warm brown eyes. "You should have come to me sooner."

"I did!" Latona protested. "Eventually. I have, now." She took a deep drag of her wine. "I was going to say something this afternoon."

"Yes," Rubellia said slowly. "I think you would have." Rubellia moved over to share Latona's couch, gathering the younger woman in her arms and stroking her hair. "Oh, my dove. Latona, I'm so sorry you've endured this." If empathy fell more strictly under the governance of Spirit, Fire still laid claim to affairs of the heart—and both elements owned their share of pride. "So—If you're willing to talk now?"

With a sigh, Latona set her cup down, and for the second time that month, told the story of what had happened to her—and to her magical talents—since Ocella's death. "I can't quite seem to govern my tongue *or* my magic these days," she finished. "But I have to, because . . . I want to do more. *Learn* more." She snatched up a slice of pear. "Not to mention it's getting a little inconvenient to keep plunging my hands into cold water every time my blood gets up."

"Well," Rubellia said, "I certainly think I can help with that aspect, at least. You even could join me here full-time, if you wanted. The Temple would delight to have you."

Latona's breath caught in her throat; there was temptation in that, to be sure, but . . . "No, Rubellia," she said. "No, I think the gods have something else in mind."

After a long, searching gaze, Rubellia gave a little sigh. "Well. I could offer you some choice words regarding my opinion of Aemilia, but I suspect they would not be helpful. And much though I might like to claim you, I think you've more of Juno's work to do than Venus's. But—" She took a sip of wine. "I do still think there's more to this matter than you're letting on. If you tell me, I may have better counsel." Latona tried to give a dismissive shrug, but suspected her blushing cheeks were giving her away when Rubellia added, "I promise, I am well-versed in keeping secrets."

"Then I shall confess, there has been someone nudging me along." Her mouth crinkled up at one end. "Someone . . . intriguing."

Rubellia's soft bistre eyes were full of understanding. "A male someone, unless I miss my guess. And not your husband?"

Latona chewed her lip, thinking of scintillating dinner conversations and walking up and down the less fashionable hills. Of a man who wanted so much for himself, with such determination, who looked out at the city of Aven and saw limitless potential. Of the strength of his belief in his ability to effect the necessary changes—and the strength of his belief in her.

She nodded.

Rubellia stared at her in a way that actually reminded Latona of Sempronius. They both had a way of looking *into* a person. But where Sempronius had a needle-focused intensity, Rubellia's method was softer. She did not cut through to secrets, but simply waited, so kind and understanding, until you felt there was no need to hide them. "Oh, my dear," she said at last. "You *are* in trouble, aren't you?"

"If I'm not yet," Latona said, "I'm at least pointed in that direction."

Rubellia plucked at a bunch of grapes thoughtfully, rolling one purple fruit between her fingers. "This potential paramour . . . would he be free to return your affections, if you could give them openly?"

"He would." Sempronius had not been married since before Ocella's dictatorship, when Aebutia had died. Latona had often wondered why he hadn't found himself a new wife, as eligible as he was. Certainly no few society dames cast their eyes at him, on their own behalf as often as their unmatched daughters'. And yet, for years now, Sempronius had remained *solus*.

"Then, if I may make so bold as to suggest it, my honey, I must suspect that it is not truly Herennius that's holding you back. If he were all—well, that could be dealt with easily enough. A bit of fuss, for certain, some inconvenience and awkward questions—but wouldn't that be worth it?" She popped a grape daintily in her mouth.

Latona fussed with her woolen wrap, twitching it into a more pleasing arrangement. "You're right," she confessed. "But it isn't only that. The man in question comes with . . . complications of his own." Rubellia nodded, still chewing on her grapes; her silence encouraged Latona to fill the space. "He is . . . quite political."

"So is your family."

A soft snort escaped Latona. "Not like he is."

"Your father may well be censor soon."

"It still doesn't . . ." Latona shook her head. "My father and brother have their goals, but their ambition compared to this man's is as . . . as a hearth fire to the sun." Rubellia's eyebrows perked up. "Taking up with him would mean thrusting myself into quite a lot of chaos." She remembered Rabirus's thinly veiled threats and the blind terror of Ocella's reign. The exhaustion of holding such close control over herself, never knowing who to trust, who might be watching, never daring to so much as breathe at the wrong time. The rumor-mongering, the jeopardy to her reputation and her family's. These were the things that prickled, suggesting that her father was, perhaps, right in his assessment that obscurity was better for her than esteem.

"My curiosity grows by the second," Rubellia said. "So you would not welcome finding yourself the focus of so much attention?" She quirked an eyebrow. "Even though you wish to assert yourself more as a mage?"

"I don't *know*, is the thing," Latona said, quickly and honestly. "Once I would have thought, no, certainly not. I was never meant to be the one who . . ." She rubbed at the bridge of her nose. "Aula was always the political one, with her terribly involved husband and her ambitions." And what had it earned her? Blood on the tiles, an empty bed, a fatherless child.

But for Latona to set her course by such a brightly burning star? Few knew what extraordinary, burning zeal he harbored in his heart—but he had told Latona, had shared his secrets with her. *'And he would never allow me to be less than all I could be.'* The thought of it sent a little shiver down her spine, though whether of fear or of titillation, she could no longer tell.

There was danger there, to be sure, but oh, such opportunity as well. Every time someone told her "no," every time someone reminded her of her place—Rabirus, Aemilia, even her own father—it only seemed to make the desire to act burn hotter. She had never been the sort to defy for the sake of defiance, she had not a rebel's heart, but now? *'What a temptation.'*

Rubellia's hand tightened around her wrist. "Latona," she said. Her voice was carefully calm but with a note of fear, the sort of tone one might use if there were a poisonous snake in the room. "Latona, the fire . . ."

∞∞∞∞∞∞∞∞∞∞∞

Latona gasped. While she had been contemplating, the flames of the garden's small fire had doubled in size and gone white with heat. These were hungry, angry flames, devouring what fuel they had and reaching for what else might feed them. Latona cast about for a jug of water, started to bolt to her feet—

But Rubellia kept a fierce grip on her, surprisingly strong, and it held her in her seat. "If you did this," Rubellia said, "then you can control it. You said you've been able to—"

"Not— Not once it's flared up like this. I've been able to stop it happening, but not—"

"We can fix this." She sounded every bit the teacher, as though this were no more than an exercise. "Remember that Fire exists as potential. As you wake it, so can you return it. Quench it back into embers." Gritting her teeth, Latona focused her mind on banking the flames.

It didn't work. Licks of blue were sparking up in the midst of the heat. The stones lining the pit glowed orange and crackled. "I'm not sure how, Rubellia. Not when it flares like this."

"Don't think of returning it to nowhere. I imagine it as a separate chamber of my heart, reserved just for this. Breathe deep and draw it in."

Through her panic, Latona tried to visualize as Rubellia suggested. Old fears bubbled up—that Aemilia had been right, that she could not control herself, that she was dangerous. But she locked those emotions away, thinking only of Rubellia's steady presence and quiet faith. Rubellia believed she could do it.

The hairs on the back of her arms stood up, but she felt a warming inside her, in her blood. With Rubellia's words in mind, Latona found herself thinking in terms of potential—not just releasing the impetus that sparked a fire back into the world but taking it into herself.

Slowly, the flames faded back to orange. The stones cooled to black. Rubellia released Latona's wrist. "Well," Rubellia said, "you certainly know how to liven up an afternoon, Latona."

"Rubellia, I'm sorry—"

Rubellia waved a hand. "Fascinating."

That startled Latona out of her self-pity. "Fascinating?"

"Mm-hmm." Rubellia's hand cupped Latona's cheek, stroking softly. "Latona, I perceive two things. One is that it is no surprise, after so many years of tamping it down, that your magic yearns to be free."

There was sense in that. The relief she had felt at Ocella's death, the lessening pressure to stay hidden, the way it surged along with high emotions . . . "And second?"

"More esoteric," Rubellia said. "I feel you're right in thinking that . . . the gods have decided to alter your course. Or perhaps they always meant this for you. Venus and Juno have laid their hands heavily on you." She tilted her head to the side, smiling sympathetically. "The only pity is that they are not always so good at explaining their whims to us mortals."

Latona laughed lightly, as much to keep from weeping as anything else. "Do they say why that is, when you're a priestess? Is that a secret of the temples? The gods were once quite clear in what they wanted, back in the day, popping down from Olympus to issue instructions or to bed pretty girls and likely lads."

Rubellia laughed, too. "It is a matter of debate, one of the mysteries yet unsolved. Perhaps the gods seek to wean us from their direct control, like children." She tucked a finger under Latona's chin, tipping it up so that she had to sit up straight. "But I do know that they would not choose an unworthy vessel. If they have chosen you for some purpose, it is because you are clever enough and strong enough to bear it."

Latona crinkled her nose. "So you're saying the gods *want* me to make a spectacle of myself?"

"I'm saying they seem to be giving you a choice: make yourself prominent, or immolate in your own fires." She tilted her head, dark curls swaying. "If the city sees you as a grand mage—if you *force* them to see that, to give you the respect you should have had as a priestess of Juno—then you will be a woman of great consequence, Latona." Rubellia smiled. "And then, I think, you'll find it much easier to do Juno's work in the city without impediments." She kissed Latona's cheek. "Come back and visit me more often. We'll practice. The Fire will dance to your will, soon enough, and Aemilia can make of that what she likes!"

❖ NOVEMBER ❖

XXII

"We're not just going to put down the revolt, we're going to make sure they bloody well *stay* down." Autronius Felix sat astride a bench in the Forum surrounded by several friends, some his fellows from military service, others the young bucks of distinguished families, including Proculus Crispinius and Publius Rufilius. He was gesticulating wildly as he pontificated on what had become his favorite topic: the necessity of war in Iberia. "We were too lenient the last time. We didn't push past the coastal regions, and we should've. As long as we let those tribes stay active on our borders, we're going to have trouble from them. So, we need to end the trouble. Permanently."

The military-minded men nodded, but Proculus shook his head. "We would be perfectly fine just bloodying their noses and sending them back to their hovels. There's no need to take the whole of Iberia."

"We control the mouth of the Baetis," Felix said. "We ought to control the mouth of the Tagus. Come on now, Proculus, if you're not going to listen to me, then you respect Sempronius Tarren's opinion, don't you? He's spoken quite—"

"Yes, I know, I hear his speeches in the Curia, too. But I still think you're over-reaching. My brother was stationed in Gades for a year before Ocella. It's not like Numidia, Felix. Iberia is vaster—and more populous—than most people realize. We can't keep multiple legions stationed there to keep the people pacified, not with the northern tribes raising a fuss every time we turn our backs. The Lusetani certainly aren't going to march over two mountain ranges to get to us, and they're not a seafaring people. We have nothing to fear from them."

"If we don't teach these barbarians a lesson, the others will be encouraged—"

"We can teach them a lesson without needing to—"

"As will our enemies in the east," Felix overran him. "If Parthia knows we can't defend our provincial borders, then we jeopardize our standing all around the Middle Sea. We could lose everything that the last two centuries have built. And that's without even taking into consideration the value of the territory itself."

Publius Rufilius, who had been blinking back and forth between them, looked impressed. "Sweet Juno, Felix, you *have* been paying attention to forum matters."

Felix shrugged his muscular shoulders. "It benefits me to do so." He had never considered that his noted career as a profligate carouser should be mutually exclusive with political awareness, and the more time he spent in Sempronius's company, the more he felt encouraged to use the brain the gods had given him as well as the brawn.

"I still think you've mis-interpreted," Proculus said. "Sempronius wants to go to Iberia, but I don't think he means to hold it. Not with Aventan legions."

Felix shifted himself on the bench as a group of priests wended their way towards a temple, the backs of their rough-woven gray togas pulled up as hoods. Each bore a dish in his hands, filled with dirt, so far as Felix could tell. Conversations in the Forum often suffered interruptions by passers-by, and though magic was not permitted within the Forum, non-thaumaturgical religious rituals could hardly be avoided. Felix thought nothing of it until one thin priest tripped over his robes, spilling his burden all over the ground. Some of it puffed up, smudging Felix's legs and those of his fellows. "Steady there!" Felix said, catching the man by the elbow before he could tumble entirely.

"My apologies, sir!" the priest said. "So sorry, so very sorry." He had a reedy voice, with a slight whistle to it. Felix rolled his eyes, ever impatient with dodderers.

"No harm done to us, old man. It'll wash. But you'll have to start the whole damn ritual over again, won't you?" He smiled as he said it, but the priest scurried off the way he'd come, muttering to himself in alarm. Felix shook his head and shrugged.

"How on earth to hold it if not with legions, then?" asked Rufilius, picking up the thread of conversation.

"Alliances," Proculus said. "Put good men in charge—those who fight alongside us to subdue the radicals—then bring their sons to Aven for education. Show them our ways and let them turn Aventan on their own, rather than put ourselves to the expense of maintaining such vast provinces."

"Hells, the both of you," Rufilius snorted, fluffing up his fair hair. "You're both turning politician on me."

Felix laughed. "Only till I can get back on the march, friend."

"It's the same theory your father eventually came 'round to on Albina, Rufilius," Proculus said, "little though we've been able to implement it. Friendly relations will get us much farther than brutal subjugation."

A frown creased Felix's typically merry countenance. "And you think this is what Sempronius intends?"

"From what I gather—"

"Do you mean Sempronius Tarren?"

The group turned towards the new voice. A rope-muscled man in a red tunic sauntered towards them, his legs splayed wide. He had several other men of similar aspect following behind him. "And what if we did?" said Rufilius, squaring his body towards the newcomer.

The man sniffed, grinning over his shoulder at his friends. " 'S'nothin'. Just that I wouldn't be sitting in the Forum proclaiming my loyalty to a man like that."

"A man like what?" This time the question came from Proculus.

The newcomer snickered, scuffing his feet in the dirt. "It's just there's a word for a man who talks big talk about going to war, putting down rebel tribes . . . a man who stands up at the Rostrum and makes pretty speeches . . ." The man came close enough that Felix could smell the oil on his recently-scraped skin, "but who turned tail and *ran* from trouble when it came calling at his own door."

Felix did not remember getting to his feet but seemed to have been propelled there. His muscles tightened, as they had each time he had ridden out against Numidian raiders. "Say it."

The man glanced back at his comrades, his lip curling in an ugly laugh. "Coward." He looked Felix up and down appraisingly, then jutted his chin out, stepping yet closer. "And if that's what we call him, then what do we call the weak-bellied fools who follow him?"

Felix's fist impacted the other man's face with a satisfying thwack. What happened next, he could hardly tell. A roaring went up in his ears: the shouts and hollering of his fellow soldiers, Rufilius and Proculus surging forward, the dust from the street scraping beneath his sandals.

◊◊◊◊◊◊◊◊◊◊◊◊◊◊◊

Latona and Merula were walking back from the markets on the far side of the Forum, crossing from the Via Sacra to the Via Nova, when Latona suddenly staggered. It no longer surprised Merula, who put an arm behind her mistress's back. "Fire or Spirit, Domina?" she asked in a hushed tone, pulling Latona off to the side of the road.

"Spirit." Latona's throat was tight, her heart suddenly racing with a wash of violent energy, hot and angry and pulsing. Her hands clenched into fists. They yearned to lash out, to pound into flesh, though the sensation could not have been more foreign to Latona. "Something's happening, this isn't . . . isn't normal . . ." Latona's teeth were closed around the savage impulse, but she ground out, "Need you to find out . . . Go see . . . Forum . . ."

"I am not leaving you here, Domina," Merula said.

Latona gestured vaguely towards the nearby row of painted columns. She didn't trust herself to move very much. Her limbs cried out for brutal action, and she would never forgive herself if she struck Merula. "Over there . . . The garden . . . I have Pacco . . ." Latona was glad she had brought one of her father's men on the shopping trip; one of Herennius's would have carried the tale to her husband.

Merula followed her gesture towards the small garden behind the Temple of Vesta. "I am not liking this, Domina," she said as she guided her mistress. She barked orders at Pacco, then muttered in Phrygian as she settled Latona on a bench. As Merula dashed off to try and find out what was happening in the Forum, Latona uncurled her hands and placed them flat on her thighs.

'Clear your head, damn it all to Tartarus, clear your head!' Latona forced her focus towards the source of the unwanted energies. This went beyond the empathic flood that had opened in her at the Cantrinalia. Something was *driving* this power, cruel and hungry. Her fingernails pressed into her legs, prickling through the fabric of her stola. *'Follow that thread . . . Don't let the tide take you . . .'*

She squeezed her eyes closed, forcing herself to breathe in the slow patterns that Rubellia had recommended. The invading sense of pandemonium was hideously dizzying—but she realized she *could* keep it from swamping her entirely. The ferocious influence fought her, though, buffeting her whenever she tried to grasp hold of the strand that might lead back to the instigators. Each time she thought she was getting close, some new burst of turbulent rage would spin her off in another direction. Of one thing she became sure, however: there was magic at play. Whether creating, enhancing, or directing, she could not tell, but something beyond natural human emotions was present.

Merula trotted back a few minutes later. Latona, her eyes still pinched closed, felt rather than saw her approach. "Is a fight in the Forum, Domina. Looks ugly. Many men, no weapons that I am seeing, but they are doing plenty of damage with fists. And—" She hesitated, ruffling a hand through her short-cropped dark curls. "I could be mistaken, Domina, but I am thinking I see . . ." Her lips twisted in a brief hesitation. "Er, friends of yours, taking part."

Latona's eyes shot wide. "Who?"

"The young handsome one. Golden-haired."

"Publius Rufilius."

"His face might be getting more interesting, if you understand me, Domina."

"Who else?"

"The rough pleb. The one they call Felix."

Latona grasped Merula's arm. "Go—Go to that college, on the Esquiline—Sempronius Tarren's friends. They'll know what to—"

"I will, Domina," Merula said. "But Pacco is taking *you* to Ama Rubellia, now."

<hr />

By the time Merula reached the Vatiniae collegium, her lungs burned from effort, and her legs felt weak and shaky. Still, she held her shoulders straight and her chin up as she pushed through the tavern's paint-stripped wooden door and cried, "I seek the master of this collegium!"

Even at this early hour, the tavern was full of the college's men, business associates, and attendant hangers-on. Most glanced up at her only briefly, then returned to what they had been doing. One man near the door put his hand on her shoulder. "Think you're in the wrong place, mouse. Let's go—"

"No!" Merula dug in her heels, struggling as he attempted to usher her out. "This is important, you stupid—" She lapsed into a string of descriptors in her native Phrygian, none of them complimentary.

"Hold up." A man rose from a nearby table—and seemed to just keep on going, tall well above the average. Merula thought him familiar; a man of that bulk was hard to forget. He stepped closer, waggling a thumb at her. "I recognize you. You belong to that patrician lady, with the golden hair and the, ah—" He started to make a gesture approximating the lady's figure, but seemed to think better of it upon seeing Merula's glare. "The— religious garb, yeah? All in pink?"

"Yes!" Merula exclaimed, pushing the other two men unceremoniously aside. "You are one of the Vatiniae, yes?"

"I am. Vatinius Nisso. But if it's the college's master you want, it's my brother you mean. Hey, Obir!" he hollered over his shoulder. "He'll be out in a minute." Nisso folded his arms over his massive chest, grinning as his brother approached. "What's the trouble, little bird?"

"Fighting in the Forum. My domina—the Lady Latona—she tells me run here quick, get you to help."

Obir, though elder, was shorter than his brother, but they shared the same short noses, coiling dark hair, and mirthful brown eyes. He listened as Merula told them everything she knew about what was going on in the Forum, then flicked his eyes over at Nisso. "The Senator did say for us to look out for the Lady."

"Forum's not our turf," Nisso said, shrugging. "We get involved there . . ."

"Then the Senator will likely be all the more grateful to us. C'mon, brother. A powerful patron's gratitude is nothing to shrug off, as we know already." He jerked his chin meaningfully up at the ceiling. Merula followed his glance and observed that the roof had been recently re-tiled. "Besides, you might get to break a few bones, and won't that be fun?"

"I think," Merula broke in, "that my mistress means for you to be *stopping* the fight."

"Easiest way to do that is to drop a few of the combatants, birdie," Nisso said, tweaking one of her curls. Merula swatted at him.

Obir turned to the room, and at a whistle, three of his mean leapt to attention. "Round up a few more of the boys. We'll see if we can't knock some sense into those fools down in the Forum. Nisso, go to the Aventine and find Sempronius Tarren. If he's not home, one of his slaves should know where to find him. You, girl." Obir gestured at Merula as he threw a cloak over his shoulders. "Show me what's going on, then you can scurry back to your mistress, eh?"

XXIII

By the time Obir and his men arrived on the scene, the brawl had grown, as the initial combatants had been joined by other partisans or by passers-by simply interested in a good fight. Felix looked possessed, his eyes wide with fury yet unseeing as he slammed his fists again and again into the other man's face. Blood poured from his own nose, but he hardly noticed. Rufilius, Proculus, and the other Popularists in the fray also bore a similar violent vacancy.

Obir waded into the fracas, heading straight for Felix—a man well-known to him from his frequent carousing in the Subura as well as his association with Sempronius Tarren. "All right, lad, that's enough—" Obir went to grab Felix's arms, to drag him off of his opponent.

Felix rounded on him, knuckles impacting Obir's jaw with a loud crack. He showed no awareness of who Obir was or that he meant no threat, but fought like a demon. Whatever their initial instructions to subdue the fight, the men of the college weren't about to stand for an attack on their master. The fray surged with new energy, some men yelling "For the people!" and others "For Aven!" and others yet their own personal battle cries, to the legions they had once served or the collegia that owned their allegiance now. Fists flew and elbows smashed into noses, knees rammed into soft bellies and heels drove into ankles. And through it all, Felix fought with no sign of slowing, never so much as flinching in pain, nor recoiling from a single blow.

"Enough!"

Sempronius had finally arrived, though the shout did not come from him. Felix's brother Marcus was at his side, face red and fists clenched. He made a swift, pounding gesture down towards the earth—a grounding spell that rolled through the combatants like a tide. Some froze in place. Others sank to the street as though suddenly overcome by the desire for sleep. Felix straightened slowly, leaving off the bloody pulp of a man beneath him. He swayed drunkenly, then crashed to his knees.

Sempronius rubbed at his forehead, mastering the urge to start bellowing recriminations. They would do him no good now. Felix and the others were clearly still insensible.

Obir approached him. "Sir, we tried to do as we thought you'd want, just subdue them, but . . ." He made a helpless gesture. "Like demons, they were. Nothing would stop them."

"I understand, Obir." Sempronius murmured.

"And I'll thank you for bearing witness to that effect if I get hauled before the Augian Commission for use of magic in the Forum," Marcus added, massaging one hand with the other.

"Obir, if you and your boys could see Rufilius and Proculus to their homes, I would take it as a kindness."

Obir snorted. "That's the pretty boy with the bleeding nostrils, and the short thick one what got kneed in the goodies? We can manage them."

"Come to me in the morning and I'll see you properly thanked for your troubles." Sempronius glanced sideways at Marcus, whose nostrils flared as he struggled to calm himself. "Marcus, think we can wrestle your brother to my domus? I should like to ask him a few questions."

"And I'd just as soon our father not see him like this," Marcus said, "though I've no doubt he'll hear tell of it soon enough."

Sempronius and Marcus were both strong men, but Felix was built like a bull. Each of them heaved one of Felix's arms over his shoulders, and together they began to stagger their way out of the Forum.

As they started up the Aventine, Sempronius turned back, glancing over the crowd. With the fighters dispersing, the Forum swiftly returned to normal operations. Soon, not even the spray of blood in the sand would stand witness to the fight. Obir and his men led a dazed Proculus in the direction of the Palatine, while Nisso and others ushered a wobbling Rufilius towards the Caelian.

Beyond them all, standing in the shelter of the marketplace, Sempronius saw a golden-haired woman, supported by her slave-girl, watching the combatants as they dispersed. *'I should have known,'* he thought, with a warmth in his chest that surprised him. *'That's another one I owe you, Lady.'*

◇◇◇◇◇◇◇◇◇◇◇◇◇◇

Vibia had been visiting when Nisso burst in with news of the brawl, and she was hardly about to leave without the full story. When Sempronius and Marcus hauled Felix in, her eyes went wide, and she barely let them settle him into a chair before rushing forward. "Let me see him." Her nose was crinkled as though offended by a putrid smell. With the flat of her hand, she pushed Felix's head back, her fingers flexed to keep them out of contact with him. She rotated his head from side to side, then she fixed him dead in the eyes. "Ugh." Vibia stepped back, shaking her hand vigorously. "Fracture magic. The *nasty* kind. He reeks of it." Her irritated gaze fell on Marcus. "I'd have expected you to know that."

"Earth can't see the workings, Vibia," Sempronius reminded her. Whatever it was had been subtle enough that it hadn't prickled his own Water-based sensing abilities, but of course, it was always easier to pick up something within one's own element. "She meant no offense, Marcus." Beside Sempronius, Vibia sniffed, as though to say Sempronius had no idea what she intended. "Vibia, do you think this is what instigated him to fight?"

"Him and all the others, I'd guess. Someone *wanted* blood in the streets." She sniffed a few times, then knelt by Felix's feet. Her fingers rubbed briskly at his calf, and came away coated with a thin umber powder. "Wanted it badly," she said. "Wash him, please. In a basin. Catch every bit of it that rinses off and throw it in the river. And someone bring water for me. I don't want this putrescence in the house any longer than I must." As Corvinus and another slave hauled Felix off towards the kitchen for a good dousing, Vibia held her dirtied hand far away from herself, pacing in the atrium. "*Filthy* magic," she said, more to herself than anyone else. "Literally and symbolically. At least if I'm going to curse someone, I do it properly, with a tablet. This is just . . . *ugh.*"

"Vibia," Sempronius said, settling his arms across his chest. "Explain, please."

She turned back to him and Marcus. "It's old Truscan magic, really. Hardly anyone uses it anymore, but they do teach us about it. It pollutes the senses. Will pollute the soul, given long enough." With loathing, she raised her fingers to her nose and inhaled carefully. "Yew bark. Anise. Mustard seed. I'd guess burial ashes and possibly crushed bones, too. From a crucified slave, if the caster could get a hold of such." A slave came in with a dish of water for her, and she gestured impatiently for it.

"Can you figure out who did it?" Sempronius asked. "Or ought we to call in the Augian Commission?" The same men who guarded against the use of magic in the Senate could also be summoned to investigate crimes of a thaumaturgical nature.

"If I went to where they were dusted, I might be able to trace it." She looked sharply up at Marcus, still rubbing her hands clean. "You said he was in the Forum?"

"Yes."

"Sons of Dis." Vibia shook her head. "With all the people tramping through . . ."

"Like trying to have a dog scent across running water," Marcus said, understanding. "I doubt there'd be a strong enough signature left for even the Commission to piece anything together."

'Just as well,' Vibia thought. She loathed the idea of bringing the Augian Commission anywhere near her brother and his close-guarded talents.

"Should we be worried about the cursed dirt affecting other people?" Sempronius asked. "If they've stepped in it?"

"Hard to say." Vibia's face was screwed up in concentration. "It would depend on how the mage bound the spell—if it was *intended* for Felix and his friends or not."

"It didn't seem to affect Obir and his men," Marcus offered.

"Or you two, for that matter. I'd guess we're safe." Vibia rubbed at her forehead. "I'm going to have a headache for *days*, Sempronius, you do know that?"

A moment later, Corvinus escorted Felix back into the atrium. Still mildly disoriented, but lucid now, he stammered, "Brother— Senator— I . . . I can explain."

"I very much doubt it, lad," Sempronius said, gesturing for Corvinus to help Felix sit. "You were cursed."

"Thoroughly," Vibia put in, still pacing around the border of the impluvium pool.

Felix looked back and forth between them, eyes innocent and astonished. "Cursed? But— Why? Who'd want to curse me?"

"Been trifling with some priest's daughter?" Marcus asked, scowling.

"What? I— No! Not that I know of, anyway."

Sempronius put a hand up to quiet his protests. "What's the last thing you remember before the fight?"

Felix cast his eyes from left to right as though hoping to find the answers etched on the walls. "I was in the Forum . . ."

"Yes, Felix, we'd figured that part out on our own," Marcus said. "And?"

"And I was talking with the lads about the Iberian campaign . . ." Felix made a vague gesture in the air. "Some ugly bastard came up to us, face like the wrong end of a camel . . . started in on us about . . ." Clarity suddenly blossomed on his face. "About you, Senator." Sempronius said nothing, but gave a small nod. "And then everything sort of went blurry."

Sempronius and Vibia exchanged a small, significant glance. Then Sempronius helped Marcus haul a yet-unsteady Felix to his feet. "We'll straighten this out."

"And wreak some vengeance, I hope," Felix said. "Being cursed . . . and in the Forum!"

Marcus put an arm around his brother's back to support him. "Look at it this way, brother—Perhaps you were just receiving payback now for something you did earlier in life."

"Or something I've yet to do?" Felix said, managing a small grin.

"Take him home, Marcus," Sempronius said. "Though you may want to stop by the Temple of Asclepius on the way and have someone see to his hands."

Felix looked at his knuckles as though just realizing they were raw and bleeding. "Yes . . . I think that'd be good . . ."

Sempronius and Vibia stood alone in the atrium for a few minutes after the Autroniae departed. Vibia had her arms folded across her chest, staring blankly at the door. "I didn't like to say it in front of everyone, brother," she said, "but what happened to Felix was highly illegal."

"Of course it was," Sempronius said, confused. "The use of magic to incite—"

"No," Vibia said. "Not just the *leges tabulae magicae*," she said, referring to Aven's body of laws that pertained only to those with magical blessings. "That was not only Fracture magic. That was *Discordian*." Sempronius's head jerked towards her sharply. Vibia nodded. "To go after the emotions like that, to incite violence in a public place . . . That was bread and oil to the Discordian cult."

"There aren't meant to be any left in the city," Sempronius said. He had no praise for most of Ocella's pronouncements, but banishing the Discordian cult had been one of the Dictator's finer notions. He had done it because he feared their disruptive power, not out of piety, but the effect was beneficial nonetheless. Discordia represented the darker aspect of Fracture, the uncontrollable chaos beyond the neat lines of Janus and the circling wheel of Fortuna.

"Someone forgot to tell them that, then," Vibia replied. "I'm not mistaken."

"I had not assumed you were. I am merely surprised."

Vibia snorted. "You hide your nature. Is it so surprising they might hide theirs in order to practice in secret?"

"Fair enough."

Vibia regarded her brother for a long moment. However traditional her typical inclinations, in this, she heartily agreed with Sempronius. A man should not be barred from the full expression of his abilities by ancient restrictions. She could never quite feel as calm about the threat of discovery as Sempronius did, though, could not shrug off the terror she felt whenever she contemplated his exposure. But Sempronius, as ever, would do as he willed. "I assume that you'll be conducting your own investigation."

"Of course," Sempronius said. "I imagine I'll be able to track it. It will be weeks before I can use the mirror, though." Vibia nodded. Shadow magic did best at the dark of the moon, and the new moon had passed at the end of October, a few days previous.

"Well," she said, "give me a target. I'll prepare a most . . . appropriate response."

XXIV

Neitin knelt hip-deep in the water near the shore, letting the cool water ripple over her thighs. Her hair was pinned atop her head to keep it dry, and the sun warmed the back of her neck. She cupped her palm and poured water over her shoulders, rubbing at her skin to sluice off a thin layer of gray dust.

They were near a town that had once belonged to the Vettoni, their allies, but had been taken over by the Arevaci. No longer. Ekialde and his men had waited until the people were in their fields, bringing in the last harvests, then laid waste to the unprepared populace. All the men were slaughtered, and most of the women. Some children were spared, but only those who showed promise as warriors or armorers, or who were pretty enough to keep as slaves. They were Arevaci, the enemy. Ekialde assured her they deserved no better.

What was left of the town would be returned to the Vettoni, though what use they would find in a smoking wreck, Neitin could scarcely imagine. Ekialde had told his men to strip the fields and larders of everything they could carry with them, then set fire to the rest. Hours later, the flames were dying down, their thick black smoke fading to a wispy haze.

Neitin stood and put her back to the charcoal tendrils still curling their way above the tree line. Her younger sisters played and splashed nearby, laughing and chattering. Nothing seemed to disturb *their* good cheer. Two talked of nothing but the handsome young warriors they intended to marry, and the third had been practicing with her bow, hoping to convince Ekialde to let her join a raid. To them, the war seemed a great game. They all supported Ekialde without question, and they all thought Neitin the luckiest woman of the Lusetani.

Their chattering and teasing was preferable to the strange reverence some others of the tribe approached her with now, as though she too were god-touched like her husband. The women wanted her to bless their hearts and wombs, to ensure happy marriages and healthy children. The men brought her gifts, hoping she would intercede with her husband on their behalf—not for favors or political gain, but to have Bandue bless and protect them. After months of such behavior, Neitin had still not figured out how to respond to these requests. *'All because I married him before, when he was just a handsome young hunter.'*

At times, she felt horribly disloyal. She was tired of tramping through forests, up and down mountains, across vast expanses of rock and brush. Neitin wanted to go home—to the village left so far behind them, where a tree protected her husband's life. Or even back to her father's village where the Tagus broadened and flattened before meeting the Endless Ocean. She thought sometimes of packing a mule and going, to bear her child somewhere safe, far from smoking fields, butchered corpses, and hungry ravens.

But she did not. Ekialde was not only her husband, but *erregerra*, proclaimed so by the elders and the magic-men. She didn't like them, particularly not his sly uncle Bailar, but they spoke with the voice of the gods. Neitin could no more fight that than sprout wings and fly back to her village.

And so she knelt in the river, letting it bear away her fears and prayers alike.

"Not too cold yet?"

Neitin recognized her husband's voice, but did not turn. "Pleasant," she said. "Invigorating." Her sisters, snickering, made their way back to shore and started retrieving their tunics from the shrubs where they had draped them. As none of them suffered from an abundance of modesty, Neitin suspected they had more interest in giving her a moment alone with her illustrious husband than with concealing their nudity.

Neitin heard a splash and a plunk as he entered the water behind her. His arms came around her middle, one hand cradling her belly, the other cupping her breast. "It's safe? For the child?"

"The water?" Neitin said, laughing. "What could be better for our baby, than to be cradled in Nabia's loving arms?"

"Hmm . . ." Ekialde toyed with her nipple idly, rolling it in his fingers like a bead. "I suppose there is some sense to that. Though if you really think so . . ." Moving swiftly, he lifted her off her feet, hooking one arm under her knees, the other supporting her back. Grinning impishly, he made as though to fling her into the deeper water.

Neitin squealed and flung her arms around his neck. "No! Husband, don't you dare!"

"It's only water, my star!" he argued, swinging her back and forth as though he truly would throw her. "Don't tell me you fear Nabia, now!"

"No! No!" Neitin kicked her legs, as though that would do any good, but in truth, she was pleased. Mischievous, teasing, as bright and energetic as the sun—this was the young man she loved and had married. She wanted his lips curved in a smile, not coated in blood.

◇◇◇◇◇◇◇◇◇◇◇◇◇◇◇

They both returned to camp thoroughly drenched, for Ekialde had not been able to resist giving Neitin a dunking, and Neitin had clung to him with such strength that he had gone under as well. Arm-in-arm, they walked the short space to the cluster of tents a little ways away from the still-smoldering fields. The usual evening bustle was ongoing: men and women stoking campfires, parceling out nuts and fruit, skinning the rabbits and deer that would be their dinner. If Neitin could forget the glint of bronze blades in the fading sunlight, she could almost pretend it was a simple hunting excursion, an almost festival atmosphere. Though Ekialde took smaller bands of warriors along with him when he scouted, he had allowed Neitin to bring enough women and servants with her to make wherever they camped feel more like a proper home.

Neitin's sisters scurried forward when they caught sight of her, clucking their tongues. They bundled her off to her tent for a change of clothing in no time, but the youngest paused to pass a message along to Ekialde. "Great *erregerra*," she said, bowing her head in the warrior's fashion. "Your scouts have returned with word of our nefarious enemy. They await your honored presence at the largest campfire."

Ekialde's eyes followed his wife towards their tent as he listened. He had, for a little while, cast off the heavy cloak of the *erregerra*, and it shamed him now to realize he had enjoyed feeling again so buoyant, so carefree, even if just for a few moments. *'But that is a boy's lightness,'* he reminded himself. *'The gods expect better of you.'* And so he nodded. "I cannot greet them thusly, wife-sister," he said, gesturing at his sodden garments. "Please tell them I will join them as soon as I have changed."

One of her sisters must have told Neitin about the scouts' return, for the cheerfulness had faded from her eyes by the time he reached the tent. She said nothing to him as her sisters re-dressed her and rubbed at her long dark hair with towels. Ekialde did not try to bridge the gulf that had opened up between them again, for as much as he loved her, the burden of the *erregerra* was neither something she could understand, nor that he could explain. And so he donned one of his finer tunics, belted his sword about his waist, and slipped the golden coronet around his brow before stepping out into the night.

His heart lightened again when he saw which scouts had returned: his good friend Angeru and the band he had dispatched to seek news from farther away from the Tagus. "We have word," Angeru said, "of Aventan soldiers, proper ones, with the red crests."

This was what he had been waiting for. "Where?"

"They seem to be in two groups," Angeru replied. "One is too far south for us to reach—yet."

Bailar sent his nephew a significant glance. "It seems we should redouble our efforts to win over the southern tribes," he said. "With their assistance, the south would not be beyond our power to take—and to hold." Ekialde gave him a curt nod that both acknowledged and hushed him, then gestured for Angeru to continue.

He did so with a grin. "The other group could be well within our ability to strike. Word comes from the Vettoni that some five hundred or so Aventan soldiers traveled into their lands. They have allied with the craven Arevaci and appear to be heading towards Toletum."

"Toletum?" The question came from one of Neitin's relatives, a gray-bearded old warrior from her father's village. "So far inland, so swiftly?"

"They would have faced little opposition along the way," said another elder. "Too many of the central and eastern tribes remain unpersuaded."

Before his counselors could enter a discussion regarding the reticence of the coastal peoples, Ekialde held up a hand for silence. "What else do we know?" Ekialde asked. "How many in total? Have they bought any other tribes over to their side?"

"The Vettoni were unsure, *erregerra*." Angeru glanced at one of his comrades as though to affirm what he would say next. "But they suggested—they would not go so far as to swear, mind you, but it was heavily implied—that the Aventans picked up many of the coastal peoples along the way. Horse-riders, for the main part, but they may have some archers with them as well."

Ekialde paced around the fire, rubbing at his beard. "We need to know more," he said. "Angeru, I will send you out again, and others, to learn their numbers. And I will send messengers to our allies, telling them to press towards Toletum."

"Do you think we can take the town?" another warrior asked.

Ekialde could feel the pressing heat of so many eyes on him. It was for an *erregerra* to be bold, yes, but not foolish. Bandue had his own wisdom.

"Not yet," he admitted, though he kept any defeatist tone out of his voice. "But we may be able to stop them getting in. They must mean to winter there." It was a matter Ekialde had given some thought to himself. He could not keep his own people on the move as he had through the summer—particularly not his wife, who would be growing heavy as the snows set in. The Lusetani would need shelter, too. "If we can prevent them from entering the city, they will not find Iberia comfortable in another month or so." The counselors nodded and murmured their approval. "Then," Ekialde proclaimed, "that will be our aim."

XXV

"But why did Felix *do* it?" Galerius asked over the breakfast table on the morning following the brawl. "I know the boy's reputation, but I would have thought even he would know better than to spill blood in the Forum."

"Word amongst the mages," said Marcia, " is that he was magically provoked."

Galerius nearly dropped the pear he had been about to bite into.

Marcia confirmed her words with a nod. "He was found to have been tainted—cursed, in fact."

Galerius did not trouble to ask how Marcia had come by this news. Missives and information were ever her province. "Then the question becomes, who would do such a thing? Felix is a bit of a rascal, but no more than any other young buck in the city. Who could hate him so much?"

"That's the wrong question," Marcia said, with quiet certainty. "Better to ask: Who would benefit most from causing chaos in the Forum? And then, who would see Autronius Felix as the ideal vessel for causing it?" Marcia let Galerius chew on that thought for a moment, then rose from her seat, gesturing toward the atrium. "Your clients are waiting, though I think this morning you would be wise to postpone their matters in favor of arriving early at the Curia."

"Too right, wife," Galerius said, sighing.

◇◇◇◇◇◇◇◇◇◇◇◇◇◇

Even before the session formally convened, trouble was brewing. Galerius entered the Curia to find Buteo in full stride, declaiming Felix to anyone who would listen. Considering the way his voice reverberated off the walls, that included everyone who had arrived thus far, whether they willed it or no. Buteo had his knot of supporters nearest him, including Gratianus, his pick for the consulship. "How can we countenance it?" Buteo asked, sweeping an arm wide. "How can we enjoy learned debate, the rhetorical gifts of our forefathers, when opinions are enforced with fists? When words are drowned out by bloodshed?"

Galerius scanned the crowd for Marcus Autronius and found the stocky Earth mage as far away as he could be and yet remain in the building. His arms were folded as tightly across his chest as his toga would allow, but he gave no other sign that he was listening. *'Thank the gods for Marcus's even temper,'* Galerius thought.

"Yet here is the true author of the debacle!" Buteo had grown, if possible, even louder, pointing now at Sempronius, who had just entered. "He, who has been courting the lowborn mob for weeks, of course his followers would incite chaos in our streets! And all this in the name of the elections—of his desire to gain high office! Will we allow it? To reward a man with high office when his supporters disturb the civil peace? To place the trust of the nation in a man whose bosom friends brawl in the very Forum?"

For a moment, Galerius thought Sempronius would pass on to his seat without comment, but he paused near Buteo and cast over his shoulder, so low Galerius almost did not hear it, "You might remember, Buteo, that it does take two sides to make a fight—but generally only one to end it."

"Insolence!" Buteo barked, and launched into a fresh stream of invectives. Sempronius strolled along to his seat, giving the bombast no further notice.

Rabirus eventually took Buteo in hand so that session could open. In some ways, holding session at all was farcical, since no legislation could be formally implemented until after the elections and since there were no magistrates to make recommendations to. Instead, the Senators had to take direct votes on matters deemed to be of immediate importance—which this morning, to Galerius's dismay, seemed to involve complaints about the quality of sesame imports.

As such, when Galerius noticed Aulus Vitellius bustling in late, he was exceedingly grateful for the interruption.

"Aulus Vitellius," the interim censor croaked in chastisement. "Session has already begun."

Aulus nodded in recognition, though he did not move to his seat, but rather stood in the center of the Curia. "Reverend fathers," he began, "I apologize for my tardiness, but when you hear the news I bring, I suspect you will understand my reason. I beg leave to place a matter before you which needs our swift attention, though we had previously determined to hold off discussing it till the end of the year. As I was preparing to leave my house, I received a letter—" This he produced from within the folds of his toga. "It is from my son, Gaius Vitellius, who is currently leading a vexillation of the Eighth Legion in Iberia." Aulus was uncharacteristically tense, his knuckles white around the scroll. His lips were pale and all the muscles of his face tight, clamping hard around each word he spoke. "He was sent to scout the region and see what truth there was to the rumors of discontent among the local tribes. Instead, he seems to be fighting a full-scale war with a mere two cohorts!"

"Now, really—" began Rabirus.

"He writes—" Aulus said, rolling over the objection, "from the Iberian interior, thusly: 'The situation is worse than we feared. While our coastal cities remain, nominally, at peace, the citizens there are terrified. Those dependent on trade from the mountains for their welfare are facing sharp, sudden poverty, and the rest still live in terror of the Lusetani and their allies coming down out of the heights. Many feared, until Tribune Mennenius or I came to rally auxiliaries from them, that Aven had abandoned them to be ravaged. This fear is prevalent, I must stress, regardless of who the citizens are—Iberian, Tyrian, or Aventan themselves.

"'Further inland, our allies are nothing less than under siege. Their fields are set afire. Their orchards are hewn down. No merchant caravan can travel safely. The rebels have set up blockades and ambushes, several of which we have ourselves encountered and fought our way through. Tribune Mennenius sent word from farther south—I intend to meet him in Toletum—of a sizable settlement entirely destroyed. Its men were killed, its women raped, its children hauled into slavery or sacrificed in bloodthirsty rites.

"'We have succeeded in rallying several of the allied tribes, scattered though they are. I am more grateful than I can say to the brave warriors who have chosen to ride with us, without whom we would be an easy target for annihilation.'" There was murmuring at this, the senators stunned that a tribune of Aven would admit such vulnerability. Aulus Vitellius held up a hand and continued. "'I speak not in disdain of my men, who have suffered since leaving Albina, yet who charge on with admirable determination. But there are fewer than a thousand fighting men between the cohorts, and the enemy seems to multiply daily. The Tartessi, who have holdings within a day's ride of Gades, have failed to respond to any of our messages. The Bastetani declare themselves with us in spirit, but are already so devastated by the Lusetani as to be of no practical use. All the tribes farther west have fallen in with the Lusetani.

"'Worst of all is their war-king, the leader who has set all the others in an uproar. He is called Ekialde in his own tongue. They seem to revere him as half a god. He is said to drink the blood of those he slays and to make enchanted armor out of their bones. Others say he cavorts with dark spirits, fiends and wraiths—*lemures*, as we would understand them. There are even reports that he can use his nefarious powers to call them on the battlefield.'" Aulus paused a moment as a ripple of whispers rolled through the Curia. "'I have not witnessed it myself, as we have not yet engaged with his main force.'"

More whispers, but Aulus still held the scroll up high, with a fierceness in his bright green eyes that made it plain he was not yet finished.

"'I have written the same to Governor Sallust, who dispatched this vexillation in the first place, but Father, I implore you to take this matter to the Senate. Two cohorts are not enough to hold this peninsula together. I doubt it will even be enough to move the Fourth out of Gades, but that would be a start and might buy our survival until spring. I was sent to determine the truth of the rumors, and that report I make: They are true. Iberia is seized by terror. Our allies plea for the protection we have promised them. Send help. By all the gods, send it quickly.'"

Aulus let the scroll snap closed. "Venerable fathers," he said, "there can no longer be any doubt of the seriousness of the situation. Iberia is in an uproar. It is time to prepare our legions in aid of our allies and our own men. We must organize now so that they may march as soon as the spring thaw comes."

As Aulus finished, a flurry of hushed whispers rose from the third row of the Curia. Rabirus made a small hand signal towards his fellows, apparently prompting Buteo, who shoved a hand between a young conservative tribune's shoulder blades. The man stumbled forward, bleating, "I interpose my veto!"

The tribune then had the singularly unpleasant experience of a hundred pairs of eyes turning in his direction simultaneously. "You interpose your veto on *what?*" snarled General Strato, rising from his bench.

"On— On discussion of this topic." The young man gulped.

"Tribune, there is no legislative motion being put to the Senate," said the interim censor. "Therefore, there is nothing for you to veto."

"But—"

"Tribune," the censor said, more forcefully despite the reediness of his aged voice, "the very reason this body decided to delay determination of the Iberian matter until December was so that we could gather information and begin discussions, should we deem preparation necessary. Young Vitellius's report has made that matter simpler for us."

"We also wanted to wait for a full quorum to debate the matter," Rabirus corrected, "which meant waiting until after the elections."

Galerius stood. "The decision of whether or not to go to war belongs to the Centuriate Assembly," he said, "not to this august body. With this new information, I suspect they will make that decision quickly."

"Until then," Rabirus interposed, rising as well, "we have no cause to discuss it here!"

Galerius turned slowly to face Rabirus. "With respect, sir, that was not precisely what I was going to suggest."

"Nonetheless," Rabirus said, squaring his posture against Galerius's, "it is sensible. We should not waste our time discussing an eventuality that, gods willing, will never come to pass."

Sempronius and Strato were on their feet in the same instant, which prompted Buteo to enter the verbal fray. His strident tones set off a chain of shouting and jostling, with Marcus Autronius rising to plead for calm.

Feeling a headache start to pinch at his temples, Galerius sat back down.

XXVI

"Fools, the whole lot of them," Sempronius said, his voice dangerously low, as he sat across a couch from Vitellia Latona later that night. They were at a dinner party thrown by the Crispiniae, where they were not the only ones discussing the Iberian news in feverish whispers. Aulus Vitellius's attention had been much in demand, but Sempronius had immediately sought out Latona, as desirous of finding some solace in her brilliant emerald eyes as he was of hearing her opinions. "What harm does it do to *talk* of a thing? They hinge their whole lives on . . . on inaction!" Such a thought was abhorrent to Sempronius Tarren. Offensive, even, anathema to the mandate of his soul.

Latona smiled mirthlessly. "Sempronius, you should know better than anyone what treacherous little creatures words can be. Of course they fear them."

Aula, who was sitting next to her sister but had been turned backwards in conversation with Proculus Crispinius, swiveled back about. "What are we talking about?"

"Gaius's letter," Latona said.

"Ooh, I was so proud when I heard what Father did, storming in all hellfire," Aula said, popping a grape in her mouth. "Word of that will spread to the people, many of whom would stand in favor of the campaign. They're already talking about it. Pass word through the macellum of the goods to be brought home—wine, metal, slaves, whatever you think will have them salivating the most—and they'll stand by your side in a heartbeat."

Sempronius arched an eyebrow, impressed by Aula's grasp of the situation. "And how are you aware of their preferences, Lady Aula?"

Aula swallowed her grape and grinned. "I have my ways. I've never found that it hurts to keep an ear open to what whispers drift up from the valleys."

"She's being deliberately vague," Latona said, nudging Aula's foot with her toe. "She has a contact in the Subura, a wine-merchant's wife who's a distant relation to us."

"Ooh, how dare you give away my sources?" Aula pretended to scowl at her sister, then threw a grape, which Latona snatched out of the air.

"You'd better hope our hosts didn't see that," Latona said, mock-chiding.

"You hear that the plebs believe it, then," Sempronius asked, "what's said about the land in Iberia?" He had been sounding out his own contacts among wine-sellers, forgers, and foundries, but it was always advantageous to have information confirmed from multiple sources.

"Some do. Some are uncertain of the risk involved." Aula glanced around the room, then jerked her chin in the direction of a pair of men talking to Appius Crispinius in a corner: an ambitious up-and-comer, Naevius, and his brother. "But men like the Naeviae, who missed out on the land grab in Pannonia—they'd be willing to have Aven take the chance. And, of course, where Aven colonizes, someone has to do the building. Plenty of work for our brickmakers and architects. If there's marble alongside the metals our brother says you military men will be tripping over yourselves to get at, so much the better."

Sempronius wondered how many people, glancing at Aula Vitellia, would guess that under bouncing copper curls lay a mind capable of calculating the intricacies of international trade, supply and demand of goods, and the political ramifications of economic fluctuations. He looked at Latona, clever and caring and more talented than she would let herself realize, then at little Alhena, in whom he sensed untested depths, and he had to admire what the Vitellian family could produce. *'Given the right chance, these women could take over the city.'*

All three women were admirable and intriguing, but Latona was the one Sempronius could hardly drag his attention away from. A thoughtful expression sat on her lovely face while her sister chattered. "The Optimates are hardly ones to stick up their noses at profit," she said. "It's a bit of a wonder they aren't scrambling to claim their piece of it in Iberia."

"Ahh, but there is risk involved," Sempronius said, leaning towards her. "And the men who are not willing to take the risk are eager to stop anyone more intrepid from benefiting by such temerity. After all, if we brave sort march off to glory and gain, their choices are dismal indeed: stay at home and risk being called cowards, or go on campaign and undoubtedly prove themselves so at the first engagement." The sharp glint was still in his eyes, but there was also a teasing light to his features now, and both women laughed.

Mirth left Latona swiftly, though. "Sempronius," she said, "what of Gaius's report about this . . . this Ekialde's dark magic?"

"I can tell you they were not as well-received in the Senate as his more concrete information regarding the allied tribes," Sempronius said. "Accusations of blood magic and necromancy are common smears against our enemies, after all."

"But they may yet be true," Latona said.

Sempronius nodded allowance of that possibility—particularly considering what had just happened to Felix. "There are more ways than ours of practicing magic, and we know very little about the native Iberian methods. Learning more about it will be one of the benefits of a conquest—assuming, of course, that we don't kill all of their practitioners before they can tell us anything."

"There are many who would say we should know as little as possible about it," Aula pointed out. "That we should kill them before their methods can infect ours."

Sempronius exhaled in a little huff, remembering a speech of Buteo's from before the Dictatorship, excoriating Numidian strains of magic that had not yet assimilated with the Aventan system. "Yes, there are many who would say so," he said, "and I am hard-pressed to think of a more wasteful point of view."

"These fool men consider that which is different to be dangerous," Aula said as she reached for more grapes.

"Exactly so." Sempronius sighed; it was the sort of attitude he had fought for many years already, and that he knew he would spend the rest of his life fighting. Men like Buteo clung to the way things had always been, oblivious to the influence of a changing world, seemingly unaware that the noble old system they strove to uphold had already begun to fall around their ears. It had been crumbling for generations before they had even been born. The first cracks had shown as soon as Aven began to expand outside the Truscum region, setting its sights on the waving wheat of Alalia, the vital ports of Sicilia, and the rich and ragged coastline of Ionia. Yet the Optimates saw every change not as an opportunity, but as an insult to the *mos maiorum*, a challenge to the gods and their ancestors. It infuriated Sempronius, that they could be so blind to reality, so stubbornly impractical.

At that moment, Herennius appeared at Latona's elbow, taking abrupt hold of her arm. "Wife, I require your assistance." His eyes were not on Latona, but rather on Sempronius, as he spoke. "I want to talk to Old Rufilius about some land he has going up Liguria way, and the goat doesn't appear in a good temper tonight. See if you can't *charm* him into a better mood."

Latona stared blankly at him, then glanced back at Sempronius and her sister. "You will excuse me." As Latona rose, shaking off Herennius's grasp, Sempronius witnessed several submerged communications. Herennius's lip curled in disdain for his wife's powers, even as he was willing to make use of them. The contradiction was naked, ugly. In Latona, he could see a swelling resentment—not only for Herennius's officious behavior, but also for the embarrassment of being commanded to perform on cue. '*A man like him should tremble even to approach a wonder like her, and yet he treats her like chattel.*'

Aula slipped over to claim her sister's vacated seat, noticing how Sempronius's eyes followed Latona's retreating form. "She's quite an asset for him," Aula said, too casually.

"It was an advantageous match for Herennius, to be sure," Sempronius replied.

Astute Aula did not miss the tension in his jaw, nor the delay with which his gaze returned to her. "Oh, yes, in many ways," she continued, her voice pitched high and airy. "Not to aggrandize myself, but my family is of quite good blood, excellent social status—a fine thing for a patrician with provincial roots. It opens many doors for him that might be closed otherwise, and her gifts help give a little extra push. In return, she has a measure of safety and security in an uncertain world." She sighed, twirling one of her ringlet curls around her finger. "Still, sometimes I do wonder . . ."

She let the thought trail off, then turned her attention back to Proculus. Though Sempronius knew perfectly well what she was doing, the manipulation still had the intended effect. He wondered, as he had before, and as Aula intended him to remember now, if the benefits of the match for Latona in any way matched the obvious drawbacks—and what might be done to alter her circumstances more favorably.

◇◇◇◇◇◇◇◇◇◇◇◇

The leading Optimates also met that night to discuss Aulus Vitellius's news, in Rabirus's neatly-ordered triclinium. "No sense of— of dignity! Any of them!" Buteo roared. "The Vitellians are all rabid Popularists, but I expected better of Galerius Orator than to support his nonsense. Strato with his constant war-mongering, the Autroniae and the Naeviae with their common blood polluting the Senate. And Sempronius Tarren. *That* man!"

"He's shameless," Gratianus put in. "I'm sure he means nothing good by it. No demagogue ever does."

"Demagogue! Yes! Exactly!" Buteo's toga flapped about his bony form as he gesticulated. Everyone else was reclining, finishing off the last plates of dinner, but Buteo had not been able to stay still all night. "Say that word in the Forum, and often, Gratianus."

"I do," Gratianus said mildly, leaning back against a stack of pillows and settling his hands over his generous midsection. As the Optimates' best chance at a consulship, he had been carefully governing his rhetoric in public speeches—though Buteo often hectored him to show less restraint.

"It's why we must protect the people of Aven from him," Buteo continued. "It's up to *us,* the *good* men of Aven, to make the weighty decisions they cannot."

"Oh, save the speech for the Forum, Buteo," Cornicen said. "It'll do more good there."

"They have no respect for the *mos maiorum,*" Rabirus said. "It's what comes of allowing all this foreign influence into the city. It dilutes the proper Aventan standards." Rabirus and Buteo both viewed the Republic's founders as nothing less than divinely inspired, led by the gods, not by whim. Why else would Aven be so different a place than any other society, different even from those Athaecan city-states or Tyrian lands where so many of the first settlers had come from? The city thrived because it followed the mandates of the gods in its organization; to challenge that was sacrilege, and would doubtless bring the city to ruin.

A shift of fabric in the corner caught Rabirus's eye: his son, fidgeting on the lowest couch. Lucretius the Younger was twenty-two, still studying the law in preparation for his eventual career in the Senate, but his friends were all mad for war and its supposed glories. *'Too impatient to earn acclaim the proper way, through quaestorships and the courts. No, no, they all want the coronets of honor to propel their careers.'*

That thought served to provide Rabirus's next topic of condemnation. "What a shame it is," he voiced, adjusting himself on his chair, "that the legions have become so—so egalitarian."

Buteo eagerly picked up the thread. "Yes. Yes! There was a time when a man had to be *fit* to serve, had to have *quality.* He had to be able to provide his own arms for the defense of the state, had to have some *investment* in it. Now! Ohhh, now, thanks to fifty years' degradation, *any* man can enter the army and find his way to glory, never minding his own wealth, never minding what it costs the state to keep him!"

"Any free man," corrected Cornicen "Be that fair, at least."

"But for how long?" Gratianus said. "How long before we strike down that barrier as well?"

"Don't be absurd," Cornicen replied. "There's no one in Aven—no, not even Sempronius Tarren, Buteo, don't give me that look—who would be that disgraceful. We're not Parthian potentates, to set slaves to do our fighting for us."

"For how long?" Buteo said, more forcefully. "A hundred years ago, it was unthinkable that the shiftless men of the Head Count be allowed to stand in our defense. Today it is unthinkable that slaves might do so. What will be left to be unthinkable in another hundred years?" Rubbing at his beak of a nose, Buteo huffed. "We should never have gotten involved in the Iberian peninsula to begin with. It's too dangerous, all this expansion." Buteo pounded his fist on the table. "Maritima, Alalia, Sicilia—What do we need with those lands?"

"Grain," Cornicen said, his even voice a stark contrast to Buteo's stentorian echoes. "Wheat. Flax. Oil." He laughed, and Buteo glared. "Good heavens, Buteo, friend, don't tell me you don't see the value in that."

"Dangerous," Rabirus said. Though his voice was quieter than Buteo's, there was a darkness in it that warned he was wearying of debate. "Every time we expand, it brings new peoples into the city, and we don't need them. They unsettle things, they overcrowd, they give the Head Count ideas."

Cornicen smiled, a little too serenely. "Ah. Truly, a cataclysm in the making."

"I believe our friend's point," Gratianus said, seeing the glint in Rabirus's eyes and rushing to speak first, "is that we could do without Iberia just fine. Let the Tyrians have it, or the barbarians, if the Tyrians can't defend it."

"The Tyrians?" Cornicen asked, laughter still in his voice, though more incredulous than genuinely amused. "What Tyrians? Old Tyre is empty and New Tyre never got back on its feet after the Numidian Wars. The men in their colonies are as much Iberian as Tyrian—and as much Aventan, in some cases!"

"That's another problem with the whole mess!" Buteo railed. "And it goes back to the legions again. We bring in all these men, these men who have nothing, no property, no land, but when they are discharged, oh, *then* they must have something!"

"Unnecessary, when good men serve in the armies," Rabirus said. "But when it's this rabble, we must find land to reward them with."

"And where do we find land?" Buteo said. "Not in Truscum, by the gods, at least we haven't sunk that far yet, to give away our homeland. But where, then? How do we find it? By conquering! Eliminate one problem, and we could quite eliminate the other, I believe."

Gratianus strove to retain a neutral expression, caught between his admiration for the principles Buteo and Rabirus espoused and his all-too-acute awareness of the lucrative opportunities that an Iberian campaign would provide. Cornicen, though, just shook his head. "It's not that I don't see what you mean, Buteo," he said. "Your trouble, friend, is that you were born two hundred years too late. Your virtues are so noble, so correct—but so impractical."

"Then think of this," Rabirus said, striding swiftly towards Cornicen, "Do you want men like Sempronius to have such power over the armies? Do you want to arm men who will be more loyal to their Popularist commanders than to the state?"

That actually earned a moment of quiet regard from Cornicen. "You think he would do as Ocella did?"

Buteo opened his mouth, but Rabirus held up a hand to forestall him. Pragmatic Cornicen would be moved by rational arguments, not by Buteo's righteous yowling. "I fear it. His rhetoric about equality, about expanding rights and partnering with lesser nations for mutual good—these are ploys, to put more power into his hands. We have seen this before, and the nation barely survived."

Cornicen shifted the weight of his toga higher on his shoulder. "Survival is . . . an interesting term, to apply to nations," he said. "I know what you fear from men like Sempronius, but I wonder if you have his measure correctly. There is a simple truth, and he may just be addressing it differently than you would: Our world is getting bigger, whether we like it or not."

"I *don't*," Buteo interjected.

Cornicen sighed. "Then it is fortunate that you seem to have no end of energy to fight the tide. I think it would quite exhaust me."

"Then you show yourself weak," Rabirus said, waving a hand dismissively. "I have little use for weak men."

As Rabirus gritted his teeth at Buteo's lack of perspicacity, Cornicen rose from his couch. "Have it your own way," he said, "but consider this: a little leniency, a little *bending*, might do more good than harm. Otherwise, you risk losing the city entirely to men like Sempronius Tarren."

As Cornicen took his leave, Rabirus noted the reactions of the others:

Buteo's protuberant nose was held high, but Gratianus shifted uncomfortably in his seat. *'And then there is my son . . .'* Young Lucretius's eyes had followed Cornicen out, and Rabirus misliked what he saw in them: not quite approving, but too keen, too curious. *'That,'* Rabirus thought, as Buteo launched into a rant about the declining standards of popular poetry, *'will bear watching.'*

As soon as their guests departed, Rabirus took to his study and wrote a letter to Pinarius Scaeva, the Fracture mage Cornicen had pointed out to him weeks earlier. *'Better to remove the instigation,'* Rabirus thought. *'If we strike off the head of the snake quickly, perhaps that will stifle the venom.'* Without a charismatic and ambitious leader, the movement would have less forward momentum.

Rabirus knew he had to be the one to make these decisions. Buteo was obnoxious and disliked; however noble his goals, men would be reluctant to follow him. And Gratianus had to keep his nose clean. He could best serve the Optimate cause by appearing above the fray and appealing to moderates. *'And so it is I who must take the difficult actions . . . I who must stain my soul, for the good of the city.'*

Using Felix as a diversion had not worked so well as he had hoped, thanks to Aulus brandishing inflammatory letters. *'But perhaps that was a weak tactic to begin with. Time to attack our problem more directly.'*

◇◇◇◇◇◇◇◇◇◇◇◇◇◇

"You'll need a better answer, about the expense," Galerius said as he and Sempronius left the Crispiniae's dinner together, their torch-bearing attendants lighting their way through the dim streets. "I don't just mean for the Senate or for the electorate. I mean for *me*."

"Yes, I know. I've had some thoughts." Sempronius had spent many afternoons sequestered in his study with Corvinus and Djadi, calculating and recalculating figures, trying to account for every potential variable. "Fortunately, Ocella didn't leave the treasury in a dismal state."

Galerius chuckled. "Quite the opposite, actually. For all the man's faults . . . We have had worse custodians of the public funds."

"It still won't be enough, though."

"The Tyrians?" Galerius suggested. "They're the ones begging for aid, insisting Aven defend their trading interests. Surely we borrow money from them."

"No," Sempronius said. "Not borrow. We will request that they shoulder some of the burden, and if they do not accede quickly enough, we will demand." Not the gentlest of diplomatic measures, but the protection of Aven could not be taken for granted. Sempronius meant to follow through on Aven's promise—but Tyre would have to contribute to the cause. "But we'll still have to raise funds, and we can only borrow so much from abroad. Bithynia and Abydosia will be more than happy to loan, but—"

"—but they won't be shy about calling in the debt, either." Galerius sighed. "And so much of the funding will have to come from the equestrian class."

Those men, wealthy but not ennobled, nestled below the uppermost echelons of society, could be forward-thinking and eager to seize opportunity, or they could be even more hidebound and intractable than men like Buteo and Rabirus. "If we balance out a property tax—or perhaps an import tax—with loans from some of the most prominent, men like Papirius Dolus, we might meet with more success. Then we—"

Something pricked at Semponius's attention, and he found his gaze wandering. He could see nothing out of the ordinary: the slaves before and behind them, with mostly quiet houses beyond their orb of illumination. Carts and donkeys would be crowding the streets below, but here on the wealthy, mostly residential Palatine, few other people were about. Yet Sempronius sensed someone . . .

"Sempronius?"

He shook his head, turning his attention back to Galerius. "Yes. Then we pay the people back out of the proceeds."

Galerius glanced sideways at him. "Tax them up front and then issue a remittance after the war?" Sempronius nodded. "Hard to think there'll be enough left for the people after you've paid out the legions."

"I don't just mean the spoils of war," Sempronius said. "I mean . . . I mean any of a hundred things. Conquest is not my goal; coalition is. For the rebel tribes as well as our allies. Far more profitable, if we think about it properly. If we tread them into the dirt, they only pay out once. If they remain our valued allies, then their bounty is renewable. Tariffs on goods they want to trade into Aven, an additional property tax to settle inside our cities, port fees and security fees, a levy on anyone granted Aventan citizenship—"

"Careful there," Galerius said. "There's many men won't like the idea of selling the citizenship—and I'd be among them."

"Not *selling*, friend," Sempronius said swiftly. "Just . . . asking for a contribution from those good men whom we've already determined are worthy of the honor."

Galerius mulled that over. "A fee which, you could argue, speaks to the investment that men like Rabirus fear immigrants can never make to the state."

Galerius was still talking, but Sempronius's attention felt fish-hooked away from him again. His thread of Water magic, he realized, picking up on magic in use somewhere. Not a signature he recognized, nor a pattern he could easily catch. His eyes strayed to the shadows beyond their circle of light. *'Someone is watching . . . someone is following . . .'*

"—it's an unusual proposal," Galerius was saying. "I think you may have a hard time selling it to the Senate."

Sempronius chose not to mention that, when it came to enfranchising Iberia, his preference would be to act first and sell the idea afterwards.

"But if you convince enough equestrians," Galerius went on, "then they may convince their patrons . . ."

"Let me send you some of the notes I've made, based on reports from merchants in Gades and Tarraco," Sempronius said, dragging his attention back again. "If they don't convince you, well, say as much, and I'll try to figure something else out."

"To convince me or to adjust the plan?"

"Whichever seems more sensible."

Galerius laughed. "That's what I like about you, you know. It's how I know you're not the demagogue they fear. Well, I'm this way." They had reached the split in the road, and Galerius nodded northward.

"Safe journey," Sempronius said. "I'll send Corvinus over with the reports in the morning."

As soon as they had rounded the corner, Sempronius gestured for Corvinus to fall into step with him. Their circle of light was smaller and dimmer now, without the Galerian attendants in addition to Sempronius's own. "Tell me what you sense." Corvinus was a weak mage, more sensitive to his element of Water than truly able to manipulate it, but Sempronius knew that if he could pick up on the threads without trying, so could Corvinus.

"I'm not sure, Dominus," Corvinus replied. "I've been getting . . . flickers. Like someone's just checking in."

"I don't like that."

"Nor I, Dominus."

XXVII

Following the river towards Toletum did not prove as simple as Tribune Vitellius had hoped. They had volleyed back and forth across the Arevaci territory for the first several days, so that Bartasco could gather warriors to come with them and consolidate his civilians under the protection of those left behind.

Vitellius had been surprised, too, that Bartasco had collected a few magic-men to join their company. The Iberians had star-readers, though their methods bore little similarity to Aventan astrologers, as well as men who blessed the water that the troops drank. *'What Governor Sallust will make of this . . .'* Vitellius had thought as he made brief mention of it in a report that he sent north. Thanks to the prohibition of Mars against magic on the battlefield, Aventan legions hardly ever traveled with mages, except perhaps an Air-dedicated avian specialist here and there, to send reports with enchanted birds. *'Hopefully Mars won't take offense at the actions of our allies.'*

Once they began to march in earnest, it proved even more difficult than the charge up from the coast. In that direction, at least, there had been proper roads part of the way. Here, the terrain was natural, rocky, and uneven. The river basin sluiced through hard rock, leaving little room to march along the banks, and it careened drunkenly around the pointed peaks. Sometimes the hills crashed so suddenly into the river that the army had to abandon the banks entirely, ascending to narrow paths through the forest.

It was not the way an Aventan legion liked to march, stretched out in a thin line, and the vulnerability of it was making Vitellius irritable.

He was, however, learning quite a bit about the Iberian tribesmen who accompanied him. Most Edetani rode horses, but the same was not true of the Arevaci, many of whom had fallen amiably in line with the legionaries, marching along with packs and shields. For all that he was their chief, Bartasco was, more often than not, among the pedestrians.

"He has never trusted horses," Hanath said, laughing. "They sense it and do not like him much, either. But," her shoulders moved in a shrug beneath her patterned cloak, "I think it just as well, in some ways. The lads like it, that he will walk with them. And if trouble should come," she added with a grin, "I can always ride to his rescue and sling him across the back of my saddle."

Hanath, Vitellius found, was an education unto herself. He had encountered female warriors before. The northern Albine tribes had some, though to Vitellius's dismay, the rumors about them riding bare-breasted into battle had proved unfounded. They were rarer among the Iberians, but Hanath had a few Arevaci girls riding attendance on her, all at least passingly familiar with a bow and arrow. Hanath's favored weapon was the spear, which Vitellius recognized as a Numidian design, not Iberian. Vitellius had considered warning his men not to meddle with the Arevaci maids, but it proved unnecessary. Hanath had more than taken care of that on the day they watched her bring down an ibex with such force that the spear-tip came out the unfortunate creature's other side.

From Hanath, Vitellius was making an effort to learn more of the Iberian language—though she warned him that many of the tribes had their own dialects, and that the Lusetani might remain incomprehensible, for all her tutelage. "It was quite a trouble for me, when I arrived!" she said, as she and Vitellius rode at the head of the winding column. They had come out of a rocky pass that morning, where the Henarus opened up into a broad lake. The water was nearly teal and too murky to reflect the surrounding peaks. Hanath had assured him it was a good sign, for the tributary river turned westward from here, cutting further inland towards Toletum and the Tagus River. "You see, I was born in Numidia, but hardly grew up there. I spent more time on boats than I did on dry land, with my father and brothers. And we came to Iberia often. More, after you Aventans decided to make war in our land," she said, a faintly chiding note in her voice.

"After we were *invited* to settle a territorial dispute between members of your own ruling family," Vitellius corrected.

"Yes, well," Hanath snorted, "you settle things with considerable force." She waved a hand. "But, had you not, I might never have met Bartasco. His people trade in Tarraco, you know, and I spent so much time there as a girl, I could speak the coastal dialect quite well. But then he wanted to bring me inland, and suddenly I had to learn the Edetani and Arevaci tongues as well." She rolled her eyes. "It is fortunate I was young and eager. I think now I would be too stubborn to learn."

"I feel much the same about Athaecan," Vitellius confessed. "I don't think any Aventan would bother to learn it if it wasn't forced on him in his youth. But you speak Tyrian as well, don't you?"

Hanath nodded. "Numidian is my mother-tongue, Tyrian my milk. Most traders of my father's sort speak both, and Athaecan as well."

Vitellius realized, with a bit of shame, that Hanath utterly trumped him when it came to languages. He had only Truscan, Athaecan, and a smattering of the Tennic argot that the soldiers stationed on the border tended to pick up. Yet here was a woman who seemed to have learned twice as many languages by the time she had married. *'Perhaps we Aventans could learn something from that.'* To cover his blush, he coughed. "So, since your husband does not ride, who was it that taught you?"

"My eldest brother," Hanath replied. "Though I confess, I did not give him much of a choice. I decided I was going to learn to ride, and he decided it was better to teach me right than watch me crack my head open." She gave him a sidelong glance, her dark eyes merry. "You are thinking I am an abnormal woman, yes, Tribune?"

"Not at all," he replied. "I was actually thinking you remind me a bit of my eldest sister."

Hanath slapped her thigh. "You are a man with sisters!" she crowed. "I had wondered where you came by your good sense. So, does this sister of yours ride astride? I did not think you Aventans let your women into battle."

"No, no," Vitellius said, chuckling at the mental image of Aula in a cuirass and scarlet cloak. "I don't mean in that way. But I see her in your determination."

His mouth twisted up at one corner, and Hanath watched him in silence for a moment before asking, "You miss them, don't you?" Vitellius nodded. "How long has it been?"

"Five years," Vitellius said. "I got letters from them regularly in Albina, but . . ."

"Not the same."

"Not quite." Something in Hanath's careful silence prompted him to add, "Not at all. It's strange, the way life seems to freeze and go on at the same time. Father dispenses advice, and my sisters pass along gossip, and I can hear their voices in their words . . . and yet I have a niece I've never met."

Hanath shifted in her saddle. "It has been long since I have seen my family, too. It's different. I chose to stay with Bartasco, and he is my heart now. But still, I will offer a prayer that you may return to them, Tribune."

And then the somberness passed as swiftly as it had fallen upon her. "But not before you teach these bastard Lusetani a lesson, eh? You've made us a promise, and I intend to make you stick to it!"

∞∞∞∞∞∞∞∞∞∞∞

As the afternoon wore on, the legion wound its way to the southern side of the lake. The river took a sharp turn to the west around a ragged cliff of ocher stone. *'Even the rocks here look odd,'* Vitellius thought. The orange hues were unlike the mossy tones of Albina or the grayer rocks of the Apennine Mountains. The trees were different, too, more colorful than those in Truscum, where the forests were mostly pine. The Iberian hills were striped amber and vermilion and crimson at this time of year, in distinct strata up the mountainside. It was beautiful—but strange.

'Perk up, Tribune,' he told himself. *'You're slinking into enemy territory with five hundred men and the winds of winter nipping at your heels. This is no time to get homesick.'*

No sooner had they cleared the rocky spur than Vitellius found himself nearly face-to-face with a bearded man on a horse. Vitellius had just enough time to think that he had surprised as much as he had *been* surprised before noticing that the fellow was not alone—and that one of the men behind him was reaching for a sword.

"*Shields!*" Vitellius bellowed, drawing his own blade. "*Formation!* Hold lines!" A horn answered him, carrying the message to the rest of the cohort. The group ahead of him was small—only a dozen, if there weren't more of them lurking nearby. Small, but armed, and angry.

For as much time as he had spent drilling the infantry, Vitellius remained a nimble cavalryman. As his opponent swung at him, Vitellius danced his horse out of the way. He had no intention of fighting like that, though, not with only himself and a few other mounted men at the head of the column. Instead, he wheeled about, splashing his horse into the water alongside the cohort, which had arranged itself into tight lines, five across, with remarkable speed. The path was too narrow to allow for more, but it would be enough. Vitellius raised his sword. "Repel cavalry!"

The first rank of shields snapped together into a firm wall, while the two lines behind them brought up their *pila,* the javelins particular to the Aventan legion. Their iron shanks gleamed briefly in the sunlight before, at a whistle from a centurion, the legionaries loosed them into the air.

Horses screamed, but men mostly just made sickening burbles when they caught a spearhead straight in the chest. Four of the enemy warriors went down in the first volley. A few others had brought their shields up in time, but were then forced to abandon them. The genius of the Aventan *pilum* was that it broke beneath the head upon impact, so it could not be thrown back, but stuck in the shield, weighing it down and rendering it useless.

A second whistle brought another rain of javelins. The remaining horses were in a panic, and their riders were unable to control them. Vitellius turned in his saddle, looking for the Edetani and Arevaci cavalry—and there they were, eyes fixed on him, awaiting their order. "Cavalry forward!"

He saw the mad grin spreading across Hanath's features as she galloped ahead of the Edetani riders, spear in one hand, shield on her left arm, reins tied about her waist. They came down the left side of the tightly packed cohort, some of them rushing through the water. Vitellius felt an urge to push forward with them, but that was not a commander's role. Instead he watched as his allies made short work of their remaining foes.

The opposing force did not immediately turn tail and flee, however. One of the Edetani auxiliaries caught a cruel blow across his shoulder, cutting to the bone and spraying hot blood across man and horse alike. Howling in agony, he fell back, but the warrior next to him paid back the injury, sinking his spear deep into the offender's chest. A backhanded swipe from a blade caught another of their opponents across the back, and though his leather armor protected him, the force of it knocked him from the saddle. The first line of Aventan legionaries spread his guts across the dirt before he could so much as sit up.

Finally, the last two of the enemy tried to run. Hanath caught one before he could even turn his horse around, spearing him with the same accuracy that had felled the ibex. Two Edetani rushed up on either side of the last man, stabbing from both sides.

And then it was over, and all fell quiet again. At a nod from Vitellius, the centurions blew their whistles in a signal to relax formation. Vitellius's chief centurion, Calix, came forward with Bartasco while the Edetani chased down those horses still alive. "Scouts, I think," Bartasco said, cleaning his sword with a scrap of an enemy's cloak. "Or there would have been more of them."

"We should have left one alive," Vitellius said, sighing. "For information." A real general, a proper commander, he felt, would have thought of that. Vitellius had thought only of eliminating the immediate threat. *'So much yet to learn . . .'*

Hanath had dismounted, spiked her spear into the dirt, and was strolling among the bodies. "Vettoni," she said, pointing. "Look."

Vitellius did, but whatever she saw meant nothing to him, though Bartasco nodded in agreement. "Err . . ." Vitellius said, neither wanting to advertise his ignorance nor willing to miss out on potentially vital information. "Vettoni, you say?"

Hanath kicked the corpse a bit, so that his arm fell back from his chest, exposing a brooch of fine-wrought copper holding his cloak to his tunic. "This style of metalworking is peculiar to their tribe. We've seen enough of it on the raiders around our towns." She kicked him again for good measure.

The injured Edetani auxiliary had been brought down off his horse by two of his fellows, and was now lying on the flat stones at the river's edge. Vitellius turned to Calix. "Find one of our medics. See if there's anything that can be done for him." He rubbed his chin as Calix scurried off. "Scouts . . ."

"At least none got off to warn the main force, wherever it is," Bartasco said. "But," he squinted down the river, "we may not be able to avoid them."

"You think they've guessed we're heading for Toletum?"

Bartasco rubbed at his beard. "Maybe. Maybe this was just coincidence—lucky for us, unlucky for them. But if word has reached them that there are Aventan forces in the mountains, then yes—Toletum would be the most obvious choice."

Vitellius nodded his agreement. From what he knew, it was by far the most defensible town in the region. If the Lusetani knew anything at all about Aventan methods, they would know the cohorts would want to winter there. *'And with Governor Fimbrianus setting such an excellent example of a legion tucking in, down in Gades . . .'* he thought, with a snort.

"The Vettoni seemed ill-prepared," Hanath said. "I think this was guesswork, no more. They may have scouting parties along all the likely routes."

"They may have *traps* along the likely routes," Vitellius said.

"So," Hanath said, "the faster we can get to Toletum, the better."

"The faster?" Bartasco said. "Or the safer? If we took a different route . . . through the forests, instead of alongside the river . . ." He looked to Vitellius. "What will it be, Tribune?"

After a moment's consideration, Vitellius answered, "Faster. We stick to the river." He met Bartasco's eyes. "Your men are used to marching in these forests, but mine are not. If we could be sure of evading any other Vettoni or Lusetani forces, it might be worth it, but if we got caught out in that terrain, it would be worse than on more open ground." Vitellius caught Calix by the shoulder as the centurion returned with a medic. "Tell the men to march prepared for battle from now on. We may meet with more Vettoni between here and Toletum. We did good work today, but we could yet meet with a larger force. We must stay alert." Not for the first time, Vitellius wished his vexillation had included an Air mage amongst its non-combatants. A man blessed by Mercury could send a pigeon to find a man on the move rather than a home roost. Vitellius wanted to rejoin the two cohorts, and he wanted his friend Mennenius at his side, should they encounter further troubles.

XXVIII

CITY OF AVEN

"Latona!" Aula, with her usual degree of patience, came rushing into the atrium where her sister waited. "I'm sorry to have kept you, I was only half-dressed when they said you'd arrived, Lucia delayed me with—oh, never mind that." She rushed forward and clasped her sister's hands. "You have news? Did you go to the Temple? Is it—" But her enthusiasm dimmed, seeing the look on her sister's face. "Oh dear. What is it, my honey?"

"I did go to the Temple of Ceres," Latona said. "Three times. But I'm afraid . . . I'm afraid I was mistaken, Aula."

Aula's face fell. "They read your water? Did the trick with the rabbit? Made you drink that awful milky stuff?"

Latona nodded to all. "They did, they did. I must have miscalculated. Herennius wasn't pleased."

Aula wrapped an arm around Latona and bundled her off to a secluded sitting room, chattering the whole way and leaving a confused Helva standing in the atrium with Merula. "What's the matter with your lady?" Helva asked.

Merula shrugged. "She thought she might be breeding, but she isn't." She did not offer that the Domina and her husband had had a row fit to bring down the rafters, considering that little of Helva's business.

Though sorry for her mistress, Merula was secretly glad. Even if a baby would mean something good came out of what her domina had to endure, Merula did not think she could find it in her heart to joy over another Herennius coming into the world.

Helva was mumbling her consolation, which Merula shrugged off. "You have any?" she asked. "Babies, I mean."

Helva paused for a moment, and Merula braced for a telling-off for her insolence. But then, with a little noise that might have been a sigh, she said, "One. Not long after Domina Vipsania brought me here."

"Who was he?" Merula said, then amended herself, "if I may be asking."

"Yes, you may ask," Helva said. "His name was Ulix, and he was Dominus Vitellius's steward at the time. Domina gave us permission to wed. She knew I was breeding before I did. It's a talent of Water, you know, to sense that. And then . . ." Something clouded her pale eyes, making Merula sorry she had asked. "And then they both died. A flux went through the city, and it took them both, along with half the household, and the Domina's first son."

Merula was quiet a moment, then said, "I sorrow for you."

"It was long ago. I've long since stopped feeling pain over it." Her voice was as placidly uninflected as ever, but Merula was not sure whether or not to interpret that as a true lack of emotion. "But I thank you anyway."

"Tsch," Merula said, leaning against the wall for a brief moment, before Helva's sharp eyes made her straighten up. "So much death in one household, all at once? What a tragedy."

Helva's mouth quirked up on one side. "More tragedy than you know. The dominus hasn't had a decent steward since."

Before Merula could ask anything else, they were interrupted by their mistresses' return to the atrium. This time, Aula was fully dressed, apparently ready to go out.

"Oh, it isn't your fault, Aula," Latona was saying as they walked towards the door. "The gods know I distress myself over it plenty. Honestly, it's just that . . . the humiliation of it, of wondering if everyone's calling me barren behind my back—"

"Not in my hearing, they aren't," Aula bit off, green eyes flashing angrily. "And if I ever heard they were, I'd take them down a peg, and no mistake."

"I suspect no one would be foolish enough to let such words slip in front of you, dear." Latona sighed. "But I'm sure some are thinking it. Blessed by Juno and Venus, and yet I can't manage to produce *something* positive out of this marriage."

Aula chewed on her lower lip, hating the expression on her beloved sister's face. Defeat was not something she was used to seeing on Latona's proud features. "Well. Put it out of your mind for the moment, anyway," she said, forcing cheerfulness into her voice. "We'll go out shopping, and then do you know what? Maia Domitia has asked me for dinner, and I'm sure she wouldn't mind a bit if you turned up as well. You know she's fond of you."

◇◇◇◇◇◇◇◇◇◇◇◇◇◇

When the two eldest Vitelliae and their attendants departed, Mus, who had been watching from behind a column, crept across the house to her mistress's chamber, finding her, as usual, flat on her back in bed, staring up at the ceiling. "Domina? Your sisters, they go."

It took a moment for Alhena to register this, but at last she stood. "Dress me, then."

For weeks now, Mus had been helping her mistress keep a secret. Alhena had taken to slipping out of the house whenever she thought she could go unnoticed. It was easy enough. No one in the Vitellian household paid much mind to who came and who went. Aulus Vitellius had never been the sort of man to stifle his daughters' freedom.

"Where did they go?" Alhena asked. From this, she could gauge how much time she would have.

"Shopping and dinner," Mus said, fussing with the drape of Alhena's stola. "Some lady's house." She had not caught the name. Alhena nodded, grateful for the respite. Dinner bought her several hours of freedom. She felt Mus hesitate, then heard her say, "Your sisters, they worry, Domina."

Alhena drew the mantle up over her head, pulling the edges forward to conceal her profile. "I know," she said. And she did. They might not have always expressed it in the best ways. Aula had little patience and a quick temper and tended to snap; Latona seemed discomfited, not so much by Alhena's behavior but by not knowing what to do about it, and so she went sad-eyed and distant. But Alhena knew how much they worried, and how much they cared. She knew it from the gentle stroking of her hair or her back in quiet moments. She knew it from the little trinkets and trifles that showed up in her room—new hair ribbons, bits of poetry, sketches, rings. She knew it from the fresh flowers and fragrant garlands hung in her chamber. She knew it because, when she did decide to emerge for meals rather than taking them alone, somehow the table was always set with her favorite foods, ideally designed to tempt her appetite. They loved her, and they were concerned, and showing it in the best way they knew how. "It isn't as though I don't appreciate it," she said. "But they don't know what to say."

"And they do, at the temple?"

Mus's question was genuine, not provocative, and Alhena did not mind it. She sighed though, thinking of what it was that drew her back to the Temple of Proserpina so often. "They understand." Proserpina understood grief all too well, as the priestesses had reminded her. She knew what it was to mourn. She spent half her eternal life surrounded by the spirits of the dead, after all. For Mus, however, Alhena framed it in different terms. "No one there offers to introduce me to some young man or another. They don't urge me to come or go, to be more active or more sociable. They don't tell me it's time to be getting on with my life."

Aula and Latona might not have actually said those words, but Alhena could see it in their eyes. The priestesses let her have her misery. They were *used* to misery. The Temple of Proserpina was a sanctuary for the bereaved, a place to weep and to lament. Not a day passed but some broken-hearted unfortunate came to light a lamp at the altar or to add her tears to the impluvium pool.

"And besides," Alhena said, "they can help me with . . . with my talents. It's clear to me that I must get better control of this. Maybe if I had . . ." Tears sprang to her eyes, and she felt Mus's hand on her shoulder. "Nothing warned me, Mus. For all that I saw, nothing told me I wouldn't have a life of contentment and joy with Tarpeius. Just those clouds, at the end—and what good did that do?" Alhena never wanted to be caught off-guard like that again. She had barely survived the pain the first time around. She did not think she could do so again. She didn't intend that, but she knew such things were not always in her control.

And so she went to the Temple of Proserpina, for training as well as for comfort. She left her father's house with her gray mantle pulled forward around her face. Looking down at her feet the whole way, she walked down the Palatine, through narrow streets to the Apulian forum. She came and went, and made no accounting for her hours. And she did not tell the sisters she loved, for she could not find the words to make them understand.

◇◇◇◇◇◇◇◇◇◇◇◇◇

If Aula and Latona were somewhat derelict in their duties to their sister, it was not for want of care for her, but because they were both over-occupied with their own affairs. Aula spent most of each day out of the house, unless she had specifically determined to receive guests of her own. With ever-present Helva trailing in her wake, and usually flanked by a pair of sturdy attendants, Aula walked and walked. She felt as though she had covered a thousand miles in a few weeks, from the Aventine to the Quirinal and everywhere in-between.

She did not troop forth merely on social calls. With Aulus standing for censor and Gaius's career to be made or marred by the Iberian venture, Aula had set to laying the foundation for future success with a focused passion. Those connections and alliances she had once thought to exploit on her husband's behalf, she now employed for Gaius's benefit. "He's practically fighting a war by *himself* over there," she cooed in tricliniums across the Palatine and the Caelian. "Positively covering himself in glory, especially for a tribune."

Latona had also been spending more time with new company and revived friendships. She and Aula had both, since the Dictator's death and the subsequent awakening of Aventan society from its terrified hibernation, been getting re-acquainted with some girlhood companions, but Latona had also decided to renew magical connections. *'Aemilia can bar me from the libraries, but she can't stop me talking to other mages or plumbing their resources.'* Marcia lent her a philosophical text, which she was thoroughly enjoying, and she spent a happy afternoon in one of the city's parks as Terentilla used her Earth magic to lure partridges, sparrows, and rabbits into their laps. It was surprisingly pleasant to associate with women who could talk not only of husbands and babies and housekeeping, but who also had opinions on religious and ethical matters.

She had also been spending more time in the company of Sempronius Tarren's social set—the Autroniae brothers, the younger Crispinians, the Domitiae, along with their sisters and wives. It was a merry group and no mistake, full of the wild young bucks and strong-headed Popularists who gave the Optimates such headaches. Latona enjoyed their company partly because they reminded her of how young *she* still was, just twenty-two, for all that she was a wedded matron. It was a fine thing, to feel so young and strong, rather than like a withered crone, entombed before her time. But it was Sempronius whose presence drew Latona in, just as it was his voice echoing in her mind: *'. . . who is, I think, destined for more,'* that had helped to spur on the defiance driving her. Though the year was dwindling, Latona felt like she could sense springtime ahead, for the first time in years.

Like Aula, Maia Domitia had been widowed by Ocella's proscriptions, left alone with a young son, an infant daughter, and her family's too-illustrious name. She had spent a year in unofficial exile in Athaeca, hoping to avoid further notice. Her nature was calmer than Aula's, but still more sanguine than melancholy. Only rarely did Latona feel sorrow flit behind her countenance, when she remembered those dark days and their losses.

The talk that evening, however, was not so serious. Maia's brothers were eager to set up a new marriage for her, and she solicited the Vitelliae's opinions on the suggested grooms. "Heavens, no, not Young Crispinius." Aula rolled her eyes. "He's so serious—and so timid! The man never seems to be able to make up his mind about anything."

"That might do very well for her," Latona said. "Dear Maia isn't quite as—"

"Frivolous?" Aula said, grinning.

"*Adventurous* as you, I was going to say." She plucked an almond from the nearest bowl.

"Well, I suppose timid husbands might have some advantages when it comes to ruling your own roost, but *I* think you should set your sights on Young Rufilius," Aula said, fluffing up her pillows. "Might as well be a handsome fellow, if you're getting a choice about it."

"Him?" Maia said, laughing. "Too young."

"He's older than all of us," Latona pointed out.

"Yes, but it takes men so much longer to mature," Maia said. "They're like stubborn grapes. Pluck them too early, and they're no good for anything."

"And if you wait too long," Aula said, "then they shrivel up and haven't any juice left in them!"

"And of course some will just be sour no matter what you do," said Latona.

"The only way to be sure, really," Aula said, wriggling impishly on her couch, "is to sample the vintage before you commit to the vine."

"Aula, you're terrible!" Maia said, but all three were laughing heartily.

"Domina?" The women looked up, wiping away tears of mirth, to see the Domitian steward. "I am sorry to interrupt, but a messenger arrived with an invitation for you." His eyes moved to the Vitelliae. "It was meant for the Dominae Vitelliae as well. I hope I was not too forward in telling him I would pass it along to you."

"Not at all," Aula said. "Spare the poor man a bit of hiking up and down the hills."

"What was the invitation?" Maia asked.

"Galerius Orator invites you all to his villa near Tibur in three days' time, for a banquet followed by a day of hunting."

"How lovely," Maia said. "A hunt's just the thing for fall. So long as the weather holds, of course."

"Did he say who else would be attending?" Aula asked.

"I did ask who else was invited, Domina," the steward replied. "I do not know who has accepted, but in addition to his own family, Galerius Orator has invited the Terentiae, the Crispiniae, the Rufiliae—" Aula winked at Maia, who threw an almond at her. "—the Autroniae, the Ulpiae, the Camillae, the Ardae, and the Semproniae." There was the look from Aula again, and Latona could not deny the heat rising on her cheeks.

"Well, that's a fair assembly," Maia said.

"And a fair mix of Popularists and moderates," Aula added. "Clever man, Galerius."

"A man who wants to be consul ought to be. Send a reply back accepting on my and my brothers' behalf. I can speak for them," Maia said. She settled back against her cushions, reaching for the dish of dried apricots. "As though Maius or Septimus would miss a hunt. It's been too long since they've had the chance to kill something. If they can't charge off to war, at least they can vent their spleens on a hapless deer."

Aula wore a broad, cheerful smile that was a bit too enthusiastic for Latona's comfort. "I'm certainly game!" she chirped. "And I'm sure I can speak for Latona as well."

Latona nodded. "We'll have to see if Father or Alhena wants to go."

Aula snorted. "Alhena's as likely to attend a hunt as Maius Domitius is to miss it."

◇◇◇◇◇◇◇◇◇◇◇◇◇◇◇

"You're sulking." Rabirus did not look at his son as he offered this criticism, but kept his eyes firmly fixed on his speech for the next Curia meeting. He was quite proud of this one; it invoked Terminus, god of boundaries, as a warning against Aven over-extending its reach with too many provinces.

"I'm not sulking, Father," Young Lucretius said.

"You are, and it's unmanly. If something's troubling you, either do something about it or find more suitable entertainment."

Young Lucretius sank into a chair with all the grace of a lead weight, his arms hanging limply off the sides. "All the other young men are going up to Tibur tomorrow. Galerius Orator's hosting a hunt."

Rabirus put down his stylus and folded his hands on top of his desk. "I seriously doubt it's *all* the other young men in the city. Who do you mean?"

"The— well, the popular ones, Father."

Rabirus sniffed. "Popular*ist*, you mean." He took up his stylus again. "I'd think you would know better than to mourn the loss of such company—particularly to me."

"It isn't only that, Father, it's practically everyone who's been training in the Campus Martius. All the officers-to-be, even the ones who aren't aligned with . . . with that set. Even Ardus Fabian and the Ulpiae are going. But of course . . ." His voice trailed off, but his father knew what he wasn't saying. Of course, even the famously moderate Galerius Orator wasn't going to invite any member of the Rabirae to his country estate.

Few of Rabirus's friends had sons the age of his own—most were already out on campaign, or else still under the care of grammarians and rhetoricians. It was a shame. Friendships forged at that age could last a lifetime—as could rivalries.

Rabirus gave no outward sign of his consideration, but his mind was working. Galerius Orator's home was near Tibur, not far from one of his own rustic estates. "I understand you're upset at not being invited," Rabirus said. His son sat up slightly, hearing the unfamiliar note of consolation. "Perhaps it would do you good to get out of the city for a bit, too. Galerius Orator isn't the only man with a villa. I'll see what I can arrange."

Young Lucretius leapt up, his features transformed with enthusiasm. "Thank you, Father," he said. "You're right. Of course. A bit of— of fresh air, really. I'm sure I'll feel much improved."

"Yes, yes. Go on now. I'm busy."

Young Lucretius left with far more spring in his step than when he'd slunk in, leaving his father to think.

Pinarius Scaeva had caused quite an uproar earlier in the month, but it had not had the desired effect. Aulus Vitellius had swept away the scandal with his son's news from Iberia. Ludicrous, overblown, tall tales, but the Senate had seized upon the new conversation rather than chastising Felix or blaming Sempronius Tarren's war-mongering. Pinarius assured him that he was working on other means to stymie Sempronius's efforts—but magic of this sort could take a while to work, and as the elections drew nearer, Rabirus grew impatient.

'But perhaps there is something that would not require Pinarius's absence from the city, but could be effected far away, leaving no trail . . .' Rabirus and his son would travel with a coterie that befit their station: slaves, attendants, cooks, litter-bearers, horsemen—and hunters.

Opportunity, he knew, could manifest in many ways.

◇◇◇◇◇◇◇◇◇◇◇◇◇

TAGUS RIVER, IBERIA

A pair of warriors came to Otiger's tent, pitched behind Ekialde and Neitin's in recognition of his status as her relative. The taller of the two had a deer slung over his shoulders, but it was the smaller who spoke. "We would have your blessing, honored one."

Otiger looked up at them, still squatting over the mantle he was piecing together for his niece. Then he glanced towards the clustered tents of Bailar and the other magic-men, on the other side of the fire circle. "You are mistaken. The man who gives blessings here is Bailar, favored of the *erregerra*."

The two soldiers glanced at each other, then the taller dropped the deer in front of Otiger. "We have brought you a deer, downed by our own hands."

Nodding, Otiger set down his bone needle and prodded at the dead beast. "Good knifework," he said. "You chased it down?"

"Against the side of a cliff."

"A young and spry one, too," Otiger observed.

"Honored one," the shorter warrior blurted, "we would have the traditional blessing. Favored Bailar's ways are . . . well enough, for those who seek them out. But we . . . our fathers told us what Bandue wanted from such as us."

"We would take the strength and the speed of the deer," said the other. "And its silence. We are to be sent out scouting."

"Too many scouts have not returned."

"We wish to return."

Regarding them coolly, Otiger thought through the consequences. Bailar was sure to be displeased, but Neitin—Neitin would be delighted to learn that not all of Ekialde's warriors had been entirely won over to the darker magics. The *erregerra*, he suspected, would care little who did the blessing or how, so long as his fighting men did their duties. These young men believed in Ekialde's cause, if not Bailar's methods. *'And me?'*

Otiger had no abhorrence for using the blood of men in his magic, when time and occasion warranted it. Such things had their place and their purpose. *'This Bailar, though . . .'* Observing him in the past weeks, Otiger had come to question his practices. His fondness for using men's blood bordered on mania. He demanded it even when the blood of deer or birds would suffice just as well. Sometimes it seemed the war-band was sent out with no purpose but to bring back fresh victims for the draining. It was overuse. If nothing else, the gods would soon stop listening. A gift was most precious when it was most rare.

And so Otiger nodded.

In due course, the beast was drained of its blood, and Otiger anointed the warriors' foreheads, lips, and hands with crimson smears, chanting all the while. The men beamed when it was done. "Thank you, honored one," the shorter of them said. "Now Bandue will know where to look for us. Such protection is invaluable."

"We will skin the beast and bring you the hide and meats," said the other.

"The bones, too, if you don't mind," Otiger said. "There's always use for them. But string your bows with the sinews." He patted the deer's sightless head. "Best to waste no part of an animal given over to the gods."

The young warriors agreed cheerfully and trotted off, looking fresher and stronger than when they arrived. Otiger allowed himself a small smile for a job well done.

He had to hold on to that satisfaction an hour later, when Bailar came looking for him. *'The man knows so much so quickly,'* Otiger thought, and would have shivered, but perhaps it was no strange thing after all. The warriors had their friends and would have explained their anointments.

"Friend Otiger," Bailar said, approaching. Otiger did not rise, but continued his work on the mantle. Magic-men had no rank between them, and he owed Bailar no homage. "I understand you've been blessing some of the war-band."

"Scouts, I think they said. They came to me."

Bailar's lips were pressed thin. "Some might say you were trying to undermine my authority here, friend," he said, "and by extension, the authority of our blessed *erregerra*."

"Might they?" Otiger said, unconcernedly placing another stitch. "How unfortunate. If you hear anyone saying such, be sure to send them straight to me. I will happily disavow them of the notion."

"You are new to the camp, and your affection for your niece may have clouded some of your awareness of how things run here." A pause. He clearly wanted Otiger to ask, but Otiger had no intention of satisfying him. Bailar cleared his throat. "*I* speak for Bandue here. It is my sacred trust and responsibility."

Another stitch, pulled slow. "No man owns the gods, friend Bailar. A magic-man should not need reminding."

XXIX

CITY OF AVEN

Galerius's estate was half a day's ride up the Via Valeria, posited in the foothills of the Apennine Mountains. "I hear there's a grove sacred to Faunus nearby," Aula said, making herself comfortable on a pile of plush blue pillows. "That should be good luck." She and Latona were sharing an enormous litter with Vibia Sempronia and Appia Crispinilla; Alhena had, as ever, declined the invitation, and Lucia was still too young to come along to such an event. In addition to the slaves bearing the litter, they were accompanied by Aulus, Sempronius, Vibia's husband Taius, both Autroniae brothers, and Rufilius, all on horseback, along with a coterie of attendants bearing hunting equipment and fresh clothes for the next day. They would arrive at Galerius's villa in time for dinner and would hunt on the morrow.

Because the streets were clogged with pedestrians, beggars, donkeys, and other litters, it seemed to take as long to get out of the city as it would take to get up into the mountains. Sempronius's habit of pausing to strike up conversation with any passer-by he recognized had Vibia huffing in frustration. "Brother!" she called out, peeling back the curtains just enough to peek out at him. "Must you check in on the family history of *every* benighted soul in the city?"

"Of course not, dear sister," he said. Spying Latona peeking out behind Vibia, he winked. "Just the ones that can vote."

Vibia flung herself back, sighing in irritation. "It's a wonder he makes it home some days. I've never known a man to get so sidetracked."

"I think it's quite noble of him," Crispinilla said, her voice fluttering in a way that prickled Latona's nerves.

"Could we open the curtains, please?" Aula asked. Never well-suited to idleness, the prospect of spending half a day trapped in a litter already had her fidgeting.

"It's too cold," Vibia answered, drawing her woolen mantle back up over her wavy sable hair for emphasis.

"Oh, it's hardly—"

"Maybe when we get out of the city, Aula," Latona said, to forestall a quarrel. "We must be near the gate by now."

But the litter was coming to an unsteady halt. "Ugh, not more traffic."

"No," Latona said, peeking out onto the road. "I don't think so . . ." Then she laughed and pulled the curtain back farther. "Look! We're to have more company on the Via Valeria." Quinta Terentia stood nearby, dressed modestly though not in her formal Vestal's garb. With a straight nose set in a narrow face, deep olive skin, and curling raven hair, she had a severe look to her. With her was her younger sister Terentilla, perched atop a horse and grinning with sheer delight as the breeze caught her unbraided hair—a stark contrast to Terentia's precision.

"How wonderful! Hello, ladies!" Aula called, waving.

"A Vestal on the hunt?" Felix laughed, wheeling his horse about. "Galerius really is throwing a fete for the ages!"

Terentia's smile was small but genuine. "I'm sorry to spoil your fun, Young Autronius, but no." Though not strictly forbidden, it was not customary for a Vestal to leave the city until after her retirement; few did so for anything less than dire matters of state. "I couldn't think of leaving Vesta's hearth to anyone else while the *mundus* is open. It's Terentilla who will be joining you."

"Hail, Penthesilea!" Felix made an elaborate bow from horseback, which Tilla returned, grinning at the reference to the famous Amazon.

"She insisted on coming along—"

"Certainly did!" Tilla chirped.

"—and I simply wanted to see her placed in the custody of those I trust." Terentia looked pointedly at the ladies in the litter.

Tilla leant down to brush a kiss on her sister's cheek, then cheerfully spurred her horse up to join the men. The slaves bearing the litter lurched into motion, and Vibia motioned for Aula to close the curtain again. Aula conceded only after Latona gave her a good nudge with her foot. "Are the Vitelliae, er, much-acquainted with Quintilla Terentilla?" Crispinilla asked.

Latona pressed her lips together slightly, piqued on Tilla's behalf at the implied judgment of the high-spirited girl's character. "I am," she said. "I think she's a darling, and such a refreshingly *genuine* person."

"She's half-wild," Vibia said. "You would never know she's the daughter of one of the city's oldest patrician houses, to look at her. Why her parents didn't take her in hand years ago, I'm sure I don't know."

"Perhaps you should ask them the next time you see them," Aula shot back, though keeping her tone light and sweet, "since you have such a care for their family's affairs."

"Tilla has blessed Diana's spirit in her," Latona said, in as conciliatory a voice as she could manage, "and we cannot fault her for that."

"Perhaps not," Vibia said, "but I don't see where that negates the necessity for good manners."

Latona settled herself in for a long ride—but not before catching a telltale flutter of Aula's eyelashes that suggested her sister was suppressing an impolitic comment.

◇◇◇◇◇◇◇◇◇◇◇◇◇

TIBUR, CENTRAL TRUSCUM

It rained for a good portion of their journey, though even that did not drive Tilla inside the litter. Like the men, she simply pulled on a cloak treated with lanolin and went on riding and chatting. The ladies in the litter gossiped, read, and napped by turns, until late afternoon brought them to Galerius Orator's villa. It was prettily situated within sight of the town of Tibur, a little ways off the main road. The Anio River, source of many aqueducts, frothed and churned its way down from waterfalls, and beyond, the Sabine Hills had bald patches where autumn's leaves had already fallen, but streaks of green pines striped them up and down.

Like his domus in Aven, Galerius's rustic villa was modestly decorated and slightly old-fashioned, but it was spacious, with plenty of guest accommodations. "I've sacrificed to Jupiter that this drizzle may clear up by tomorrow," Galerius said as he welcomed them to his home, "and Marcia's been reading the winds. She feels confident this will all blow over."

Once the other groups of travelers had arrived and everyone had settled into their rooms, dried out, and re-dressed, they gathered for dinner—a less formal affair, even in the Galerian household, than they would have had in the city.

Vibia Sempronia was less at ease in this company than her brother was. Popularist more by familial association than by true conviction, she often thought her brother's compatriots rather too rough and rude a crowd. Not Galerius and his wife, of course. No one could challenge Marcia Tullia for propriety, and Vibia had only agreed to come along on the trip because she was the hostess. *'But the rest of them . . .'*

Their parties were a little too wild for her taste, their speech too coarse, their opinions too radical. Worse, the women of the group were too forward. While Vibia certainly never scrupled to speak politically with her husband or brother, she did so in private. The Vitelliae, the Domitiae, the Crispiniae all apparently felt comfortable voicing their opinions in public—at dinner tables or luncheons, at the theatre, at the gardens. *'Astonishing, really, that Aula hasn't stormed the Rostra yet,'* she thought, watching as the copper-haired woman joked with Young Rufilius, smacking him lightly on the arm.

Too, the Popularist men often lacked the dignity that Vibia felt appropriate for the sons and daughters of Aven's most esteemed houses. *'Felix I could forgive, I suppose,'* she thought, *'but a son of the Rufiliae ought to know better.'*

It bothered her, too, to look at the elder Appia Crispinia, twenty-nine years old and fecund as ever, growing round with the weight of her fourth child. Though riding up with the garrulous Vitelliae and younger sister Crispinilla had been something of a trial, it had been preferable to sharing a litter with a woman who seemed capable of bearing one. Appia and her husband, Maius Domitius, had been about an hour behind the first group, accompanied by the rest of the Domitiae and a pack of older senators, men more of Galerius's tenor, all of them standing for praetor or aedile in the upcoming elections.

Vibia had chosen a couch well away from the Crispiniae and had not been entirely pleased when Vitellia Latona had elected that part of the room as well. She had no way of knowing that Latona was equally as discomfited by Crispinia's conspicuous fertility; she only saw that Latona was occupying ever more of Sempronius's time and attention.

"The old guard is *determined* to keep the worthy equestrians off the lists as long as they can," Sempronius was saying to Latona as the servants set venison, thrush, and salted turbot out on the tables. "Your father will have quite a fight ahead of him when he wins office."

"Your confidence in him is warming," Latona said.

Sempronius shrugged. "He's well-respected and well worth the position. But with Buteo and Rabirus bludgeoning in every challenge and additional qualification they can think of . . ."

"Has Rabirus given you more trouble?" Latona asked. "Not with the rolls, I mean, but with—"

"—the temples?" Sempronius sighed, and Vibia found her fingers clenching in irritation.

Latona had been the first lady with whom Sempronius had shared his project. Vibia had only found out when he had come home complaining of Rabirus's interference. He had taken Vibia to the site as well, but Latona had gotten there first. Though not as prone to vulgar behavior as her sister, the second Vitellian daughter discomfited Vibia even more. She was, Vibia felt, slyer than Aula, cannier, and perhaps more dangerous, if she ever took it in her head to be so. *'And now he's finishing the woman's sentences.'* Sempronius's wife, sweet and dutiful creature that she had been, had never infringed upon Vibia's influence with her brother, but this woman, though married to another, seemed to have gotten her hooks in.

"Nothing overt," Sempronius continued, "but I can sense him circling." He had mentioned to his sister the strange press of magic following him in the streets; Vibia could feel some comfort that Latona did not know about *that*. "I've had Nisso and Obir put their ears out for me, as well, and Obir did hear something about—"

But a sudden bellow from Felix cut him off. Vibia winced. In addition to their other faults, Sempronius's friends were so *loud*. "Sempronius! Sempronius, Proculus is having me on about the Lusetani again. Tell him how we'll roll right over the bastards—err, sorry, ladies—and come home covered in riches."

Sempronius shifted himself towards the other couches, but shook his head. "Sorry, Felix, but I can't agree with you there."

"What? But, Sempronius, no one's more in favor of the campaign than you—"

"Not because I think it will be easy." Vibia knew well enough that her brother would never think an easy conquest worth his attention. A man was measured by the strength of those he defeated.

Scowling, Felix said, "But with the training of our legions and the quality of our commanding officers—"

Aulus Vitellius laughed grimly. "And no fine generals have ever lost battles? We'd be fools to underestimate the Lusetani. Barbarian is just a word for someone who wears different clothes than we do. It's certainly no guarantee of an easy conquest."

"They've no government to speak of," said Rufilius, "just a bold man who's decided he wants to be king and thinks he can make a good show of it by roughing up our allies."

"You're wrong there, son." His father, famous for his conquest of the Albine Mountains, still had a voice that could silence a legion's worth of dissent, and it hushed even Felix's fervor. "Reports indicate they have organization—didn't your son say so, Aulus?"

Vibia felt a pinch of unease from Aulus, saw the strain of it on his face as he nodded. "This war-chief of theirs has proved efficient at bringing the tribes together and making use of their various talents."

"It's not like Numidia, lads," Albinicus told his son and Felix. "These people are tribal, but not nomadic, and their idea of leadership is deeply tied to their religion, just as much as ours—perhaps more so, in some ways."

"If you can call it a religion." Felix had found his tongue again. "Drinking blood and praying to trees and—"

"Do not mock the gods of other people," Latona cautioned. It was an impudent interjection into the men's conversation, in Vibia's opinion, but Latona played it off with a teasing smile. "Remember, we fine Aventans borrowed most of ours from other nations."

"From Athaeca, Lady!" Felix objected. "From civilized people. Not from savages."

Vibia felt another ripple of unease, this time from Galerius Orator, but it was his wife who spoke next. "Religion is far too serious a matter for an evening such as this." Her voice had a cool thread of magic in it, the power of rationality cutting through the high emotions. "Let's have a game, instead. I heard an excellent riddle at Appia's last party. Dear, would you be so kind as to share it?"

'Neatly done,' Vibia thought, gratified to have her respect for her hostess validated. Much though they tried to outstrip their plebeian origins, the Autroniae still had little sense of appropriate behavior. 'Felix may have been magically manipulated into that Forum brawl, but I suspect it hardly took much prompting.'

Sempronius was not yet ready to abandon the topic of Iberia, and as Appia launched into a recitation and the others set to guessing, he bent his head back to Latona and said, "Your father hears often from Young Vitellius?"

Latona nodded. "As often as the post can manage, that is. Sometimes we hear nothing for weeks and then get four or five letters all at once."

"And you write to him as well?"

"I do. I've a packet to send to him soon, in fact."

"Might I give you something to include with it?" Sempronius asked. "I'd like to sound him out on— well, it's not the sort of thing he'd comment on in official dispatches."

"Certainly you may," Latona answered. "Though you must promise to tell me what it's about."

Sempronius laughed. "Another time, I certainly shall. But Marcia is right—we should set such dull matters aside tonight." And with that, he leaned over to offer a suggestion to Appia's riddle.

The evening ended early, as the hunt would start at daybreak. Vibia was all too ready to retire with her husband—but as they started towards their comfortable guest room, she saw her brother walking down the opposite corridor with Vitellia Latona. Her cheeks were candescent with wine and laughter, and as she leaned against the brightly-painted wall, her hips angled towards Sempronius. He was canted towards her, not quite whispering, but Vibia felt sure that whatever he said would not be fit for public discourse. For one startling moment, she thought he meant to accompany her, or pull her into his own chamber—but then her sister joined them, all smiles. Aula was forward enough, or drunk enough, to tip forward and kiss Sempronius's cheek, then she took her sister's hand and pulled her into their room. Shaking his head good-naturedly, Sempronius turned a corner towards his own chamber.

And Vibia could breathe a little easier.

XXX

The morning of the hunt dawned, as Galerius had predicted, free of rain, though thin gray clouds still paled the sun's light to a suffusing glow. Those who would hunt were up at dawn for a light breakfast provided by Marcia, then off into the woods, accompanied by packs of hounds and spear-bearing slaves. The men on horseback would, in truth, do little of the hunting. Local plebeians had been hired to guide them, slaves would stir the bushes and guide the dogs, and trained hunters might even make most of the kills. Nonetheless, the noblemen all had bows or spears, as suited them, in case the opportunity for action presented itself.

As they rode into the forest, Sempronius's thoughts were uncustomarily preoccupied. Latona's conversation the night before had been as stimulating as ever, and she had been a picture of loveliness, with soft azure wool pooling about her curves and an emerald mantle pinned in her hair, bringing out the brilliance of her eyes. He could not be sorry that her husband had, once again, chosen his provincial concerns over attending his wife at a social gathering, but he faulted the man's choice anyway. *'Herennius has a jewel, and he wastes his time counting pebbles.'* Sempronius could not fathom it. If Latona were merely beautiful, it might have been understandable—but a woman of intelligence, grace, and magical talent was an invaluable partner to any Aventan man of ambition.

And that was the trouble. Herennius was a thing incomprehensible to Sempronius: a man without initiative, lacking not only the hungry, chasmal *need* that so drove Sempronius through life, but even the customary sort of motivation to spur him on. A woman as extraordinary as Latona could never find happiness with someone so . . . pedestrian.

From Aula, Sempronius received a steady stream of hints. Nothing so overt that it could be called gossip or that Aula could be accused of revealing her sister's secrets. Just enough to add detail to the picture. Herennius had not yet turned wife-beater, at least not that Sempronius could discern or that Aula had let on, but he punished his wife for her exceptional qualities in other ways. Dismissal and disregard cut deep.

Small, petty men often lashed out, belying their own insufficiencies.

But why the lady would put up with it, why she would stay shackled to such an unworthy creature, that was the question. Sempronius might have felt pity for him, hopelessly outmatched in life with just enough wit to be aware of it, had his petulance not contributed to Latona's melancholy. *'She deserves support, encouragement. If she learned to trust her own strengths, there's so much she could achieve.'*

Perhaps if his thoughts had not been so occupied, Sempronius might have had attention to spare for Shadow's warning press at his mind, or his mundane five senses might have alerted him that their band was not alone in the forest.

◇◇◇◇◇◇◇◇◇◇◇◇◇◇

Most of the ladies, Marcia and Tilla excepted, had opted for a relaxing lie-in, a luxury the noise and bustle of the city rarely afforded them. Equally refreshing was the liberty of not needing to rise to manage their own households. Marcia had all in hand, and when they did drift from their rooms, they found tables set with fresh fruits, new-baked breads, and olive oil from the first press of the season. Latona rose before Aula, who had drunk more deeply the night before. Just as when they were girls, Aula had pulled a pillow over her head to shield the morning's light.

A party of men returned to the villa for the midday meal—some of the older senators, worn out by a few hours' hard riding, and some of the younger men, more eager to spend time with the ladies than to chase down another deer. They spread on out several blankets underneath a patched sky, enjoying the sweet air brought in by a cool and gentle breeze. Galerius had a smartly-dressed coterie of slaves attending on them, and they saw to it that the dishes of nuts and fruits never went empty—nor the glasses of warmed wine.

Felix and Rufilius had shucked off their togas and were wrestling good-naturedly in the grass, and several of the ladies were admiring the spectacle. Crispinilla's mouth hung slightly agape, Maia Domitia stared with avid appreciation, chewing absent-mindedly on one of her fingernails, and Aula, who had finally appeared just in time for lunch, shamelessly applauded every throw and fall. Latona could not fault them; dark-haired Felix and golden Rufilius were both fine specimens of Aventan manhood and well-worth the watching.

Terentilla, for all her boundless energy, had decided to take a break from the hunting as well. "I like it well enough," she confided, plopping her brown limbs down on Latona's blanket. "But really it's the riding and the chasing I like. The killing itself . . ." Her nose wrinkled.

Latona nodded, understanding. Spirit did not have so close an affinity with animals as Earth did, but it was near enough that she could guess Tilla's discomfort. "It can be overwhelming. I'm content to partake in the bounty without needing to be present for its fall."

"Exactly so! I mean, I like a roast venison as much as anyone, but sometimes it seems a bit unfair, to chase them down with hounds and horns. Sometimes I feel it should just be bow and arrow against the wilderness."

Latona had to smile. "Diana's instincts would serve you well, I'm sure."

Tilla rolled onto her back, ignorant of the disdaining glances being sent her way by some of the other women. "I'm so glad Terentia convinced Father to let me come, all the same. I hadn't been out of the city since Sextilis, and—"

But Latona, despite her fondness for Tilla, was no longer listening. A heaviness had swarmed her senses, dizzying her. "Something's wrong," she said, staggering to her feet.

"Latona?" Tilla reached up for her hand. "What is it?"

"I don't . . . I don't know . . . but something's . . . ah!" She clasped a hand to her chest. A lance of pain had gone through her suddenly—a shock of fear, but more than fear, outrage and indignation. "Someone's hurt." She looked around, half hoping to see that one of the ladies had sliced her palm while cutting fruit, or that one of the wrestlers had accidentally landed a blow in a too-sensitive area. No such signs of distress manifested, however, though her own actions were garnering some attention. She closed her eyes, concentrating on the thread of Spirit magic that had called out to her. "On the hunt. Someone's been injured. I'm sure of it."

Tilla searched Latona's face, then leapt to her feet and gave a loud whistle, drawing attention away from the wrestling. "Boys!" she hollered. Crispinilla wrinkled her nose at the unladylike volume, but Tilla did not notice. "There's trouble in the forest. Who's up for a ride?" Without waiting for a response, she whipped back around to Latona. "Can you keep a seat?" Latona nodded. She was no great equestrian, but she had enough skill not to embarrass herself. "Good. Hoy! Felix! Put those damn muscles to good use and help the Lady Latona up behind me!"

A few minutes later, Latona clung to Terentilla's back as they thundered down the forest path, Felix and Young Rufilius flanking them. Tilla took instruction from Latona on which way to go, though Latona had only the aching compulsion in her chest to guide them. Up one hill and down another, along the banks of a rippling stream, and then they encountered a group of the hunters racing back the opposite direction. Tilla's horse whinnied in objection as she pulled him up short. "Terentilla?" someone asked, and Latona recognized her father's voice, though her face was pressed into Tilla's shoulder. "What's going on? And—Latona?"

She looked up to see not only her father but Marcus, Albinicus, and Sempronius on horseback. They had evidently left their attendants behind with the others, and on closer inspection, the reason why was obvious. Sempronius had an arrow sticking out of his upper arm, the shaft bobbing awkwardly with each step his horse took.

"She sensed it!" Tilla said. "We didn't know precisely what it would be, but she knew something was wrong, someone was hurt."

"Where did that come from?" Latona asked.

"Daughter, it's none of your—"

"We don't know," Marcus said. "Just—out of the woods. No one saw who loosed it."

"We can't stay here," Albinicus said. "He needs to—"

But no one needed to tell Terentilla that. She rounded her horse and took off back towards the villa at a gallop, leaving Latona to clutch desperately at Terentilla's tunic for balance. Once back at the house, Tilla and Latona rushed past the confused picnickers, hurrying to tell Galerius's servants to be ready for an injury. The men were not far behind, ushering Sempronius. Tilla looked perfectly ready to stay and help, but Aulus shooed both women out. "Go and calm the other ladies," he said to his daughter. "Tell them it was an accident. A stray arrow from another hunter." Latona's instincts were still bristled, and she suspected it was nothing so simple, but she nodded and tugged Tilla back outside, where Marcia was already attempting to restore normalcy.

∞∞∞∞∞∞∞∞∞∞

In Galerius's office, Marcus settled Sempronius into a chair while slaves brought in clean linens and fresh water. Galerius threw open the shutters, flooding the room with sunlight. Felix angled Sempronius towards the window and bent over him, inspecting the wound. "No good pulling it out. Best to push it through."

Sempronius nodded, though he was grimacing. "Do it, Felix." It was rough, battlefield medicine, but most soldiers learned how to do it sooner or later.

"Brace yourself, then," Felix said. He grasped the shaft of the arrow and broke it a fist's width from Sempronius's skin. The jostling of the wound jarred a slight moan out of Sempronius, though pride made him bite it back as swiftly as he could. "Worse to come," Felix muttered. "Someone wanna give him something to bite down on?"

"Just do it," Sempronius growled. "Marcus, hold my arms, please."

Despite the severity of the situation, Felix grinned. "I appreciate you not wanting to punch the man who's helping you." He waited until Marcus had come behind the chair and had a firm grip on Sempronius's forearms, pinning him to the chair, then gripped what was left of the arrow shaft. "One . . . two . . ." And before Felix could say "three," he pushed on the shaft, hard and fast. This time, Sempronius could not swallow a cursing cry as pain, hot and twisting, lanced through his arm. Felix adjusted him to get a grip on the arrowhead. "Now, now, Senator, my brother's a pious man, and you're gonna curse like that in front of him?"

Sempronius laughed mirthlessly. "I'll make an appropriate apology to all offended deities later. Just get the damn thing out, Felix."

"Yes, sir." With a swift, jerking motion, Felix yanked what remained of the arrow out of the back of Sempronius's arm. Sempronius cursed another blue streak, but gestured with his other arm for someone to bring water to cleanse the wound. He had expected the pain to ebb after the arrow was out, but instead, it was spreading, an ache growing down towards his elbow and up towards his neck. His fingers, numb and stiff, were slow to respond when he tried to flex them. And his magical sense prickled with Shadow's warning of foul deeds done.

Felix brought the arrow up to his eye to inspect it. "Um." he said, rotating it between his fingers. "Does this look odd to anyone else?"

Marcus Autronius took the arrow and held it to his nose. He sniffed twice, then dropped it. "Poison."

Everyone in the room startled, except Sempronius, who closed his eyes, half in resignation, half wincing. "Poison?" Aulus said. "But that would mean . . . We thought it was an accident!"

Sweat was beginning to glisten on Sempronius's forehead, and his jaw started to chatter. Shadow's sense made him acutely aware of the blackness already spreading in his blood, and for the first time, he worried that his control might slip and cause him to give himself away. "Fetch . . . Latona . . ." he said.

"Latona?" Aulus asked. "No, nonsense, why would my daughter—"

"Fire magic," Marcus said. "That's what you mean, isn't it, Sempronius?"

"Of course." Galerius had picked up the reasoning. "She might be able to purge the poison."

"What?" Aulus's face went ashen. "Latona doesn't have any training as a healer! It's not just inappropriate, it's absurd—"

"Try . . ." was all Sempronius could manage, but Marcus finished for him.

"Let her try, at least! We may not have the time to get him into Tibur to a physician—if there's even one there who could help. We *certainly* don't have the time to get him back to Aven."

A deep frown creased Aulus's face, but he gave a stiff nod and left the room, returning a moment later with Latona in tow. A worried pallor had taken over the usual golden glow of her face. Sempronius nodded at his arm, summoning the strength to speak even as the darkness pressed at him. "Been poisoned, Lady Latona. I need . . . need . . ."

Marcus took over again. "He's fading fast, Lady. We need Fire magic to purge the poison. No one else here can do it, and by the time we found an antidote or got him to a priest or a physician—"

"But—" Latona's jaw hung open as she glanced between Marcus, Sempronius, her father, and the other men in the room. "I— I can't, I don't know how, no one ever taught me— I've never done anything like this."

Sempronius shifted in his chair, choking back a groan of pain. "Latona." Her eyes snapped to his. He saw her terror, her insecurity, writ clear on her face even without the insight of his magic. "You can. I believe this."

XXXI

The moment, long and horrible, seemed to hang in the air. Sempronius's deep brown eyes were unfocused and going red around the edges, and though he was trying not to show his pain, his breath was ragged and labored. There was not just a plea in his gaze; there was a command, to do as he believed she could. As ever, his confidence in her eclipsed her own.

'You have to try.'

There was nothing else for it. Latona had no idea if she was capable of this magic, but she could not condemn Sempronius through her own insecurity.

She shucked off her mantle and tossed it at someone—she wasn't even aware whom—then stepped close to Sempronius. "I need fire," she said. "Bring a lamp, please." Marcus came near with one. "Hold it steady, here." She placed one hand around the clay, feeling the warmth against the hollow of her palm. Soon she had the thread of it—the heat and the spark, a source for her magic to draw on. *"Please,"* she whispered, not certain who she implored, and then she pressed the palm of her other hand over the puncture wound.

Fire was not the strongest element in healing magic. Water did best, or Light, but Marcus and Marcia were the only other mages present, and neither had those talents. Fire could purify, though, and that was what Sempronius needed now.

Latona squeezed her eyes shut, trying to forget how many of the most important men in Aven were about to witness her attempt. *'Venus and Vulcan, look here and guide me. Hunt it out,'* she thought. *'Let the magic seek out the poison and burn it clean.'* A warmth tingled in her fingers and spread out across Sempronius's skin. With effort, she managed to focus it tighter, forcing the magic into the wound, probing the envenomed flesh.

Sempronius hissed in pain, but Marcus, standing behind her, held her arm so that she could not draw it back. Was that a surge of Earth energy she felt, steadying her? "Keep going," he said. "He'll be fine."

Latona wanted to tell him that she didn't know if it was working, but she forced that thought from her mind. Such weakness and waffling would ensure failure. She focused in on the purging heat, ignoring Marcus whispering behind her, ignoring her father's pacing, ignoring everything but the beat of her own heart, the warmth of the lamp, and the pulse of the magic. Harder still was ignoring what came from inside Sempronius: his pain, the whirl of his panicked emotions, the stress of keeping them under control, and a dark haze that she could not identify, but suspected had to do with his impending unconsciousness. *'Focus, focus . . . true, Claudia never taught you these skills, but you've read the theory, you can do this. If you don't do this, Sempronius dies.'* And that thought harrowed, but Latona could not allow that fear to divert her attention.

The purging magic operated by channeling through healthy flesh with ease, pushing back when it encountered obstacles. The poison had its own peculiar sensation, a devouring rot like the sickly mush of an overripe plum. When Latona's magic came against it, she drew the Fire through herself and encouraged it forward to burn through the infectious taint. There was a rhythm to it, of push and pull, and soon she had her magic flowing through his blood in relentless pursuit of the impurities.

After a few minutes, she felt Sempronius's body relax, no longer instinctively fortifying itself against an intruder. The release of tension sagged through her as well. "I think . . . I think that's done it . . ." she said, stepping back. She felt arms holding her up and realized only then that her knees had gone out from under her. Marcus had caught her, awkwardly, as he still held the lamp, then passed her off to her father. A slave had stepped forward with a damp cloth to wipe her hands clean of Sempronius's blood. "He's . . . he'll be all right. Though he really should see a proper physician as soon as possible." She regained her feet, bringing herself upright as Sempronius, with some effort, hauled himself out of the chair. Latona remembered what Rubellia had warned her about, the propensity of Fire magic to overheat. "I may have accidentally given him a fever." It was a known hazard of using Fire magic to heal, a reason that Water and Light were preferred.

Around them, the rest of the men burst into conversation, speculating on who might have loosed a poisoned arrow in the woods near Galerius's villa. But Latona hardly heard them. Her blood pounded in her ears, and in her chest she felt resonant *satisfaction*. *'I did it. I did it. There was a challenge, and I met it.'*

"Thank you, Lady," he said, taking an unsteady step towards her. He made as though to kiss her hand, but used the opportunity to draw himself close to her ear. "How did you know?" Sempronius's voice was hardly a whisper, nowhere near loud enough for the others to hear. "When you and Terentilla came to us in the woods. How did you know something was wrong?"

Her cheeks colored. "Spirit magic. I felt . . . I felt your pain." It bespoke the connection between them, one that she felt tightening now that she had sensed the danger so immediately.

He pressed her hand, admiration shining through the exhaustion in his eyes. "You are an astonishing woman." His voice was still low, but its warm flow curled right around Latona's heart. Then he released her, stepping back. "Galerius, I'm afraid I may have to trespass on your hospitality a day or so longer than planned. I don't think I'm up to riding quite yet."

"Of course," Galerius said. "I'll send out riders immediately, to see if they can find who loosed the arrow."

"Thank you, though I doubt they'll have much luck." Sempronius rotated his arm experimentally, wincing. "I suspect whoever is behind this is a long ways off by now."

"Sit back down, man," Felix said, half-shoving Sempronius back into his seat. "We've still got to sew you up."

"Quite right. As soon as this is done, if someone would be so good as to fetch my sister. I imagine she's beside herself with worry."

"Come, my dear," Aulus said, taking his daughter's elbow. "No need for you to see this."

There was a fierceness in his gaze, though not anger, and with her magic still primed, Latona could feel the source of it: fear, old but rippling. *'Of course,'* she thought. *'Years of trying to keep me unnoticed, and now I go and successfully perform magic beyond my training in front of Aven's foremost men.'*

Aulus squeezed her arm lightly. "You need to rest." It was an order, not an observation. Latona thought about challenging him, and if she had felt the burrowing resentment she so often did from Herennius, she might have. Her father's sternness, though, came from concern, and so she relented. Loath though she was to be parted from Sempronius, she let Aulus lead her back to the chamber she had shared with Aula.

XXXII

True to his word, Galerius had dedicated his resources to finding the attempted assassin, but by the time he and Sempronius returned to Aven, a few days after the rest of the hunting party, their efforts had not yielded any new information. Sempronius appreciated the effort, but he suspected there would be no clues to uncover, at least not through traditional means. All the men who might want him dead had capacity enough to cover their tracks. *'One more thing to ask the mirror.'* The moon was on the wane, and soon, Sempronius would be able to search for answers in his own reliable fashion.

In the meantime, he had to tender his thanks to the woman who had saved his life.

Sempronius set out for the Palatine Hill once his arm had healed sufficiently. Though Latona had purged the poison, and likely anything else that would cause infection, the wound still ached. His whole upper arm was covered in an ugly purplish-red bruise, which made donning a toga even more uncomfortable than usual. The Asclepian priest who had seen him upon his return to the city had wanted Sempronius to rest for weeks—but that was a luxury a candidate for office could not afford.

With him were Corvinus and two household slaves bearing baskets of fresh goods, just in from his country estates. Despite their excellent quality, Sempronius felt it a meager tribute. It *was*, however, an appropriate gift from a widowed senator to a married woman, nothing that would raise eyebrows or set tongues wagging. He would have come bearing bolts of Seric silks, golden bangles, and jeweled pendants, but such luxurious offerings would be sure to cause a flutter. While a buried mischievous instinct relished the notion of stirring up Latona and of flouting Herennius, Sempronius could little afford a scandal, not with the elections so close.

He had considered books, such as he had given the youngest Vitellia after the Cantrinalia, but further contemplation of the implications forced him to discard that, too, as too personal. If anyone mistook such a gift to the unwed Alhena for a courtship token, it was fodder for gossip, but not infamy. The same to another man's wife was a different matter. So, appropriate, impersonal fruit it was.

Sempronius called first at the Vitellian house, where Aulus was happy to receive him, although Aula seemed truly dismayed to inform him that Latona was at her husband's domus on the Caelian Hill.

More ill luck followed: Numerius Herennius was not only in town, but at home when his steward admitted Sempronius to the atrium. "Sempronius Tarren," he said, caution riding high in his voice. "What brings your honored personage to my house?"

"I was hoping to speak with the Lady Vitellia," Sempronius answered, careful not to use the familiar form of her name.

"What is your business with my wife?" Legs splayed apart and arms folded across his chest, Herennius evidently thought he was doing a reasonable impression of an imposing figure. Sempronius's eyes caught the uncomfortable angle of Herennius's shoulders, the nervous flicker of his gaze; Shadow observed the suspicion near-brimming from the man. Herennius reeked of petty insecurities.

Beyond Herennius, Sempronius also caught sight of a dark-haired young woman peering around a column: Merula, who scurried off towards the back of the house. "She did me a good turn at Galerius Orator's hunt," Sempronius said. "You may have heard there was an accident with a stray arrow. The lady has more talent in healing than she realizes." Herennius's nostrils flared in an incredulous huff. "I wanted to deliver a token of my appreciation." Sempronius gestured at the baskets. "Fruit and berries, to grace your tables, with my thanks."

"Yes, well," Herennius said, "I shall pass on your gratitude. I'm sure the lady will be exceedingly receptive." Herennius's words were polite, but his tone belied his bitterness. "I'm sure you have important business to be conducting elsewhere, Senator. Do not let me delay you."

Herennius's short-sightedness was to Sempronius's advantage, and he had no compunction about using the man's flaws against him. "The lady acted with both bravery and compassion," he said, "though perhaps she has been too modest to speak of it herself. I am greatly in her debt, and I cannot consider myself well-discharged of my duty until I have expressed my gratitude, in person."

Herennius's face reddened, but before he could say anything else, the lady in question appeared. Merula, at her elbow, was whispering hurriedly to her as they walked along. She glided forward, wearing what Sempronius recognized as her publicly gracious smile. *'How often does she have to wear that in her own home?'* Hardly looking at her husband, she nodded in greeting to Sempronius. "Senator," she said, her voice cool and careful, "It is a pleasure to welcome you to our house. I hope nothing is amiss?"

"Nothing indeed, Lady Vitellia. I only wanted to express my gratitude for your assistance in Tibur."

Herennius hurried to respond before Latona could. "Give the gentleman your thanks so he can be on his way."

"Not without taking some water, surely," Latona said.

"He has no need to—"

"Sempronius Tarren is a friend and an ally of my father's," Latona said, her voice growing louder and harder. "It would be churlish indeed to deny him the courtesy of our house." She pressed her lips thin before adding. "Please, husband, don't feel that it should keep you from your appointments. I know you were on your way to the emporium. You may consider your duties as a host discharged." She laid one hand on his arm, gesturing to the door with the other.

Herennius shrugged her off more roughly than was necessary. "He does not pass beyond the atrium. Your girl will stay here, as will my steward." Glaring from one of them to the other, he snapped his fingers at an attendant, who passed him a cloak. With the barest attempt at a civil nod to Sempronius, Herennius stalked from the building.

Some of the tension ebbed out of Latona's body as the door shut behind him. "I apologize for my husband," Latona sighed. "He has much on his mind."

Sempronius could have played along with her deflection, but somehow, it no longer seemed appropriate. This woman, this incredible woman who fascinated him, had saved his life and yet dared not trust her own talents. If civil manners dictated he allow her to apologize for Herennius's bad behavior, then Sempronius could no longer be civil.

"No," he said. "That isn't it."

Latona blinked in surprise. "What do you mean?"

Sempronius glanced at Herennius's steward, still standing by the door with Corvinus and the other Sempronian attendants, and Latona took his meaning. She gestured him into the atrium, and they sat on two benches that came together at a right angle by a fluted column. Merula sat in a chair behind her mistress, but Sempronius knew she was loyal to Latona and would keep her secrets. He pitched his voice low enough that the steward would not overhear. "Your husband doesn't like me, plain and simple," he said. "And he knows that you do, and that makes him nervous. And . . . I think he is threatened by you."

"Threatened?" Her laugh was brittle, false, which told Sempronius that he had hit the mark. He smiled slowly as comprehension dawned.

"Sweet lady," he said, "who taught you that being extraordinary was dangerous?"

◇◇◇◇◇◇◇◇◇◇◇◇◇

Sempronius had a way, when he chose, of disarmingly intense eye contact. There was otherwise nothing remarkable about his gaze; his eyes were plain brown, quite normal. But he could fix a person with a concentration like a stalking panther, and, feeling quite the doe, Latona found herself unable to break the gaze.

"The world," Latona said, scarce above a whisper. "Sempronius, you know—how many people learned that lesson under Ocella?"

"I spent two years in Abydosia learning it," Sempronius said. "But some dangers must be faced down, not avoided. You are strong enough to bear it. By the gods, Latona, think what you have borne, without breaking." She shook her head, and his hand jerked slightly, as though he had reached out to grasp hers, but, mindful of observing eyes, caught himself only just in time. "You are stronger than you know. Your cleverness, your goodness, your power—you could set this city spinning if you chose to."

She started to protest, but couldn't find the voice. What *had* she dreamed of, in the days before Claudia's death? Who might she have been, if the High Priestess of Juno had had the cultivating of her life?

"You know that, deep down," he pressed on. "And I promise you that your husband senses it. *That* is the seed of his resentment. The pigeon knows he has no right to love an eagle."

This time, the tightness in Latona's chest, the quickening patter of her heartbeat, had nothing to do with her magic. "You— You should not talk that way."

"I should, and I mean to," Sempronius insisted. His voice had the same strange, unshakable certainty it had on the day of the Cantrinalia, when he had told her of his plans for Aven—the tone that harbored no thought of failure, no concession that the world might turn out in any way but how he wished it. "Someone ought to. It would be a sin if you went through life yoked to such a lesser creature, unaware of the indignity." His fingers dropped onto her arm, just below her elbow, so lightly that she almost would not have felt it—but his skin was warm, a contrast to the cool autumn air breezing in from above, and his touch soothed. "He certainly has his place in the order of the world, but he is not the man for you, Vitellia Latona."

"And what sort of man *do* I need?" Latona breathed. She knew full well what she was doing, what she was inviting, the chaos she feared, but she could not have stopped herself for the world. She felt it in him, too, the yearning; Spirit magic sang between them, glimmering with the promise of their connection.

"A man of ambition," he said. "A man who appreciates all that you are, and who will not let your talents wither unappreciated and uncultivated."

"So I should look for a man who will shamelessly use me for his own purposes?" she questioned, light mockery not quite covering the concern in her voice. It was what her parents had feared, after all.

He gave a soft chuff of laughter. "A man who will make you a partner," he said. "Who would cherish your bravery and your goodness as much as your talents. Who would take pride in seeing you in all your glory, not seek to dim you for fear of standing in your shadow. Someone beside whom you could brave down the dangers that the world imposes on extraordinary people. You, Latona, deserve a man who sees you, as you are, and who adores you for that."

No onlooker could find anything scandalous about how they were sitting, yet Latona felt the intensity of his gaze as intimately as an embrace. Her heart thundered; her fingers ached with the heat of unspent energy. When he continued, the passion in his voice could, Latona was convinced, have stirred the gods themselves to do his bidding.

"You could be the greatest lady in Aven. You *should* be. But you need a husband equally worthy—a husband with drive, ambition, vision—a husband strong enough to take the reins of this city and guide it to its destiny. You deserve a husband who is your match." Those words hung heavy between them, and Latona caught herself thinking, *'Please, Sempronius, please . . .'* But a cough from Merula reminded them both of the censorious eyes upon them. Sempronius drew back, and Latona was ashamed to realize she lurched slightly at the sudden loss. "And Herennius," he continued, "is not that man—not a man with common ambition, much less a man with an extraordinary destiny."

Latona wet her lips and looked down at her lap, trying to re-center her composure before speaking. But ardor rode too high in her blood to be set aside. She flicked her gaze back up to him, provocative, challenging. "And you, Sempronius Tarren? Are you so worthy?" She was almost afraid to hear the answer.

There was a secret, hiding in the corner of his smile; probably there were dozens of them, peeking deliberately out so she would know they were there, but refusing to reveal themselves in full. "You would have to ask the gods, Vitellia Latona, for the answer to that question. But all things are possible."

"You certainly make it seem so."

They stayed like that a moment, though Latona was unsure whether they were appreciating each other or sizing each other up. Then Sempronius stood, breaking the spell. He gestured to two of his servants. "My purpose in coming, lady, was to thank you. You saved my life."

Latona blushed. "A lucky instinct, Sempronius."

"Latona." There was something desperate written on Sempronius's face. "Why will you insist on diminishing your successes?" When Latona had no ready answer, he sighed. "Well. You did save it, whether you'll own it or not, and as I am exceedingly fond of my life, I am thus most grateful for your efforts." At another brisk signal, the slaves uncovered the baskets, revealing piles of elderberries, blackberries, plums, peaches, and cherries. "From my estates in Umbria."

"You've had an excellent harvest, by the looks of it," Latona said, drawing down the mask of courtesy as bastion against her discomfiture. "This is a generous gift, Senator, and I thank you for it."

"It is but a token," Sempronius said. "No gift could equal the generosity of spirit you have displayed." He stepped in closer to her, dropping his voice again. "Unless, perhaps, I could find the words to convince you to see yourself as I see you."

He took his leave, and when he did so, Herennius's steward gladly returned to his usual duties. Latona's chest ached as though she had been sobbing, and her fingers were a-tingle with the magic brimming in her. *'Discipline,'* she reminded herself. *'Don't let your emotions . . .'*

She could not force the thought to completion.

'I should weave. Or I should practice as Rubellia recommends. Or I should . . . I should . . .' The unfairness of the situation welled inside her chest: that fate and her father had consigned her to Herennius, that she had such trifling outlets for the power dammed up within her. *'That Sempronius Tarren . . . That I cannot, that I may not . . .'*

Merula was quicker this time; she doused the nearby clay lamps with a bowlful of water from the impluvium pool before Latona even realized she had heated them to the point of shattering. It wasn't enough. Latona felt ready to immolate. *'There were heroes in the Golden Age who could not merely manipulate fire, but summon it, shoot it from their very fingertips, like Jupiter wielding a lightning bolt.'* Near-choking on her frustration, Latona felt the temptation. *'Dangers be damned, I want to set a blaze.'*

Another few lamps popped into short-lived balls of flame, swiftly knocked into the water by Merula. Then Latona slumped to the floor, wishing she were a child who could scream and rail and throw a tantrum. Instead, she stuck her hands in the impluvium pool, and when that proved insufficient to settle the heat under her skin, splashed water on her arms and face as well. *'This is what Mother and Father feared, this is why Aemilia says you're unfit, this is why you scare yourself . . .'* But the familiar castigations had lost some of their power to flagellate. *'Sempronius isn't afraid. Nor Rubellia. They believe you can control it—and the emotions behind it. Having a temper needn't, in itself, be a danger. And the force of your emotions could be a strength, not a weakness.'*

Merula plunked down beside her mistress; her face spoke volumes, though her lips were tight. Latona sighed. "Very well, Merula," she said. "Chide me."

"It is not being my job to chide you," Merula said. "And, I am getting swift with the water, so there is little harm being done there." Then, after a beat, "It is being my job to *protect* you. Which will be harder if you are doing something that makes Dominus Herennius beat you." Latona looked at her sharply, though more in surprise than reprimand. "I am hoping it is never coming to that, Domina, but . . . A married woman may not do as you wish to do, I think." Then she muttered, low enough that Latona could pretend not to hear her, "Though there are ways of fixing *that*."

◇◇◇◇◇◇◇◇◇◇◇◇◇

By the time Sempronius returned home, Vibia had been sitting on a chair in his study, drumming her fingers on her thigh, for quite some time. "I came to call," she said, without turning to look at him. "But they said you were out."

"Obviously," Sempronius said, coming around to stand behind his desk. "But as it was a brief excursion, I know you can't have been waiting long."

Vibia sniffed. "You should be resting. The physician said—"

"Corvinus is already doing an excellent job mothering me; I'm sure he does not need your help."

Vibia scowled briefly at the freedman, who had trailed in behind Sempronius, bearing a stack of messages. She had never been comfortable with the fact that he knew of his master's hidden magical blessing, but she had to admit he'd done an admirable job keeping the secret. "They said you'd gone to the home of Numerius Herennius."

"I had."

"I was unaware you had business with him. I always thought he was only an incidental Popularist because of family connections."

"You are correct in that assessment, but my business was not with him. It was with his wife."

Though she had expected the answer, it twisted Vibia's gut nonetheless. "Ah."

"Vibia," Sempronius said, weariness in his voice, "you are being tedious. If you have something to say—"

"Are you in love with Vitellia Latona?"

Vibia felt the jolt of shock ripple out of him, though he gave no external sign of his discomfiture. "I beg your pardon."

"You may yet need it," Vibia said. "You are, aren't you?"

Those who knew Sempronius less well would never have caught the hesitation, the twitch in his jaw, but Vibia saw it, flickering there in the breath before he replied, "I hold her in very high admiration. She is a grand lady of estimable family, superb intelligence, and considerable charm. And she *did* just save my life."

This time, Vibia weighed her words before speaking. Pique had got the better of her with the initial question. "Take care, brother, that your admiration does not grow less appropriate."

Sempronius started to fold his arms over his chest, then winced at the pain in his shoulder. "What is your objection?"

"I think there are better places to set your sights," Vibia sighed. "An *admiration* for a woman from a more moderate family might do you more good in the election, for one thing. But that consideration pales next to the danger that Latona poses to you. Have you even considered that?"

"If you mean because she's married, I think I can handle—"

Vibia flapped a hand irritably. "That's on your own conscience, and hers. No. I mean because she's a Spirit mage."

"Because she's a—"

Vibia's eyes flicked over at Corvinus, who was observing from the doorway, his pale face expressionless. "No one lurking around out there, I take it?" He nodded. "Good." Vibia turned back to Sempronius. "Because she could find you out. If she manages to fully harness that power you've detected in her, then if you slip up at all, she might discover you. And frankly, brother, it troubles me if you're so besotted that that had not occurred to you."

His face took on a stubborn set. "What makes you think it hadn't occurred to me? I am as careful around her as I am around Marcia Tullia or the men in the Augian Commission, all of whom have a lot more practice than Latona in discovering the signatures left by magic."

"I hope so," Vibia said. "For your safety, brother, I do dearly hope so." She hesitated, weighing her next words: they were hard on her tongue, but she had avoided this point of fissure for too long. "That isn't the only danger of her magic. You know what they say of her."

"Oh?" Sempronius gestured for Corvinus to come and unwind the toga from his shoulders. "Do I?"

Her eyes narrowed. "Now *you're* being tedious." Vibia rolled her shoulders, searching for words that were tactful yet precise. "You were in Abydosia for some time, brother. You weren't privy to the rumors in Aven towards the end of Ocella's reign."

"No," he agreed. "Marcia and Galerius rarely passed along *gossip*."

"Ocella took an interest in her, after he murdered her sister's husband—"

"Tread lightly, Vibia."

"—an interest she was not seen to repudiate or disavow, and I simply wonder at the wisdom of associating with someone whom others perceive as a dictator's mistress—"

"No." Sempronius's tone was so sharp that Vibia blinked in surprise. "Her association with Ocella was no kind of—" His face tightened, making Vibia wonder what stories he *had* heard, in Abydosia or since returning. Would Latona herself have dared to speak of it to him? Vibia could not imagine such a breach of the bounds of appropriate conversation— but then, Vibia could not imagine doing many of the things the Vitelliae did. "She was as much victim to Ocella's predation as anyone he proscribed or exiled. It would be unjust for anyone to use against her the actions she took to survive—as unjust as blaming me for fleeing to Abydosia, or General Strato for staying in the field."

Vibia took his measure. She knew her brother well enough to know when not to pick a fight—and to know when he spoke with true conviction. She nodded her concession to him, though she retained private concerns about Latona's tendency to captivate powerful men. "If you say so, then I shall speak against those rumors as I hear them."

"And I shall thank you for it."

"I just—I want you to take care." She sighed, feeling a touch defeated, wondering if this was a battle she had lost before even taking the field. "You have such grand vision, brother. I worry sometimes that the smaller things slip by you."

Sempronius's stance softened. He drew near to Vibia, clasping her by the shoulder and kissing her forehead. "Your concern is well-meant, and I shall endeavor to take it as such. I value your observations and opinions, as they have been invaluable to my political career for more than a decade. But I do believe I can see to my own personal affairs."

Vibia, though, remembered close-bent heads at dinner tables, glances exchanged across crowded rooms, and the readiness with which Sempronius trusted those of whom he thought highly—and she did have to wonder at the wisdom of it.

XXXIII

There was snow on the mountaintops.

Vitellius stared at the ragged crests a long time, praying it was just some trick of the light from the rising sun, but as Phoebus Apollo drove his chariot higher in the sky, Vitellius realized there was nothing for it: snow had fallen in the higher reaches.

"Damn."

"Double damn," said a voice behind him—Mennenius. If there had been anything good about the past few weeks on the march, it was that the second cohort had caught up to them, doubling their strength to the near-thousand it should be. "How close are we to Toletum?" Mennenius asked.

"Three days, perhaps." Hanath's voice, this time. Mennenius startled; he had not yet gotten used to her habit of injecting herself into any conversation she saw fit. "The river has turned more southward, and the banks open up a bit. It should be easier marching from here." She smiled at Vitellius. "Fear not, Tribune. We will get you there before the snows find us."

Around them, the men were busily breaking camp. The strict order of the Aventan legion was among its chief assets. Every man knew his duties at dawn and dusk. Each camp was arranged the same way, every tent in the same proximity to the others, wherever the site. If the legionaries were similarly troubled by the appearance of white caps on the surrounding peaks, none let it interfere with their work.

By the time Vitellius finished his supervisory rounds and returned to his own half-deconstructed tent, two messengers were waiting for him—one with a scroll from Governor Sallust, and another from Fimbrianus in Gades. Sallust's was just what he had expected: an acknowledgment of his efforts thus far and a slew of questions about the allied tribes. There was a note of concern about their magic-men, but far more interest in their numbers, positions, and skills—information to pass on to whoever took over the Eighth from him after the upcoming elections. Fimbrianus's letter, though—

"There's a scowl," Mennenius said. "What on earth does that say?"

"I'm being ordered to stand down," Vitellius said.

"Stand down?" Mennenius looked aghast.

"Mm. Governor Fimbrianus accuses me of stirring up trouble. Says I'm inciting the tribes to violence."

"But the violence was going on long before—"

"Yes, and everyone knows that." Vitellius frowned, thinking of what he knew of Fimbrianus. Aulus had never thought much of him. *What would Father say about this? And what would he have me do, with contradicting orders?'*

Mennenius was casting about in confusion. "We can't very well just pack up and abandon our allies now! Not when we've promised to—"

"I know," Vitellius said, still glancing at Fimbrianus's over-long letter. *'A great many words to say "Go home." '* He snorted. "No. Even if it weren't craven and ignoble to take our leave, I doubt we'd make it halfway to Tarraco without getting slaughtered by those we betrayed." Hanath, he suspected, would take great joy in running him through with that spear of hers, should he prove false.

"So what do we—?"

Vitellius worried the inside of his cheek. Fimbrianus was from a powerful family, and he was, in theory, in control of the region. *'But if I must make an enemy . . .'* He let the scroll snap shut. "Governor Fimbrianus is not my commanding officer," he said. "Governor Sallust says press on, so press on I shall." He glared down at the offending roll of paper. "And if my father has anything to say about it, we may hope for reinforcement." Behind him, legionaries were packing up his desk. "That letter, it seems, will have to wait till we make camp this evening."

Any further discussion was forestalled by the arrival of a scouting party, racing in from the half-struck rows of tents outside. Their leader saluted Vitellius. "Sir! We've news."

Vitellius's heart jumped, but he knew that to rush would undermine his authority. So instead he nodded, then looked at the rest of the scouts. "See to the horses," he told them. "They need food and water before we march. Now, then, Dorsus, isn't it?"

"Yes, sir."

Internally, Vitellius sighed, glad to have gotten it right. With a thousand men reporting to him, he could not hope to remember all their names, but he tried to keep track of the centurions and the specialists. "Dorsus, what's your news?"

"An enemy camp, sir," the scout said. "Vettoni. Might be the same group that sent out those scouts we ran into upriver."

"Where?"

"Not far. There's a stream that feeds into the Tagus, and they're a little ways up it. Either they don't know we're here, or they don't much mind."

"How many men?"

"Two hundred and odd."

Vitellius nodded, then turned to the centurions who had gathered nearby, lured by the scouts' return. "Assemble one cohort. The other should continue striking camp. I want the Edetani cavalry with me. They're best at riding on these rough paths. I want four ready to bolt if we need reinforcements from the Arevaci infantry. Dorsus, stay and speak with me further. I want to know as much as you can tell me about the terrain."

A chorus of "Yes, sir's" echoed back at him, and they all dispersed to their duties. *'Is this how Generals feel?'* Vitellius wondered if it was worth wearing an enormous plumed helmet and standing beneath a distinctive standard, both of which rather increased one's odds of attracting a volley of sharp and pointy objects from the opposing side.

Dorsus sketched out a quick map of the nearby area for Vitellius, pointing out that the Vettoni were camped on a bluff near a sparse outcrop of forest, a little farther west of the river. "How dense is the forest there?" Vitellius asked.

"Nothing like Albina," Dorsus answered. "We should be able to get through without dividing ranks."

"Excellent. Then we can approach through the forest," Vitellius gestured on the map, "rather than charging through open fields. Maybe take them a bit by surprise, and block their chance to retreat."

Once the cohort was assembled, Vitellius knew that it was his duty to make some sort of speech. His throat felt dry. *'Tribunes aren't supposed to have to do this,'* he thought. *'It wants a legate, at the least. There should be someone else.'* But there wasn't, and even Mennenius was looking at him expectantly. Vitellius mounted his horse, rode to the front of the line, and decided to keep it simple. *'At least I don't have to pitch my voice very far.'*

"All right, men!" he said. "Seems there's some Vettoni bastards nearby who think they can rough up Aventan allies and not pay for their audacity. I intend that we show them different! We will *show* them how Aven defends its friends!" He paused, letting the men get a few good bellows out. Then, "I hear tell that one of their chieftains has proclaimed himself a king. Not just any king, but a god-touched king." There was some murmuring at that. Aventans had no use for kings. "He claims he has divine right to slaughter innocents! To lay waste to fertile fields! And what do we think of that?" A chorus of booing. Vitellius caught Hanath's eye, where the Arevaci and Edetani cavalry were mustered. "Our allies tell us this self-appointed god-king is a fraud! Will we let *them* be dishonored by his perversion?" A gambit, to get the men to cheer the Iberians, and Vitellius was not disappointed; the cohort shouted their willingness to stand by their allies. "Will we stand idly by and shame Mars with our reticence?" Again, a chorus of "No!"s. "Then let us march out and make these Vettoni regret their arrogance!"

The men cheered and stomped and rattled their shields, but as far as speeches went, Vitellius knew it would not be one for the annals. It had done its work, though, and put the fighting spirit into his men. *'Look here, Mars,'* he thought as they rode out. *'We are men of the Eighth Legion, and we go to battle in your name. Lend us the strength of your arms, the fire of your belly, the glory of victory. Look here and know us.'*

∞∞∞∞∞∞∞∞∞∞∞

Vitellius stood with the cohort's *signum*, the pole-mounted emblem of their pride and strength, and watched the Vettoni come on and on, with better form than the northern tribes. But that troubled him little. Calix and the other centurions knew their business. These men were not much blooded, but they had seen action along the borders, and no amount of hellish screaming, mud-smeared faces, or glinting axes would make them break their lines. Not even coming face-to-face with the occasional female warrior disturbed them, not after watching Hanath and her spear. Vitellius's lines held, and would continue to hold.

Still, it was unnerving, how many Vettoni seemed to be able to take blows and yet return for more. A man he would have sworn he had seen gutted would rise again, bleeding and howling, yet still able to fight.

By Vitellius's calculations, their line should have broken in under a quarter of an hour. When the battle went past that, Vitellius had a chilling thought: the nature of Iberian magic, such as he knew of it, was rooted in blood. Aventans regarded it with a mix of fear and disdain, considering it inferior to their elemental system. *'But what,'* Vitellius wondered, *'if it somehow affects the fighters? If it gives them this power, to keep fighting when they should fall?'*

Beneath that thought was another, more chilling: that this Iberian magic might border perilously close to necromancy. Vitellius had yet to witness such, but he had heard the rumors. *'How could we fight that?'* Aventan magic could not even be used on the battlefield. *'But the rules of their war-gods are different from those of Mars.'* How could the legion conquer troops rendered nigh-invincible by blasphemous magic?

But there was no time for that now, not while Vitellius had a battle he *could* win. If there was magic behind the Vettoni's endurance, it finally wore out. Their line faltered, and as soon as Vitellius saw it start, he called out, "Wedge!" The troops reformed themselves into a penetrating shape, the better to force their way into the Vettonian ranks. After another moment, the Vettoni faltered entirely. A centurion drove his gladius deep into the stomach of one of their apparent leaders, and that set the rest to running. Vitellius raised a hand to signal to the cavalry to ride them down as they retreated.

Well-disciplined, the infantrymen stopped forward motion and held their position as soon as the cavalry took over. Only when the Vettoni were all dead or fled did Vitellius give the order to break ranks and fall to spoil. "Calix!" he called.

Calix turned, saluted, and anticipated Vitellius's question. "I don't believe we've lost any, sir, though we've a few wounded that will need tending to."

"Good."

"Should we head back to camp, sir?"

Vitellius was about to answer when something caught his eye: a faint tendril of smoke reaching above the hill beyond them. It had not been visible from their camp near the river. "Take the legionaries and return to camp with any prisoners," he said. "Take them to Tribune Mennenius. The auxiliaries will come with me."

As soon as the riders crested the hill, Vitellius saw the source of the smoke: a town, or what used to be one. No building was left whole; most were smoldering ruins of mud and thatch. Strewn through what had been streets, Vitellius saw bodies, some bloodied, some burned.

Hanath pulled her horse up alongside Vitellius. "This was an Arevaci town," she said, her voice as cold as the north wind. Vitellius had stopped wondering at the fierceness of her loyalty to her adopted people, but the fury of it blazed in her pitch-dark eyes. That alone would not have harrowed Vitellius—he had seen skirmishes enough in Albina, knew the ugliness and the rank stench of death—but these were not soldiers. It took Vitellius mere moments to trot from one end of town to the other, taking in everything: a blacksmith's tools strewn about a yard, one smeared with gore; torn cloth lying across a threshold; a woman's body pitched half-over a fence; a lone bleating goat wandering aimlessly. *'Civilians. Near enough to their own people . . .'* These things had happened with Aventans, of course, during the Truscan Wars, but that was two generations past, nothing Vitellius had ever witnessed. *'It's war. This happens in war.'* But Aventans didn't kill civilians if it could be avoided; it was not only ignoble, but wasteful.

<hr/>

When Vitellius returned to the half-struck camp, he dismounted at the gate, marched straight to the quaestorium, where some half-dozen Vettoni prisoners had been taken. Calix was there, still spattered with the gore of battle but apparently unconcerned by it, as was Mennenius. "Vitellius," Mennenius began. "What happened out—?"

"Later," Vitellius said, not wanting to discuss the matter in front of the prisoners, just in case they understood more Truscan than they let on. "Calix, get information out of these dogs. Find an auxiliary who can understand the Vettoni dialect."

"Yes sir," Calix replied.

"If they won't talk, flog them." If the prisoners understood him, they showed little sign of it, staring defiantly back. Mennenius, on the other hand, had gone wide-eyed, bewildered at his friend's sudden ferocity. With the scent of smoke still in his nostrils, Vitellius was in no mood for leniency or diplomacy. "Flog them, beat them, notch their ears, cut off their toes, I don't care what you have to do, but bloody well do it. I want to know everything there is to know about their numbers and where the bastards are hiding. And if they haven't talked by the time we're ready to move, drag them behind the wagons, and we'll try again when next we make camp."

XXXIV

CITY OF AVEN

There were times Merula fantasized about killing her master.

She would never go through with it, of course. Not even Lady Latona's favor could protect her from the consequences of such a transgression. She knew what Aventan magistrates did to slaves who even raised a hand to a citizen, and she quite preferred to live a long life with all limbs and extremities intact. But Merula had watched Herennius's condescending indulgence towards his wife turn to cool disregard and now, it seemed, outright contempt. Since the Dictator's death, he freely expressed the festering resentment that his wife's association with Ocella had generated, and so Herennius had begun to test, with far more frequency, the spare ration of patience that Merula's gods had seen fit to give her.

On a drizzly afternoon shortly before the Kalends of December, Herennius strode into the room where Merula and the Domina were embroidering. "Wife," he barked. Ruddy color was high in his cheeks; he was either excited or angry about something, but Merula could not tell which. Latona took her time finishing a stitch, laying the work carefully in her lap, then looked up at her husband. "You will join me in my chamber. Immediately. Prepare yourself as is necessary." As an afterthought, he jerked his head at Merula, "Leave that here." Without waiting, he huffed in a circle and left the room.

Sighing, Latona rose and handed her needlework to Merula. Merula stuffed it hastily in a basket, trotting along behind Latona as she walked towards Herennius's bedchamber. "Domina? Domina, do you need—"

"I think I can manage to undress myself without assistance, Merula, thank you." The sigh remained in her voice, trailing resignation.

"Not what I am meaning," Merula said. There was a twitch in her fingers, and she was acutely aware of the sensation of cool metal against her skin, where her knife was strapped to her thigh. "If he hurts you, Domina—"

But Latona shook her head. "It will be no more than uncomfortable, as always." Her eyes flicked heavenward. "And I daresay I will not have to endure any discomfort for long." She put on a falsely bright smile. "And who knows? If I get a child out of it, then it's all for good."

Merula was not sure of that. As there was nothing to be done for it, she had no choice but to leave Latona at the chamber door and bundle herself down to the kitchen. She had been sitting there for an hour, helping the cook, Caenis, to slice vegetables for a stew, when one of the other slaves, a slender Ionian woman called Philotis, came in sniffling. "What's wrong?" Caenis said, without turning from the table where she was peeling onions.

"Dominus beat me," Philotis said.

"Beat you?" Caenis asked, arching an eyebrow. Such would be unusual in the Herennian domus, where the steward ran a firm enough household that extreme corrections were not often necessary.

"He *hit* me," Philotis said, her full lips turned in an exaggerated pout.

"What'd you do?"

Merula read naked indignation on Philotis's face. "I didn't *do* anything. Or fail to do anything, thank you very much. I was just in the wrong damn place when he was in the wrong damn mood." She spat on the ground. That roused Caenis to look over her shoulder where Philotis's words had not, and with a roll of her eyes, Philotis rubbed the damp spot out with her bare foot. "He hit Ivorcus today, too," she added, "because he didn't think his toga had been properly starched. His foul temper is showing."

Caenis shrugged. "Could be worse. I know perfectly well you haven't had a real beating since you entered this house, and even if the Dominus ordered it, old Tembri is so weak it'd feel like a tickle. What's a slap here or there?"

"Easy for you to say," Philotis sniffed. "He never hits *you*."

"It's a stupid man who hits the slave who makes his food," Caenis said, with a little laugh. "But don't go thinking I've never felt the back of a master's hand. My last, he was a devil for it, damn near every day. At least he was too busy fooling around with the pretty boys to meddle with me, so I thanked the gods for giving me tits instead of a prick." She snorted derisively. "You can stay in here and sulk if you like, but make yourself useful."

Still looking aggrieved, Philotis plunked herself down on a stool next to Merula and started shucking peas. "I've had my fill of it, I don't mind telling you," she said, "and in another year or so, I expect I'll have enough saved up to buy myself from him, and see if anyone ever lays a hand to me again."

Caenis snorted. "There'll always be someone willing to take on that job, I'm sure."

Philotis pointedly ignored her. "What about you, Merula?" Philotis asked. "Are you saving up?"

Before Merula could do more than shrug, Caenis chortled, slapping her hands against her thighs. "What should she want freedom for? So she can give up her nice, cushioned cot in the Domina's bedroom and go live in a tiny fifth-floor insula with three other freedwomen?" Caenis shook her head. "It's not worth it, my honeys. I know. My brother, he saved for his freedom, and it's gotten him nowhere good. He can vote, but his vote means nothing." Another snort. "Head Count, urban tribe, who cares? He makes money, but it all goes to pay for the shithole he lives in. And the food he eats now!"

"Maybe we're not all as stupid as your brother," Philotis said, though she proved her own intelligence by muttering it too low for Caenis to hear. She cleared her throat, then said louder, "Even if my own prospects weren't good—and I think I could do quite well working for a seamstress, thank you very much—I want my children to be born free." She elbowed Merula, looking for support. "Don't you think that's better?"

Merula had been taken from her home in Phrygia so young that she could hardly call it to her memory in more than fragments of scent and sound. Still, she had to admit that, though free-living had done her parents little good, it would be different to be manumitted and bestowed with Aventan citizenship, as all freed slaves were. "Better opportunities, I am thinking," she allowed.

"There. See? Merula agrees with me." Caenis's eyeroll indicated what she thought of that. "What would *you* do, then?" Philotis asked.

Merula had given the matter some thought, all too aware that, though her life with Vitellia Latona was easy enough, should the domina die—as women did, all the time—her prospects would be far better as a freedwoman than as a slave. The trouble was that her desire was nothing she could voice to someone like Philotis, so she only shrugged. "Find work. I am having skills enough."

In truth, Merula had been around Aventan society enough for some of it to have rubbed off on her, particularly the instinct for turning a profit. It had occurred to her that her mistress had hit upon something potentially useful, in training a female bodyguard, and Merula thought that she could earn fair wages teaching others to do as she did—a sort of *ludus*, like the gladiators had. It was an outrageous notion, she knew, but the idea did make her smile.

"What was it got Dominus so upset, anyway?" Caenis said. "Think he'll stay angry through dinner? I may need to change the menu."

Philotis smirked. "Best find some larks, then," she said. "I heard him and the domina screaming at each other before he came out and slapped me for having the nerve to clean the atrium. Apparently the dominus's manhood failed him at the critical moment. He blamed the domina. He yelled, she yelled. Then I heard a crash, something breaking, and then he stormed out and hit me."

Merula made a little hissing noise under her breath, then cursed a streak in her native Phrygian. Though neither Caenis nor Philotis could understand the words, her tone implied enough for Caenis to glare at her. "He can do with her what he likes," Caenis said. "She's as much his property as you or I, but she gets far greater compensation for it, so I won't be shedding too many tears for her fate."

Merula rose. "I should see to her. And *you*," she said, glaring at Philotis, "I should cuff you myself for not telling me when you first come down." She bounded up the stairs to the main level of the house, glad for her own sake that she did not encounter Dominus Herennius on her way.

◇◇◇◇◇◇◇◇◇◇◇◇◇◇

There was no moon in the sky as Sempronius settled down in front of the altar in his atrium. The day's rain had petered off, leaving a soupy fog in its wake, but that did not trouble Sempronius. To the contrary, it would provide an excellent conduit for his energies.

He had dismissed all his servants but Corvinus from the main level of the domus. With deliberate care, he refreshed the offerings on the smooth-worn stone. He had brought sand from the Forum, to help focus the magic on the pertinent issue, and this he sprinkled in a circle around himself before kneeling in front of the obsidian mirror, his hands resting palms-up on his knees.

With the heavy aroma of balsam and myrrh incense thickening the air, Sempronius murmured the usual invocations, then repeated a call for favor, over and over again, chanting as he allowed his mind to fall into the right patterns. It took time to suspend his thoughts between the mundane and the spiritual, striking the perfect balancing point, where his mind could hold on to the crux of the matter yet let go enough to allow the gods use of him. And he could not scant the effort today, not when he had to be sure that the divine powers could find no fault with him. Breathing in the smoke emanating from the incense on the altar, Sempronius felt his awareness slide into place, and he gazed down at the obsidian mirror.

Yet the haze of gray did not clear. No images faded into discernible form on the glossy surface. Sempronius frowned. Shadow's answers were ever tricky to corral, but the element did not usually play so coy with him. He repeated the incantation in a low voice, blocking out all external stimulus. Neither the press of the floor against his knees nor the rustling of leaves, neither the coolness of the air nor the wafting incense could be allowed to distract him. He acknowledged only the sleek surface of the dark mirror.

There was a tendril—a wisp of information, no more, but it danced out of Sempronius's mental reach whenever he tried to grasp it. A deliberate tease, the information there yet unrevealed.

Still murmuring to his gods, Sempronius redoubled his focus, peering through the layers of obfuscation, willing the haze on the dark mirror to part for him. *'Show me. Show me the man who stands in my way, the man who cursed Autronius Felix, who tracks me through the streets, who favored me with a poisoned arrow, and show me how he is doing it.'*

Sempronius pushed harder at the mist, determined to chase the elusive hint into a corner and pin it down if necessary. Images started to clear on the obsidian mirror, but Sempronius did not allow his relief to relax his concentration. The Forum. The area where Felix had gotten himself in trouble, near the Temple of Castor and Pollux. The Via Sacra, the tribunal . . .

A lancing pain flashed in Sempronius's mind, nearly knocking him flat. The obsidian mirror flared with a hot white light, obliterating the images that Sempronius had so painstakingly summoned. Only with effort did Sempronius manage to keep hold of the mirror itself, whose cool surface now burned like heated iron. *'It's just an illusion,'* he told himself, setting it down carefully in front of the altar, only removing his fingers from it when he was sure it was stable. He looked at his hands; the flesh was red, but not blistered.

Corvinus had bolted forward at the first sign of trouble. "Dominus?"

"Send for my sister. Tell her it is urgent. Let no one else in this part of the house."

He sat, rump inelegantly on the floor, contemplating the still-blazing mirror until Vibia arrived. "Brother!" She rushed to kneel by him, though hesitated to reach out a hand, unsure of what had happened. "Corvinus said there was trouble, but he wasn't sure—"

"The mirror." Sempronius nodded at it. "I was attempting to hunt down whoever ensorcelled Felix in the Forum and tried to murder me— whether they are the same person or not—but nothing would come. Just mist. I got it to clear enough to see the area where Felix was cursed, but then . . . this." He made a sweeping gesture. "It's as though the mirror is in riot. And there's a pain in my head like you wouldn't believe."

Vibia frowned at him, then at the mirror, then back at him. Then she rolled up the sleeves of her woolen under-tunic. "May I?" she asked, reaching towards his head. Sempronius nodded.

Her fingers against his temples did nothing to lessen the pain. Instead, they focused it, bringing all the sparks to two focal points. His hands clenched into fists, pressed tight against his thighs as Vibia probed.

"Well, that's the oddest damn thing I've ever encountered," Vibia said, rocking back on her heels.

"You have always had a way with comforting words, sister."

"Would you rather I tiptoe around it?" she snapped. "This is bizarre magic, and I don't know any gentler way of putting it. Someone's used Fracture magic to set wards." Sempronius's face screwed up in confusion. "I know. I've never heard of such a thing." Vibia rubbed at her own forehead. "I suppose it's not entirely non-sensical. Like cutting a trench around a camp instead of building up walls. All the same, very odd." She pinched at the bridge of her nose. "The good news is, I don't think it was meant for you specifically. It's just a guard against anyone who comes poking about."

Sempronius nodded. "That is good news. If anyone knew to put up magical wards against me, specifically . . ." He did not need to spell out the disaster that would presage.

"And it means it likely won't stick." Vibia pushed to her feet, and Sempronius rose, too, though his head was still rolling with pain and dizziness. "Get a good night's rest and it should clear itself. And tomorrow, figure out how to track down your quarry through more traditional means."

◇◇◇◇◇◇◇◇◇◇◇◇

"Of course it's Rabirus." Corvinus stood over Sempronius's desk, his eyes roving over papers. Most were in Sempronius's handwriting, though a few were in Vibia's. Others were Corvinus's own, with occasional additions in Djadi's neat script. Notes on politics, notes on alliances, notes on personal intrigues—and notes on Fracture magic. "Forgive my saying so, Dominus, but that seems fairly obvious."

"I concur with your assessment," Sempronius said. "But *how*?" He pulled a paper from the stack. "If he's attacking me with Fracture magic, he must be using a Fracture *mage*. I've accounted for all the ones in the city, but I haven't been able to connect any of them to Rabirus." He waved a hand over the list. "Several in the Temple of Janus, as expected. One in Fortuna, one in Orcus, one in Castor and Pollux . . ."

"That's a lot in temples," Corvinus commented.

"The alternatives for a Fracture mage can be bleak." Sempronius tapped his finger on a few other names on the list. "Beggars and madmen . . . Without the discipline of a temple, the more powerful Fracture mages can quite go to pieces." He frowned at one name, whose story he knew. "Though for this poor woman, it was Ocella's hard usage, not lack of control, that did her in."

Corvinus nodded his understanding. "And you think there's nothing to fear from those in the temples?"

"There could be quite a lot to fear," Sempronius said, "but I had Marcus ask around. He says the High Priest of Janus swears up and down his people are quite devoted, hardly ever notice the world outside their rituals." He frowned, thinking of the fog on his mirror, the things it would not let him see. Something near the Forum, but that scarcely narrowed matters down. The Forum was the heart of the city, surrounded by temples and administrative buildings. Thousands of people streamed in and out of it every day. "As for the others, the acolyte at Orcus and the priest of Castor and Pollux hardly have enough power to find a door with, and the girl at Fortuna has potential but is scarcely sixteen. None have known political connections to the Optimates."

"Unlikely then. What about these?" Corvinus pointed to three other names on the list of Fracture mages: a gambler, a bookmaker, and a landlord of one of the cheapest insulae in the Subura. "They would be easy enough to pay off."

"An excellent inclination, Corvinus, but I've had the Vatiniae look into them. They say there's no indication of a connection—or that they have enough power to cause the mayhem my unknown opponent has." Sempronius rubbed his forehead, smudging it with a bit of ink, and bent once again over the list. "Two children, no worries there. Vibia vouches for Rufilia Mulagonis, little though I think she likes to. And that's all of them inside the city."

"Do you think it could be—"

"Someone outside the city?" Sempronius drew a breath, then released it slowly. "I have to confess the possibility, considering the poisoned arrow at Tibur." He rose from the desk and began pacing. "If this mage is acting at Lucretius Rabirus's direction, then the likely purpose is to disrupt my political aims. That business with Felix in the Forum, meant to cast aspersions on my associates and thus the Popularist cause . . . the arrow, so soon after we began debating Iberia in the Senate . . ."

"And that sense you've had, Dominus, of someone or something following you in the streets," Corvinus said. "I've noticed it happens when you're on Forum business, not social."

Sempronius looked to him, startled. "I had not realized that." The omission surprised him.

Corvinus bowed his head slightly. "It is my duty to make note of such minutiae."

"Well done." Sempronius paced a few more moments, the only sound in the room the occasional flick of a page as Corvinus continued picking through the notes on the desk. "The advantage of a Fracture mage as an opponent is that they can easily become reckless."

"Dominus?"

"Just a thought. Our best hope of finding out who is working against me may be in waiting for them to make a mistake—or pressuring them into making one."

◆ DECEMBER ◆

XXXV

Autumn turned to winter with unseemly haste. A cold and biting air swept over the city, prompting sensible men to stay close to a high-functioning hypocaust.

The senators of Aven, it could be argued, were not sensible men.

The Curia was cold brick and ancient, unforgiving timber, heated only by a fire pit in the middle of the room. *'If we had consuls,'* Sempronius thought, glaring down at the empty chairs from his bench, *'they, at least, would be warm.'*

Still seething over his inability to discover the source of his troubles, Sempronius was in no mood to deal with the bickering and maneuvering of his peers. The shouting started well before session formally opened. New reports had come in from Tribunes Vitellius and Mennenius, lamenting the depredations suffered by the Arevaci allies. Mennenius, who had talent as a cartographer, had included a map of the destroyed villages they had found, and Aulus had thrust these under the noses of practically everyone in the Forum over the past few days. "Half the Iberian Peninsula seems to be up in arms," shouted General Strato. "We can delay no longer!" There was much pounding of fists and shouting, both approving and castigating.

"What matter is it to us if the inland tribes squabble amongst themselves?" Buteo asked, rising. "Our settlements on the coast are safe, are they not? Do those scribblings of a tribune show any attacks within two hundred miles of the coast?"

"Seven hells, Buteo, do you truly fail to see why we must stir ourselves?" countered Quintus Terentius. Throughout the autumn, he had stayed neutral on the Iberian question; Sempronius considered his support a sign that the tide was moving in the right direction. "Our coastal settlements need access to goods from the inland. Every report that comes from Iberia tells that the rebel tribes have pushed further out. They could be at the gates of Gades before long!"

"Every man in the Senate can guess why you're in favor, Quintus

Terentius!" bellowed Buteo in reply. "Hoping to find a new wife among the Lusetani, are you?"

There was a deal of laughter, as much of it good-natured as mean-spirited, and even Terentius himself grinned, feeling no shame for his family's reputation for making eccentric bridal choices. "Perhaps we all ought to look to the west for our next wives," Terentius said, gesturing broadly. "For it seems they breed impressive men. It might improve our stock!"

Throughout another hour of bickering and trading jibes, Sempronius remained quiet, partly due to a lingering headache, but also because he was sorting out what he most wanted to say. Aven's possible fates danced in his mind's eye, echoes of what he had seen in his obsidian mirror, shifting and uncertain—but all pointing, at this first crux, towards Iberia and towards his own hand in shaping Aven's work there. To further his goals of expansion and financial success for Aven, he had to have victory in Iberia. To have victory, he had to have an army when the new year rolled around; to have an army, he had to have first pick of the praetorships, a mandate to command. Sempronius listened, considered, and at length, counted heads.

Then he signaled that he wished to speak. "Gentlemen, I have a proposal."

"Of *course* you do," muttered Rabirus.

"When I first broached the matter of Iberia, this august body determined that more information was needed." He gestured towards Aulus, who had in his lap every message that he had received from his son in the past few months. "We have information. We have *not* heard from Governor Fimbrianus in Gades—a silence that speaks of the Governor's unwillingness to risk the Fourth Legion outside the city walls! We have information. Every scrap of it calls for action." His outstretched hand pointed next towards Buteo. "Some in this body would question the need for action. If there is fighting, allow them to fight. If there is murder, allow them to kill. What business is it of ours?" His fingers curled into a fist, and his voice exploded as though he were on a battlefield, not in the Curia. "They are our *allies*!"

Several men startled visibly. Sempronius was glad about it. He was known for his cool head, keeping his voice moderate however outrageous his ideas. When Buteo bellowed, no one thought it strange. When Sempronius did, it was worth the noticing.

He took care not to make it seem like a loss of control. A deep breath steadied him, kept his face from reddening. His arm resumed the normal speech-giving posture. "Our allies, venerable fathers. Men to whom we have pledged ourselves. Women and children who think of Aven as their shield against destruction. If we fail them now, we disgrace ourselves. We dishonor ourselves, our ancestors, and our gods. We prove to the world that Aven is not a nation that can be trusted!" Sempronius adjusted his stance to a less aggressive posture. "This is not the reputation I wish for our nation to hold, gentlemen. This is not a reputation to be proud of. Could we allow the Iberians to slaughter each other? Withdraw our troops, leave our allies to fend for themselves? Certainly we could. But it would be morally reprehensible, and the other nations of the Middle Sea would rightly despise us for it."

He kept his hand up, a signal that he was not done, and even Buteo looked too shocked to interrupt.

Sempronius weighed his next words. If he called for a division and lost, it would impair his reputation at a critical moment. If won, he would gain votes from the citizens who supported the war but could alienate those who didn't.

But he heard his own words ringing back at him. He wanted war in Iberia for his own purposes, true. He wanted to win an election and lead an army. But he also believed what he had said: Aven had taken on a re-sponsibility. Sempronius would not suffer the shame of the city, *his* city, failing so utterly.

"We said we would wait for more information. We said we would wait for December. Well, gentlemen, December has arrived. The year draws to a close. I call now for a division on the question of going to war in Iberia."

As soon as he dropped his hand, the Senate erupted in turbulent con-versation. The interim censor eventually had to pound his walking stick on the floor for attention. "A division has been called for!" he wheezed. "Those in favor of opening the gates of war for an Iberian conflict will move to the left. Those opposed will move to the right."

Aulus was first to move to the left, still pointedly holding the stack of reports from his son, and Generals Strato and Albinicus, with Sempro-nius himself, followed almost as swiftly as Rabirus and Buteo moved to the right. Gnaeus and Marcus Autronius looked unsettled, but also moved left; Sempronius could only imagine the row at home if they ab-stained and Felix got wind of it. Herennius rose slowly, glaring at Sempronius—but he glanced at Aulus and then moved left. *'I'll take a grudging vote,'* Sempronius thought. *'At least the Vitellian marriage alliance has some kind of benefit.'* Cornicen wavered, too, but at a sharp look from Rabirus, moved right.

As the men continued to divide, Sempronius's jaw tightened; it was too evenly split for his comfort, and a great many men seemed unprepared to make the decision, alarmed by the suddenness of Sempronius's call.

When Galerius Orator rose, his face impassive, and moved left, more began to follow. Sempronius released a breath he was unaware he had been holding. Galerius's support moved many of the prominent moderates. Then more of the middle-rankers, the back-benchers. Followers, all of them, too weak to decide on their own, but Sempronius could hardly chide them for that in this moment. Soon two-thirds of the room was on the left.

"Motion passes," the interim censor said. Buteo looked fit to burst. "The first matter of business following the elections will be the preparation for war in Iberia, and the Senate will recommend a course of action to the Centuriate Assembly."

Sempronius, cautiously, smiled.

⬦⬦⬦⬦⬦⬦⬦⬦⬦⬦⬦

"You have a plan. *Tell* me you have a plan."

Several of the Optimates, all men who had moved to the right with alacrity, were gathered at Rabirus's house. His son stood in the corner, goggling at the infuriated outbursts and venomous invectives. Most of those had come from Buteo. Ally though he was, Rabirus was suppressing the urge to kick him. Buteo was wonderful at making a lot of noise, and certainly he had done his duty at the Rostra nearly every day for the past month, but when it came time for action, he looked to Rabirus. Not just looked to him, *demanded* it of him, as though Rabirus alone had such agency.

Rabirus hoped he had sense enough not to mention Pinarius Scaeva now. Not everyone crowded into his study would understand Rabirus's decision to engage the services of so unsavory a character. *'I had to call upon him. I had no choice. For the good of Aven, for the good of the Republic . . .'*

Before Rabirus could think of a reply that was suitable for this audience, however, Buteo had moved on to chastising Cornicen. "And *you!* Took your time in voting, didn't you? You've a lot of nerve even showing your face here, after that—"

"Has it occurred to you, Buteo," Cornicen broke in, "that just because a man is your enemy does not mean he is necessarily always wrong? There are advantages to going to war in Iberia, as you and I have discussed before. I see nothing shameful about considering one's response to an important question before making a decision."

"It's craven and self-serving, is what it is," Buteo snarled. "You're as bad as the rest of them."

"Obviously not," Cornicen shot back, "or I wouldn't be here, now would I?"

"Stop," Rabirus said. "This is getting us nowhere. We have only a few days before the election to determine how to turn this to our favor."

"The trouble with the praetorial elections," Gratianus put in, "is that the Centuries are, by and large, for war. Even the officer classes may back him," he went on. "The younger men are spoiling for war, and many others will follow Aufidius Strato and Rufilius Albinicus's lead."

"Then we must focus our efforts on those who will not," Rabirus said. "The older men, wiser and steadier. Those who saw how much effort we've wasted in Numidia and Phrygia, who know the expense of campaigning."

"And who value the *mos maiorum*!" Buteo waved an arm in the air. "You all act as though this is merely a matter of— of practicality! As though the very foundation of the Republic were not at stake!"

Cornicen looked about to argue the merits of practicality, so Rabirus jumped in first. "Of course I prize the *mos maiorum* as highly as you do, friend."

Buteo sniffed, as though to say no one could possibly hold the ancient traditions in a regard that compared to his worship of them.

"But we must face the reality that not all the men of the Centuries are made of such stalwart moral character. We must appeal to their lesser natures—long enough to win the elections at least. Now." He gestured to a slave, who approached with a tablet. "Let us decide how best to divide our resources over the next few days. Who do we most need to talk to?"

The Optimates spent the rest of the evening in tactical discussion, determining how to make use of Cornicen's pragmatic streak, analyzing where to deploy their consular candidate, Gratianus, and tactfully deciding with whom Buteo's strident moralizing would do them good rather than harm. Soon they had a list and a plan, targets for public speechmaking and private conversations alike. Rabirus prayed it would be enough to turn the tide against the Popularists.

Only when the others had gone and his son had disappeared to his chamber did Rabirus catch Buteo by the elbow and hiss, "Of course I have something planned. Pinarius Scaeva promised me that Sempronius Tarren will never see the praetorship. He is not a man who makes such pronouncements idly."

"Forgive me, friend," Buteo said, nostrils flaring, "but your pet mage has taken his sweet time about it. What's he done since that fumbling excuse for action with Autronius Felix, hm?"

"He assures me—"

"No doubt he does!" Buteo huffed. "He's being paid well for it! But I tell you, Rabirus, he's working too slow for my liking. I know you prefer the subtle press of the shadows, but sometimes, a blunt object will remove an obstacle just as well."

Rabirus rubbed his forehead. Buteo's strident nature made him a strong but sometimes inconvenient ally. "Certainly no one could accuse you of subtlety, friend," he said, "but surely you see the need—"

"What I see," Buteo said, "is that we should overlook no opportunity to keep someone as dangerous as Sempronius Tarren out of power."

XXXVI

The following evening, Sempronius accepted a dinner invitation from the Autroniae. "Felix will be dancing on air," Gnaeus said. "He's desperate to start talking strategy with you."

"There'll be no living with him now," Marcus added. "If he talks of anything but Iberia between now and spring, I'll be astonished."

Sempronius nodded, but whatever the Autroniae might think, he knew that winning in the Curia was only half the battle. Now he had to ride that victory to another. A campaign in Iberia would do him little good if he was not the one leading it.

At Marcus's suggestion, Sempronius had brought the Vatiniae brothers to dinner with him. Their star was rising along with Sempronius's, but even so, they would never be accepted for meals in houses like the Galeriae's or the Crispiniae's. The Autroniae, however, were only a few generations removed from freedmen. They weren't about to turn their noses up at Mauretanian immigrants. Obir and Nisso got along famously with Felix in particular, trading stories about fighting desert nomads, theorizing on how best to take on the Lusetani.

The night was well advanced when Sempronius and the Vatiniae took their leave. As was his habit, Sempronius chose to walk rather than ride in a litter, the better to observe the life of the city. The night was cold, but between thick woolen cloaks and the warm flush of wine, none of the men minded. Since he had Corvinus with him as well, Sempronius would have parted ways with the Vatiniae at the bottom of the Quirinal, but as his clients, they insisted on walking him at least as far as the Circus Maximus, even though it meant traipsing in the wrong direction.

The Subura was never quiet, even at night. They avoided the more well-attended streets, full of brothels and rowdy taverns, picking their way through the relatively peaceful maze of insulae and shops that curved around the low slopes of the Carinae. Eventually, the haphazard avenues would careen into the Via Sacra, and they would be in the decidedly less disorderly side of town.

As they passed through the markets, an enormous cart, laden with amphorae, blocked their way. They veered into a narrow alley, intending to dog-leg back—

A heavy body impacted Sempronius from the right side. He pushed back, hard, thinking at first it was just some drunkard, staggering his way home. Then he saw the flash of metal, caught by the light of the waxing moon, and noticed two more men hurtling towards them through the alley.

Sempronius was unarmed, but the Vatiniae certainly were not, and even Corvinus had a little knife at his belt. Amid punching, grunting, and shoving, Sempronius heard the wet suction of a blade entering flesh, but in the press of bodies and the darkness of the alley, he had no idea who had been stabbed. He parried a thrust aimed at his chest, then grabbed the man's arm, gave it a twist, and swung him hard into the wall, using the attacker's own weight and forward momentum against him. When the man fell, Sempronius stamped hard on his hand, forcing him to relinquish the blade.

Corvinus and Obir were holding their own, but—Sempronius's stomach lurched—Nisso was slumped against the wall, his hand clutched to his belly. Sempronius recovered his attacker's blade and started for one of the other men, but Corvinus put his own knife between the man's ribs. The last man standing, realizing it was now, at best, three against one, dropped his blade in front of Corvinus and took off down the alley. Sempronius's attacker, though his head was bleeding, had recovered enough to stagger to his feet and follow his comrade. "Should I track them, Dominus?" Corvinus asked.

At least one of them would not get far fast. But the streets here were a labyrinth, so easy to disappear into, and Nisso was bleeding. "No. Vatinius Nisso needs help."

"We are near your sister's house, Dominus."

"Lead the way," Obir said, heaving one of Nisso's arms over his shoulder. Sempronius moved to take the other. "And quickly, lad!"

∞∞∞∞∞∞∞∞∞∞∞

Sempronius pounded on the green-lacquered door so loudly that a neighbor cursed out the window at him. The petite Ionian slave who answered recognized him, but was clearly confused. "Dominus Sempronius— Domina Vibia has already retired for the night, and Dominus Mella is still at—"

"Wake my sister. Now." He pushed past the little man and ushered Obir and Nisso in as quickly as he could. Even in dim light, Sempronius could see that Nisso was in a bad way. His tunic was dark with blood, his eyes rolling and unfocused as Obir supported his weight. "Get him a couch," Sempronius ordered the slave, who was standing gape-mouthed, shocked at the sudden intrusion of chaos into their house. "And send a boy out, find a healer and bring him here immediately. And someone bring lights!"

Sempronius was not his master, but the door-slave rushed to obey, fetching the steward first, then scurrying to the other errands. The steward, in turn, woke Vibia, who rushed bleary-eyed into the atrium, clutching a wrap around her tunic. "Sempronius, what in Juno's name—" Vibia began, but Sempronius heard the note of protest in her voice and held up a hand.

"We were ambushed," he said, as two slaves dragged a couch over and helped to ease Nisso down onto it.

"Amb— What happened?"

"We were on our way back from the Autroniae's, passing through the Subura," Sempronius said. "Three men came out of nowhere, daggers out."

"Thieves?" Vibia asked, though there was more hope than certainty in her voice.

"We were meant to think so, Domina," Obir said. "Yet they seemed to have no interest in our purses. We left one dead in the alley, but the other two ran like rabbits once they realized—" Obir cut himself off, grimacing. He had injuries as well, though nowhere near as dire as Nisso's: an ugly welt raised on his cheek, a slashing cut over his left eye, and splashes of blood drying on his arms.

"This was no robbery," Sempronius said. "They didn't take anything. Just stabbed and ran, as soon as we started to fight back. I apologize for bringing this to your doorstep, but we were nearer here than my home or theirs."

"Of course."

"Send one of your men to the nearest collegium. Say there's a dead man around the corner from them that I want investigated, and I'll pay for their trouble." Sempronius doubted there would be enough evidence for him to bring a suit against anyone, but he wanted whatever information there was to gather. "Tell them to knock on the surrounding doors, ask if—" Nisso gave a groan, refocusing Sempronius's attention. He knelt beside the couch. "Obir, give me your knife." Sempronius used it to slit

Nisso's tunic up the side. Behind him, Vibia turned demurely away. Nisso groaned as Sempronius peeled the sodden fabric away from his skin. "I'm sorry to jostle you," Sempronius said, "but I need a look at this." Nisso gave no response. His breathing had grown labored, and Sempronius wondered if he could hear.

Sempronius had seen enough skirmishes during his early military service to know a lethal gut wound when he saw one. The stench of blood and bowels was nearly overpowering, enough to prompt Vibia to remove herself from the room. A clean puncture wound might have been salvageable, but the tearing rent across Nisso's midsection was wide enough for Sempronius could see the knotty pink expanse of his intestines. He was hemorrhaging blood that covered Sempronius's hands and stained the couch. His brow and cheeks were drenched in sweat, and his mouth gaped open, his lips working wordlessly. Pluto's mark was on him: a dark shade, which Sempronius's Shadow magic saw all too clearly, that spoke of inescapable death.

Feeling heavy, Sempronius stood and walked to Obir. "I'm sorry, friend. But . . . your brother is beyond aid." Obir staggered backwards, looking suddenly ten years older. "We've sent for a healer, but, I've seen this before. The wound was deep enough to tear open his insides. It allows poison into his blood." He gestured towards the shrine, standing in an alcove off the atrium. "If there are any gods you would like to say words to on his behalf . . ."

Obir nodded dumbly, and as he walked lead-footed to the shrine, Sempronius returned to Nisso. "Corvinus," he called. "Tell someone to bring me a basin of water."

It was a branch of his magic that Sempronius rarely exercised. Water was the conduit of the soul, and Shadow the province of the Underworld; together, Sempronius had the power to ease a man's passing. And it was magic he could work subtly, especially with the household in such disorder and Obir oblivious in his grief.

Corvinus placed the basin beneath Nisso's couch. Sempronius sunk his hands into the water, turning it pink with Nisso's blood. "I call upon you, Lympha, Reader of Souls. I call upon you, Pluto, Lord of the Underworld . . ." As he whispered, he could hear Obir at the shrine, praying in a mix of Truscan and Maureti, to the gods of both lands, his voice low and choked with tears.

When Sempronius finished his incantation, he placed his dripping hands on Nisso's cheeks. "Go in peace, my friend," he said. The magic flowed through him, through the water, a dark wave that crossed from one realm to the next. Passing so near the shades of the underworld, Sempronius could feel its magnetic pull, but he watched without blinking as the spark of life, still fighting so desperately, through so much pain, finally faded from behind Nisso's eyes.

Sempronius's muscles ached as he stepped back and allowed Corvinus to wipe the blood from his hands with a fresh towel. Corvinus took both the towel and the basin of water away. While Obir prayed and wept, Sempronius kept watch over the corpse.

At length, Obir finished his supplication and returned to stand beside Sempronius. His eyes streamed tears freely as he looked down at what had been his brother. "He always fought well," Obir said. "But these bastards surprised us. He never had a chance to draw his knife."

"I would like to pay his funeral expenses, if you would allow me," Sempronius said. He might not know who, precisely, had been behind the attack, but the Vatiniae would never have been involved had they not been attending upon Sempronius. It conferred an obligation that Sempronius did not think he could ever fully pay.

"I thank you, Sempronius," Obir said, his voice thick with sorrow. "But we are members of a burial club."

Sempronius nodded. "All the same, if you should wish a monument for him, mourners, anything of that sort, I will provide it."

"You have always been a worthy patron to us."

Sempronius laid a hand on Obir's shoulder. "I will leave you to say your farewells. My sister's people will see to it, if you need anything." He went to seek out Vibia.

She had gone to the portico at the top of the garden, and she looked even paler than usual. "There is a dead man in your atrium," Sempronius said. "A man who was my friend and client, so I pray you, spare me any chiding until tomorrow, at least."

Vibia swayed, drawing her wrap even tighter around her. She swallowed her discomfort, however, and asked only, "Do you know who did this?"

"I can only suspect," Sempronius said. "And it will be easy enough to track. There was no magic to this, just thuggishness."

"They fear you," Vibia said. "If they did not, they would content themselves with the usual corruptions. Not curses in the Forum, poisoned arrows, and blades drawn in the dead of night."

"Some of them, it seems, got a taste for bloodshed under Ocella."

Sempronius paced along the line where the light spilling from the house gave way to the darkness of the unlit garden. Rabirus or Buteo, it hardly mattered which was the hand behind this particular atrocity. They were a matched pair of black nags. Buteo, who loved the idea of the republic so much he could not see its reality, and Rabirus, who had learned brutality at a dictator's elbow. Sempronius knew them to be ruthless, but he would never have guessed them so entirely unscrupled as to attempt an assassination mere days before an election. *'And all because I outwitted them.'*

Vibia let her brother walk out his irritation, his grief, and whatever else drove him to kick at fallen leaves and swear under his breath for several minutes before speaking again. "Be careful, brother," she said. "You know I support you, but it will be hard to effect change if you are dead."

"I promise you, sister," Sempronius said, looking up at the stars, "I have no intention of dying at these men's hands."

"No." Vibia followed his gaze. "No one ever does."

XXXVII

"There is a price." Bailar held a fresh-whetted knife in one hand, a bronze bowl in the other. Despite the biting cold, Ekialde knelt, bare to the waist, under the bone-white full moon. "Another man's blood can give you strength, but if you wish dominion over another, or to extend your protection to another, for that, it will require your own."

Bailar had consulted the stars and determined that the time was right for Ekialde to take the next step in his path as *erregerra*. Drinking blood to absorb power was easy; any man could do it, though not all would feel the hand of Bandue upon them if they did. But Bailar, clever and wise and always seeking, had come to Ekialde with some ideas drawn from ancient tales and half-forgotten superstitions.

Ekialde had not been sure at first. Some of what Bailar suggested verged on darker magics than he felt comfortable with—certainly darker than Neitin would approve of. *'But I have all my people to think of.'* Was it not the duty of an *erregerra* to bear burdens on his tribe's behalf? And Bailar assured him these actions would help him to protect the Lusetani.

From Ekialde's shield arm, he drew a thin red line. Bailar caught the blood in the bronze bowl, then handed it over to another of the magic-men. The gray-bearded fellow had a lump of clay in his hand, which he rolled in the blood slowly, letting the earth soak up Ekialde's life. As he massaged the clod, he muttered, words that Ekialde could not hear and knew were beyond his understanding. He did not question these mysteries, but trusted in his uncle and his gods.

Once the blood had been absorbed, staining the russet clay a darker shade, the magic-man held the bowl up to Ekialde. "Place your hand upon it."

Ekialde extended his left hand, ignoring the fresh sting from the moss-staunched wound as he stretched out his arm. The clay was warmer against his palm than he had expected.

Bailar stood at Ekialde's elbow and whispered the correct words to him. Ekialde repeated them aloud, focusing the blood's power. "I, Ekialde, *erregerra* of the Lusetani, I call down the strength of Bandue, the love of Nabia. I have spilled my blood, willingly, for another. Her name is Neitin, and she is known to you. Let my strength be her guard, let my care be her comfort. Protect her as she is your daughter; protect her as she is an *erregerra*'s wife; protect her as she bears my blood, within and without."

The magic-man bearing the bowl nodded approvingly, and Bailar patted his nephew's shoulder. "Well done, sister-son. It is a noble venture."

"I will etch it with protective symbols and fire it into a tablet," the gray-bearded magic-man said, "and so long as your wife wears it, Bandue and Nabia will draw her under their cloaks."

Ekialde wondered whether he should tell Neitin, considering her distaste for the practice, that it was no mere charm but linked to his life's blood. If he did, she might not wear it, and keeping her and the babe safe was as important to Ekialde as his conquest over the Aventans. *'And what better to protect her than my own blood? As it lives within her, it will hang about her neck and shield her.'*

Neitin, he suspected, would not see it that way. Perhaps it would be best that she not know what ritual had gone into the charm's making.

The gray-bearded fellow shuffled away, towards another campfire, but Bailar remained, still gripping the knife, already gleaming with Ekialde's blood. "There is the other," he said, "if you still wish to try."

It was stranger magic, and harder. Bailar had confessed that he had never heard of a man in living memory performing it. But then, when had there been such need? When had there been an *erregerra* with the strength and will enough to try it?

Ekialde held out his sword-arm.

This time, Bailar cut deeper and longer, for this magic required far more blood. Ekialde's breath caught in his throat, but he was careful not to cry out or wince in pain. The gods would not tolerate such weakness in their *erregerra*.

Bailar caught this blood not in a bowl, but in a drinking vessel of fired-clay. Its long neck opened into a broad belly, and Ekialde could hear the splash of his blood against the rounded interior. When the belly was full, Bailar stoppered the vessel with bit of wax, then walked over to the fire. Ekialde watched as Bailar, too, muttered words over the blood, rolling the vessel back and forth between his hands over the flickering warmth.

As Bailar worked, Ekialde thought of the Vettoni who had been unable to stop the Aventans from reaching Toletum. They had a strong-hold now, the shelter of walls to skulk behind, roofs under which to avoid the snow. If the Aventan commander was wise—and Ekialde had to assume he had *some* brains, if he had made his way to Toletum with as few men as reported—then he would have brought in stores from the surrounding community as a guard against straining the city's resources. They would be fed and warm through the *mendi*'s harshest months.

Ekialde's question, then, was whether to try and lure them out or to trap them within the city walls. He knew little of siege-craft; a society with few walled cities had little need for it. But to capture Toletum would be a grand success, proof to the gods that their faith in him was justified. To try to capture it and fail, however . . .

Staring into the flames, Ekialde tried to open his mind to the voice of his god. Bandue, he was sure, would help him choose rightly. Ekialde could take advice from his own war-band and from the leaders of the other tribes, but an *erregerra* was expected to *know*.

Perhaps the god was looking elsewhere that night, however, for Ekialde heard nothing but the crackling of the fire and felt nothing but the prickling cold of the winter wind.

At long last, Bailar came back to him. Despite the chill, his brow shone with sweat, and his pale brown eyes had a strange luminescence to them. Bailar had not experienced difficulty communing with the gods. "It will take three days to prepare," Bailar said. "I have the necessary items, but I will need to be in seclusion for the next two nights. See to it that no one disturbs me."

Ekialde nodded. "And when it is done? What am I to do with it?" Bailar had told him this magic would help him to bind his enemies to his will, but he had offered only scant details on how it would work. Ekialde had no need to know the higher mysteries, but the action of casting the spell—that, he suspected, was an important detail.

Bailar held the stoppered vessel aloft. "It will require both dedication and cunning, for you will have to be within proximity of your foe. Cast this on a man, once I have transformed your blood to the potion, and he will be yours to command. The magic compels the mind."

Ekialde scratched at his beard, gazing at the moon's light bouncing off of the curve of the clay. "And how will that serve me in battle? To compel a single man?"

Bailar arched a dark eyebrow. "Choose the man carefully."

TOLETUM, CENTRAL IBERIA

Vitellius and Mennenius's cohorts made it to Toletum shortly after the Kalends of December. The city's walls were, as Hanath had promised, unimpressive by Aventan standards, hardly more than a pasture fence in some places, but that mattered little. Toletum had natural defenses that did far more than its mud-bricked barricade ever would.

At the south of a U-shaped riverbend, the town lay cradled in the water's arms. Because the Tagus cut deep into the terrain, Toletum sat atop a magnificent hill, visible for miles in the distance, tantalizing and teasing. Its houses and temples shone like gold above the sharply inclined riverbanks, where leafless trees and ocher stones tumbled down to the winding river. Any attacking army would have only one side from which to approach, as any attempt to dare the riverbanks would result in a steep climb, harried by falling rocks at best, by arrows and oil if the city were defended.

A siege was of more concern. The same topography that protected Toletum from assault also made it easy to cut off. From what Vitellius had learned from the Arevaci and Edetani, the Iberians knew little of siege-craft, but he did not want to take chances. Already he had his men building wooden screens to protect the switchbacking pathways from the town to the river. On the one flat side of the city, they were digging trenches, immediately under the walls and at staggered intervals from there to the forest. If the Lusetani proved cleverer than reported, Vitellius had plans.

In further preparation, he had urged the people of Toletum to welcome what refugees the city could hold but also to bring in all the stores they could, that the extra mouths not prove burdensome. He had sent out the Arevaci and Edetani with specific instructions to salvage anything they could from abandoned or sacked towns. Thanks to these efforts, the granaries of Toletum were overflowing, the pens and pastures teeming with goats and cattle. He hoped it would not come to rationing, that the Lusetani would not be able to hem them in before spring, but he had a math-minded centurion drawing up distribution charts anyway.

The cohorts had not been in Toletum long when a packet of letters found them, shuffled up from the coast by the network of riders Vitellius had dispatched between the allied tribes. He sent more missives out than he ever received back, as it was far easier these days for his couriers to find merchants leaving Iberia than those willing to risk themselves inland.

One letter was from Governor Sallust, back in Albina, formally authorizing Vitellius to extend his command of the excursion into the new year. *'An honor,'* Vitellius thought, *'and a curse.'* The Senate could send no reinforcements until after the elections. *'And I may not know their outcome until spring . . . Nor my own fate, to stay here, be recalled to Albina, or finally go home.'* He would be loath to leave the allies he had gathered up, the men and women who had placed their trust in him. *'But I would, I confess, not mind being able to shift some of this burden from my shoulders . . . see my father and sisters . . . meet my niece . . .'*

There were also two more letters from Fimbrianus, again insisting that he disengage and go back to Nedhena. These, Vitellius hardly glanced at before consigning them to the brazier.

His father's letters—three of them, all from early November—decried the inaction of the Senate, the constant delays and roadblocks thrown up by the Optimates. *'Keep writing, as often as you can spare the time and the riders,'* Aulus instructed. There were two letters from Aula, stuffed full of Forum intrigues and Palatine gossip. Lucia had added her name and a small picture of what Vitellius presumed to be a lion. Aula further said that their youngest sibling had been socially withdrawn, taking little pleasure in the usual amusements of patrician life. Vitellius wondered if he should be worried—but Alhena, a girl of nine when he left Aven, was nearly a stranger to him. He did not know what advice or comfort he could offer her, and he was sure whatever the trouble was, Aula and Latona could, between them, handle it.

One letter came from an unexpected source: Sempronius Tarren, someone Vitellius knew more by reputation than by conversation. Sempronius had already been campaigning when Vitellius was a stripling, and Vitellius himself had been abroad too long to have met him often in Aven. From his father, Vitellius knew that Sempronius was a fierce Popularist, one "determined to put the cat among the pigeons," in Aulus's words, and that his campaign for the praetorship stood in large part upon his intent to go to war in Iberia. His name had featured in a few of Aula's and Latona's letters as well, always in high regard. *'So what does he want with me?'*

The letter opened with formalities and pleasantries enough, and a note that Latona had been kind enough to add this message to the packet, but Sempronius wasted little ink getting to the heart of the matter. *'From your admirable father, I have heard of the challenges your vexillation has faced. A thousand men certainly seems inadequate for the scope of the difficulty there, though I have heard only praise for how you have managed it. I hope you will not find the following idea presumptuous of me: If you think it would help win you support, you might suggest that Aven would offer the full citizenship to auxiliaries who serve us well and complete full terms of enlistment. No promises, of course—but I shall do everything in my power to see that we repay those allies who keep faith well and truly. Write me back, if you can, and let me know if you think such action would be a boon to us in the region.'*

Vitellius nearly dropped the letter when he read that. What Sempronius suggested was extraordinary. Citizenship had been awarded to Aventan auxiliaries in the past, certainly—but rarely with full rights in the first generation, and never to all members of an assisting tribe. Their leaders, a noble few who proved themselves in battle, these were the men Aven honored with citizenship.

Perhaps Sempronius only meant it as bait for the allied tribes, a promise he never intended to pay, but from what Vitellius knew of the man, he didn't think so. The idea did have merit. Giving more Iberians a firm stake in Aven's interests would benefit the war effort—though Vitellius worried over the rippling implications it might have for the city after this conflict was settled. Still, he would certainly chew the suggestion over. As yet, the allied tribes seemed willing to help and grateful just for the vexillation's presence, although harder times could provoke the need for grander payoff.

That letter he also committed to the brazier, suspecting Sempronius would little thank him if it fell into the wrong hands.

Last, a small wooden box, with a note from Latona. A broad smile broke over Vitellius's face. A pair of thick woolen tunics, socks, and a focale, the neck scarf which military men wore to keep their armor and baldrics from chafing—all hand-woven by his sister, and as such, bearing her magical gifts. *'Dear brother,'* her note read, *'may these keep you warm and safe, and see you through whatever may come. I know it is the fashion for men in your situation to think of no god but Mars, but I have asked my ladies to look after you as well. Wear these, thank them, and think of your family.'*

Vitellius lifted one of the tunics to his face, breathing in the scent. After so many days on the road, it in truth smelled like little but wool and dust, but nonetheless, Vitellius fancied he could catch the aromas of home: the earthy aromas of pine resin and terracotta tiles, the luxurious scent of lavender perfume, incense from the altars, and the fragrant flowers of his sisters' gardens.

"Sir." The interruption came from Dorsus, who was swift proving one of Vitellius's finest scouts. Where he had learned to ride as well as the Edetani, Vitellius had no idea, but he was grateful for the man's skill. Vitellius gestured for Dorsus to spill his news. "We found some villagers wandering along the riverbank. Said their villages have been destroyed by a marauding band."

Vitellius set the letters on his desk, weighing the stack down with a rock. "Arevaci villagers?"

"Bartasco says no. Their dialect's a little different."

Vitellius frowned. "Are the marauders still in the area?"

"By the villagers' reports, yes. They were weary with running from them."

"How far?"

"They'd been fleeing for three days, they said. But they're certainly not moving at legion speed."

Vitellius nodded, considering what to do. Part of him was loath to leave the security it had taken them so long to reach, and he did have to contemplate the possibility of a trap. Even if the villagers weren't in on the subterfuge, the Lusetani could well be taking advantage of the situation. But the Aventans had committed themselves to protecting their allies—and a show of force against the marauders might convince more Iberians to join with the Aventans. "Find Centurion Calix. We'll take one cohort out tomorrow morning and leave the other here to continue improving the city's fortifications."

XXXVIII

CITY OF AVEN

Sempronius Tarren rose at dawn on the Ides of December. Corvinus dressed him carefully in a freshly-chalked *toga candida*. His only jewelry was the signet ring on his middle finger: a falcon in flight, cut into carnelian. He went first to the top of the Capitoline Hill, offering his respect and a white ram to Jupiter, then proceeded north, out the Servian Gate, to the Field of Mars.

The morning would be spent in last-minute campaigning. After months of bribery, direct and tangential, and weeks of regulated speech-making at the Rostra, the final morning served as the last chance to impress someone enough to affect their vote.

No sheep pasture, Sempronius was sure, had ever had so much wool in it as the Field of Mars on this December morning. Thousands of men crowded the low-lying plain crooked in the bend of the Tiber, mingling, jostling—and many were armed. Outside the walls of the city, soldiers could bear their short swords along with the rest of their regalia, and many did. Red cloaks were prominent throughout the crowd, throwing the white-togaed candidates into starker relief, and many of the men, whether legionaries proud of their service or officers looking to impress, had belted on their blades.

It had never made Sempronius nervous before. But then, before, no one had killed his friend while attempting to assassinate *him*.

Sempronius sighed, worked a crack out of his right shoulder, and assessed the scene, sorting out which men he needed to track down and speak with. The Fifth Class, consisting of property-less men, always voted last—if they got to vote at all, since the Officers' Class and the first three classes of general citizens nearly always reached majority. It galled Sempronius to know he could little afford to spend his morning with anyone but the equestrians and the First Class. The senators would have made up their minds about him already, and the lower classes did not hold enough influence—however crucial they were to filling out the ranks of the legions or keeping the city fed. He had pitched his programs to the lower orders of the populace, had feted and feasted them on the

Aventine and the Esquiline, but today, he had to aim higher. Lifting his chin in resigned dedication, Sempronius sighted wealthy Papirius Dolus across the field and began negotiating his way through the crowd towards him.

⬦⬦⬦⬦⬦⬦⬦⬦⬦⬦⬦⬦⬦⬦

Aulus Vitellius had, like Sempronius Tarren, bestirred himself early to go make his final campaign speeches. The women of his household waited until later in the day to venture forth. They would not be allowed on the Field, but by afternoon, when the campaigning ended and the voting began, the surrounding streets would throng with women and non-citizens, eagerly awaiting word of who would be the first men in years to rule Aven with electoral authority. With Herennius already at the Field— as a member of the First Class, not an officer, since he had never served in the legions—Latona came to have lunch with her sisters before they would join the spectating masses.

She arrived on the Palatine, however, to find the house in an uproar. Lucia was in the atrium in her nurse's arms, staring wide-eyed at the door to Alhena's sleeping chamber, where Aula stood, pinching the bridge of her nose. Aula was only half-dressed, her copper hair still loose about her ears. As Latona drew closer, she could hear muffled sobs coming from inside Alhena's room. "What's going on?" she asked.

"Alhena won't go," Aula said, making an irritated gesture.

Latona peeked inside the room. Alhena was still in her sleeping tunic, collapsed on her bed with her arms thrown up over her face. Mus knelt by the edge of the bed, stroking her hair and singing in her native dialect. "Well . . ." Latona said, quiet and careful, "that's not particularly a surprise, is it? She hasn't been fond of crowds lately."

"It's not just that she won't go, it's that she doesn't want us to go, either," Aula said. "She saw me getting ready and started pitching a rather extraordinary fit. Howling and tearing her hair and I don't know what else, but she's terrified half the servants. Even *Lucia* hasn't wailed like this in years. And I'm about out of patience for it!" She raised her voice on the last sentence, leaning pointedly into Alhena's room.

Latona laid a hand on her sister's shoulder, guiding her in the other direction. "You go finish getting ready. I'll see what I can find out." Aula grumbled but conceded, allowing Helva to chivvy her back to her own chamber and the ministrations of her *ornatrix*. Latona stepped inside

Alhena's room and cleared her throat. Mus shuffled back slightly, not looking up at Latona, but not fully moving away from her mistress, either.

Still sniffling, Alhena dropped one arm from her face, blinking owlishly at her sister. "Latona?"

"Yes, darling, I'm here."

Alhena sat up in a swift, sudden motion, diving forward to clasp Latona's hands. "Aula said you're going out to the Field, to watch the vote. Are you? Is she right?"

"Well, of course we are, dove!" Latona said, freeing one hand to wipe the tears from Alhena's cheek. "We must be there for Father. I understand, of course, if you don't want to join the press, I imagine the streets will be quite—"

"Please don't."

It was the "please," as much as the scared, girlish tone of her voice, that caught Latona's attention. When Alhena was just being prudish and supercilious, she would say something arch like, 'I wish you wouldn't.' This was different. "What's troubling you? Did you see something?"

"I don't . . . I don't know, precisely." Alhena twisted the corner of her mantle between her fingers. "It wasn't . . . It's been so long since a vision was like this. It was such a strange dream, and Aula woke me up before I could . . ." An impatient huff. "I don't think . . . I didn't get all of it. Whatever the message was . . . But it seemed you were in a cage of splinters . . ." Her voice was dwindling, as embarrassed as uncertain. "The walls were closing in on you, piercing your heart and lungs and mind, all the golden light flowing out of you . . ." Tears flowed freely again, dewing her pale eyelashes and streaking her skin. "Please don't go, Latona, if you do, I just know something horrible is going to happen."

Latona sank down onto the bed beside her. "I can't imagine what such a vision might mean, darling."

"Neither can I," Alhena said, "but there was such pain . . ." She broke into sobs again, crumpling forward until her head was buried between her knees. Latona rocked her gently, she wasn't sure for how long, but eventually the sobs faded to sniffles, then to wheezing breaths. Just like a child in a fit, Alhena seemed to have wept herself to sleep, too exhausted to stay conscious.

Rising gently from the bed, Latona laid a hand on Mus's shoulder. "When she wakes, make sure she takes some water," she said.

"Yes, Domina."

She found Aula in the final stages of preparation, adjusting the folds of her emerald-green mantle. "Well?"

"She's had a vision, it seems," Latona said. "Something about me in a box of splinters—a cage. She thinks . . . well, she thinks it was interrupted when you woke her up, but she's quite distressed over it. Worried, for me."

Aula's face softened slightly. Alhena had seen disaster before, and they all knew how deeply it affected her, particularly since Tarpeius's death.

"She's asleep now."

"Good." Aula gestured for Gera to bring Lucia forward. "Then I think we should still go."

"Do you?" Latona glanced back at Alhena's chamber. "She was quite insistent . . ."

Aula rubbed at her temples. "Latona, you know how much I love and care for her, but she's had me at my wits' end this morning, and this election is too important for us to miss. It would be *noted* if we weren't there to support Father. That could weaken his influence as well as our own." Latona nodded; Aula's political instincts were, as ever, acute. "Alhena's young enough that her absence won't be remarked upon. If she's asleep, that's probably the best thing for her. With any luck, Mus will have the sense to dose her with vervain should she wake back up. You don't really mean to miss the vote, do you?"

"Well . . ." Latona said. "No." She was particularly disinclined to miss it since Herennius had forbidden her to go out. "But if there is something to Alhena's vision—"

"We can tell Mus to send someone with a message if she wakes up and has anything more specific. But you said yourself, she didn't see a complete vision. No doubt getting woken out of it startled her, and I'll apologize for that later, but for all we know, whatever she's seen might be half-formed or years in the future. Anyway—" Aula took her by the elbow. "What on earth could happen to you between here and the Campus Martius?"

Since Aula had a valid point, Latona re-wrapped her own mantle and let Aula hustle her towards the door. Aula kissed Lucia farewell, snapped her fingers to their cordon of attendants, and strode out into the street. Aula seemed to relax as soon as she took a deep breath beneath the brumous sky. "I'm starving. Let's find food along the way."

◇◇◇◇◇◇◇◇◇◇◇◇◇◇

The morning did not start resoundingly well for the Popularists, though Sempronius had expected no differently. The officers' class, largely composed of senators, supported Galerius Orator's bid for the consulship, due to his moderate sensibilities, but were mixed on who they wanted for his colleague. The more military in nature, as well as those with mercantile aspirations for Iberian goods, went for General Strato; the Optimates pulled considerable sway for Decimus Gratianus.

The praetorial slots were even more jumbled, with Sempronius Tarren sharing the *primus* votes with Lucretius Rabirus and Ulpius Turro. When the first few Centuries returned their choice, it looked like Turro might pull ahead—a middling choice between Sempronius's ambitious Popularism and Rabirus's heel-dragging conservatism. Even those who supported war were not fully certain who they wanted in charge of it, some doubting Sempronius's youth and experience, some questioning the authenticity of his motives. Sempronius had expected that suspicion and was grateful that many had at least chosen pliable Ulpius over intractable Rabirus as an option.

It was only when the First Class of enlisted men began to vote that Sempronius risked a small smile. These were the men—plebeian but with some wealth to their names, the citizens of the Aventine, the Viminal, and the Quirinal—who Sempronius had spent so much time, energy, and sestertii wooing. The old men had caught the scent of wealth from Iberia; the young men had Bellona's fever, yearning to defend Aven's rights and reputation on the battlefield. The First Class put Sempronius even with Rabirus and Ulpius for the *primus* slot. Then the Second Class started to vote—men neither wealthy nor impoverished, most of them families on the rise, hungry and ambitious. The representatives of their Centuries tallied results and stepped forward.

And Sempronius's name surged towards a majority.

◇◇◇◇◇◇◇◇◇◇◇◇◇◇

On the edge of the Field, Latona was growing agitated. "I don't know what you're so fussed about," Aula said. "It always takes forever. I mean, *obviously* it was well and good to reform the voting process so the officers couldn't just run all over the other classes, but I must say, it must've been a speedier process back in the day, and—Latona, *why* are you so fidgety?"

"It's a tense day." Unable to maintain the still and dignified posture that befit a matron of her status, Latona felt an itching in her palms and a tightness in her chest.

"Well, try to nail your feet down, would you? You're worse than Tilla today, I swear." Aula rolled her eyes.

Latona tried to do as she bid, but within another moment, her magical sensibilities pricked up, setting a hot flush on her skin, even where it was kissed by the frosty air. She had guarded herself against the high emotions around the Field, but this was different. She sensed an element, stronger than it should be, in the heart of the city, a pulsing source of energy calling out to her talents. "Something's wrong." she said. Her breath hung in the air, and before it had faded—

"Fire!" someone yelled, and in that moment, Latona realized, with awful certainty, what Alhena had been so worried about.

XXXIX

Black plumes rose from somewhere behind the Capitoline Hill—Transtiberium, perhaps, or the Aventine. The cry of "Fire" echoed throughout the Campus Martius, putting a halt to the voting halfway through the Third Class.

Despite his concern, Sempronius wanted to spit, or curse, or kick someone. By the Second Class's votes, Sempronius was leading in the praetorship lists, and Galerius Orator nearly had a majority for consul. He was certain that the Third Class would secure the necessary proportion, with no need to proceed further. Now, the vote would have to be started again on the next religiously appropriate day. The frustration put a coiling knot in his stomach. He wanted the matter settled so he could begin enacting his plans—but an event like this might be viewed as judgment from the gods, and could cause the Centuries to change their minds.

He shook off his grievance. Fire in Aven was the gravest danger, could wipe out entire neighborhoods in minutes, tearing through the jumbled insulae, overlapping rooftops, and haphazardly constructed stalls. On a day like today, with the breeze kicking up from the west, Sempronius shuddered to think what the consequences could be. He cast about for men he knew would be of use, who could keep their heads in a crisis—Galerius, Aufidius, Rufilius, anyone who could help organize the necessary bucket brigades.

Then someone, shoving through the crowd, passed word that the Aventine emporium was the center of the blaze. And Sempronius no longer considered this the most unfortunate of coincidences.

◇◇◇◇◇◇◇◇◇◇◇◇◇◇◇

Latona stared at the darkening sky beyond the Capitoline Hill. The smoke was coming from the Aventine, near the river. "I have to go," she heard herself say.

"Well, of course we must," Aula said. "Pacco, Haelix, clear a path, all hell's going to break loose here in a minute. Get us home the fastest—"

"No," Latona said. A racing tingle on her skin urged action, her magical gifts bubbling to the surface not from lack of control but in response to a need. *'I can help. I must help. My duty . . . Juno's work . . . my city . . .'*

"No?" Aula's voice was shrill with fear and confusion. "What do you mean, no?"

Latona pulled her eyes away from the columns of curling pitch crawling sun-wards. "I have to go help."

A brief silence followed her proclamation, then Merula, Haelix, Helva, and Aula all started talking at once. "Domina, you cannot be thinking to—"

"My lady, the streets are not—"

"The danger is too great, if your father or husband—"

"Latona!" Aula's screech put the others to shame. "Sweetheart, you can't be meaning to go." Her head bobbled uncertainly between her sister and the smoke in the south. "You can't!"

Latona had already unwound her mantle and flung it over Aula's shoulder, then, upon consideration, she began unpinning her over-gown as well. "Domina!" Merula objected.

"I'll move faster without it, and it's one less thing to worry about. If anyone sees me, they'll just take me for a pleb, I'm sure. I won't be recognized."

"Domina, that is not what I am meaning—"

"Merula, stay here. That is a direct order," Latona said, flinging the gown over Aula's shoulder as well, leaving her clad in a simple cinnamon-brown tunic. When she saw the frown creasing Merula's brow, she added, more softly, "My dear, the danger I'll be facing is nothing you could protect me from. Stay with Aula. See her home safely." She gripped her handmaid's shoulder tightly. "It's going to get rough out. Get them back to my father's home, quickly, before it gets worse."

Merula's jaw had a tightness to it, and her eyes were burning with an insolence another mistress might have had her whipped for. But she nodded sharply. "I will see it done, Domina." Latona cupped her cheek fondly.

Helva was glancing towards the crowd, and Latona guessed she was thinking of darting off to find Aulus or Herennius. *'Well, let her. Much good may it do either of them.'* Latona looked instead to Aula. "I can do this. I can help. It's a fire, and I—"

"You're not trained for *this*." Aula objected. "Latona, this isn't putting an influence on someone at a party or keeping the hypocaust properly balanced!"

"I know that!" Latona said, her voice rising. Around them, the crowd was starting to panic. The Centuries had broken up, and though some of the senators appeared to be bellowing orders, more of the men were paying attention to their centurions. "Bona Dea, Aula, don't you think I know that? But I know, I *know* I can do this. I've been working, I've been studying—I don't have time to explain now." She could not find the words fast enough to explain to her sister what had been happening to her over the past few months. Rubellia's training, Sempronius's encouragement, the growing certainty that she had more capability in her, the call she felt she had to answer—all as though she had been preparing for this very moment, when she could use her magic for genuine good, to protect the city. "I may not be High Priestess of Juno, but I am not a child, I am not a novice, I have this power in me, and *I know I can help.*" Aula's eyes were sparkling with tears. "I promise, I will come home safe and explain everything later."

"Latona—!" Aula stretched out a hand, but Latona was already gone, darting with surprising speed through the pressing crowd. Aula let herself be steered in the other direction, heard Merula shouting at people to make way, threatening to punch someone who shoved her.

Aula tried to ignore the nauseated whorl seeping into her stomach. She had insisted on this. She had told Latona not to worry, not to pay Alhena any mind. And now she wished, with every scrap of her being, that she had not done so.

◇◇◇◇◇◇◇◇◇◇◇◇◇◇

Latona followed the river past the Fabrician Bridge, curving around to the warehouses that lined the Tiber River beneath the Aventine Hill. To a mage with the talent to see the elemental forces at work, as Latona's Spirit allowed her, the scene was a crazed tangle of colored light and swirling scents. There was so much happening at once that the air buzzed with it, a low-level crackle like heat lightning in a summer sky. A patchwork of mages moved in concert, combining their powers to control the blaze. The city had a number of talented Water mages, not only the priests of Neptune and Lympha, but also among the men who worked on the aqueducts, and they were out in force. If there were any advantage to the fire's location, it was its proximity to both the river and the Aqua Appia. Methods both mundane and magical were in use to draw down the water—but there was only so much the Water mages could do without accidentally triggering a flash flood, trading one sort of trouble for another.

That was where the Earth, Air, and Fire mages came in: Earth could smother, Air could starve, and Fire could bank its own. Plebeian and patrician, priest and layman worked side-by-side. There were even a few other women in the mix, though not many, and all plebs. Latona thought she saw Marcus joining a line of Earth mages, but she moved in the other direction, where a net of red-glowing energy attempted to shape and subdue the raging flames. Without a word, Latona fell in line beside them, holding both hands before her and splaying her fingers, adding her strength to their attempt.

Before she could align her mind to the appropriate energies, though, a sudden shout distracted her. "Lady!" Latona turned to see a man in a striped tunic scurrying towards her: a patrician Fire mage, the High Priest of Helios. Latona had never liked him; the man had fallen in line with Ocella a little too eagerly, and he had very firm ideas about the *mos maiorum*—and where women fit into it.

"Honored priest," she said, her voice falsely bright. "Well-met."

"Lady, this is no place for a woman of your pedigree and—"

"I am here," Latona cut in, "and I can help. I promise not to jeopardize myself, nor to do anything that might hinder the efforts of the bucket brigades. But I have been blessed with a gift, by Vulcan as much as by Venus, and I intend to use it."

But the priest's brow was still furrowed. "It is not proper, Lady, and it is dangerous. If a woman of your pedigree were to fall victim to—"

"Jupiter's thunder, man!" someone else yelled—a plebeian Fire-forger, from the looks of him. "If the chit can help, let her help! Don't waste *your* time and energy arguing with her!"

The priest's lower lip jutted out, but he looked at the flames, gave a curt nod, and shuffled away towards another knot of mages, muttering something that sounded suspiciously like, "So long as no one blames *me.*"

And there, Latona thought, was Aventan practicality at its finest.

She refocused her attention on the flames.

XL

Sempronius found Obir in the crowd, along with a pair of familiar centurions. Together, they worked to organize a response to the crisis. Centurions, Sempronius knew, were invaluable in a tight crunch. Legionaries might mock them, hate them, envy them—but by the gods, they would follow their orders almost instinctively, even if they were not under arms.

He had been unable to find Galerius in the growing chaos, but Strato had taken a group of men up to the Aqua Appia to try and bring down water in larger numbers. Others were working to draw it up from the river; yet more were armed with axes and hooks, pulling down buildings to create firebreaks. Already, though, the flames were spreading further down the wharves, jeopardizing grain storage—alarming at any time, even more so at the onset of winter.

Through the turmoil, Sempronius's magical senses were prickling. Water was weaker in him than Shadow, but he could feel the river to his right, the aqueduct to his left, the thin tendrils curling out from each as the bucket brigades set to work. Unfortunately, he could also feel the lack of moisture in the air, the dry snap in the wind that made wood ignite at the slightest provocation.

'The Aventine. Of course it would be the Aventine.' Not just the Aventine, *his* Aventine. He could little ignore the proximity of the fire to so many of his projects—the improvements to the docks, the Aventine Triad temple complex, the intended site of his Temple to Victoria. He did not know, of course—but he suspected. The thought made him bite the inside of his cheek as he hoisted another bucket, passing it to the legionary standing beside him.

◊◊◊◊◊◊◊◊◊◊◊◊◊◊

'You can do this. It is just as you've practiced, only . . . bigger. And you can do it because you must. Open a vault within yourself, like Rubellia said.' As Latona drew on the energy of the flames, she felt a strange pulse of magic deep within the conflagration. *'No, not a pulse . . .'* More of a crackle, as

when pottery overheats in a kiln. Within the net of criss-crossing magics, something she could not identify disrupted their harmony, preventing the efforts of the assembled mages from working together optimally. When Latona reached her own magic out to probe it, to try and discover its source, she felt her control shudder.

The power flowing into her suddenly felt too much. She was full, too full, overwhelmed with it, as when she had set oil lamps ablaze. If she lost control now, with so much raw energy swirling along the Aventine docks, with such flagrant potential already ablaze, she would be facing an utter catastrophe.

'No.'

With all her willpower, she stamped down on the compulsion. *'I will not lose control so easily. I will not.'* Whatever fissure lurked within the flames, she could not let it shake her focus. Calling Rubellia's teachings to mind, she drew a deep breath, closed her eyes, and opened the gates inside her. *'Venus and Vulcan, look here . . . Vulcan, help me reach the fires. Venus, let my heart be strong enough.'*

She was no longer just banking the fire, no longer trying to calm the flames back down into embers. Instead, the power flowed backwards. The expulsive energy she normally used to push flames along was instead filling her, hotter and stronger than the wisps of fire she had practiced on. It felt like swallowing sunlight, like her very blood was open and accepting the blaze into it. She should have been terrified. She wanted to laugh. A strange inebriation suffused her, tingly and pleasant despite the dire circumstances. Latona drank in the warmth, making it part of her blood.

When she opened her eyes, there was no longer a blaze in front of her. Flames licked the sky to the left and right, but the warehouse in front of her was cool and still. She swayed slightly, leaning forward to rest her hands on her thighs. *'I am going to pay for that later.'* Latona's lungs ached with the effort, and her fingers itched. *'If it starts to feel like it will overwhelm me, I swear, I will go dunk myself in the Tiber.'* Her hands felt heavy as she raised them to push a sweat-damp mass of soot-stained golden hair back from her face.

Only then did she notice that the other Fire mages nearby were staring at her. *'So,'* she thought, dropping her hands again. *'Not entirely as inconspicuous as I might have hoped.'*

The plebeian Fire-forger, who had earlier shouted at the priest, proved most practical. Moving forward to take her by the elbow, he guided her towards a side street. "If you can do that again, go. Now."

Whether she had just impressed or terrified Aven's other Fire mages, she would not now hesitate in front of them. Gathering the skirt of her tunic in her fists, she followed the call towards the line of warehouses along the riverbank.

As Latona passed one large and recently-painted emporium, she became acutely aware that she could not draw in another fire without expelling some energy first. *'If I try, I'll shatter into a thousand pieces.'* Her skin danced with a warm, crackling glow, redder and brighter than it should have been—not unpleasant or painful, but certainly strong enough to remind her of her mortal frailty.

As she turned the corner, she came across a row of citizens—plebs of the Aventine, none with any magic to them that she could see, passing buckets against the flames. It hardly made a difference; they were drawing from a public fountain, but one splash at a time did little to quell the conflagration. Latona could feel their panic, their fear, but also their determination. *'Oh, you glories of Aven!'* Fierce pride and bravery drove them onward, and Latona swelled with admiration for them—but they were tiring, wondering how much good they could really do.

Almost reflexively, she sent a burst of heartening energy their way—and the pressure inside her eased as well. The energy she had absorbed from the flames rejoiced to find a new outlet. Latona could feel flagging limbs gain new strength, could see the buckets hoisted higher and faster. Latona had no idea if it would actually help them battle the flames more efficiently, but it helped them believe they could. And that was important, too.

She kept up the stream of encouragement, letting it feed the conviction already present in the plebeians' hearts. Fire's raw power settled into a new pattern, shaped and guided by Spirit, and as it flowed out of Latona, a suffusing relief took its place. Her skin cooled and the tingling sensation faded.

That thought spurred her on as much as the need to keep working against the blaze, and with new eagerness, she rounded a corner to take on another building.

◇◇◇◇◇◇◇◇◇◇◇◇◇

Atop the Palatine Hill, Vitellia Alhena paced anxiously on the portico of her father's domus. The flames on the Aventine were well visible from there, an effulgent orange glow beyond the rooftops. Dark clouds in a deepening sky made it seem much later in the day than it was.

Alhena's hair was still in disarray, and she still wore only a tunic and loosely wrapped shawl, but her eyes were clear and dry. The terror had ebbed when the critical moment had passed. Nothing she could do now would protect her sister from the pain, and that realization, strangely, lightened Alhena's soul.

She could not stop it from happening, but perhaps—*perhaps*—she could change the story. She had not, after all, seen the end.

Alhena looked at Mus, then nodded sharply, as though confirming something they both already knew. "Towards the Aventine, then," she said. "I'll need sturdier shoes than these. And a heavy cloak." Even through the growing haze of Proserpina's gift, Alhena remained, in essence, a practical girl.

Mus did not need to be told to move quickly.

◇◇◇◇◇◇◇◇◇◇◇◇◇◇◇

The sun, Latona presumed, was sinking, though the sky was so dark it hardly seemed to make a difference. She had no idea how long she had been working. Her limbs were exhausted, both her heels were bleeding, and her hands were chapped from the cold—but her heart soared.

She rounded a corner, thinking that she may have reached the southern end of the fire and ought to cut back up towards the Porticus, when she stumbled, as though she had been shoved between the shoulderblades. The ground beneath her seemed to have shifted, though when she fell to her hands and knees, she discovered it perfectly solid. "What—?" Her awareness of the flames and people alike went suddenly cold, as though her magic had been severed and redirected. She gasped as something inside her lurched, like a tenterhook cast into her ribcage.

"Tsk, tsk." An unfamiliar voice, from a man whose hooded robes covered his face. "Didn't realize how much of *yourself* you were putting out there, did you?" A derisive snort. "Spirit mages. I don't know why everyone makes so much of you."

The robed figure made a strange gesture with his hand. Pain shuttered through Latona's head, like hot nails driving into her skull, and then her vision exploded in a sudden burst of white light.

XLI

She was not unconscious—not quite. Vaguely, as though it were happening to someone else, Latona felt her body lifted, hauled a short distance, then dumped unceremoniously on the ground. Only then did the world begin to piece itself back together, color and definition returning to her vision.

She seemed to be in one of the emporium warehouses. Her eyes darted immediately to the rafters, but she saw no sign of smoke nor flame. "It's definitely her." The same voice as before, talking to someone else: a blurry figure draped in chalky white. "I tracked her through the emporium, and it's the same signature as—"

"Quiet, Pinarius." When Latona was able to focus her eyesight, she recognized the other figure. Then she pushed herself up—or tried. She only made it onto her knees before she felt a seizing chest pain. An outside pressure, squeezing. "Try not to tax yourself, Lady. I need you out of my way, but I would not see you permanently harmed. I have no desire to spill patrician blood."

"Lucretius Rabirus." It was hard to speak with the strange, drawing pang inside her ribs. "Why—?"

"Because, Vitellia Herenniae," Rabirus said, "you have been the mystery thorn in my side for months, though—" He gave a mirthless chuckle. "I will confess, I had no idea it would be you that Pinarius brought me."

Though her head was wagging with exhaustion and confusion, Latona reached out with Spirit magic to get a sense of Rabirus's aims, his purpose—but no sooner did she send out a tendril than she felt herself slammed back down. It took her a moment to realize that the effect had not been physical; she was still on her knees, but she felt as though the wind had been knocked out of her, and her vision went hazily gray again.

Rabirus shot Pinarius a look. "What was that?"

"She was trying to use magic," Pinarius said, "to figure you out."

A soft, chuffing laugh. "Ironic." Rabirus strolled a bit closer to Latona. "I've been trying to figure her out, too." He stood above her, looking down. Latona still felt staggered, but her jaw set in defiance. "Dictator

Ocella wondered. He thought you might have untapped resources. He even had his pet mages watch you for signs. But you disappointed him. So why now?"

"I don't know what you—"

"Don't play coy," Pinarius said. "I've enough Air in me to track the signature when it's blazing like yours was today. Truly extraordinary, but you did call too much attention to yourself."

"Yes." Rabirus looked contemplative. "Apparently you've been leaving that signature all over the city for months now. Quelling riots, breaking up brawls . . ." A muscle in his cheek twitched, belying his false admiration. "Purging poisons."

"You," Latona said, making another attempt to stand. The pain in her chest was like an anchor, weighting her to the rough warehouse floor. "You tried to—"

"And now," Rabirus overran her, "this. Putting out fires at twice the speed of a whole team of Vulcan priests and fire-forgers? Astonishing work, really. And this was supposed to go so well."

Latona's head was reeling, though she was no longer sure if it was from magical interference or the bizarre circumstances. "You set the fires," Latona said. She looked to the Fracture mage. "With your help." That was what she had felt, the fissures helping destruction along, all of his making. Fracture magic could speed things up, if a man wanted a fire to spread swiftly: a crack in an amphora of oil here, a weakened timber frame there, thatching made brittle. This man, though, went beyond that, to the dancing edge of chaos, where Fracture magic tipped past the brink of balance and into madness. The flames were only the vehicle for his purpose: panic and strife were what he bred and spread. Had anyone else had stumbled into his magical traps? Had they shaken other mages' control as they had hers? For now she could plainly see that was what they were meant to do. Rabirus would have known the city's mages would descend upon the Aventine in force to control the blaze, and so he instructed his creature to impede their efforts. "Monsters," Latona said. "The both of you."

"Do not think I did so lightly," Rabirus said, "but sacrifices must be made. Sempronius Tarren is a menace, one who will prove a greater threat to our sacred nation than even Ocella, if he advances unchecked. Everything I have done has been to protect the city from greater evils." The smug mockery faded, replaced by an expression at once darker and more sincere. "You know that feeling. Isn't that what you think you're doing? We have the same aims, even if yours are misguided."

"Burning down the city hardly seems to be to its benefit."

"Sometimes, a fire purges," Rabirus shot back. "*You* know that. Sempronius and his dangerous ideals are the true poison, and Aven cannot be healthy while they infect her. You were right to hide your gifts from Ocella. He used mages for his personal perfidies and vendettas, not for the betterment of the city. But now, if you chose, if you followed the *right* advice—"

Latona shuddered at the acquisitive hunger she now saw in Rabirus's eyes. This was the danger, this the threat she had been told to fear: owning a power that men would want to twist and use. She wet her lips, or tried to. Her mouth was parched. "If you think to gain my help in your purge," she managed to say, "then I am afraid I must disappoint you."

"Yet you would not so disappoint Sempronius, would you?" Rabirus asked. "Will you violate the *leges magicae* on his behalf? Use your influence to sway elections, to enthrall the populace? Is that why you were at the Field of Mars today?"

"I would never act with such disregard for—"

"Never say never," Pinarius intoned.

"He has a point," Rabirus said. Dropping his voice, he added, "After all, who would have ever thought I'd find myself in collusion with such as him? If you keep on this path, Lady, you will discover that playing this game means making very strange decisions sometimes."

"Even if I *were* as morally bankrupt as your pet over there," Latona said, with a vicious glare in Pinarius's direction, "it wouldn't matter. Sempronius doesn't need illegal sorcery and underhanded tricks any more than he needed to lick the boots of a Dictator. He's out-maneuvered you before and he will again."

Surprisingly swift, Rabirus moved forward and seized Latona's chin. Latona resisted the urge to bite him. "My, you *are* enthralled, aren't you? How immodest." He searched her face, making Latona ashamed not of her sweat and disarray, but of the tears that had sprung to her eyes when she spoke to defend Sempronius. "So his interest in making the most of you is not entirely political, is it?" Latona felt a shock of vindictive satisfaction from him: he felt he had hit upon something he could use, a chink in Sempronius's armor. "Tell me, is it the compulsion of Spirit magic, that thrusts you in among powerful men? Or just average lust?"

"I never—" But Rabirus's smirk had her own secrets knotted up in it. He had, after all, been Ocella's right hand, there in Capraia when Latona had attended the Dictator's command. "You've done far worse, just to protect your power and position," she said. "I make no apologies for what I did to protect my family."

"You might yet prove useful, one way or another. Ocella knew what he was about, collecting mages as he did. They do make fine political assets." The glint of malice shone in his eyes again. "And if you prove intractable . . . You have, I think, a sister, blessed by Proserpina?"

Latona *did* try to bite him then, but he jerked back too quickly. Her blood raged at the threat to Alhena, and she said, in a lioness's protective growl, "You go near her, and I swear, I will open your throat with my teeth."

"If you cannot be convinced, then take a warning, Vitellia Herenniae," Rabirus said, straightening up. "Whether you've been acting for Sempronius or out of some deluded notion that you're helping the city, you would do well to abandon the efforts. It would be dangerous for you to continue. But if you put your talents to a morally appropriate use, perhaps that would wipe clean the sins of your past." He gestured Pinarius forward. "I'll leave you in good custody to think it over."

As Rabirus left the warehouse, Pinarius pushed his hood back to reveal a thin face. He had a weedy look to him, almost sickly pale, with stringy gray hair sleeked back from pointy features. A bronze amulet hung at his throat, and Latona could sense malevolence pulsing from it.

Latona waited a moment, as much to pull her own senses together as to increase the odds of catching him off-guard. She dropped her head, not needing to feign fatigue, and breathed deep. However he had seized control of her power earlier, it had taken much of her strength with it. Yet there, nestled at the core of her heart, an ember still burned in reserve. As soon as she gave it a tentative probe, it woke, hungry and aching. Latona did what she could to fling the energy towards Pinarius, hoping to dazzle his senses long enough to make good her escape.

She made it about three steps.

◇◇◇◇◇◇◇◇◇◇◇◇◇◇◇

If Sempronius thought the day was unusual already, his capacity for astonishment stretched to its utmost when Vitellia Alhena, half-dressed and looking panicked, strode up to him while he was in the middle of a bucket line. "Senator! Oh, Senator, I'm so glad—I thought I'd find you near here, but I wasn't certain, I was just sort of following the instinct."

"Lady Alhena, please, slow down," Sempronius said, stepping out of the line and drawing her into a nook beside two brick buildings. "What are you doing out here? You should be—"

"My sister," she said, grabbing his tunic. "Latona. You have to find her. It has to be you. She's in trouble. I warned her that she would be, but she didn't listen, I should've *known* she wouldn't listen. And— and—" She shook her head violently, like a dog with water in its ear. "Your sister."

"*My* sister?" he echoed. "What could my sister have to do with—?"

"You will need her magic. There's Fracture at work here. It took me so long to work it out, I'm sorry, I should've been faster, but I'm sure of it now. The splinters—Fracture magic—Oh, if only Proserpina's messages weren't always so symbolically rendered—" Alhena's eyes were red-rimmed as though she had been crying, but she appeared lucid, despite her rapid speech. "Sempronius, please, I do know how I sound. Don't think I don't know that. But I am sure of this. I would not trouble you if I weren't."

Sempronius searched her face a moment longer, wondering how much she knew, what secrets her visions might have revealed. Then he nodded. "I know you wouldn't. Walk with me. We'll fetch my sister. Tell me everything I need to know."

∞∞∞∞∞∞∞∞∞∞∞∞

Before Latona gained the door of the warehouse, a suffocating pressure built all around her body, as though she had been wrapped tightly in heavy, damp blankets. Through it all was a drawing cold that reached into the core of her and fed on the warmth it found there. It squeezed stiff rigor into her muscles, the very force of it holding her upright—and then, just as swiftly, it was gone, and she crashed to the dirt floor.

"Don't test me," Pinarius said. "You haven't the strength."

Latona knew, however much it shamed her, that there was truth in what he said. She had been pouring out energy, her own mingled with what she had absorbed from the flames, with no thought of protecting herself. *'Much power but little control . . . stupid,'* she chastised herself. Inattention had made her easy prey, especially to one such as him. Fracture and Spirit were inimical elements, like Water and Fire, at once dangerous and vulnerable to each other: the sheer willpower of Spirit against the fickle edge of Fracture.

She could not surrender. *'Will not, I will not.'* Rabirus's hopes for her conversion and potential usefulness aside, instinct told her that surrender to his pet mage would mean not capitulation but death, and so her Spirit magic flared out, attempting to shield her from Fracture's predation. But his control was more refined, and every attempt she made, he simply drained away.

Propelled by defiance, she struggled to rise. Her palms scraped against the gravelly dirt, and she was only able to make it to her hands and knees. "You . . . are a disgrace to the gods." She could scarcely draw breath to speak. "You . . . sully . . . their gifts."

But Pinarius laughed. "I wear the robes of Janus, and true, he may find me wanting. But my soul answers to another." He dangled the bronze medallion between his fingers. "Lady Discordia sets a different standard."

Latona's head was swimming with the effort to stay conscious. "Discordia?" she gasped. It made sense—a twisted, sickening sense.

Pinarius knelt in front of Latona. "Rabirus may have qualms about killing so fair and fine-blooded an opponent, Lady, but I assure you, I do not." He inhaled deeply, as though catching a scent. "Your magical signature is dazzling. Coruscate. Do you have any idea how delicious it is, to break and devour a power that radiant?" Tears coursed down Latona's cheeks, and though some were born of effort and frustration, others were plain, raw fear. "So go on. Burn as brightly as you can. I will swallow every last bit of your magic down into the void, and leave you behind, a colder corpse than most."

Latona knew if she could not find a way to draw her powers back in, to restore the Spirit energy to her own body, she would soon be nothing but an empty husk. She tried to count her breaths, but with the spongy suffocation wrapped around her, it felt impossible. The blurriness in her eyes was turning to blackness, first in spots, then taking over her sight entirely. The last thing she saw before it claimed her was the door behind Pinarius opening and light from the street spilling in. A flicker of hope rose in her chest, but Pinarius Scaeva's consuming void gulped it down, and she knew no more.

XLII

"Step away from her."

If the Fracture mage was surprised to see not only Sempronius Tarren but his sister standing in the doorway to the warehouse, he managed not to show it. Sempronius's jaw was tight with a cold rage, and Vibia shook with fury for this twisted use of Fracture's power. "That's Pinarius Scaeva," Vibia whispered. "A priest of Janus." Revulsion envenomed her words.

It was worse than Vibia would immediately realize. She would see the tangle of fissures and malicious intent, but Sempronius, touched enough by Water to see *all* of his opponent's workings, could read the whole story of what had happened. Pinarius had ripped into Latona with the unforgiving force of a boar's tusk, then used her own strength against her, drawing her essence out and pouring it into a gaping maw.

'But that,' Sempronius thought, *'I might be able to do something with.'*

It made sense now—the chaos in the Forum, the trap when Sempronius attempted to track it. The aspect of Fracture that this mage was using was the sort that stole from other powers, mauling the energy of the other elements. But here, in his mania to defeat Latona's Spirit magic, the mage had misstepped. Fracture could tear open a sinkhole, but Shadow could control it.

"Vibia," he said, hardly putting breath behind the shape of the words, "break the link."

Vibia's skill was nowhere near as refined as Pinarius's, but a strong enough blast would serve the purpose. She just had to find the right point. Standing in the doorway, a place of strength for those who drew their power from edges and boundaries, Vibia groped for the point of change in the pattern—and found it echoing out of Pinarius himself, a faint and ragged fringe of panic. They had surprised him, thrown off his intentions. That was a weakness she could strike at.

Vibia sent severing energy there, pricking at his insecurity. It shook his control—a loss no Fracture mage could afford. Vibia's interference put a crack in his confidence, and that was enough to shatter the concatenation he had built.

There was a flash of bronze-tinged light, followed by a strong wave of magical energy that staggered Sempronius and nearly knocked Vibia off her feet. Latona's body relaxed, and Sempronius breathed a little easier.

Except now a new danger set the hairs on his arms prickling upright. Tearing apart the link between Latona, Pinarius, and the sinkhole of energy had saved Latona and dizzied the Fracture mage, but the maw did not disappear. A thoughtless, undirected devourer of energy—and of souls—spun between the mages, seeking something to latch onto. Of such things were the *lemures* born: haunting spirits that fed on the hearts and minds of whoever they encountered. Melancholy and madness followed in their wake.

Vibia didn't have the strength to control it, and Pinarius was still recovering from the reeling pain of having his control shattered. So Sempronius stepped forth to confront the void, intent on snapping it shut before it could spawn any hungry ghosts.

But as soon as his own magic stretched out to touch it, his resolve faded. He felt the maw's hunger as his own, a dark mirror of his ambition. It tasted him, his goals, his frustrations, and it offered a deal. Feeding one of them could feed both.

'*Use me,*' it seemed to whisper. '*Play with me. Make me your own.*'

What a temptation. To pocket a sinkhole like that in his own power. To shape it, summon it forth when he desired, create *lemures* who would feed on his enemies and sap them of their very will to stand against him. What doors that would open. What great works he could perform, with a force like this ready for the beckoning. '*It would be the next best thing to holding Death itself on a leash.*'

Sempronius's lips parted, but no words came. The world around him seemed to be fading to black; the walls of the warehouse, Pinarius's staggered form, even Latona, still prostrate, and Vibia at his shoulder, all seemed to be receding. The only thing that appeared real, tangible, was the maw's gaping whorl, calling out to him.

"*How slow it will be, otherwise. The long road to victory, so many obstacles, a slog, held back by lesser men, fighting for every inch . . .*" Its voice was like a nymph's song, lulling and seductive. "*And for what? You know the world you fashion will be superior. You know the people will be happier. You know it will work, so efficiently, prosperously. So why not just take it?*" The darkness was like what he felt when brushing against the shades of the underworld, eerily compelling, a taste of the inevitable undertow. "*Use me, use me . . . Take the power you know is your right . . . Reach out and claim what is owed you . . .*"

The abyss stared at Sempronius, enticing, and Sempronius took an unconscious half-step forward.

"Brother," Vibia hissed, and her familiar impatience snapped him back to himself.

He shook his head, clearing the haze of dark attraction. *'No. Not that way. I will strive for the world I want, but not that way.'* And he refocused his control over the maw.

It was like grabbing a bull by the horns and attempting to steer it, but Sempronius refused to let a glorified metaphysical trench get the better of him. Raging at having lost its grip on him, the maw demanded something to feed on before it would close—so Sempronius gave it Pinarius Scaeva.

Pinarius had been staggering to his feet, but fell again, seizing in horrible jerks and spasms as his own creation devoured his energy. Beside Sempronius, Vibia flinched. It was what all Fracture mages feared, falling into a hellish void of their own making. All magic could betray you, but Fracture would do it the quickest. As Sempronius watched, Pinarius's skin turned an ashy gray and spittle frothed at his mouth. Sempronius tried not to think that this was what the darkness had offered him, or of how good it felt to hold the reins of destruction. Finally, he moved to close it off—like tugging on pursestrings, slipping the greedy mouth closed.

◇◇◇◇◇◇◇◇◇◇◇◇◇◇

Vibia could not see her brother's workings, but she felt it when the chasm snapped shut. She drew a deep breath, her lungs feeling as though they had never known such relief. Beside her, Sempronius looked unsettled, his pupils unnaturally dilated. Deciding to give him a moment to himself, Vibia walked over to the two prone figures.

For her brother's sake, she checked Vitellia Latona first. The woman was breathing, though shallowly. Vibia laid two fingers against her temple, checking for signs of permanent damage done by Pinarius's vile abuse. "She should be fine," Vibia announced over her shoulder. "She'll probably be ill for days, but she'll recover." Sempronius nodded dumbly as Vibia strode over to Pinarius Scaeva. Him, she did not feel compelled to treat gently. Her dainty slippered foot kicked out to turn him onto his back, and her lip curled in disgust as she laid her fingers to his temple. "Unfortunately, he might recover as well," she said after a moment.

"I was quite hoping . . ." Sempronius's voice was dry and cracking.

"I know. So was I. He's broken, but . . ." Vibia stood, wishing she could wash her hands. "His mind might put itself back together, given time and rest. You should kill him." She folded her arms tight over her chest. She felt fragile, brittle with the effort she had expended in the past few minutes. No one knew the limits of her power better than she did. "He knows too much, now. He saw you working magic, and if you think he won't run straight to Rabirus with that information—"

"I know." Sempronius moved stiffly to stand over the fallen Discordian. "He remains a priest of Janus. Even if he has defiled the office, I have no wish to bring a deity's wrath down upon my head with his death."

"So what do you—?"

"Break his mind. Make it so he can't remember his own name, much less what happened tonight."

"Brother, I don't know if I have the skill—"

"You do," he said, stepping away from Pinarius and towards the door. "At least, you will, with help. Alhena? If you would be so good."

Tiptoeing, Alhena crept into the building. She was white-faced and clinging to her girl's arm, and Vibia could feel the crackle of her terror when she saw Latona on the ground. *'Poor mite. We should not have left her out there.'* But it had been a necessity, lest she witness Sempronius's display of power. *'However high her regard for my brother, she could not be trusted with that.'*

"Ohhh . . ." Alhena swayed uneasily as she came closer. "So that's who it was." Watching a tangle of thoughts play out on the younger woman's face, Vibia felt a pang of sympathy. Life had to be hard enough, with such unusual siblings, without the burdens of Proserpina on her as well. And Vibia knew what it was to wrestle with a demanding and unpredictable element.

"Lady Alhena," Sempronius said. "You are a mage of Time, which means, I think, you could hold some power over memory." Her nod was uncertain. Sempronius took her gently by the arm and passed her off to Vibia. "My sister, as you know, is a mage of Fracture. I think together, you could see to it that this traitor to your arts never hurts anyone else as he hurt your sister."

Alhena's beatific smile was startlingly out of place, given the circumstances. "Oh yes. I think I can do that. And it would be my great pleasure." Vibia thought she knew why. When someone wronged Sempronius, she could easily curse them with a smile on her face. Alhena, it seemed, had the same sororal instinct. Vibia approved. Vengeance could be soothing—all the more so when applied righteously.

Sempronius patted her shoulder. "Good. Can you stay here with Vibia until I send my men to bring you home and to deal with what's left of him?"

"Certainly," Alhena agreed.

Vibia was less compliant. "What are you—?" But she clamped her mouth shut as she watched Sempronius lift Latona up. She was still limp, her hair falling over his arm like a tangled golden waterfall. *'And what a pretty picture that makes,'* Vibia thought sourly.

"I'm taking her to Rubellia at the Temple of Venus. Whatever Pinarius did to her, Rubellia may be able to help."

"Not the Temple of Juno? Oh. Of course not."

"She'll be more . . . comfortable with Rubellia."

Vibia nodded curtly.

"Not regretting coming to assist me, are you?"

"Of course not, brother," Vibia said, her voice tight. "You asked it of me." She turned away from him, kneeling down by Pinarius's head. She splayed her fingers over his brow, calling the rupturing magic to her once again as Alhena bent down beside her. "And you know how seriously I take my duty to the family."

∞∞∞∞∞∞∞∞∞∞

When Latona came to, her first fogged thought was that her vision had not come back with her. Everything had gone so dark. It took her a moment to realize that night had fallen in the time since she had been hauled into that warehouse. Her next realization was that she was no longer *in* the warehouse, and only then did she notice, with as much alarm as her drowsy senses could summon, that she was being carried through the streets of Aven. "What—? Where am—?"

"Awake, are you? Good. Put your arms around my neck, if you can."

Latona obeyed only once she was able to place the voice. "Sempronius, how did you—?"

"Your sister," he said. "Alhena. She—"

"Had a vision," Latona finished. "Oh, if I'd listened . . ." Her head fell into the crook of his shoulder, and only then did she realize how utterly inappropriate it was. She wriggled against him. "I can stand."

"I doubt it."

"If anyone sees us—"

"I'd imagine everyone has more important things on their minds this evening."

"The fire!" she gasped, memory flooding back to her. "Is it—?"

"More or less under control," Sempronius said.

Latona knew she ought to make Sempronius put her down, but she felt weak as a half-drowned kitten. "So foolish . . ." she murmured. "If I hadn't run off on my own, I wouldn't have needed rescuing . . ."

"You saved my life not a month ago. I owed you one," Sempronius said.

"Please . . . put me down . . . this isn't . . ."

He did, but not before side-stepping into an alleyway between two shops. He let her drop softly, making sure her feet were firm on the ground. Even then, he found he could not release her entirely. His fingertips ghosted over her arms. She was sticky with sweat, streaked with soot, and, now, shivering in the December cold. Too, she was vulnerable—a proud Vitellian daughter who had let the glamours of confidence and unflappability drop, too exhausted to hold them up. A hunter would be poised to exploit such a display, to aim for the exposed wound. Shadow's influence tempted him, as it so often did. Usually he mastered the impulse by reminding himself of the dark road such indulgences could lead to—roads like the one Pinarius Scaeva's maw had just shown him. Yet with Latona, he felt not only his internal sense of honor, but an instinct to protect, to defend.

Unusual, but not unwelcome.

Latona's head was still swimming, and it took effort just to concentrate on what was up and what was down. Sempronius's voice penetrated the fog, though, asking, "How do you feel?"

"Dizzy," Latona said. Her voice was thready, and her palms fell flat against his chest as she tried to steady herself. Each breath felt like a precious gift, and yet her mind still floated in strange detachment from her body. Sempronius, though, was solid, and real, and warm. Touching him reassured her that she had not, in fact, died in that warehouse.

She swayed again, and he caught her under the elbows. Latona looked up into his eyes, finding herself lost in the compassion and concern she saw there.

A compulsion pattered in her heart, but this one had nothing to do with her magic. A coil of need begging her to throw worth, wealth, and reputation all away, just to know what his lips would feel like against hers. It was absurd. It was *mad*, wanting a man like this, and the only thing that made it endurable was the same thing that made it so painful— her awareness, ever more certain, that he wanted her too, just as fiercely.

"Venus protect me," she whispered as her fingers seized the front of his tunic. She went up on her toes, pressing her lips to his.

However much she may have surprised him, Sempronius responded eagerly, and the hands holding her up slipped easily around her back. This was no gentle, tentative kiss, no awkward endearment; Sempronius's mouth was hot and insistent, eliciting little shocks of pleasure that Latona felt all the way down to her toes.

He kissed with the same intensity he applied to everything in his life, and Latona felt possessed, swept up in his flood. She clutched blindly at his shoulders, clinging to him for support, and as she swayed into him, his arm locked around her waist, holding her fast. She felt, too, a tingle of warmth that came not from their close-pressed bodies, but from within her, the tangled haze of Fire and Spirit rushing over her skin and pricking up the hair on her arms.

There was something oddly restorative in it, too, as though the kiss brought her back to herself, anchoring her soul back into her body. Perhaps it was Venus driving her, giving her strength through this impossible desire.

Sempronius broke away first, though his lips drifted over her cheeks and hair before he said, "You mad, brave creature."

"I'm sorry," Latona said, making to turn away from him.

"Don't you dare apologize."

"I shouldn't have— we shouldn't— this is—" Latona pushed back from him, but her balance and strength were not yet fully restored. She swayed unsteadily, and in an instant found herself swept up in Sempronius's arms again.

"I'm a monster," he said, moving them back out into the street. "Pouncing on you like some starving animal." Latona wound her arms around his neck and refrained from pointing out that it was she who had done the pouncing. "Come on," he said. "I'm taking you to Ama Rubellia."

XLIII

Latona was able to regain herself somewhat at the Temple of Venus through the restorative power of a bath, as well as the cosseting of Rubellia and her acolytes. Little Pontia, the girl that Latona had rescued all those months ago on the Esquiline, proved particularly attentive, gently pulling a comb through Latona's limp curls. She looked so in awe that Latona might have been embarrassed, if she had had any energy left for self-indulgent emotions. "She sees you as a savior twice over," Rubellia said, when she came in with a fresh gown, so that Latona need not return home so disheveled. "There's nothing wrong with letting the girl have a hero."

Latona's error was in then heading for the Caelian, not the Palatine. She recognized the mistake before she even got through the doorway, for she could hear her husband bellowing, and the steward howling in protest.

When Herennius realized the front door had opened, he left off beating his steward and whirled about to face his wife. For a moment, Latona thought he might strike her as well. He stayed his hand, however, not that far gone. 'Yet.'

"You!" Herennius shouted, advancing on her. "You defied me."

Latona was too tired to bother dissembling. "Yes. I suppose I did." Some impish inclination to press her luck made her add, "Though in fairness, I never did agree to your proclamation that I would stay home, and in fact informed you that I had every intention of supporting my fa—"

"Explain yourself!"

She forbore to point out that was what she had been doing before he interrupted her. "I was with Aula and my father's men," Latona began. "It was all perfectly—"

"Do not lie!" Herennius bellowed. "We've had a message from your father—your sister is in a panic, wondering where you were, if you're well."

Latona closed her eyes. Had it only been a few hours ago that she had shoved her excess clothing at Aula and bolted off into danger? But

Herennius's words revealed that Aula had not given her away. "We got separated when the fires broke out," she said. "There was quite a crush."

"Trouble!" Herennius said. "Just as I predicted. You can't keep yourself away from it."

Latona discovered in that moment that she had precisely no patience left to spare for her husband. "It's certainly not as though I *wanted* to find myself in the middle of a conflagration, Herennius, and furthermore, you had no right to forbid me going out in the first place!"

His face grew florid, and as he stepped closer to her, Latona felt Merula tensing behind her. "I am your *husband*—"

"But not my master," Latona spat back. "Not my owner, Herennius."

"—and you will show me the respect I am due!"

"I show you precisely the respect you have earned!" Latona shouted, pushed beyond her ability to retain composure.

Herennius's lips were thin and white. "I am a worthy man, you know," he said. "I act with honor. I see to my clients' interests. I manage my estates well. I do not shame you."

Latona sighed, her chest feeling oddly deflated. Nothing he said was untrue. But that was, itself, a trouble. Herennius was respectable without ever being extraordinary—without wanting to try. It would have suited a great many women, but not her—not now. Not when she was beginning to discover what she herself was capable of. "We are ill-suited, Herennius, and that is a fact," she said, rubbing her forehead.

"Will you divorce me?"

Latona let the question hang in the air. She had the legal right to do so, of course, any woman did. The memory of Sempronius's lips still hanging on hers should have inspired courage, perhaps, but instead it reminded her what was at stake. *'There are already rumors about me . . . Ocella, Sempronius, too many will not see a difference.'* At least marriage to Herennius sheltered her reputation in that regard. Divorcing him without clear cause would provoke suspicion of her virtue—and knowing herself to be derelict, Latona was not sure she could face the scrutiny, not with her family's fortunes also at stake. "No," she said at last. "Will you divorce me?"

"No," he responded, much more quickly. "It would be foolish, particularly with your father about to become censor." He jabbed a finger at her. "But you will remember what I have done for you, what I protect you from. You will behave in a more suitable wifely fashion, and then . . ." He settled back on his heels with a self-satisfied nod. "Then I expect we shall get along tolerably enough once again."

A tolerable marriage. Many women would consider that a fine enough thing, as much as they could expect out of life. But the powers of Fire and Spirit had re-awoken in Latona's soul, and she found herself uncertain whether she could resign herself to so lackluster a thing as a tolerable marriage.

"So," Herennius went on, "We will go to your father's for dinner, so that he may see you are well—and you can apologize for having so foolishly worried everyone."

All Latona wanted to do was curl up in her bed, but it seemed this day would never end. "Then by all means," she said, gesturing at the door, "let us go."

◇◇◇◇◇◇◇◇◇◇◇◇◇◇◇

The meal was stiff and awkward, but Latona was so fatigued that she hardly noticed. Aulus had a scolding for her, and she did regret the hours of terror she had caused Aula, but most of the evening passed as in a fog. After dinner, Aulus and Herennius withdrew to Aulus's study to discuss what financial rearrangements might have to be made, if the elections were put off long enough to require another round of campaigning. Latona let Aula fuss and cluck over her for a few minutes, but when Gera caught Lucia creeping out of bed to try and eavesdrop on the adults' conversation, Latona took the opportunity of Aula's diverted attention to draw Alhena aside.

"We should have listened to you, pet," she said, squeezing her sister's hands.

But Alhena surprised her by shaking her head. "No. You shouldn't have. I think . . . I think it all had to happen, so that other things can . . ." She paused, frowning. "It's the oddest sensation, you know, to be so sure of something, and yet have no idea at all what it's about. If I'd seen the end of that vision, it might've made more sense, and I wouldn't have been so panicked."

"It's a good thing you were panicked!" Latona said. "You saved the day. If you hadn't brought Vibia, of all people, I don't know what might have happened."

"I brought her because she had to be there," Alhena said, with a self-conscious shrug. "I'm just glad it didn't take me any longer to figure it out. And him, too. Sempronius Tarren, I mean. I think—" She bit off her words, her cheeks flushing nearly as red as her hair.

"What?"

"Nothing. It's nothing. Just . . ." Alhena's blue eyes darted about the room, as they tended to do when she was avoiding saying something. "Your gold and his darkness. I see them together. You and he are connected, somehow." Alhena fidgeted with her hair, poking distractedly at a loose pin. "I don't know what it means, but you two are . . . a part of one another's stories, I suppose is the best way of putting it." Her hands fluttered. "I don't know, but I . . . I'm going to try to do better. To learn more. I know I've been . . . I mean, I know I haven't . . ." Alhena glanced over her shoulder; Aula was returning to the table, having wrangled Lucia back to bed. "Well. Whatever it is you're heading into, you won't go ill-prepared, not if I have anything to say about it."

She looked uncharacteristically fierce when she said it—and in that moment looked more like Gaius and Aula than Latona had ever noticed before. "Thank you, dove," she said, leaning to kiss Alhena's forehead.

"Thank her for what?" Aula said, flopping herself down.

Latona glanced at Alhena, but she gave the tiniest shake of her head—and Latona agreed. No one seemed to know that Alhena had slipped out of the house that afternoon, and Latona would not repay her courage by giving her away.

"For being my sister," Latona said, as brightly as she could manage. "And you, too." Her fingers still entwined with Alhena's, she reached out for Aula with the other hand. "No one could ask for better."

◇◇◇◇◇◇◇◇◇◇◇◇◇◇◇

The augurs looked to the skies and determined that the next clear day for the elections would be the fourth following the Ides of December. On the day before, Latona and Alhena went to the home of Taius Mella to meet with Sempronius and Vibia: Latona, to thank Vibia for intervening with Pinarius Scaeva on her behalf; Sempronius, to thank Alhena for raising the alarm. Latona felt it a little awkward to be so indebted to Vibia. They were friends, but only in the vague way their social class and familial alliances demanded. Latona had always suspected Vibia did not actually like her or Aula much—and she had difficulty mustering much fondness in return.

None of that dimmed her appreciation for what Vibia had done. "I don't know what it was that you did," Latona said, "but it must have been extraordinary magic."

"It's something we Fracture mages learn early on," Vibia said. "The most dangerous thing to one of us is another of us." Her shoulders moved beneath her mantle, but Latona felt more emotion churning in her than her affectation of nonchalance let on. "Our control has to be so precise. Perhaps that's why we're best suited to tamper with each other."

"You must have done a magnificent job of it," Latona said. "He was strong and well-prepared." What she did not say, but knew they were both thinking, was that Vibia's power was not nearly a match for Pinarius's. Latona had no idea how Vibia had managed to find the weak link in his defenses, and could not help wondering, for all her gratitude.

Vibia's gaze flicked towards her brother, speaking something that Latona could not identify. Then she sighed again. "Never discount the element of surprise."

"I'm only sorry you're not getting public credit for it." They had agreed, between them, not to make any public mention of Pinarius Scaeva or of Lucretius Rabirus's part in the whole scheme. With no proof of his involvement in the fire and nothing concrete to link him to Pinarius, there was little they could do. Latona had not even told Aula the details. Ama Rubellia knew a little, but Sempronius had offered as sparse an explanation as he could manage, and Latona had not had the strength to explain further.

"It's of no matter," Vibia said. "The price for taking credit would be far too high." Again, a little glance at Sempronius. "And don't worry," Vibia added, a dark look coming into her eyes. "Lucretius Rabirus hasn't gotten away clear, not if I have anything to say about it."

"My sister has rather an enthusiasm for righteous cursing," Sempronius said.

"Pinarius Scaeva was using *filthy* Fracture magic to do his work," Vibia said in defense—though to Latona's mind, she had no need to explain or excuse her vehemence. "It's— it's a miasma. Perverted. Rabirus knew that and set him loose on the city. He deserves everything I can throw at him and more."

"I'm more concerned," Sempronius said, "that Scaeva professed association with the Discordian Cult. I thought they were all gone from the city, but if he was nestled into the Temple of Janus . . ." Sempronius shook his head. "I dislike the implication." The man himself had been found a gibbering wreck, during the clean-up of the docks the next day. No one seemed to have any idea how a priest of Janus had ended up in an Aventine warehouse, nor how his wits had come to be so shattered—no one except the four people standing in the Mellan atrium, none of whom were inclined to illuminate the matter.

◇◇◇◇◇◇◇◇◇◇◇◇◇◇◇◇

The following morning, the elections resumed with rather less pomp and enthusiasm than they had generated the first time. The crowd was smaller, Sempronius noted. He wondered how many were absent because they assumed the electoral results would repeat themselves and how many stayed away out of superstition. If the gods were to express their displeasure a second time . . .

The speeches and negotiating were less energetic. Even Sempronius had difficulty summoning the necessary passion. He felt as though he had already spoken to everyone whose opinion was not permanently fixed against him. The good news, so far as he was concerned, was that his reputation did not seem to have been damaged by the Aventine fire. Buteo had tried to imply that the gods had singled Sempronius out for punishment, but too many men, from senators down to foot soldiers, had seen him not only organizing the brigades, but hauling buckets with his own hands. The senators appreciated the leadership; the lower classes, the willingness to work.

As such, Sempronius found the entire atmosphere of the elections far more casual. He stood discussing the fire and its implications with the Autroniae while the officers and the First Class voted. When they had finished, Sempronius found himself enjoying more of an advantage than he had during the first election.

When the final results were announced following the votes of the Third Class, however, Sempronius's good mood evaporated immediately.

He had taken first place among the praetors. The province of Cantabria, command of a legion, direction of the Iberian War, all were his for the taking. Galerius and Aufidius had won the consulship and Aulus Vitellius the censor's office. By all accounts, it was a resounding victory for the Popularists, by a wider margin than they would have won on the first try. Yet here he was, feeling punched in the stomach.

He had taken first place among the praetors. Lucretius Rabirus had taken second.

"How?" Sempronius said, clenching his fists. "*How* did that man come in second?"

"I can only assume," Marcus sighed, "that he bribed very, very well."

Sempronius was ruffling his hair in agitation, mindless of the fact that chalk from his toga had rubbed off on his palm. "I can't even begin . . ." It beggared his speech, that Rabirus, of all men, could stand now in such a position to imperil his plans to bring Aven to the glorious future of his visions.

Felix cursed under his breath. "Diana's tits, here he comes."

"He wouldn't," Marcus said.

"Well, he is."

Marcus rubbed briskly at Sempronius's head, trying to shift the white streak that he had deposited into it, but Sempronius brushed him off. He had far, far greater quarrels with Lucretius Rabirus than precision of appearance.

"Well." Rabirus pulled to a halt in front of him, flanked by cronies, wearing that slick, self-satisfied smile. By Felix's fidgeting, he wanted to punch it off Rabirus's face as badly as Sempronius did. "Congratulations, Senator. Returned first among the praetors. What an honor."

Sempronius nodded. Rabirus rocked on his heels slightly. *'If he wants me to return the congratulations,'* Sempronius thought, *'he can wait until Mount Olympus crumbles into dust.'* Not even peace-making Marcus looked inclined to offer an olive branch.

"I presume you'll be taking Cantabria," Rabirus said, "with your enthusiasm for the Iberian endeavor. Sensible, of course, most sensible." Sempronius did not dignify that observation with a response. Taking Cantabria—and its legions—to spearhead the Iberian War had been part of Sempronius's campaign, which made him wonder why Rabirus thought it worth mentioning. "In fact," Rabirus continued, "I think you've quite won me over." Sempronius arched a disbelieving eyebrow, and Rabirus's irritating little smile broke into a broad grin. "So much so, in fact, that I think I'll claim Baelonia for my province." Thunderstruck, Sempronius thought he had misheard until Rabirus continued: "Yes, Baelonia. And that means, of course, I'll be taking over Fimbrianus's legion in Gades. Control of a port city is so crucial to a campaign, isn't it?" Rabirus leaned in, the self-righteous smile melting away and his false cheer with it. "Just something for you to take into consideration when you're making your plans for this war you've thrown us into. I will be there."

Sempronius could only stare as Rabirus sauntered away, his chin held high.

Behind him, Felix cursed another blue streak.

XLIV

"Advance!"

This was not the way an Aventan legion liked to give battle. Aventans preferred to know their ground first, to set a strategic formation. Fate was giving Vitellius no such chance.

A series of skirmishes had drawn Vitellius farther away from Toletum. There had been casualties, more than a lone cohort could afford, but realizing that he had wandered near-blind into a viper's nest, he was loath to send for Mennenius and risk those men as well. They would be needed in Toletum—all the more if Vitellius's cohort never returned.

And now there was word that Ekialde himself, the Lusetani war-king, was the one drawing the Aventans from their security.

Vitellius arrived at the top of a hill north of the town of Libora only to see the Lusetani approaching from the east. It was a larger force than Vitellius had seen since coming to Iberia. More than a thousand, he guessed, and all of them spoiling for a fight. Their women and noncombatants had been left elsewhere, and their formation was far superior to that of the Vettoni marauders the Avetans had encountered before.

Vitellius quickly assessed the situation. Libora had walls, but they were neither high nor strong. If the Aventans did not reach the city borders first, the Lusetani would swarm over the defenses like so many termites attacking a bit of rotting wood. Fortunately, with the River Tagus on one side and steep, rocky terrain on the others, the Lusetanians had little choice but to attack the town straight-on, charging up the packed dirt road that ran through the depression between the hillsides. If the Aventans were to prevent them from breaching the city walls, they would have to block and hold the road.

So they ran, down the hill and towards the dusty path that came in from the east. Vitellius could at last be glad for the months of racing around the uneven Iberian terrain. His men would not now be surprised by the sudden shift of their armor's weight, nor by the rolling of pebbles beneath their *caligae*. They had learned to adapt to these conditions, allowing them to move down the hillside with alacrity, reaching the road just a few hundred paces ahead of the Lusetani.

Vitellius had only a moment to decide whether to meet the Lusetani with a counter-charge or to take a defensive position. These were experienced soldiers. But the run down the hill had cost them effort. Better to rest their legs and let the Lusetani break themselves on a solid line of Aventan shields. He signaled as much to Centurion Calix, then cried "Defensive formation!" and rode to the back of the lines with the rest of the Edetani auxiliaries. "*Pila* at the ready!" In perfect unison, the front two hundred men gripped their iron-tipped spears.

Vitellius waited. He had to choose the precise right moment for the *pila* to be most effective. As the sickle-shaped swords of the enemy caught the sunlight and glinted menacingly, not a man of Vitellius's four hundred gave any sign that the approaching horde of screaming, wild-eyed barbarians bothered him in the least. That was Aventan discipline.

Vitellius let the Lusetani draw nearer, nearer, and there were so many of them, hundreds more than they had faced in any prior engagement, but he could not let that distract him. *'This wants a general,'* he thought, *'but there is only you. Stand for Aven, Tribune, and make Mars know your name.'*

"Throw!"

A single, devastating motion. Two hundred spears sang as they flew through the air, then ended their trajectory with thuds or squelches. Many of the Lusetani were able to deflect the *pila* with their little round shields, but the heaviness of the iron tips made the shields thereafter useless. Others found the *pila* were too numerous to avoid, and their bodies created the first hazard for their fellows.

On they came, though; there were far more than two hundred Lusetani warriors charging at the huddled Aventan cohorts, even if every spear had found its mark. Vitellius did not need to order his men to draw swords; the Lusetani were upon them with a deafening crash. The first line of Aventans braced to absorb the force of the charge. Sometimes, a good check with an Aventan shield was enough to knock an opponent unconscious. For the rest, there was the legionary's primary weapon, a short sword jabbing efficiently out from behind the protective line.

The Lusetani were fast and ferocious. Their curved swords distributed force differently than an Aventan *gladius*, able to strike with the shuddering power of an ax blow. Aventan shields would not splinter or crack even under such persuasion, but the legionaries behind the shields were not always so lucky. The impact of the sword's swing, with the weight of a Lusetani warrior behind it, could stagger even the most hardily-trained soldier. Like waves beating down a rock into grains of sand, the Lusetani intended to wear the Aventan cohorts down until they broke.

Vitellius initially remained at the back of the field, where he could keep an eye on the battle as it developed. When he saw his first lines falter under the hammering force of all those heavy blades, however, he knew the time had come to lead from the front. Though the centurions were doing their best to cycle fresh men up, the replacements could not always make it fully forward in time, causing the line of locked shields to stagger—and that, in turn, made it easier for the Lusetani to worm in between the soldiers. Some injured were already collapsing, falling towards the back of the ranks, blood staining the packed dirt of the road.

Vitellius did not want to look too closely to see who would be breathing his last, or had already. He had to think of the whole, of the cohort as a unit. *'If we break,'* Vitellius thought, *'we'll be cut to pieces.'*

He was not concerned only for his own life and his men's. He knew that if this cohort got massacred, it drastically increased the chances that Toletum would fall. If Toletum fell, there would be no one to stop the Lusetani from swarming towards the coast and the rich cities there.

Vitellius scanned the battlefield and saw the cohort standard: a dog reared on its hind legs, mounted atop a high pole. As he watched, the dog dipped, as though the *signifer* bearing it had taken a blow. They were not eagles, the sacred emblems of the Aventan legion; those were back in Nedhena with Governor Sallust and the rest of the Eighth, safe from the insurmountable shame of loss. But losing the cohort standard was a mark of defeat and weakness. It would be a blow to the cohort's morale, if they fell, and a black mark on Vitellius's record as a leader.

He dismounted, yelling instructions to the cavalry as he did so. "Lead a sally on their left flank," he said. "But pull back as soon as your horses start to tire! Mars and Bellona willing, we'll need the mounts strong and fresh to chase these bastards down at the end of the day." He had time enough to see Hanath's bloodthirsty grin before the horses sprang into motion. Vitellius drew his own sword, grabbed a shield from a fallen soldier, and pushed into the ranks.

Once the men noticed his presence, the effect rippled through the cohort. Few military tribunes ever actually engaged in a fight: it was a political appointment, meant to thrust ambitious young men into the association of their elders and betters. To see Vitellius taking up a sword, risking his own neck alongside them, cheered the men of the Eighth's far-flung vexillation as little else in that moment could have. Even better were the insults Vitellius threw at them as he forced his way to the front rank.

"Come on, you callow bastards! You going to let these shit-eating, piss-swilling sons of pigs get the better of you? I want these lines firmer than a Bithynian dancing-boy's butt-cheek!"

Such were the words of inspiration for Aventan legionaries.

The clamor inside the formation was astonishingly loud. The Lusetanian swords clanged horribly when they caught at the metal-bound borders of the Aventan shields. Worse were the splintering cracks of bones splitting, the muddy squish-and-suction of swords finding bowels. Vitellius gritted his teeth and tried to set a good example. When one Lusetani launched himself high for a downward strike, Vitellius swiftly brought the top of his shield up into the warrior's chin. His neck snapped back, and he crumpled.

For a few moments, it looked as though Vitellius's surge of inspiration might have saved them—but his men were tired. The battle had gone on for too long, with so few reinforcements to cycle through the front lines. A hard check against his shield from a Lusetani warrior rattled Vitellius's teeth and weakened his stance.

And then, quite suddenly, the press of Lusetani eased up. Had Vitellius remained upon his horse, he would have seen the cause immediately; as it was, he had as little idea as any of the rankers, unable to see much past their own helmets and shields. Then the cavalry, of their own initiative, came thundering in from both sides, driving the Lusetani apart, hacking at them with long swords and spitting them with spears. Only then did Vitellius get enough of a respite to look up and see a sight that filled his heart with a joy it had not known in weeks: two military standards draped in red fabric, the emblems of Legio IV Sanguineus, the legion of Gades. Relief had arrived.

Legio IV had approached from the southeast, at just the right angle to force the Lusetani to turn away from their attack on Vitellius's cohort. With their attention split, the unrelenting force of their onslaught began to fail. So cheered was Vitellius that he hoisted shield and sword anew and gave the bellowing cry *"Advance!"* for the second time in that day. Flagging though they were, his cohort followed his initiative, charging at the Lusetanian's retreating backsides.

One among the Lusetani refused to give ground, however: a man whose long black hair was as thick with blood as with grease, whose yellow eyes lit in anger as he saw his men retreating. There was gold bound not just around his forearms and biceps, but about his brow, and he was screaming furiously in the Lusetanian tongue.

Vitellius's heart leapt. Here, at last, was the man responsible for the chaos he had borne witness to over the past months. Here was the epicenter of the turmoil quaking the Iberian peninsula. All the news from the allied tribes indicated that this uprising had centered around a single charismatic leader, Ekialde of the Lusetani. The opportunity glistened like a gem in the sunlight.

Vitellius charged him.

◇◇◇◇◇◇◇◇◇◇◇◇◇◇◇◇

Ekialde saw the high gray plumes reaching above the shield heading towards him, the point of a wedge of blood-spattered shields, and he saw opportunity. Here, *here* was a proper chance to do honor to Bandue. No merchant or villager, this, and no mere ranker among the Aventans. The man who owned those feathers would be a man of rank and worth— someone the Aventans would miss.

Someone worth ensorcelling.

The two leaders engaged each other with vicious fervor, Ekialde wild-eyed with righteous fury at the invader. Around them, Ekialde's stalwart war-band clashed, howling, with the Aventans that drove into them like a moving wall. The Aventan commander thrust at him, and Ekialde parried with such force that the man seemed to shiver. Yet Ekialde did not go in for the kill; he meant more than death for this Aventan.

He withdrew a small clay vessel, the container for Bailar's compulsion magic, from where he had tucked it, safe in his belt. "Bandue, look here! Bandue, take this man as your slave!" The Aventan gave no sign that he understood the Lusetani words, but thrust at Ekialde with his stunted sword again. Ekialde easily parried; his opponent's arm was growing weak, but that mattered little now. "Bandue, your force be mine! Bandue, use my blood to claim this man!" And with a great wheeling of his arm, he whipped the clay vessel down towards Vitellius's helmet.

◇◇◇◇◇◇◇◇◇◇◇◇◇◇◇◇

The whole thing was so strange that Vitellius barely lifted his shield in time, catching Ekialde in the arm with its reinforced edge. The vessel shattered against shield and helmet both, splashing out a hot red liquid. Blood, Vitellius realized with disgust, though it seemed strangely dark and thick, and it had a pungent, rotting odor. *'But why?'*

Vitellius made to stab at Ekialde again, but his right arm felt leaden, slow to respond to his commands. With a rush of panic, Vitellius moved his shield to defend against Ekialde's next blow.

But Ekialde stepped back, staring at Vitellius as though waiting for something. Vitellius *did* feel strange. Fuzzy-headed, though he could contribute that to the blow to his helmet. Tired, as though his muscles suddenly felt the labor of the past hour. Sedate, as though none of this mattered, not the hollering of the men around him, not the groans and cries of the dying.

But then came a flushing warmth crawling across his skin. His tunic and neck scarf took on a faint glow, or so it seemed to Vitellius's amazed eyes. The strange sanguine liquid seemed drawn to the fabric like a lodestone. The crimson wool soaked up the blood like bread sopping olive oil. Vitellius could feel it, sliding across the skin of his face, neck, and arm—and then the strange fog in his brain lifted. Vitellius shook his head, raised his sword arm, and made another thrust at Ekialde.

Ekialde's jaw actually dropped. And then he turned and ran.

◇◇◇◇◇◇◇◇◇◇◇◇◇◇

Recovering himself, Vitellius raised his sword in signal to Hanath and the other nearby cavalry, then pointed them at Ekialde's retreating form. With ululating screams, the auxiliary forces spurred their horses onward. Ekialde cut immediately up the hill, scrambling up its steepest incline, where the horses could not easily follow. Vitellius had to watch, cursing under his breath, as Ekialde escaped.

The Edetani had plenty to occupy them, as not all of the Lusetani had been swift enough or clever enough to follow Ekialde's lead up the rocky incline. As the cavalry finished off the straggling warriors, Vitellius looked around for the standards, and was gratified to find them still safe in Aventan hands. Sagging with relief, Vitellius leaned against his shield.

Vitellius was bleeding from his right arm and his right calf—the unprotected side, likely exposed during his charge towards Ekialde. But Vitellius was more concerned with his tunic and his neck scarf. They were stained with both his blood and the mystery substance, and the fabric still seemed warm to the touch. He unknotted the *focale* and threaded it through his fingers.

"Latona . . ." Then Vitellius laughed. He had no idea what the Lusetani princeling had tried to do to him, but it smacked of magic—some charm or potion that should have felled him. But Aventan magic had won out. His sister's magic had protected him.

Vitellius was still contemplating the neck scarf when he was joined by several centurions of the newly arrived cohorts from the Fourth. "Tribune!" one of them called, saluting. The others followed suit. "Centurion Papius, sir."

"Centurion," Vitellius said, not caring how much his weariness showed, "I cannot thank you enough. Had you not arrived when you did—"

The centurion was younger than many and did not have the hardbitten, leather-worn look of many of his type. Instead, he stared incredulously at the bodies around him. "I had no idea there were so many of them out here. Governor Fimbrianus only said . . ." He swallowed hard. "My apologies, sir, we should have been better prepared for the engagement."

"While I appreciate your conscientiousness, centurion, I must point out that, well-prepared or not, your arrival prevented our annihilation." Vitellius could feel his heartbeat slowing back to a normal rate. He looked past Papius at the men gathering behind him. "Are you the primus pilus, centurion, or—" But as he looked at the ranks re-forming behind Papius, he realized there were far fewer than the five thousand combatants there ought to have been. "Where— Where are the rest of you?"

"The rest?" Papius asked.

Vitellius blinked. "Yes, the rest. From Gades. You're Fimbrianus's Fourth from Gades, aren't you? Where's— Where's your commander?"

"We are, tribune, but there are no more of us coming." Papius looked truly sorry to say it. "Fimbrianus only sent one cohort out. The rest are staying to protect Gades. We were supposed to go up the coast, actually, but a scout said there was a large Lusetani force headed this way. Fimbrianus said we needed the blooding most. We're the newest recruits in the region, you see, and so—"

"He said he could spare us best," growled a rank soldier from behind him.

Swallowing his rage at Fimbrianus, Vitellius looked Papius in the eye. "Well, whatever your qualifications, it's a damn good thing you're here.

You honored Mars today." He turned to call for Calix. "Centurion, show the men of the Fourth to our camp and see that they get settled in."

Vitellius called for his horse, mounted swiftly, and rode for the camp. The centurions could see to cleaning up the site of battle. Vitellius had a letter to send.

He stormed into his tent, causing the clerk to leap up from his desk in surprise.

"Paper," Vitellius growled. "Take a letter to the Senate. Copy to Governor Fimbrianus in Gades."

The clerk took one look at Vitellius's blood-spattered, anger-lined face, and scrambled to comply. "What should I tell them, sir?"

Vitellius thought for a moment, breathing heavily. His *focale* was still gripped in his hand, and its fading warmth reminded him of what could have happened today. This was more than a simple peasant rebellion, more than a spat between clans. He had been sent, ill-prepared, into a wilderness of the spirit as well as of geography.

Though there was no touch of magical blessing upon him, his nature was full of a fire of its own, and the temper that lurked in so many of the Vitelliae burst out now. "Tell them that several dozen good men of the Eighth Legion gave their lives in service to Aven today. Tell them we now have concrete evidence that the Lusetani are willing to use dark sorcery against us. Tell them if Governor Fimbrianus doesn't stop his cowardly skulking and get his *full* legion out of Gades, then all of Baelonia is going to crumble around him—and as Baelonia goes, so will Cantabria and Pyreneia. Tell them if Toletum falls, we shall have precious little standing between these rebels and Tarraco." His hand clenched around the *focale* so hard that it hurt, but it was all he could do to keep from hurling a hapless piece of furniture across the room. The rage was boiling in his blood at the unfairness of it all, that the responsibility was thrust upon him. "Tell them that while they may not have noticed that there's a bloody war going on out here, there are a thousand Aventan soldiers all too aware of it who would be more than happy to educate them personally on the matter, if they could *kindly get off their asses and come out here to see it!*" The clerk gaped at him, too alarmed at his commander's vitriolic energy to have written more than the first few words. Vitellius came to stand over him, jabbing a finger at the paper. "Write it. Just as I said."

XLV

When Dula Autroniae announced her intentions to throw a phenomenal celebration on the third day of the Saturnalia, Aula Vitellia promptly declared it the best thing she had heard in weeks.

Once the public rites of the holiday were over, and the traditional feasting of the slaves had passed, the noble and wealthy were free to feast and gamble and drink until the week was out. Thrilled at her son's appointment to Sempronius's staff for the Iberian campaign, Dula was feeling generous, and Gnaeus was of a mind to indulge her. Sempronius Tarren had claimed the Tenth Legion for Cantabria, and the Tenth already had an illustrious reputation. Felix's career was on the rise, and with it, the honor of the Autroniae.

With all that new money of theirs, the Autroniae had bought an extensive plot on the Quirinal and built their domus in modern fashion to their own tastes. It boasted a sprawling footprint, with larger dining rooms and a grander garden than the older, more traditional homes on the Palatine or Aventine. Parties on the Quirinal were less dignified, more raucous, and if the company was not rarefied, it was young, energetic, and enthusiastic. Men and women shared couches that had no semblance of hierarchy, and the floor was piled with pillows and carpets, plush and inviting. Dula had hired a fascinating young poet known for his bawdy verses, and he stood atop a table, coming up with doggerel rhymes on the spot, teasing the guests, flattering the ladies, and skewering their political opponents.

The only mar on the evening, in Latona's opinion, was her husband's decision to join them. Their relations had been particularly strained since the fire, and they had hardly spoken in days. To Latona's relief, however, soon after Dula welcomed the guests and performed the opening rites to the household gods, Herennius wandered off, aiming himself towards a knot of business-minded men who were standing near an impluvium pool. "Ah," Aula said in Latona's ear, as all three sisters settled onto a couch nearer the flute players than the poet. "Well, that explains it. He may not see the attraction of the party, but he sees *great* virtue in the mercantile company the Autroniae keep."

Felix wasted no time dropping himself unceremoniously onto their couch. "Ladies!" he said, the flush on his cheeks indicating that he had likely been in a festive mood for some hours already. "Welcome! What a trio you make! Dressed to match and everything." Aula and Latona had both donned their identical golden mantles, Latona over her vivid fuchsia gown, Aula with an azure blue. Alhena had chosen a milder yellow. "How can a simple lad like me possibly endure being in the presence of such ravishing beauty?"

Latona and Aula both greeted him with broad smiles, though Alhena blushed, ducked her head, and scurried off to join Appia on a couch in the corner. Latona said, "I daresay you'll manage. Aren't you meant to be drilling in Campania?" She was merely teasing, however, and she was actually pleased. It was nice to be complimented, even by so renowned a flirt as Felix. "Sempronius told me he'd sent you up ahead, since he can't leave the city till after the investiture."

"The boys of the Tenth can look to themselves for a bit," Felix said. "It'll be good practice for the centurions, to make sure they can keep a handle on things during a holiday."

"Don't disguise it as strategy." Aula wagged a finger at him. "You just didn't want to miss the Saturnalia parties down here."

Felix favored them with the grin that had slain defenseless hearts on every hill in Aven. "Guilty. Sempronius Tarren had a few rather severe words for me on that count, but I believe I'd far prefer a chastisement coming from you, Lady Aula."

"Don't tempt me," Aula said with a wink.

"What else am I for?" Felix laughed. "I hope you saw the spread my mother's laid out. I think she had the kitchen girls dip anything they could get their hands on in honey." He tweaked one of Aula's curls. "Though I must say, *you* look quite good enough to take a nibble out of. Does your father know you're out on such a terribly improper holiday, keeping company with ruffians like us?"

"Our father," Latona answered, over Aula's flattered tittering, "is in the country, overseeing some matters of the enrollment there. He couldn't wait to set to work." She lifted her eyebrows meaningfully. "We are entirely ungoverned."

"Well, that sounds promising," Felix said, with a grin.

"I intend," Aula said, her eyes sparkling with mischief as she gratefully accepted a cup from one of the Autroniae slaves, "to drink deep and *enjoy* myself this evening."

"And I sincerely hope you do," Felix said. "The Saturnalia's a waste if it can't bring joy to beautiful creatures such as yourselves. Now—tell me what you think of this poet my mother's hired."

◇◇◇◇◇◇◇◇◇◇◇◇◇◇◇

As the evening wore on, the effects of the barely watered wine began to show. The music grew louder and faster-paced, the dancing more provocative, the jokes bawdier, and the laughter riotous. Dula had the hypocaust blasting hot air to chase away the midwinter chill, and the resulting ambient warmth chased away her guests' heavier layers of clothing as well. Ladies' mantles and men's togas were tossed over armrests or handed off to servants, and Latona found herself glad she had chosen a narrow-strapped linen tunic beneath her gown rather than a full-sleeved woolen one, even though she had been shivering in the litter on the ride over.

Alhena only made it an hour in the festive atmosphere before she begged off. "It's just a bit much," she said. "I wasn't quite prepared for this."

Aula fluffed up her sister's hair. "No need to apologize, my honey. It was very good of you to come out at all."

"We were very pleased to have you join us," Latona said, kissing Alhena's cheek. More pleased than they could say, in truth, considering how little Alhena had been willing to socialize all autumn. "Mus and Pacco will see you safe home."

"I'll send the litter back," Alhena said.

Aula grinned. "No need to rush it on our account."

Rubellia joined the Vitelliae on their couch and was soon persuaded into a bit of choice gossip. When the Domitiae started throwing dice at a nearby table, Aula abandoned her sister with alacrity. Gambling was technically illegal most of the year, yet not only permitted but encouraged during Saturnalia. "Don't embarrass yourself!" Latona called after her.

"It's not my fault I'm so appallingly good at it," Aula replied, grinning.

"She really is, is the trouble," Latona muttered to Rubellia. "It's absolutely maddening." She flopped back on the plump red cushions, feeling pleasantly hazy. Her mantle had come unpinned from her hair, but she could not trouble herself to rearrange it. Rubellia signaled for more wine, and they reclined with their heads sharing one rolled pillow, listening to the music and poetry which flowed as prolifically as the drink.

Felix joined the poet Urbanus on top of the table in the center of the room, and they began stomping out a rhythm together, trading verses back and forth. "What say we to the sacred past, to those who came before?" Felix challenged.

"We'll march to Tartarus to ask," Urbanus shot back. "They'll meet us at the door!"

"What say we to the fighting men, who march on hob-nailed soles?"

"Tell them to rinse with vinegar, if they visit foreign holes."

The military men in the room groaned and hissed, but laughed and pounded the tables in appreciation, too. Encouraged, Felix went on. "What say we to the lovely widows, to fair dames yet unconquered?" From her seat at the gaming table, Aula paused her throw long enough to raise her cup appreciatively.

"Bid them let us twixt their thighs, lest their youth be squandered."

Felix winked at Crispinilla, whose cheeks turned a violent pink, and she was giggling, too. If Felix hadn't charmed his way beneath her skirts yet, he might well do so by the end of the evening. At the moment, at least, he seemed to be enjoying the attention of the room too much to abandon his poetical partner. "What say we to a virgin bride, to stop her trembling fear?"

Urbanus spun out to the crowd, casting an appraising glance on them all. "We need no words for that, my friend, you'll never find one here!" The crowd hooted and applauded that sentiment.

By now the poet and his young host had most of the room clapping along with their beat. A wicked gleam entered Felix's eyes as he assessed the crowd: young, Popularist, and inebriated. "What do we say of the Optimates," he ventured, "those masters of oration?"

Urbanus's expression echoed Felix's; Latona could not imagine that he was a favorite among the conservative households. "They do excel, I must admit, in matters of defecation."

"What do we say of Lucretius Rabirus, idol of righteous men?"

"He took it up-ass from a Dictator once, and yearns to do so again."

"What do we say of our favorite buzzard, Arrius Buteo?"

"If his prick was the size of his nose, he'd have no cause for sorrow!"

And on it went, with Felix and Urbanus lambasting every Optimate of note in the city, and the partygoers lauding them for it. Latona was wiping hilarity-provoked tears from her eyes when Herennius suddenly appeared behind her couch. "I'm ready to leave," he said, voice low and gruff.

"Herennius, it's early yet." Or it was by Saturnalian standards, at least. "I had thought—"

"I did not ask what you thought of it; I said that I am ready to depart."

Latona's chin set stubbornly. "I do not wish to go yet," she said. "You may, if you like. I can share Aula's litter." She chose not to add that it had gone off with Alhena and would not be back for hours.

Herennius had a stubborn expression on his normally indifferent face. "It doesn't look well," he said, "my wife remaining behind while I go home. Particularly not at a party such as this." He flicked his eyes meaningfully over to the tables where Felix and Urbanus were now cheerfully casting aspersions on the potency and stamina of Decimus Gratianus.

"It *is* Saturnalia," Latona said. "Perhaps if you just tried to enjoy yourself a little—"

"I've no intention of behaving like some drunken libertine just because it's the end of December."

"Well, short of throwing me over your shoulder, you've no way to force me to go," Latona pointed out, more tartly than she once might have, "so you may as well reconcile yourself. Dula has thrown a lovely party. I'm not tired. I am enjoying myself. I do not wish to go home."

Her threat was not precisely true; if Herennius raised enough of a fuss, Latona would go rather than face the shame of a public row. But Herennius would not call her bluff. He chose, instead, the lesser of the two social evils. "Fine," he snapped. "Stay. I'll send someone back to guide you home at your leisure." He spat the last word as though it besmirched him somehow.

Though she had emerged the victor, the dispute had robbed her of her pleasantly hazy feeling. "My dear?" Rubellia said, laying a hand atop Latona's. "Do you need—"

Latona's cheeks burned with the indignity of it. She rose swiftly. "I think I'll take a turn in the garden."

"Would you like company?" Rubellia asked, starting to rise as well, but Latona waved her off.

"No, no. I think just a moment or two alone with my thoughts . . ." She put on a false smile and the glamour of a golden glow, though she had little expectation they would fool Rubellia. "And then I'll be back in perfectly good spirits, I'm sure."

As Latona strode off to the peristyle, Rubellia made eye contact across the room with Aula. Aula followed her gaze, first towards Herennius's retreating figure, then at Latona. Aula never could stand to see her sister discomfited, and so she plucked Sempronius by the sleeve. "Sempronius," she cooed lightly. "My sister looks troubled. I think she's gone to take a turn in the garden. Would you do me the grand favor of check-ing on her?" She moved her shoulders in an innocent shrug. "If I leave the table now, Maia here's going to make off with everything."

Sempronius regarded Aula's wholly innocent expression. "Lady Aula," he said, dropping his voice low, "you are not half so empty-headed as you like people to think."

Her eyes, so like her sister's, flashed with sudden shrewdness—just briefly, and then she was back to batting innocent lashes up at him. "I care only for my sister's happiness, sir," she said, and though her tone was flippant, the words nonetheless rang with truth.

He rose and gave her a slight bow. "I live to serve, my lady. Perhaps I can ease her troubles and your concern in a single stroke."

"Oh, I do hope so," Aula said, with another knowing little smile be-fore she turned back to the Domitiae.

XLVI

The garden was large and as ornate as everything in the Autroniae domus. Several other partygoers lingered under the portico near the doors, but Latona brushed past them with murmured acknowledgments and made her way down onto the lower garden. Few, if any, of the other guests would venture there, far as it was from the light and warmth of the house. The air had a biting chill, but Latona welcomed it, thinking perhaps it would cool her temper.

The perimeter of the garden had wall sconces with torches standing in them, and these provided just enough light, flickering and filtering through the leaves, that Latona could find her way in the lower garden. Dula had decorated with myrtle and juniper, green even in December, and several trellises bore entwining ivy at this time of year, though they would teem over with flowers in the spring. Latona slipped behind one of these and closed her eyes. She breathed deep and tried to follow Rubellia's advice, focusing on the beat of her own heart, the draw of her own breath. Once her rhythms began to slow, she let herself find comfort in the unaccustomed stillness around her. The back of the garden was far enough from the house to mute the noise of the party. Here there were only faint strains of music, the burbling of the fountain, the soft cooing of doves in their ivory cages.

A noise startled her out of her contemplation. She whirled around, ready to put on a good face and turn on the charm until she could be alone again. When she saw that it was Sempronius, however, her intentions for falsity deflated. "Oh," was all she could manage to say.

"Lady Latona," he said, stepping closer to her, within the shadowed seclusion she had found. "Your sister was concerned for your welfare."

Latona nodded, unsure of what to say. She had seen Sempronius often since the fire, but always in the company of others. It had taken the best of her art to conceal her tangle of emotions every time she remembered that night and what it had ignited in her heart, and if Sempronius ever guessed at her flustered state, he was at least good enough to pretend to ignore it.

"You look cold," he said. "Would you like me to fetch your—"

"No," Latona said, too swiftly. "No. Stay, please. I had thought to be alone, but . . ." Her pique was too high to let her prevaricate, and so the truth came out in a sigh. "Your company is better."

◇◇◇◇◇◇◇◇◇◇◇◇◇◇◇

It had never been Sempronius's way to probe, as he generally found that silence encouraged greater confidences than provocative questions, and so he stood near her, waiting. She *did* look cold, and Sempronius wished he had a cloak to offer her, but he had been so eager to follow Aula's suggestion that he didn't pause to take one. He could think of other ways to warm her, too, and certainly better ones, in his own estimation.

"I do believe I'm coming to hate that man." She spoke so softly that Sempronius might not have heard her, had his focus on her been less than absolute.

"I assume we speak of your husband."

"He wasn't always this way," Latona sighed, her gaze drifting off towards the glowing torchlight. "Or if he was, I didn't notice, or I didn't mind. I was perfectly content with him when we were first married." Her fingers fidgeted at her side. "He's been particularly cross with me ever since the fire. And he only knows I went to help down at the emporium. Not . . . anything else."

"Men often react with anger when presented with something they fear."

"That," Latona murmured, "could rather neatly sum up my entire marriage."

"I don't say that by way of excuse," Sempronius went on, "just explanation."

"I knew what I was doing," Latona said.

"Did you?" Sempronius asked. Latona looked at him sharply. Despite the events of the evening, they had never actually talked about *why* she had been there in the emporium—but he had an inkling, and one he wanted to hear her admit. "I had the story from a fire-forger, one of the Aventine men. He said you looked startled at your own actions, so I did wonder if you fully knew the danger you walked into."

"Well, I wasn't anticipating getting abducted and nearly murdered, but when it came to the fire, yes. I knew I had to try, at least. I knew it was dangerous, but I also knew it would work because it *had* to. I couldn't allow anything else."

He knew that feeling, the inability to accept an alternative because to do so meant ruin or death. She spoke with such vehemence, such passion, and beneath that, a yearning to be heard and acknowledged. It shone in her emerald eyes, fierce and defiant, and he felt a rush of affection for her. "I admire you for that more than I can express. If what you did was in one way foolish, it was, far more than that, brave and noble and *worthy* of you."

She presented such a perfect picture of loveliness that Sempronius thought the image of her in this moment would be burned in his memory for all time. Soft tendrils of golden hair fell around her face, and her lips were slightly parted, too invitingly, whether she knew it or not. "Worthy?" she asked, after a moment. "What do you mean by that?"

"It was extraordinary, Latona," Sempronius said, still so softly. "Not just the magic, but *you*. You were extraordinary. That you would risk yourself and venture so much on this city's behalf . . . That was the bravery I knew was in you." He was beaming in admiration. "You faced down the danger. You strode forth, and damn it all, because you wanted to do what was right. So, yes. I find that extremely worthy."

It seemed woefully inadequate, but she managed to say, "Thank you."

"You have no need," Sempronius said, "but you are most welcome anyway. You are a woman of great potential, Latona, and it has for too long gone unencouraged."

Latona looked back up at the lambent glow from the house. "We will be missed. My sister—"

"Is four cups in, gambling, and not likely to stir from her couch anytime soon," Sempronius said. "Not with the streak of luck she's having. And it's Saturnalia. Nights like this, Latona, were made for mischief." Somehow his hands had slipped around her waist, his thumbs sliding over the soft swell of her ribcage, so nearly brushing against the underside of her breasts. "I know you feel it. With the Fire of Venus thrumming in your veins, how could you not?"

"The Fire of Venus?" Latona half-chuckled. "What a thing to say . . ." And yet something within her tugged and pulled, whispering that *this* was something her gifts were meant for. She felt the force of it, the straining urge to call on those blessings. It was a palpable ache, pounding in her heart and swelling in her breast, a pang in the secret place between her legs. Every part cried out for her to sway into Sempronius Tarren, magnetically drawn to all that he was and all that he had to offer her.

"Your problem, Latona," Sempronius said, and he was close, so close that Latona almost felt that they were breathing together, sharing the rhythm of air and life, "is in not demanding enough on your own behalf."

Latona recognized the challenge. It was the same, in essence, as what he'd been needling her with for months—the imperative to want more, to *be* more. With the same mad impulse that had driven her towards the flames, she looked straight and unblinking into Sempronius's eyes. "Kiss me."

He smiled, then bent his head slowly to hers. His lips ghosted over her earlobe, along her jawline, so achingly gentle that she shivered. His hands gripped her tighter, pulling her body flush against his, so that she could feel the solid strength of his chest, the insinuating curve of his well-muscled thigh. When his mouth finally found hers, she wanted to sigh with relief. From such a tender initiation, Sempronius's kiss grew steadily more possessive, more demanding, and Latona was only too eager to yield.

She could feel the thrum of her blood, loud in her temples, almost a painful ache in her chest as he brushed aside the fabric of her gown and tunic, his lips following the fabric as it dropped over her shoulder. The silken folds fell just short of exposing her chest to the night air, a tantalizing strip of fabric all that stood between her sensitive skin and the stars. Sempronius's kisses scorched across her collarbone, and her breath drew shallow, hesitant, as his hand slid up to cup her breast through her gown.

Sempronius knew what a dangerous transgression he was leading them both into, but from the instant she had admitted her desire and opened that door, he did not think he could have stopped himself. He knew, as his fingers explored her curves, the swell of hip, narrowness of waist, and gentle blossom of ribs into breasts, that they would never forget her shape. Never given to such reckless risk-taking, Sempronius allowed himself to be lulled by the darkness, the supposed seclusion provided by ivy and columns—but even more, to be drawn in by her. Something in Latona's brilliant burning seduced him as thoroughly as his words did her, nudging him into forgoing the need to plan and hedge and wait. For months, he had prodded her to take a chance, to spread her wings and see how high she could soar, and now that she had, he discovered that his only choice was to take the flying leap along with her. He kissed his way up to her mouth again, holding her so close that he could feel her rapid heartbeat against his chest, could sense the heat pooling between her legs.

Only one thing could have broken the spell on them, and it came in a hissing voice: "Latona!"

XLVII

Latona whirled around, clutching at her disheveled gown, suddenly shot cold with terror. She relaxed a fraction when she saw that it was Ama Rubellia, standing a few feet away.

"You can't do that here."

It took Latona a moment to realize that Rubellia had not expressed condemnation, only concern for the setting. Rubellia strode towards them, glancing over her shoulder. "There are too many people milling about. You're certainly not the only ones with such matters on your minds. Felix is about to—well, you might have company soon, so I thought it best to come warn you."

"Rubellia—" Latona started, though not sure what she intended to protest.

"The Autroniae have some guest chambers down that way," Rubellia said, nodding towards a garden path that led down the left side of the house. "If you follow the promenade to the end, it takes you to a separate part of the house. New fashions and all that. And," she added, as casual as though it were of little consequence, "the doors have bolts."

Latona could only gape at her in astonishment. Sempronius, though, found his voice. "I'm grateful for the information, Ama Rubellia, and so shall refrain from asking how you came by it."

Rubellia's lips curled in a secretive smile. "The House of Venus hears many things. I can keep the particulars to myself while still helping others to benefit from the knowledge. I'll cover for your absence, should anyone ask." With a conspiratorial smile, Rubellia kissed Latona's cheek. "Go with grace."

Bearing the blessing of the Priestess of Venus to assuage her conscience, Latona turned to Sempronius. He held out a hand, and Latona realized she had this moment to choose. She could easily plead her virtue and return to the party with Rubellia. Or she could go with Sempronius, well and truly adulter herself, and find out what would happen if she gave vent to the embers kindling inside of her.

She gave Sempronius her hand and let him lead her down the twisting garden path.

∞∞∞∞∞∞∞∞∞∞∞

A narrow corridor ran between the row of cubicles and what must have been originally intended as the outer wall of the domus proper. Sempronius bypassed the first two, tested the door of the third, and found the room empty.

It held nothing more than a narrow, simply dressed bed and a wooden stool, as was common for guest chambers. A single lamp hung near the door, already lit, no doubt anticipating the need of any inebriated guests who had to stumble in rather than finding their ways home.

As soon as he slid the bolt on the door, Sempronius Tarren descended upon her like a starving man, clasping her head with both his hands, kissing her feverishly. Latona melted into him with a little moan, clutching at his tunic. One of Sempronius's arms encircled her waist, pulling her against him with such force that it brought her up onto her tiptoes, unbalanced. His desire was palpable, his focus as hot and intense as the sun in midsummer. The kiss felt like it could go on forever, like it was trying to make up for all the impassioned kisses Latona had missed in her life.

When Sempronius at last tore his mouth from hers, it was only to press his lips to her cheeks, her temples, into her hair. "I have wanted you, Latona," he breathed. "So long, I have wanted you."

Latona could scarcely find words for the fervor overtaking her. She had given herself to Herennius out of duty and to Ocella out of necessity, but this was her own choice, driven by heat and ravenous desire. If she were going to sin, then she intended to do so thoroughly.

Sempronius's strong arms wound around her back, holding her fast. Those arms were a surety, and Latona had the strange sense that nothing could harm or even distress her while she was in the circle of his protection. There was a rightness to it, what they were doing, despite the secrecy—and despite the illegality. *'There are higher imperatives.'*

Before she could wonder where that thought had come from, he was kissing her again, his hands exploring her body, her own roving fearlessly over his chest and shoulders and arms, gripping and caressing what she had for so long denied herself. His touch sent white-hot thrills through her veins, jolting every part of her body to a strange new awareness. She felt a warm scarlet glow rising, that tangible radiance—Venus's gifts, burning so brightly in her, and Sempronius clutching her as though he would drink it all in.

She threw him off-balance far more than he had expected. Not that he had ever expected Latona to be a casual fling, a simple tumble, easily enjoyed and easily forgotten; she was too extraordinary a woman for that, but this inebriating effect, he had not anticipated. It would be easy, so easy, to lose himself in her, to give over to the brilliance of it all. He felt an urgency that could not rest at the initial glow. Her body was warm and soft in his arms, and her lips tasted of cinnamon, and Sempronius had to have more. With one arm secure around her waist, he bent her back slightly, his teeth grazing her earlobe and nibbling down her neck.

Latona blushed to realize she was trembling like a virgin girl, though it was with eagerness, not modesty, as Sempronius finally moved to pluck the brooches from her shoulders, unpinning her gown, then tugged at the thin ties of her tunic straps. When the first side fell, exposing one breast, she drew in her breath sharply, in anticipation rather than surprise. Slowly, reverently, he bent to take her nipple in his mouth, wetting it with his tongue, giving a little suck. Somehow the sensation was so intense, so joyously thrilling, Latona thought she might fall all to pieces right then. But he kissed his way back up to her mouth, and his nimble fingers pulled the belting sash from around her waist.

Gown and tunic together fell in ripples from her body, catching slightly at the swell of her hips before slipping down and pooling at her feet. Sempronius sank to his knees, his hands sliding down her sides, glorying in every curve and arch of her body. "My goddess," he said, his voice a husky whisper.

To be the object of such intense regard should have made Latona uncomfortable, should have had her fidgeting, moving to cover herself. She knew she was being wanton in the worst possible way, utterly shameless, standing naked in one of Dula's guest chambers, with the noise from the Saturnalia revels faintly audible through the walls. She knew that. Yet all she wanted to do was let Sempronius Tarren worship her, to drown in the depths of his passion. She slid her fingers through his hair, then trailed her fingers down to stroke his cheek and curl under his jaw. "Love me," she whispered.

And Sempronius obliged.

He guided her down onto the little bed before shucking off his tunic and undergarment and joining her. His body was every bit as well-formed as Latona had guessed, broad shoulders and narrow waist and lean muscles. The fingers roving over her had calluses, well-earned not just through military training, but through the sort of labor few patrician men put themselves to. She had seen him at it, and admired him for it. And as she glanced lower, following his well-defined hip bones to the juncture of his thighs, Latona was surprised at the surge of lust swelling in her. The male organ had always seemed a strange and perfunctory thing to her before, almost comical, yet now, seeing Sempronius in the dim light of the tiny room, it became attractive, enticing.

Sempronius took his time discovering her. Aware that their time together was at a premium, he wanted to memorize every inch of her. He smiled to hear her little gasps or soft moans as his fingers traced her curves or his teeth teased at some tender spot. From breasts to stomach to hips, he left no arc unexplored, and when his hand slipped between her legs, Latona fought to keep from screaming with pure, twisting *need*. His head dipped lower, his mouth drifting over her hips, then lower, ever nearer to the part of her most desperate for attention.

Latona knew people did such things, of course. It was one of the radiant joys Aula had spoken of so glowingly. But certainly Herennius had never been so inclined, and Latona had never thought to own such bliss herself.

A hot coil burned inside her, swirling and pulsing and yearning, and when it erupted in rapture, she felt the sweetness of it rolling all the way down to her toes and back up again, wave after wave of cascading pleasure. And the glow that overtook her, the spiraling heat of her magic, Fire and Spirit surging together out from the core of her being, was stronger and fiercer than anything she had felt before. She surrendered herself to it—and so did Sempronius.

A man who rarely allowed himself to be overwhelmed by anything, Sempronius willingly gave himself over to the sweet rush of Latona's emotions. It was a danger, he knew, to let the powerful influence of her magic wash over him so thoroughly, but somehow he could not bring himself to put a stop to it.

'*This was what Anchises felt, laying with the goddess Venus,*' he thought as he kissed his way back up her body, '*when he sired on her the founder of our nation. This was how Ulysses lost himself in the arms of Calypso.*' When he looked at the radiant smile on Latona's face as she lay, half-swooning, beneath him, there could be no question that his surrender was more than worth it.

When they joined at last, Latona had to clamp a hand over her own mouth to stifle herself. The joy was too great, the ecstasy too brilliant to hold in, as though her body might simply burst apart into a thousand rays of light. It was almost a delirium, physical sensation and ardent passion, the gifts of Fire and the empathy of Spirit, all whirling together and quite overwhelming any scrap of rationality she might have held onto. Her arms fell around Sempronius's shoulders, and she clung to him near-desperately, arching at the ripples of pleasure shuddering through her body. She could feel no shame, no regret in this. The more he moved within her, the more frenzied their rhythm became, the more she felt aglow with the rightness of it.

Somehow, Sempronius summoned the presence of mind to withdraw before his own climax hit, spilling himself on the bedding rather than inside her. Even embracing this willing madness, they could only risk so much.

For several long, silent minutes, they lay entangled, panting. Latona was experiencing the extremely strange sensation of being completely exhausted and thoroughly energized at the same time. Her body was aching—in such sweet ways, but still, aching—and yet her spirit soared like Phoebus in the heavens.

Almost at the same instant, they turned their heads to look at each other. Sempronius reached out with one finger to brush a sweat-damp tendril of hair from her brow. "We can't stay here," he said, voice made soft with how little he wanted to admit that their stolen moments had to end.

"I know."

The golden cocoon of her bliss shattered, and the crash rippled through the magical haze she had cast over them both. Sempronius felt it like a trickle of cold water, though he did not need Shadow's intuition to guess at the cause of her sudden shift in mood. He leaned over, kissing her brow, her closed eyelids. "The Fates do not bring two such as us together without a greater purpose," he said. "This is not all there is for us. I swear that to you."

Latona nodded, her eyes still squeezed shut. He could not guarantee that, but it comforted her that he wanted to say it.

He dressed himself first, then gently brought her to her feet and helped her to repin her gown. "I don't know that there's much we can do for your hair," he said, entwining his fingers in the disheveled golden locks.

"At this hour of the night, I doubt anyone will find it unusual."

He stroked her cheek with his thumb, then bent to kiss her again.

Latona's hands gripped his tunic, unwilling to part from him. It was Sempronius who found the strength to break away, though he did so with a regretful sigh. "Come now, my lady," he said. "Back into the light we go."

He opened the door and glanced out, then gestured for her to come along. As they scurried back towards the garden, Latona heard muffled cries and the slapping of flesh against flesh from another of the guest cubicles. She wasn't sure if it shamed her or thrilled her, to know she was not alone in her wickedness.

It had grown colder out in the garden since they had been secluded in their little room, or perhaps it only seemed so, the merciless chill of reality dousing the too-brief dream they had allowed themselves. Latona shivered as the enormity of what they had done finally settled in. The law still allowed a woman taken in adultery to be killed by her husband or father, and the thought was no less chilling even though it had not been enforced in generations. Sempronius was in perhaps even greater danger, if it were ever known.

'*But you were not discovered,*' she thought. '*Lady Venus smiles on this.*'

"I dare not kiss you again," Sempronius said, though his lips were at her ear, and his hand lingered at the small of her back. "Not so near the house." He smiled. "I was not mistaken in you, Lady Latona. You are an unparalleled glory when you are brave enough to allow yourself to be." Whatever his intentions might have been, his lips dusted against her temple once more.

And then he was gone, melted back into the colonnades, moving to rejoin the party. Latona took several long, deep breaths, smoothing her hair back from her face and willing the blush to leave her cheeks before she also returned, hoping that their long absence had not been noted.

The mood of the party had mellowed, as the degrees of drunkenness slipped from revelry into lethargy. Aula had left off gambling and was lolling on a couch next to Maia and Rufilius, all three of them looking half-asleep. The poet Urbanus seemed to have given up ribaldry in favor of something more lyrical. However adeptly his words might skewer, the doggerel belied the extent of his true talent. His voice was smooth yet commanding, not a soldier's voice, to be sure, but no weak piping, either. It was a voice to make the Muses themselves sit up and take notice. '*Small wonder that they all look rapt,*' Latona thought, glancing at the assembled congregation as she picked her way back to her sister's side. Even some of those whose eyes had drifted closed were nonetheless nodding along with the rhythm of his verse. Only after a moment did his words manage to penetrate through the fog of her mind:

Love is ardent when discovered;
When the misfortune of lovers is made dually yoked,
They persist in that which brought about their own sufferance.
There is a story, well noted in heaven,
Of Mars and Venus captured by the ruse of her husband.
Father Mars, mad with love for Venus,
From the grim duke of war became an entreating lover,
And Venus proved neither resistant nor mocking,
For never was there a goddess bearing more tender a heart.

It seemed a cruel jest, that Latona should walk back in to the middle of this particular story. Rufilius stirred himself as she drew close, and gave up his place on the couch so that Latona could nestle in next to her sister. She dropped her head on Aula's shoulder, breathing in the rosy scent of her hair, as Urbanus told of the lovers taken in adultery, exposed, mocked by all the rest of the gods. It ended well for love, though; when Neptune's pleas for dignity finally freed the pair, they no longer had the need for subterfuge or shame and could live together openly.

'And no one thinks the less of Venus for it,' Latona thought, silently contemplating while her sister sighed dramatically over the story. *'The other gods envy Mars his good fortune, all admitting they would trade places with him in an instant. And she goes on being "laughter-loving Venus," cherished and adored by all.'*

There was a moral in it, somewhere, but Latona's heart was too troubled to sort out what that might be.

XLVIII

"You promised!"

Ekialde, *erregerra* of the Lusetani, was in a towering rage. He had dismissed all of his war-band from his tent but his uncle Bailar and was now storming in circles around it. His uncle knelt to one side, staring down at the dirt, though Ekialde was far from certain that he was displaying the shame he ought to feel. Bailar always had an answer. Probably he was just composing himself to deliver it.

Ekialde wasn't certain he wished to hear.

"You swore to me that it would work. My own blood, your workings—I did as you said. It spattered his skin, his face. I think it even went into his eyes and mouth. So why is he not now my slave?"

"You knew this was untested magic, sister-son."

"That you said would work!"

Bailar raised his head slowly. "I was not mistaken. It would have. But from what you said, it sounds as though the Aventans have protective magic of their own. If I had known, I might have been able to prepare—"

"Excuses!" Ekialde spat. He sat heavily on the edge of his bed. The shame of the entire endeavor scorched at him. Not only to lose a battle, but to have his supremacy as *erregerra* falter. Worse still, to second-guess himself, to wonder if he had done well in following Bailar's advice and experimenting with such unusual magic. *'What if Neitin was right? I thought I was doing what was best for my people . . . but does this show that the gods disagree?'*

Bailar rose and came to sit beside Ekialde. "Sister-son," he said, his voice softer than before. "Neither you nor I could have foreseen this. You are Bandue's representative, not Bandue himself. And the Aventan magic is clearly that of cowards—held close, not openly declared. We did not know this before. We do now."

Ekialde rubbed at his dark hair. "But will we have the time to correct our approach? Will my people still have faith?"

"Of course they will—if you remain their strong leader. Do not allow this to trouble you. Stride out in the morning and show them that the god still walks with you." Bailar grasped his nephew's hands, squeezing them to just before the point of pain. "And there is more. We can do more. If you are willing."

Ekialde's eyes blazed as gold as the coals in the brazier. "I want to win. I want to chase these Aventan bastards from the *mendi*."

"Then listen. We will have to learn more of them, first. More of their magic. Once we know how to work around their defenses . . ." Bailar drew a deep breath. "You would have to be strong for it. It would take much of your essence, and some of your own people might call it a perversion of the gods' will. But I think, with Bandue's own permission, we could wreak untold havoc. Blood does not only convey strength, after all."

"What do you mean?"

"Blood can do so much. It can thicken and stop up the veins. It can swell the brain, madden a man. It carries disease. We could turn the Aventans' own bodies against them. If you are willing—if you are brave enough, to stare into deeper mysteries than any leader in our memory— there is *much* we can do." Bailar's hands moved to his wrists, feeling the pulse there. The pressure made Ekialde aware of its thrum. "Are you willing? Willing to use not just magic of the blood, but of the bone? Willing to yolk your strength to the powers of Endovelicos as shadow, not sun? To summon his workers from the netherworld and use your strength to control them?"

Ekialde pursed his lips, weighing the matter. He could not be naive; there would be those who said Bailar intended dark magics, such as the Lusetani had not employed for generations. His wife would be among those critics. *'But if it would work . . . The gods wish me to rid our land of foreign influence, of that I am sure. To restore the purity of our people, I must do whatever is necessary. And if Bailar is brave enough, then so must I be.'* The role of an *erregerra* was to risk himself for his people, and that meant his soul no less than his body.

"Tell me, uncle," Ekialde said. "If it helps us defeat the Aventans, there is nothing I'm not brave enough for. Tell me everything."

◇◇◇◇◇◇◇◇◇◇◇◇◇

Neitin had waited outside the tent, hugging her belly and listening. When she heard Ekialde making his promise to his uncle, she rose, tears dewing her cheeks, and walked a little ways into the forest. She could move silently when she chose. Only her sisters noticed her passing by, and they were not about to call Ekialde's war-band on her.

The night sky was an empty slate, moonless and starless. Neitin fell to her knees, splaying her hands against the dirt. She scratched the top layer of soil loose. It was hard with the cold, but she wanted to reach something softer, more alive, not the earth that was whipped and chafed by the wind.

The dirt was even colder further down, but malleable. Neitin curled her hands into fists, then cast her gaze up to the sky. "I have no magic," she said. "I can work no great wonders. But I beg you, gods of my people, keep him safe."

They had seen the might of Aven now, had pitched the best of theirs against only a small faction of the invaders. What would happen when Aven came against them in full force?

For Neitin, the solution was simple: go home, back to the lowlands near the ocean. She longed for familiar terrain. *'What will happen if my child is born here, so far from our people's home?'* But Ekialde would hear none of this. He had set himself a course and would not swerve, not even if it meant sinking into his uncle's blood-mania.

So all Neitin could do was pray. "Nabia, for the sake of our child, do not let him fall into this darkness. Trebarunu, let us come home safe. No more of this. No more blood. No more of his uncle's wickedness."

She hung her head, dark curls falling like curtains on either side of her face. The amulet Ekialde had given her swayed between her breasts, clacking against the other charm she wore—a smooth stone with a natural hole in it, taken from the river where she and Ekialde had played. She wanted to have it blessed, but there was no magic-woman to do so, not here in this masculine wilderness of war.

✦ JANUARIUS ✦

XLIX

The six hundred and eighty-ninth year since Aven's founding drifted into the six hundred and ninetieth, the priests made their sacrifices to Janus, the new magistrates took their offices, and Sempronius Tarren, officially invested as the praetorial governor of Cantabria, could now travel north to rally his legions.

He would not be making the journey alone. Recruits from Samnium and Apulia had mustered on the Campus Martius, and these would be heading north as well, along with the non-combatants and administrative staff who had not yet departed for the training camps in Campania. Most of the Tenth was already there, in the foothills, and Sempronius's new recruits would bring the legion to full numbers. They would move farther north, into Liguria, and stay there through the winter. It was Sempronius's hope that training there, rather than on the Campus Martius or elsewhere in Truscum, would better prepare the legions to fight at the higher elevations of the Iberian plateaus.

The legions readied themselves to depart on a cold morning in the first week of January. Frost crisped the grass, and soldiers and commanders alike had donned extra togas and thick woolen socks to stave off the chill. Marching would, at least, warm them up, and so despite the early hour, most of the men were anxious to depart.

◇◇◇◇◇◇◇◇◇◇◇◇◇

Latona did not know what it was that compelled her to bundle into a plain green gown and fawn-toned mantle, hours before most of the women in Aven's polite society would be awake, and slip out of her house with Merula at her side. She did not know why her feet carried her down the Palatine Hill, through the Forum, near-deserted except for crumb-picking birds and a few public slaves, sweeping the steps of the temples. She did not know why she proceeded around the Capitoline to the gate that opened out toward the Field of Mars. Or rather, though she knew the reason for all these actions, she did not know why she allowed the impulse to rule her, rather than defeating it and staying home in her warm bed.

Her husband would be furious, she knew, if he were aware of it. It would never occur to him to look for her when he rose in the morning, though; she never went anywhere so early. Still, the risk of it thrummed in her heart.

The Campus Martius was swarming with men, some lined up in their rows, prepared to march, others still dousing campfires, packing up tents, swearing at each other, at their horses, at their inferiors, about their superiors. Mostly the men ignored her; some few, perhaps those with better manners bred or beaten into them, tugged their forelocks or gave her little nods. She did her best to stay out of the way of anyone who looked like he was moving with purpose as she wandered towards the command tents on the far side of the field, hoping she wasn't too late, hoping that the commanders had not yet assembled themselves at the head of the ranks.

Latona saw, as she approached, the nervous look of the tribunes in their early twenties heading out on their first campaign, unblooded men younger than most of the legionaries. One looked particularly pale and sweaty. Moved to pity by the nauseated expression clouding the young man's face, Latona sent a little boost of encouraging magic his way as she passed.

Latona also passed two men she definitely recognized: Felix and Rufilius. As she passed, Rufilius offered her a jaunty salute, and Felix actually winked. She smiled politely and nodded at them, but went along her way, hoping they did not attach too much meaning to her presence in the camp. And then, standing in front of a crimson-bannered tent, she found the man she had crept out of her house in the early hours of the morning to see.

Sempronius Tarren cut a fine figure in his military kit. Not all men did. The paneled kilt and short red tunic made a man with scrawny or ill-proportioned legs look positively ridiculous, and of course not everyone had arm muscles impressive enough to show off the bands around wrists and biceps to their greatest effect. Sempronius looked as fit as any of the relentlessly drilled legionaries, and Latona did not feel the slightest bit ashamed for noticing. His steel cuirass fit him perfectly—specially crafted, then, not a family heirloom. Some patricians took great pride in wearing the same armor their forefathers had worn; Latona thought that foolish, considering how poorly fitted some of those hand-me-downs could be. His segmented armor gleamed in the sunlight, polished with devoted care. He had not yet donned the shining helmet, impressively crested with stiff black horsehair; it was stuck atop a post next to him while he adjusted the saddlebags on an uncomplaining mule.

When he saw her approach, he handed the mule-tending to an eager young tribune. He stepped a little ways away from the tent and made a very correct nod of greeting, in deference to any observation by the milling crowd. She bobbed her head in reply, allowing the dull brown mantle to slip off the back of her head, draping down her back. "Lady Latona," he said. Though he looked unflustered, there was a tightness in his voice. "Have you come to see me off?"

"I— Yes, yes, I have," Latona said, feeling foolish. She realized that, absurdly, she was looking down at the red dust, not at his face, and she remedied that immediately. Unable to come up with any plausible excuse for being about this early in the day, she settled on simply telling the truth. "I wanted to say farewell."

"That's kind," Sempronius said. A smile quirked his lips. "My own sister quite declined to get up so early in the day, and bade me her fond farewells last night."

Neither of them mentioned that seeing a man off personally was the action of a wife, not a friend. Less than one, more than the other, Latona hardly knew what it might be appropriate to say and could barely master the impulse to reach out and touch him. To do so would be dangerous. Her body remembered his too well; feeling it again might undo her composure entirely.

So instead, Latona reached for her waist and tugged on a small square of fabric which she had tucked into her belt. A *focale*, largely unornamented, except for a few embroidered designs at the corners. "I've been weaving a lot lately," she explained, holding it out to him. "And I thought . . . well, I want you to have this."

His fingers brushed hers, light and brief, as he took the *focale* from her. "This is very good of you, my lady," he said. He tilted his head to the side, considering. "There is Fire magic in this, unless I miss my guess?"

"There is."

He cut her off by closing the distance between them, and Latona felt her heartbeat jump. Eyes locked on hers, he seized one of her hands in his, bending the fingers gently. He lifted them to his lips and kissed the knuckles. Latona had guessed rightly. Her heart ached to feel his warmth again, and the heat in his eyes, focused and hungry with some nameless need, showed that he felt it, too.

"This is a special gift, Latona, and you honor me by giving it," he said. "I thank you, most deeply. I shall wear it in battle and take heart, knowing that your magic protects me."

"It seemed right," she said. Socially inappropriate, perhaps, but *right*, in her bones. The scrap of crimson fabric was a connection that could link his life's blood to her talents, and thus to her strength. It was a gift she should never have had the audacity to bestow, yet here she was, and Sempronius promised to cherish it. His forefinger stroked, almost imperceptibly, against her palm, over the pad at the base of her thumb, and Latona felt her pulse leap. No onlooker could find anything improper by glancing at them, but the gesture was maddeningly intimate, sending a thrill down Latona's spine.

He pulled her close—too close, dangerously close if anyone should see them and recognize her. "Not a dozen women in all Truscum could create something like this." His lips brushed her cheek, barely pressing against the corner of her mouth, and Latona realized she was holding her breath. From afar, it might have looked like the farewell kiss a brother would give a sister, but Latona felt a heat in it that seared her to the core. He rested his head against hers, temple to temple, and murmured in her ear, low and urgent, "*See* yourself."

What might have happened next, Latona would never know, and she was spared the trial of having to find words—or of having to keep herself from twining her arms around his neck and scandalizing herself there in the Campus Martius. A horn echoed its signal across the Field, and Sempronius stepped away from her—though it seemed, to Latona, that he did not release her fingers until the last possible moment.

"I must be on my way," he said, looking off towards the edge of the field, where the men were assembling. The heat had left his eyes; he was, again, the unflappable military officer. There was still sincerity there, though, as he said, "May I write to you?"

"I hope you will." Latona felt the desire to touch him in every inch of her skin, even in the smallest, most casual way. She wanted to brush his hair back from his eyes. She wanted to go up on her toes and kiss his cheek and tell him to be safe. She wanted to press her fingers against his again, just to have one last tangible moment before he left.

Instead she stepped back as an aide brought his horse around. "I wish you well on your travels," she said, sounding formal and stilted and hating it. She watched as he donned his helmet and then, just before mounting his horse, looked back at her once more.

"May your future treat you well, if not gently, lady," he said. He stepped up on the block provided for him and swung himself up onto the back of his horse, a solid and no-nonsense looking gray beast, dappled with white spots. And then he was off, whistling to the dawdling tribunes to pick up their pace and follow him. Latona waited, watching as the commanders, legates, and tribunes took their places at the head of the legion. Then she pulled her mantle up over her hair, covering the sides of her face, and fled back, before the threatening sting of tears prickling at the back of her eyes could overwhelm her.

∞∞∞∞∞∞∞∞∞∞∞

She did not head home immediately, but strode east to the Quirinal Hill. Mostly filled with temples and administrative buildings, it was quiet this early in the day. "Domina?" Merula ventured, when they were about halfway up the hill.

"Speak freely," Latona said, her voice distant.

"I am only wondering if you found what you were looking for." Merula watched as a progression of emotions flickered over Latona's face.

"Yes. I rather think I did." Latona looked sideways and caught Merula's eyes. "And don't pretend you don't know what that was about."

"I would never presume, Domina—"

"Oh, yes, you would. Shame, Merula, you know I don't value you for your humility." Merula snorted.

Soon they reached the summit. The Quirinal overlooked the Field of Mars, and from there they watched as the legion formed their ranks: row after row of men in clanking segmented armor, polished so brightly that the Campus Martius glimmered in the light of the rising sun. Here and there a standard poked higher than the mens' heads—banners bearing numbers, animal skins flung high on spears, all the symbols blessed by Jupiter, meant to make the men take courage and fight without fear. From this distance, Latona could distinguish no individual man; the army became a single organism with thousands of limbs, twisting its way north.

Beyond them stood the triadic temples atop the Capitoline Hill, their massive triangular pediments pointing up towards the heavens. Jupiter Optimus Maximus was the largest, but the roof of Juno Maxima caught the morning light and gleamed like gold. *'Yet she is not only in the temples . . .'* Women served and were served by Juno everywhere, in every stage of life. *'So what would you have of me, lady?'*

"Domina?" Merula asked. "You are having a thought on your face."

Smiling at the expression, Latona nodded. "All my life, I have let other people have the shaping of it," she said. "My parents, afraid of my power, trying to shelter me; Aemilia, trying to ensure I would never be a threat; my husband, trying to hide me or hem me in; Ocella . . ." She let that thought drift off.

After a moment, Merula asked, "And Sempronius Tarren? What would he have of you?"

The thought rang in Latona's head. *'"Destined for more . . ."'*

"I don't know, Merula," she said, dropping her mantle a bit as the sun warmed her back. He was too clever, she suspected, to be truly altruistic in pushing her. But was his ulterior motive a benefit for himself or for the nation that he loved so passionately?

'Does it matter?' That way lay freedom, however rocky or meandering the path. Her eyes scanned the city, waking to its usual morning chaos—the city she loved no less than Sempronius did, for all its faults and foibles. *'I love it and I can protect it, if I have the nerve to try.'* Months ago, the thought would have terrified her with its sheer absurdity, but now . . .

"I will do it, then," Latona said, more to the open sky and whatever gods were listening than to Merula. "Let Aemilia or Herennius or my father make of it what they may, and be damned with their objections. I will do it. I will stretch my power and find out what the gods intend for me." Her jaw set hard, though her hands were trembling. "And let the dice fly where they may."

GLOSSARY

AB URBE CONDITA: literally, "from the founding of the city". How the Romans/Aventans measure years, in time since what we consider 753 BCE, the legendary founding of the city.

AEDILE: a mid-level magistrate responsible for public buildings, the public games, and the supply of grain to the city. Elected by the Tribal Assembly. Men generally served this office between their quaestorship and praetorship, though it was not strictly necessary to be elected as praetor.

CAMPUS MARTIUS: The Field of Mars, a large open space used for military training and for elections.

CENSOR: a magistrate responsible for maintaining the census and electoral rolls, supervising public morality, and some aspects of government finances. A man had to have served as consul to be elected as censor. Elected by the Centuriate Assembly.

CENTURIATE ASSEMBLY: One of three voting assemblies designated by the Roman constitution, which gathered for legislative, electoral, and judicial purposes. Originally a military organization, but later expanded and ranked by wealth rather than military status. Only the Centuriate Assembly could declare war or elect the highest-ranking Roman magistrates: praetors, consuls, and censors.

COLLEGIA: assemblies with legal purpose and some authority which could function as guilds, religious organizations, or social clubs. Most common were the crossroads colleges, which were neighborhood associations formed around shrines placed at intersections.

CONSUL: The highest and most prestigious political office in the Roman Republic. The Centuriate Assembly elected two consuls to serve together for a one-year term. Consuls held executive power. They convened and presided over the Senate, negotiated with foreign states, and served as commanders-in-chief of the legions.

CURIA: the Senate House.

CURSUS HONORUM: literally, the course of offices; the sequential order of public offices held by politicians in the Roman Republic.

DICTATOR: a magistrate entrusted by the Senate with full power and authority to act unilaterally. A temporary office intended to be held for no more than six months.

DOMINUS/DOMINA: literally, "master/mistress", but also translates as the equivalent of "Lord/Lady" when used in conjunction with a name.

DOMUS: house. In the city, generally referred to a free-standing building occupied by a single family.

EQUESTRIAN: one of the property classes of ancient Rome, ranking below the Senators but above the rest.

FIVE CLASSES: property classes including all those who held land but did not have enough wealth to qualify as Equestrians or Senators.

FORUM: a large open-air market, often surrounded by a mixture of temples and shops. The largest forum in Rome/Aven, generally referred to as *the* Forum, was the center of political, mercantile, and spiritual life.

HEAD COUNT: the property-less class, with no land and little wealth.

INSULA: apartment. Blocks of insulae could be five to seven stories, with the largest and most luxurious apartments on the bottom floor and the smallest and most miserable at the top.

LEGES TABULAE MAGICAE: a section of Aventan law governing the behavior of mages, particularly with regard to interactions with non-magical citizens.

LEX CANTATIA AUGIAE: an Aventan law preventing the ascension of magically-gifted citizens to the ranks of praetor, consul, or censor.

LICTOR: a civil servant who acted as a bodyguard to high-ranking public officials.

MACELLUM: a market, smaller and with fewer permanent structures than a forum or emporium.

MOS MAIORUM: the "proper way of things." An informal code based on precedent and custom, elevated to dogmatic status by the Optimates.

OPTIMATES: one of the two most prominent political factions in Aven, dedicated to conservatism, relative isolationism, and the preservation of power among the elite.

PATRONS AND CLIENTS: the basic social unit of ancient Rome was the patronage system, by which the patron, a man of higher social status and clout, served as protector, sponsor, and benefactor of the client, who in turn provided support and assistance to his patron.

POPULARISTS: one of the two most prominent political factions in Aven, favoring expansion of civic rights and economic opportunity.

PRAETOR: a magistrate ranking just below a consul. Praetors had municipal and judicial duties, but might also serve as commanders of legions or as local governors. Their specific duties fluctuated greatly at different points in Rome's history.

QUAESTOR: the first rank of the *cursus honorum*, requisite for entry to the Senate, responsible for the state treasury and audits.

QUINTILIS: the month we know as July.

SENATE: the Assembly consisting of the most experienced politicians. The Senate dictated foreign and military policy and directed domestic policy, but could not actually pass laws.

SENATORS: both the highest-ranking and wealthiest social class and those men who served in the Senate.

SEXTILIS: the month we know as August.

TRIBAL ASSEMBLY: the largest of the three Assemblies, as it consisted of all Roman citizens, divided into their "tribes," which largely referred to their family's region of origin. This Assembly was most often responsible for the passage of laws.

TRIBUNE: a title with several meanings. A tribune of the plebs acted as a check on the Senate and the Assemblies, able to exercise veto power over the actions of consuls and other magistrates. A military tribune commanded portions of the Roman army, subordinate to praetors and consuls; these were usually men in their early twenties, getting military experience before beginning the cursus honorum. Other mid-ranking officers were also styled tribune, generally those who were members of a commander's staff.

VILLA: a large home outside of a city. This might be a villa rustica, a country estate, or a villa maritima, a seaside home.

ACKNOWLEDGMENTS

This novel has been the love and labor of many years, and it could not have happened without the support, guidance, and friendship of so many people. I would like to extend my heartfelt thanks to:

Foremost, my parents, Mary and Bruce, and my sister, Cait. Never has there been a day when I had cause to doubt their support or their love. I have been brave enough to walk this path only because they have always had my back.

The friends who have supported me, loved me, encouraged me: "What are the odds the gods would put us all in one spot?"—or, at least, in a sequence of spots over the course of a lifetime, where we could all crash into each other? However it happened, I am blessed to know you.

The teachers and mentors I have been fortunate enough to encounter along the road. Some of you taught me to write; some of you showed me what was worth writing; some of you inspired me more that I can credit. Some of you did all three, and so to Carter, Ralph, and Sarah, I must add "thanks, thanks, and ever thanks".

The members of so many writing communities who have been sounding boards and partners in commiseration: the 17 Scribes, Authors 18, Debs, Fuse Club, and of course all my fellow Sirens. What grand fortune, to have fellowship with so many wonderful minds.

My Patreon supporters, for being the first to enter the world of Aven, and most particularly the honored Consuls, Marcell Williams and my excellent parents.

John Lavinus, my darling grand vizier, thaumaturgical consult, and closest confidante. Without you, dear one, I shudder to think where I might be.

And finally, my brilliant agent, Connor Goldsmith, and the pair of editors who saw this project to completion, Sarah Guan and Betsy Wollheim, with the whole amazing team at DAW Books. Thank you for helping me to shape these dreams into a story worth the telling.